Praise for Andrea Penrose's Wrexf

"Compelling . . . an intricately plotte ... set in Regency England. Its complex story line and authentic historical details bring the early days of the Industrial Revolution vividly to life. Bound to fascinate readers of C.S. Harris and even fans of Victorian mysteries." —*Library Journal* STARRED REVIEW

"Scientific discoveries combine with a complex mystery to provide an action-packed brainteaser." —*Kirkus Reviews*

"The author captures the Regency era's complexities in vivid settings, contrasting milieus, and a wealth of fascinating details . . . This thoughtful blend of derring-do and intellectual discussion should win Penrose new fans." —*Publishers Weekly*

"This book is very suspenseful and takes many turns, as the clues point first to one person, then another. Penrose is excellent at conveying the details of early nineteenth-century science and experiments with electricity. This was the era of Frankenstein, after all. The relationship between Wrexford and Charlotte is further developed in this book, and I am looking forward to seeing where it leads next." —*Historical Novel Society*

"Andrea Penrose masterfully weaves the numerous plotlines of *Murder at Kensington Palace* into a scintillating whole." —*Criminal Element*

"Charlotte Sloane and the Earl of Wrexford are a perfect crime-solving duo as headstrong and intelligent sleuths bucking the conventions of society." —*RT Book Reviews*

"The relationship and banter between the two stars of this series is incredible. Readers will look forward to seeing Charlotte and Wrex again (and, hopefully, very soon)." —*Suspense Magazine*

"Thoroughly enjoyable . . . with sharp, engaging characters, rich period detail, and a compellingly twisty plot, Andrea Penrose delivers a winner . . . fans of C.S. Harris and Kate Ross will be rooting for Charlotte Sloane and the Earl of Wrexford. Devilishly good fun!" —**Deanna Raybourn**, *New York Times* bestselling author

## Books by Andrea Penrose

*Murder on Black Swan Lane*

*Murder at Half Moon Gate*

*Murder at Kensington Palace*

*Murder at Queen's Landing*

# MURDER AT QUEEN'S LANDING

## ANDREA PENROSE

KENSINGTON
PUBLISHING CORP.

www.kensingtonbooks.com

KENSINGTON BOOKS are published by

Kensington Publishing Corp.
119 West 40th Street
New York, NY 10018

First Kensington Hardcover Edition: October 2020

ISBN-13: 978-1-4967-2286-7 (ebook)
ISBN-10: 1-4967-2286-8 (ebook)

ISBN-13: 978-1-4967-2285-0
ISBN-10: 1-4967-2285-X

First Kensington Trade Paperback Edition: September 2021

10 9 8 7 6 5 4 3 2 1

Printed in the United States of America

*To Darius "Jake" Roy, David Jiang, and Brett Gu*

*Intrepid heroes of Saybrook*
*Thanks for letting me write you into my story. I look*
*forward to reading all the wonderful chapters you're*
*going to write in your own lives.*

# ACKNOWLEDGMENTS

Writing entails much solitary effort, which makes me even more grateful for all the wonderful people who help bring a book from that first faint glimmer of an idea to the printed (and digital) page.

Many thanks go to my wonderful agent, Kevan Lyon, for her guidance and encouragement in navigating the ever-changing waters of modern publishing. And I'm incredibly grateful to my fabulous editor, Wendy McCurdy, whose suggestions and counsel always make me a better writer.

I'm also sending heartfelt shout-outs to special friends. . . .

To "Professor Plotto," whose astounding breadth of knowledge—from the esoteric to the sublime—is a source of constant inspiration. (As are the diabolical plot twist suggestions!)

To my amazing blog group, the Word Wenches—Joanna Bourne, Nicola Cornick, Anne Gracie, Susanna Kearsley, Susan King, Mary Jo Putney, and Patricia Rice—who are always there with a cyber crying towel and a virtual slug of single malt scotch! I'm extraordinarily lucky to have such wonderful brainstorming partners and beta readers. But most of all, I'm extraordinarily lucky to have such wonderful friends. . . .

To Lauren Willig, for our Yale Club cookie brainstorming sessions . . . to Deanna Raybourn and Beatriz Williams, for all the fun and inspiration of tossing around creative ideas . . . to the Saybrook Fellowship, whose collective creativity and scholarship are constant reminders that books and ideas make the world a brighter place . . .

And lastly, hugs to all the PR, production, and art staff at Kensington Books. You guys are the best!

# PROLOGUE

"Halloo?"

A sudden gust of wind moaned in answer, its salt-sharp swirls tugging at the shoulder capes of the gentleman's elegant overcoat. He took a tentative step into the narrow alleyway between the unlit warehouses, then drew in a shaky breath as his soft-as-butter Hessian boots sank deeper into the muck.

"I must be mad," he muttered. But he couldn't afford to ignore the summons, no matter that every bone in his body was howling that what it implied couldn't be true.

"One, two . . ." Wincing at the squelch of every slow, sucking step, Hessian Boots felt his way along the grimy brick until he found the iron hasp of the fourth door. As promised, the massive padlock was unfastened, and the age-dark oak creaked open at his touch.

Fear slithered down his spine. It was dark as a crypt inside.

"Would that I could retreat," he whispered. *To carefree days of sun and laughter, of privilege and pleasure.* But there was no going back. The only choice was stumble ahead and try to find a way—

A hand seized his arm, yanking him deeper into the gloom. The door thudded shut behind him.

"W-what the devil—"

"Shhhh!" hissed his captor, shaking him to silence. "Stay quiet, or you'll get your throat cut."

Hessian Boots felt panic rise in his gorge. "But *why?*" he demanded. "What your note implied is . . ." A swallow. "Impossible."

A laugh, low and mirthless, as a flint struck steel and a tiny flame sparked to life. Flexing his black-gloved fingers, his captor shifted the single candle and pulled a packet from inside his coat. "See for yourself. I've made copies of enough documents concerning Argentum to prove that what I said is true. Unlike you fancy, fork-tongued serpents, the numbers don't lie."

In the flickering light, the oilskin seemed to dip and sway through the shadows, like a cobra about to strike.

*Argentum.* Ye gods, so it wasn't a bluff. The man knew.

"How did you discover all this?" demanded Hessian Boots, keeping his hands fisted at his sides. He had been told that the venture was a closely guarded secret, known only to a privileged few.

"Never mind. What matters is that you need to stop it."

"But . . ." *A ruse*—this was a filthy ruse to destroy all the imagination and hard work that had gone into the venture. Argentum would create a whole new world of opportunities for the future, so of course, there were those who would try to stop it.

By whatever means it took.

"But I can't stop it," lied Hessian Boots. "It's too late for that."

"You had better pray you're wrong," said Black Gloves.

Despite the damp chill swirling up from the river, sweat was dripping from his brow, the salt stinging his eyes. "W-what do you—"

A fierce bark suddenly shattered the nighttime stillness, its echo reverberating against the close-set buildings.

"You hear that? The night watchmen and their hellhounds

arc starting to make their round." Black Gloves pressed in closer. "We can't afford to linger."

Hessian Boots felt the packet being thrust into his coat pocket.

"Good versus Evil . . . Read the documents and then you must decide which side you're on. Trust me, your life will likely depend on your choice."

The flame sputtered and went out, shrouding them in a darkness blacker than Satan's maw.

His thoughts were spinning helter-pelter, so it took him an instant to react. "What do you mean? Who are you?" he demanded.

But a dull *thunk* and a flutter of chill air was the only answer.

After a heartbeat of hesitation, Hessian Boots edged his way to the door and found the iron latch. Pressing his forehead to the dank wood, he gritted his teeth to stop them from chattering.

*Damnation—surely this must be some devil-cursed nightmare.* He squeezed his eyes shut, willing himself to wake. But the prickling splinters against his skin and the foul-smelling mud seeping through his boots were all too real.

A hound barked again.

The sound roused him from self-pity. *Escape—I must escape.* He wasn't the only one at risk.

After easing the latch up, Hessian Boots opened the door a crack and ventured a peek. And thankfully saw naught but a shadowy gloom. Darkness, he realized, was now a blessing, not a curse.

Spotting no sign of life, he darted to the corner of the warehouses and after a small pause, ducked low and ran to take cover among the hogshead barrels stacked by the loading area.

The gate where he had entered wasn't far. Another few minutes . . .

But then a blade of lantern light sliced through the thick fog, stirring pale curls of mist.

Heart hammering, Hessian Boots held his breath as fear suddenly fisted around his chest. It had to be a ruse! His partners had warned him that jealous rivals would seek to stop the venture if word of it somehow got out. Black Gloves had likely passed on falsely incriminating documents in order to foment mistrust and dissention. Or . . .

He forced himself to swallow his terror. Or perhaps there was an even darker explanation. . . .

His thoughts began to spin, specters tangling with suspicions. Nothing was making any sense.

It seemed to take forever, but at last the sounds of the patrolling guard faded away. Which seemed only to amplify the ominous groans and creaks from the nearby wharves. *Rusty metal . . . rotting wood . . .* Hessian Boots released a sigh as another menacing thought crept into his head. . . .

*The worn-out bones of those who toiled in endless misery to make the rich even more obscenely rich.*

"What a bloody fool I've been," he moaned.

Water slurped against the barnacled pilings, the receding tide giving way to the stench of decay.

Hessian Boots slipped free of the barrels and hurried to a narrow cart path that led through another warren of windowless warehouses and out to the side gate set in the dockyard's perimeter wall. Hugging close to the shadows, he quickened his steps.

*A right turn and then a left turn . . .*

A shove knocked him off-balance, and suddenly he was falling, falling—

"You can't go that way," warned Black Gloves, yanking him upright and pushing him back into the shadows. His shoulder hit hard against jagged brick as smooth leather-clad hands forced him into a narrow passageway between two windowless buildings.

"They're waiting at the gate," added Black Gloves. "There's another way out. Follow me. The stone landing ramp can be crossed at low tide."

Digging in his heels, Hessian Boots tried to shake loose from the other man's hold. "Let go of me! I'm not playing any more of your filthy games." He fumbled at his pocket, trying to reach the packet of papers and fling it into the mud.

"Don't be daft." Black Gloves tightened his grip and pulled him closer. "Trust me, if we try to leave by the gate, we're dead men."

"I don't believe—" His words died in a gasp as a dribble of moonlight caught the lethal flash of steel.

Black Gloves had pulled a knife and was angling the blade upward.

"Damn you to hell," rasped Hessian Boots, fear turning to fury as he heard someone else scrabble into the narrow passageway.

*A trap!*

He lashed out a kick that buckled his captor's knee, then lunged and seized the hand holding the knife.

*Punching, kicking shoving, swearing*—Hessian Boots was vaguely aware of a third man joining the fray. *Friend or foe?* Impossible to tell. Reason had given way to the primal, primitive instinct to survive.

Steel sliced a gash across his knuckles. Recoiling, he swung a wild punch and heard a grunt of pain. The blade flickered, a quicksilver gleam against the dark blur of bodies.

Hessian Boots punched again and for an instant felt a sticky wetness beneath his fingers before a blow from behind knocked the wind from his lungs and sent him careening into the wall.

*Run!*

Was it a shout from Black Gloves or merely his inner voice of self-preservation?

*"Run!"* The cry came again.

Dizzy, disoriented, Hessian Boots gasped for breath, squinting through the gloom as the two thrashing shadows spun toward him. A strange cacophony filled his ears: the thrum of his own blood pulsing through his veins . . . amplified by a strange thudding.

And then suddenly from the maze of warehouses rose flashes

of light bouncing wildly off the bricks, punctuated by shouts and snarling barks.

It was the thought of gnashing teeth tearing at his flesh that roused him. Evading a grab at his coat, Hessian Boots pushed away from the wall and plunged deeper into the passageway, following it blindly until at last he saw a glimmer of lamplight and the silhouette of the stone landing ramp up ahead. Slipping, sliding, he raced across the still-wet muck and somehow managed to reach the street.

*Run!*

Gut churning, legs pumping, boots pounding the cobbles, he willed himself to go faster, praying for escape from the hounds of hell snapping at his heels.

# CHAPTER 1

"No." The Earl of Wrexford gave a critical squint at the waistcoat. "Absolutely not."

His valet gave an aggrieved sniff. "You can't mean to attend tonight's gala ball dressed in unremitting black. You'll look like an undertaker."

"You would rather I look like a street fiddler's monkey?"

Tyler bristled. "As if I would ever suggest something so vulgar." He ran his hand over the exquisitely embroidered silk. "This particular shade of cerise embellished with midnight-dark thread is both stylish and sophisticated."

The earl made a rude sound. "Then you may wear it yourself. Preferably in the laboratory, when you are cleaning up the most caustic of our chemicals."

"*You* are an arse," grumbled his valet. "And a fashion philistine."

"And might I point out that *you* are my humble servant."

"Not for long, if you insist on having such a boring wardrobe. A man of my rare talents needs challenges."

"Then go to the workroom library," drawled the earl, "and

fetch the book on Benjamin Silliman, so you can read up on his experiments with minerals." He ran a hand through his hair, earning another huff. "I wish to see if we can replicate his results with acid on quartz. And then, assuming the results are what I expect, I have an idea I wish to try."

Tyler's look of injured outrage quickly dissolved into one of curiosity. "Hmmm, acids, eh? Are you perchance thinking of adding vitriolic acid to Silliman's original mix?"

Wrexford was considered one of the most brilliant chemists in England, but most of his research was done in his private laboratory as he didn't work well within the hierarchy of London's prestigious scientific institutions. His sarcasm tended to offend people. Tyler, who served as his laboratory assistant as well as his valet, was one of the few people who could tolerate his mercurial moods.

"Perhaps," answered the earl.

"I'll have the summaries from my reading and all the supplies assembled by tomorrow." The valet tucked the offending waistcoat under his arm and turned for the dressing room. But after a step, he paused. "Won't you at least consider the silver and ebony stripe? It has the sort of subtle textures and elegance that Lady Charlotte would appreciate."

*Charlotte Sloane.* Wrexford hesitated and looked away to the leaded windows, where the darkening night shadows were teasing against the glass. *A lady of infinite textures, woven of complexities and conflicts.* Though that, he admitted, was rather like the pot calling the kettle black.

"I don't think Lady Charlotte gives a fig for how I'm dressed for the evening," he replied.

After all, she cloaked herself in quicksilver shadows. *And secrets—oh-so-many secrets.* An involuntary twitch pulled at his mouth. One of the more surprising ones he had discovered was the fact that having assumed her late husband's pen name, she was the notorious A. J. Quill, London's leading satirical artist.

They had first clashed when Wrexford had become the subject of her razor-sharp pen—that a highborn aristocrat had been accused of murder had had all of London abuzz. But they had come to form an uneasy alliance in order to find the real killer.

Much to their mutual surprise, a friendship had developed. Though that was too simple a word to describe the bond between them. It had grown even more complicated over the course of several more murder investigations, in ways impossible to articulate. And recently, it had taken another twist—

Tyler let out a huff, drawing the earl back from his musings. "She's a gifted artist and a sharp-eyed observer. Of course she'll notice all the little details that add color and texture to a blank canvas—or the lack thereof." Another rude sound. "So don't blame me if she decides you're a man of no imagination or taste."

"Oh, please, Tyler, don't tease Wrex into a foul humor," came a voice from the corridor. A moment later, a tall, fair-haired gentleman attired in elegant evening clothes entered the sitting room of the earl's bedchamber There was a certain insouciance to the not-quite-perfect folds of his cravat and rakehell smile.

"Lady Charlotte will be nervous enough making her first foray into a Mayfair ballroom without having to endure his sharp-tongued sarcasm." Christopher Sheffield fixed the earl with a wary look. "Please try to refrain from misbehaving tonight. Especially as you tend to do it deliberately."

Wrexford raised a brow. "Are you really chiding *me* for bad behavior?"

Sheffield had been the earl's close friend since their days at Oxford. The younger son of a marquess, he was allowed no responsibilities for running the vast ancestral estates, and his imperious father kept a stranglehold on the family purse strings, doling out naught but a tiny stipend. Bored and frustrated,

Sheffield retaliated by drinking and gambling to excess—a pattern of behavior that did no one any good.

His expression pinching to an oddly pensive look, Sheffield crossed the carpet and took a seat in one of the armchairs set by the hearth. "Perhaps I'm trying to change."

"Well, that calls for a drink," quipped Tyler as he moved to the tray of decanters on the side table. Sheffield was very fond of the earl's expensive brandy.

Sheffield dismissed the suggestion with an airy wave. "No, no. I wish to keep a clear head."

"Are you ill?" queried Wrexford.

"Ha, ha, ha." Assuming an injured look, his friend slouched deeper into the pillows. "Actually, I was hoping to discuss something—" He stopped short as he caught sight of the waistcoat Tyler was carrying, and then started to laugh in earnest.

The valet fixed him with a pained look. "Pray, what's so amusing?"

"The idea that Wrex might wear that." Sheffield made a face. "Ye heavens, he would look like one of those peacocks from the court of King Charles I. You know, the ones painted by what's-his-name, the flamboyant, good-looking fellow who was a great favorite with the ladies."

"Anthony Van Dyck?" suggested the earl.

"Yes, that's him." His friend looked rather pleased with himself. "As you see, I didn't sleep through every lecture at Oxford."

Heaving a long-suffering sigh, the valet stalked out of the room.

Sheffield's smirk lingered for a moment and then gave way to a more uncertain mien. "I daresay Lady Charlotte is feeling nervous about making her first grand entrée into Society."

Another of Charlotte Sloane's secrets had recently wrought a great change in her life. The daughter of an earl, she had been disowned by her family for eloping to Italy with a man beneath her station. And then, after becoming a widow, she had dared to forge an independent life for herself within the dog-eat-dog world of the lower classes through talent, grit, and determination. But the recent murder of her cousin—and the arrest of his twin brother for the crime—had forced her to step out of the shadows and back into the glittering world of the beau monde in order to find the real culprit.

Wrexford moved to the side table and poured himself a brandy. "I daresay she is." He lifted his glass. "You're sure you won't join me?"

A curt wave dismissed the offer.

He shrugged and took a swallow, allowing the liquid fire to prickle against his tongue.

"What if it turns out that she hates this new life?" Sheffield rose and began to pace. "You know how she despises the hypocrisy and selfishness of the aristocracy. She's already made some small compromises, but she'll have to keep making even more changes to fit into her new world, and . . ."

His friend gave a troubled sigh. "And once you change, there's no going back."

"Change is an inexorable part of our existence, Kit," he replied. "With every tick of Time, we're moving ever closer to our mortality. Our lives are in a constant state of flux. Try as we may, we can't stand still."

"Thank you. That makes me feel ever so much more sanguine about the coming evening." Despite the quip, Sheffield looked even more unsettled.

The earl sensed they were talking about more than Charlotte's challenges. "The idea of change frightens us all, Kit."

"Not you." His friend came to a halt. "Nothing rattles you."

*Ah, would that it were so*, thought Wrexford.

"You have the gift of sardonic detachment," Sheffield went on. "You can laugh at the absurdities of our human foibles rather than find them terrifying."

"Terror is also an inexorable part of our existence," he said quietly. "To claim otherwise means there's no blood pulsing through your veins."

"But how—"

"Don't fret over Lady Charlotte," counseled Wrexford. An oblique answer, perhaps, to the real question his friend was asking. But Sheffield was a clever fellow. "She has courage, resilience, a sharp sense of humor." He paused. "Most importantly, she has friends. Terror loses its power when you're not facing it alone."

An odd glimmer seemed to spark beneath Sheffield's lashes. "Did I just hear you say a good word about the power of friendship and love?"

"Heaven forfend. You must have imagined it." Wrexford quaffed another swallow of brandy. "But getting back to what you started to say a moment ago . . ." He quickly changed the subject, having no wish to pursue the topic of emotions. "You wish to discuss something?"

"Yes." His friend looked away for a moment. "A rather important matter, in fact."

"Ah." The earl's lips twitched. "I take it you've run through your quarterly allowance and wish to borrow some blunt for brandy and revelries."

Sheffield stiffened. "I'm aware of my reputation—admittedly richly deserved—as a beef-witted fribble. So you've every right to be sarcastic. But I wish . . . I wish to change." He drew in his breath. "And so . . ."

Wrexford put down his glass, cursing his rapier tongue.

"And so I have a business proposal to present to you," blurted out Sheffield as he pulled a sheaf of papers from the leather portfolio he had tucked under his arm. "Assuming, of course, that you're willing to listen, instead of falling into a fit of laughter."

*Am I really such an unfeeling friend?* The thought wasn't a comfortable one.

"Let us go down to the study," he replied, "where we may spread out your documents and have a careful look at everything."

"Thank you." Sheffield's look of gratitude made him feel even more like an arse.

The earl led the way down the stairs to a comfortable room filled with carved bookshelves, leather armchairs, and an overstuffed curio cabinet of scientific oddities. The massive desk had a well-used look, its age-mellowed pearwood top nearly invisible beneath the stacks of scientific journals and books on chemistry.

Wrexford quickly cleared a space for his friend's papers and then took a seat as Sheffield arranged his documents in several neat stacks before clearing his throat.

"Seeing as we shall soon be capering in a ballroom, I won't dance around the tree. I would like to ask you for an investment to start a business." His friend gestured at the papers. "You will find all the details there—what it is, why it will be profitable, the financial projections for the first phase of operation." A pause. "And the number of shares you shall receive in the company."

Sheffield tugged a little nervously at his cuff. "Please take your time in reviewing the material. If you have any questions, I shall endeavor to answer them."

A silence settled over the study, stirred only by the whispery flutter of paper and the muted crackling of the banked coals in the hearth. As Wrexford read through the pages, he found himself growing more and more impressed. The details of the business were presented in an articulate and well-reasoned outline, and the projection of profits was quite conservative. All in all, it appeared a very professional proposal.

He looked up. "I take it you have partners in this endeavor?"

"Yes," answered Sheffield. He didn't elaborate.

Curious, the earl replied, "Might I ask whom?"

His friend hesitated and averted his eyes. "I would prefer not to say, if you don't mind."

Wrexford couldn't help but raise a brow.

"*Not* for any unscrupulous reason," added Sheffield hastily. "I think you'll approve of them. But at the moment, I'm not at liberty to reveal that information."

"Very well." Wrexford decided to respect the request but then went on to ask some lengthy questions related to the matter of costs and profits and the actual running of the business. He could easily afford the requested investment, but it wasn't a paltry sum. And he knew that if the business failed, his friend would feel ashamed of squandering the earl's money.

Sheffield answered the queries with a calm confidence, showing an excellent understanding of the proposed company, including his own role. "Because of my family connections and my entrée into Society, I've assumed the main duties of raising investments. But I'm also involved in choosing what imports will appeal to the aristocracy. One of the partners is highly skilled in doing the complex financial projections, and one of them has expertise and contacts in the world of shipping."

After a bit more probing, Wrexford was satisfied. "It appears a very solid plan." He scribbled out a note and sealed it with his signet ring. "Take this to my banker tomorrow and he'll give you the funds."

His friend expelled a breath, a flicker of relief lighting beneath his lashes. "Again, my thanks. I owe you a debt of gratitude, Wrex."

"Actually, you don't," he replied. "I've no intention of taking any stock from you. I'm happy, simply as a friend, to invest in your future, and wish you great success."

"No!" Sheffield fisted his hands and made no move to pick up the promissory note. "I'm not asking for charity." There was a tone in his friend's voice that he had never heard before. "This is a business deal and will be done as such—or not at all."

"As you wish," agreed Wrexford, though a frisson of unease tickled down his spine. He fervently hoped that his friend's partners were competent. If the company failed, Sheffield would, he feared, take it very hard.

His friend gathered up the papers before pocketing the note. "You had better begin dressing," he murmured, glancing at the mantel clock. "The ball begins soon, and you've promised to lead Lady Charlotte out for the first waltz. You can't leave her standing like an abandoned flower, left to wilt in the shadows of the wall."

The chiding, however oblique, stung. "Do you truly think I would leave Lady Charlotte in the lurch?"

Sheffield flushed. "No, of course not! But . . ." His words trailed off in a muted rustling as he placed the documents back in his portfolio.

"But what?" asked the earl softly.

There was a heartbeat of hesitation before his friend reluctantly replied, "But there are times when your sentiments are . . . difficult to discern. They often flicker between day and night . . . reflecting the warmth of the sun or the coolness of the moon."

It was an astute observation, admitted the earl. "Perhaps it's simply my fate to be contrary. The dark and light sides of my nature are constantly at war with each other."

Sheffield fixed him with a searching stare, but before he could reply, Wrexford turned the conversation back to the ball. "Lady Charlotte won't lack for support as she reenters the world of the beau monde. I'm well aware that pomp and glitter are needed to impress them and ensure her acceptance into Polite Society—an ironic moniker, seeing as they are, for the most part, naught but a pack of well-groomed, sharp-clawed feral cats."

The earl gave a shrug. "Be that as it may, I've taken care of arranging the right partners for her. And don't forget that her cousin Nicholas, the new Lord Chittenden, and her good friend Lord Sterling will be there to lend moral support."

"Well, then," murmured Sheffield. "It appears there's no reason to worry. The evening should spin along with nary a slip or stumble."

There was a spun-sugar, fairie-tale splendor to the scene. The curling grand staircase of pure white marble led up to a landing, where two massive urns of pale pink roses flanked a thick gold-threaded burgundy runner, its sinuous velvet beckoning the invited guests to enter. . . .

Lady Charlotte Sloane slowed her steps and drew a deep breath as she eyed the ornate archway leading into the ballroom. Music floated out of the open doors, the notes twirling a merry dance with the effervescent laughter and discreet clink of champagne glasses. Diamond-bright light from the crystal chandeliers illuminated the jewel-tone sparkle of the ladies in their sumptuous gowns and the muted elegance of the gentlemen in their evening finery.

It was the stuff of every wellborn schoolgirl's dreams. . . .

To her horror, Charlotte felt a prickling against her eyelids. *Damnation—I ran all the way to Italy to escape living in just such a gilded cage.*

"Chin up, gel," murmured Alison, the dowager Marchioness of Peake, taking a firmer hold of Charlotte's arm. "I imagine you've faced far more fearsome challenges than stepping into a crowd of overfed aristocrats."

"Remind me again why I'm doing this." She squinted. The glitter was hurting her eyes. "At seventeen, I was wise enough to know I'd never survive as a pasteboard cutout, corseted in the tight strictures of Society."

"Yes, but now you're ever wiser, because you've learned how to make your own rules," replied the dowager.

*Rules.* Ever since she could remember, Charlotte had chosen to live her life breaking every possible blue-blooded rule in the book.

*Choices, choices.* Her recent decision to step out from the shadows and reenter the world of the beau monde had allowed her to find her cousin's killer. But the triumph had not come without a cost, for now there was no going back to her previous life, where anonymity had allowed an unfettered freedom and independence.

And so, here she was—a world-wise widow who was more at home in the slums than the fancy salons—attending her first formal ball. The irony was even sharper as she made her living satirizing the world of indolent excesses, along with the ladies and gentlemen with whom she was rubbing shoulders.

"And," added Alison, "you're doing this because you're rather fond of your doddering old great-aunt and know how much I'm looking forward to stirring up some gossip among the pompous prigs and featherbrained widgeons of the ton." Her blue eyes took on a sharp-edged gleam. "Life was becoming sadly flat before you stepped back into my life. And what fun is it if one loses the reputation of being a Holy Terror?"

A smile touched Charlotte's lips. Alison had been the only adult member of her stiff-rumped family who had understood—and encouraged—the wayward girl whose curiosity and imagination refused to be confined within conventional thinking.

"It's you who gave me the courage to fly in the face of conformity," she murmured.

"Oh, pfft. It's not as if you've done anything *really* outrageous."

*Ha!* She and the dowager had only recently reconnected, and her great-aunt didn't yet know the full scope of Charlotte's . . . eccentricities.

Alison thumped her cane on the carpet, cutting short any further musings, and quickly led them through the requisite greeting of their hostess.

"Now come, let us enjoy the pleasures of wine and waltzing until dawn." *Thump-thump.* "Remember, we are here to enjoy a night of revelry." The dowager waved for a footman to bring over his tray of champagne. "And we may begin by joining those two young jackanapes by the refreshment table."

Charlotte's face wreathed in a smile—a genuine one—when she spotted her cousin Nicholas and her childhood comrade in mischief. Jeremy, who through an unforeseen quirk of family travails was now the very wealthy Baron Sterling, looked up and met her gaze with a grin.

"Well, well, here I go away from London for several months and all hell breaks loose," he murmured as he came forward and leaned in to brush a kiss to her glove.

A cold-as-ice shiver raced down her spine. It was true—the murder of Nicholas's twin brother and his subsequent arrest for the heinous crime had plunged her and her friends into a dark and dangerous netherworld of unimaginable horrors as they refused to give up on proving him innocent. Without the help of . . .

"Thank heavens for Wrexford," added Jeremy. "Granted, he's an arrogant and irascible devil, but he possesses the intelligence and iron will to beat Satan at his own game."

"We were lucky," she said softly.

All trace of humor died in his eyes. "So I heard." Charlotte herself had come perilously close to sticking her spoon in the wall. "I should have returned from the North to help."

"Your friends needed you," countered Charlotte. "And none of us dreamed that things would take such an unexpected turn."

"Yes, well, murder has a way of drawing you into all sorts of unpleasant surprises," replied Jeremy, who had been caught up in one of their earlier investigations. "I fervently hope that from now on, you and the earl will stop tripping over dead bodies . . ."

He paused and raised a brow. "Ah, speak of the devil."

# CHAPTER 2

Charlotte slowly turned, the flutter of her fancy silks stirring a pebbling of gooseflesh on her bare arms.

Wrexford was easy to spot in the crowd. Tall and broad shouldered, his Satan-dark hair falling over his collar in unruly tangles, he was dressed entirely in black, save for the touch of starched white linen at his neck.

His evening attire was exquisitely tailored, she noted. However, his scowl—also black—was cut from a different cloth.

He disliked pompous prigs even more than she did.

Feathers bobbing, a gaggle of turbaned matrons scattered at his approach, clucking like helpless chicks whose henhouse had just been invaded by a wolf. A murmur ran through the room—Wrexford was known for his volatile behavior—as the earl stopped and looked around.

Their eyes met.

And a glint of emerald sparkled through his lashes as the scowl softened, allowing his lips to curl ever so slightly upward.

Charlotte drew in a breath, suddenly feeling as if she had just swallowed a flock of butterflies.

*What an odd sensation,* she mused. It must be the champagne that was making her feel so fluttery.

"Wrexford!" called the dowager, breaking away from her conversation with Nicholas to wave him over.

"Milady." The earl executed a faultless bow. "How very naughty of you to cast all the fresh-faced young beauties in the shade." Looking up with a spark of unholy amusement, he lowered his voice to a mock whisper. "Intelligence and experience in a lady are far more alluring than simpering smiles and vapid conversation."

A snort sounded in answer. "What fustian, sir." Alison waggled her cane. "However, at my age, the prattle of a charming rogue, fustian or not, is rather welcome."

"Me, charming?" Wrexford arched his dark brows. "God forbid."

Charlotte shifted as he greeted Nicholas and Jeremy . . . and then went very still as he turned to her.

"Lady Charlotte."

It took her an instant to realize he was reaching out to perform the usual ritual of bestowing a kiss upon her hand.

She hastily fumbled to place her palm atop his knuckles.

"You look . . ."

Charlotte waited for one of his usual sarcastic witticisms.

"Lovely," he finished.

Her jaw went slack.

"The color suits you," he added. "It's . . . elusive."

Madame Françoise, London's most exclusive modiste—and also part of Charlotte's extensive network of sharp-eyed informants who kept her apprised of all the hidden secrets and scandals of the ton—had chosen a smoky slate-blue hue for Charlotte's gown, and the watered silk had an intriguing aura of mystery as it subtly shifted shades depending on how it caught the light.

"Elusive," repeated Charlotte dryly, quickly composing her emotions. "I daresay I'm the only lady here who'll receive *that* word as a compliment." A pause. "Assuming it was one."

"Surely by now you know better than to expect platitudes from me."

"I do." She tugged at her glove, feeling oddly jumpy, and then quaffed another sip of her champagne. "As a man of science, you're dedicated to searching for truths through logic and empirical evidence, rather than emotion or wishful thinking. So, of course you recognize that no matter how costly or alluring the fabric, one can't make a silk purse out of a sow's ear."

Wrexford took her arm and drew her away from the others to a more secluded spot by the doorway leading to the side salons. The musicians, she realized, had left off playing a stately concerto and were tuning their instruments for the start of the dancing.

A spurt of panic rose in her gorge.

"Relax, Lady Charlotte," counseled the earl. The steadiness of his hand seemed to still her churning innards. He watched as the Royal Duke of Cumberland and several of his cronies strolled past them. "Remember, you know all the deepest, darkest foibles and scandals of everyone in the room. It is they who should be feeling on the verge of puking."

"How very reassuring, Wrexford," she drawled. "You certainly know how to calm a lady's delicate nerves."

A chuckle rumbled in his throat. "Would you rather I appeal to your mercenary side? Just think of all the juicy little details you'll gather firsthand for your satirical drawings now that you have entrée into the inner sanctum of the aristocracy."

The earl had a point. For her, this wasn't about flirting and frivolities. Yes, her job put food on the table and allowed an independence few ladies of her class ever achieved. But she did it because she had a passion for fighting hypocrisy and the misuse of power and privilege.

*Good versus evil.* She knew Wrexford thought her pitifully naïve to believe that light could vanquish darkness. . . .

A none-too-gentle tug roused her from her reverie as he

plucked the glass from her hand and set it aside. "Stop wool-gathering. They're striking up the first waltz."

Charlotte didn't need to look around to know all eyes were upon her. It felt as if dagger points were dancing over every inch of exposed skin.

"Just imagine they're all naked," he murmured.

"Must I?" She let out a ragged exhale, and the knot in her belly suddenly loosened. Leave it to Wrexford to say something so spectacularly outrageous that she couldn't help but smile. "Now I'm not nervous. I'm merely ill."

He laughed. And then, as the first notes of the lilting melody began, he swept her into a twirling turn and all rational thoughts went spinning away.

*A sow's ear?* Pulling Charlotte a touch closer, Wrexford guided her through another intricate figure of the waltz. *Is that how she sees herself?* To him, she possessed the quicksilver grace of a forest wood sprite, a beguiling mix of dark and light dipping and darting through the shadows, eluding all attempts to cage her spirit.

She confounded him. Challenged him. And yes, infuriated him when she charged into places where angels should fear to tread.

His breath caught in his throat at the memory of their recent investigation. He had never been so frightened in his life as when he had opened the door to a secret chamber, uncertain of whether he would find her dead or alive.

"You're scowling," murmured Charlotte.

He shook off his dark thoughts.

"You're supposed to be helping me make a good impression on the beau monde, and instead they'll think I'm an ungainly oaf who is squashing your toes."

"I'm notorious for scowling." Her silken gown, as ethereal and changeable as a puff of smoke, fluttered around her slender hips as they moved as one in harmony to the music. "And for being a dangerous, mercurial fellow with a hair-trigger temper."

Her lips twitched. "Your bark is far worse than your bite. But be that as it may, you could be Satan Incarnate, but the fact that you're an earl adds luster to my first dance in Polite Society." A pause. "So do try to appear as though I'm not driving you to distraction."

Wrexford couldn't hold back a smile. "There. Is that better?"

She nodded uncertainly and looked away. They spun through the next few turns in silence.

"Forgive me if my sharp tongue has caused offense," he finally said. "As you well know, I see the world through a rather cynical prism."

"Oh, it's not you, Wrexford. I've become quite comfortable with your sarcasm." Charlotte sighed. "The trouble lies with me. I . . ." She stepped through a turn with unconscious grace. "I never imagined I'd be here. And I suppose I'm still trying to come to grips with how my life has changed."

"Change is an immutable part of life," he said. "We grow, we evolve, and we learn to look at things from new perspective. And we come to feel differently about things than we did in the past."

His words seemed to surprise her. "When we first met, you claimed you didn't have any feelings."

"Perhaps I've changed."

Charlotte met his gaze. A current was swirling in the depths of her eyes, but he couldn't quite fathom its meaning. "I think we've both changed."

Wrexford held his breath and waited for her to go on.

"But . . ." She allowed a rueful grimace. "I couldn't begin to say how." Another spin, another twirl. "Or why."

"Some things defy words," he agreed.

"And yet—"

Whatever she was going to say was cut short by the music ending.

All around them, the fluttering blaze of colors stilled as the other couples began to leave the dance floor. Wrexford released his hold on her and stepped back. "I see Sheffield and Lady Cordelia have arrived and are with Lady Peake and the others. Shall we join them?"

"Lady Charlotte!" Sheffield greeted her with an appreciative smile and placed his hand on his heart. "On with the dancing! Let joy be unconfin'd—"

"I beg you, Kit," interrupted the earl. "If you're going to misquote poetry, at least choose someone other than that arse Lord Byron."

"You don't find the baron's poetry romantic, Lord Wrexford?" asked Lady Cordelia Mansfield, the corners of her mouth giving a telltale twitch. Like the earl, she didn't suffer fools gladly.

He looked down his long nose at her. "I find any excess unpalatable—to wit, add a cup of sugar to your tea rather than a spoonful, and it will make you gag."

"I take my tea unsugared, so I quite agree with you," replied Cordelia.

"I thought all ladies swooned over Byron," protested Sheffield, though he, too, looked to be biting back a grin. "What about you, Lady Charlotte?" he queried, turning to her.

"I hate to disappoint you, but I'm afraid my sentiments are the same."

"Thank heavens." Sheffield expelled a theatrical sigh. "Now I don't feel quite so intimidated in offering my humble self for the next set." A mischievous twinkle danced in his eyes. "You see, I could never pen a poem. It takes too much thinking—and thinking makes my head hurt."

Charlotte laughed and happily accepted his hand. Sheffield had come to be a close friend, and although he was considered a charming fribble by most of Society, Charlotte was well aware that his seemingly reckless behavior masked a sharp intelligence and steadfast loyalty.

"I shall try to make sure that dancing doesn't make your toes hurt," she replied. "But I can't promise."

"Stop your gabbling and move your feet, Mr. Sheffield," chided Alison. "The music is starting."

*Spinning, spinning, spinning.* The laughter, the music, the colors—aswirl in the bright blaze of candlelight, the ballroom was beginning to blur. Charlotte blinked as she capered through the steps of a lively country gavotte, suddenly feeling overwhelmed by the noise and the crush of the crowd.

It felt as if she had been dancing for hours—after Sheffield and her cousin had come the Duke of Roxleigh and Lord Winchester, two of the most august aristocrats in London, followed by a dizzying procession of more prominent gentlemen. . . .

"Thank, you, sir," she murmured a little breathlessly as at last the dance came to an end.

Her partner smiled and offered his arm. "Would you care for some champagne before the next set begins?"

Desperately in need of a quiet respite, Charlotte replied with a fib. "Alas, I've a tiny tear in my hem, so I'm afraid I must forgo the pleasure of another dance in order to withdraw and have one of the maids help repair the stitching."

"But of course." He inclined a gentlemanly bow and escorted her to the side doorway leading out of the ballroom.

After thanking him again, she slipped into the corridor and headed for the rear of the mansion. But instead of turning right for the withdrawing room, Charlotte darted down the darkened passageway to her left, intent on finding a deserted room where she might sit quietly and collect her thoughts.

Spotting a half-open door, she ducked inside and found herself in an unlit foyer. Straight ahead was an archway leading into an alcove. From the faint glow of light illuminating the framed prints on the wall, there appeared to be a main room around the corner.

A game room, perhaps?

Drawn by a flutter of a cool evening breeze—a window seemed to be open—and the thought of a comfortable armchair offering a safe haven from the glare of the ballroom, Charlotte took a few quick steps, her silk dancing slippers moving noiselessly over the Oriental runner. She was about to turn when a sudden muttered huff warned that she wasn't alone.

"What the devil do you mean by showing up here in such a state and sending a footman to summon me here?"

A lady's voice.

*Ye heavens. Surely it wasn't . . .*

"I-I'm sorry," a man's voice answered, sounding slurred and disoriented. "I know I shouldn't have come here, but . . ." He let out a ragged sigh. "But I've had a bit of shock."

"You look like hell. Sit and pull yourself together while I pour you a glass of brandy."

Charlotte shrank back against the wall, not daring to move, and held her breath as the rustle of skirts was followed by the clink of glass against glass.

"Here. Drink." A gasp. "Good Lord, your hand is badly scraped and bleeding."

"I can explain—"

"Shhhh! Not so loud!" warned the lady. "The last thing we want is for someone to see you in this condition."

Their voices dropped to an urgent but indistinct murmur, punctuated by the sound of ripping fabric.

"Stop squirming. I need to bandage your palm."

Charlotte ventured a quick peek and felt her heart hit up against her ribs. It *was* Cordelia, and the smoky light of the small oil lamp showed that the man with her was her brother, Jameson Mansfield, the new Earl of Woodbridge since his father's recent death.

However, at the moment, he looked more like a vagrant wastrel. His boots were filthy, and his disheveled coat and breeches were streaked with muck. As for his face, he looked like he had been in a fight.

She ducked back into the shadows as Woodbridge scrubbed a hand over his bruised jaw and shifted in his seat.

"What happened?" asked Cordelia in a tight voice. The clink of glass seemed to indicate she was pouring her brother another measure of brandy.

"I wasn't thinking clearly. I—I ventured somewhere I shouldn't have gone . . ." His voice trailed off as he paused to draw a labored breath, and when he spoke again, it was in an agitated whisper.

It was well known that footpads prowled through Hyde Park and its adjoining streets, looking for drunken gentlemen whose fuzzed wits made them easy prey, thought Charlotte. It appeared Woodbridge had been careless and had paid the price.

"The devil take it, Jamie. How could you have been so stupid?" muttered Cordelia.

Charlotte didn't blame her friend for sounding exasperated. She had met Jameson Mansfield, and he had struck her as less pragmatic and perceptive than his sister. The encounter had also revealed that the late earl's profligate spending had left the two siblings with mounting financial pressures.

Woodbridge cleared his throat. "Hear me out, Cordy—"

"Not now," cut in Cordelia. "Leave by the same way you came in, and go home. I'll return to the ballroom and take my leave." Skirts rustled. "And pray that no one notices that part of my petticoat is missing."

Charlotte didn't wait to hear any more. Embarrassed at having accidentally witnessed such a painfully private family matter, she quickly retreated and hurried through the shadowed turns of the corridor until she reached the aureole of light spilling out from the side doorway of the ballroom.

Pausing for a moment, she smoothed her skirts and steeled

her spine as the sinuous lilt of music and laughter spun through the perfumed air.

*Elegance and glamor. Gaiety and revelries.* But she, of all people, knew that beneath its glitter, the world of the beau monde was not quite as perfect as it seemed.

Cordelia and her brother occupied the very highest rung of Society and, by all appearances, lived a gilded life. And yet their elegant tailoring and fine silks apparently hid family financial troubles.

Just how dangerous were they?

London offered a multitude of sins. Had the need for money driven Woodbridge to one of the gaming hells in the stews? Or . . .

Charlotte felt a frisson of unease. Since she was an artist who made a living uncovering secrets, her senses were attuned to noticing the smallest details. So she couldn't help but wonder why the air in the game room had held a whiff of brine, and the mud on Woodbridge's boots had been speckled with bits of oyster shells.

# CHAPTER 3

Wincing as a dappling of cheery sunlight danced through the windowpanes, warming the sheaf of blank watercolor paper on the blotter, Charlotte gingerly took a seat at her work desk.

"Mmph." The movement, though slight, drew another grumble of protest from her lurching stomach. "It seems that I engaged in one too many gavottes with a sparkling glass of champagne last night."

Pleasure had its penance. No matter that she wished to crawl back under the bedcovers, she had a drawing due today.

Steepling her fingers, Charlotte contemplated the top sheet, its pristine white hue seeming to stare back at her with a taunting challenge flickering up from its rough-grained surface.

"Right," she murmured. "The city has been unnaturally peaceful of late. Why, even the Prince Regent has stirred no new scandals. So . . ." A sigh. "What other foibles are there to skewer?"

Her gaze strayed over to the recent editions of *Ackermann's Repository* stacked on the side table. The journal's on-dits on Polite Society were often useful for sparking an idea, but they, too, had been awfully tame of late.

"Oh, come." A sigh. "Surely I can think of *something* to ridicule. Scandal and secrets are my bread and butter."

Alas, her mind, like the paper, remained blank.

She tried to concentrate. Her thoughts were usually well focused, sharpened, no doubt, by the fact that peace and quiet put no pennies in her purse. But this morning they kept waltzing to their own tune, spinning and twirling like the dust motes dancing in the gold-flecked light.

*Dancing.* The word stirred a different sort of flutter in her belly.

Waltzing with Wrexford, she mused, had been oddly wonderful . . . though, of course, those two words made no sense together.

"But then, neither do the two of us," murmured Charlotte, then reminded herself that work must take precedence over personal lollygagging. She reached for her quill and penknife and began shaping a sharp point.

And yet her damnable wayward brain seemed to have another idea in mind.

*Wrexford.* His name—like his physical presence when he sauntered into her pleasant little parlor—seemed to shove all else from her thoughts. She wasn't precisely sure how that had come to be. At first blush, he wasn't a gentleman to make a girlish heart flutter.

*Irascible. Arrogant. Sarcastic.* His scientific mind valued cold-blooded logic over tender sentiment.

Putting aside her newly sharpened pen, Charlotte picked up a pencil and began to doodle. But as with most things in life, such a starkly simple first impression had given way to a far more nuanced portrait. She stared down at her caricature, with its sinuous curls of too-long hair—the earl was always in need of a barber—and subtle shading that softened the hard line of his jaw. Strange how comfortable she had become with the austere planes of his face. Rather than just the starkly chiseled edges, she now saw all the subtle contours and vulnerabilities that made him . . .

That made him Wrexford.

Their relationship had taken a number of twists and turns, the way all too often darkened by danger. And of late, it had taken a new spin . . . one that still seemed to have both of them off-balance. Perhaps if in the future they stopped tripping over dead bodies, they could begin to sort out their personal feelings. . . .

"The future? Ha!" Shoving aside her musings, Charlotte crumpled the sketch and drew a fresh sheet onto the blotter. "I had better concentrate on the present."

After several long moments, a sigh of relief slipped from her lips as she suddenly remembered the bit of gossip McClellan, the redoubtable woman who served as both maid and general taskmaster in their little household, had mentioned at breakfast. A highwayman had apparently accosted a carriage last night on Hounslow Heath and robbed the lone traveler of a princely sum of valuables.

That the victim was the notoriously eccentric Duchess of York, wife of the king's second son, would delight the masses, who, along with having a soft spot for the romantic image of a dashing highwayman, loved nothing more than to laugh at the follies of their betters. The duchess's marriage was not a happy one, and she had taken up residence at Oatlands, the family estate in Surrey, where she lived alone, with a vast menagerie of animals to keep her company.

She was said to be particularly fond of her pugs and pet monkeys.

Repressing a grin, Charlotte reached for her paint box and began mixing a batch of garish colors. Already she was imagining the drawing's composition—the carriage, with drooling dogs peering from all the windows and a capering monkey dressed in a footman's livery throwing a coconut at the pistol-wielding highwayman. After all, the public needed to laugh as well as ponder the serious issues that often resonated in her satire.

With a few quick pencil strokes, she drew in the basic outlines, then reached for her pen. . . .

A loud pounding on the front door nearly caused Charlotte to spill the inkwell.

"Now what?" she murmured after expelling a harried sigh.

"Oiy, oiy!" cried a reedy voice as McClellan admitted the caller. "There's been a 'orrible murder down by the wharf where de rich skivvies bring in their puffers from the east!"

"Hold your horses, Skinny," called Charlotte as she hurried down the stairs. The rail-thin streetsweep, never easy to understand under the best of circumstances, tended to mangle his vowels when he was excited. "And please repeat what you just said—at a walk, not a gallop."

"Oiy," snorted the lad in frustration. "Ye didn't skibble wot I jez sed?"

Charlotte smiled at McClellan. "Perhaps ginger biscuits would smooth out the rough edges of Skinny's tongue."

The boy was part of a small band of urchins—all friends of Raven and Hawk from their time of living on the streets—who regularly gathered information for Charlotte. Their eyes and ears had also proved invaluable in previous murder investigations.

"Indeed," agreed the maid. "I daresay a jam tart and a cup of sugared tea would help, as well."

"Aye, that would do the trick." Skinny's pronunciation was suddenly greatly improved.

Charlotte looked down at the boy's muck-encrusted shoes and gave a mental wince before saying, "Excellent. Now come have a seat in the parlor while McClellan fetches the refreshments."

"Where's Raven and Hawk?" asked Skinny as he scampered to one of the pillowed armchairs, leaving a trail of dried dung on the carpet.

Charlotte furrowed her brow, suddenly realizing she hadn't yet seen her young wards.

The brothers had first come under her wing while her late husband had still been alive—two half-wild street urchins who ran errands in return for scraps of food and a place to sleep. But they had come to be a family, tied together by love rather than blood. In fact, she had recently become their legal guardian, though how that had come about was rather complicated. . . .

She sighed. A maid proficient in wielding a pistol and picking a lock . . . two streetwise-beyond-their-years urchins . . . and herself, a lady with so many personas she sometimes feared her true self was becoming blurred beyond recognition.

Theirs was, admittedly, an exceedingly eccentric household.

McClellan's brusque cough brought her back to the present. "I believe they went out before you awoke."

"To do what?" she asked.

"As to that, I really can't say."

"Hmmph." Charlotte pursed her lips. "Well, I do hope Raven remembers that he has a mathematics lesson with Lady Cordelia later this afternoon." Though whether his tutor was in any frame of mind to recall the appointment was another question.

However, she pushed that thought aside on hearing Skinny start to squirm. For her, adding up all the elements of a murder was a far more intriguing challenge than a page full of numbers.

Wrexford tightened the sash of his dressing gown and poured himself a cup of coffee.

"I must be getting old," he muttered. In the past, a night of dancing and drinking champagne wouldn't have left him feeling as if a spike had been hammered through his skull.

Though in truth, he admitted after swallowing a sip of the

scalding devil-dark brew, it was unlikely that the ballroom revelries were responsible for his throbbing head. They had been surprisingly pleasant. Dancing with Charlotte was . . .

He suddenly recalled her musings on how some things defied words. What a pair they were—conundrums wrapped in conundrums. And yet, strangely enough, that thought provoked a smile.

*A mistake.* The tiny facial movement sent another sharp stab through the back of his head.

Wrexford took another swallow of coffee and then began massaging at his temples. The fault for his present condition lay in his workroom, not the Countess of Lexington's opulent mansion. On returning home from the ball, he had taken a moment to read over the books that Tyler had left out for him regarding Silliman's experiments. One thing had led to another, and he had stayed up until well past dawn, working at close quarters among the fumes of some potent acids.

*Ah, but science requires sacrifice.*

After picking up his cup, the earl ambled out of the breakfast room and headed for the rear of the townhouse, curious to see how the experiments were progressing. To his surprise, he heard voices emanating from the workroom. One of them was Tyler's. And the other . . .

"Ah, there you are, milord." A big, beefy man turned from studying the esoteric objects displayed in the curio cabinet and eyed Wrexford's sleep-tousled hair and unshaven jaw. "Apparently, there's no truth to the old adage 'No rest for the wicked.'"

"On the contrary, Griffin, I've been sleeping the sleep of the innocent," Wrexford retorted. He and the Bow Street Runner had first met when Griffin had suspected him of a gruesome murder, but they had since become allies rather than adversaries and had worked together in solving several other deaths. "So please swallow any further attempts at humor. I've not yet had my breakfast."

A smile curled at the corners of Griffin's lips. "What are we having?"

"Bloody hell, how do you survive when you're not feasting off my largesse?" grumbled Wrexford. Their meetings usually took place at a tavern, with the earl purchasing a very handsome meal in return for the Runner's help in working through the conundrums of a case.

"Very poorly," shot back Griffin. He gave an appreciative sniff as a footman discreetly knocked, then entered the room, bearing a large tray of covered dishes.

The earl blew out a long-suffering sigh. "You might as well set an extra place, Tyler. Otherwise he'll stay for supper."

The valet dutifully cleared a spot on the massive desk and carried over an extra chair.

"Much obliged, milord," murmured the Runner.

Wrexford slouched into his seat and poured a fresh cup of coffee. "So, to what do I owe the pleasure of a visit—other than the need for you to fill your growling breadbox?"

"The fact that you're the most learned man I know." Griffin helped himself to a freshly baked muffin. "Does the word *argentum* mean anything to you?"

"Anyone who's had the classical languages thumped into his head can't help but know it," the earl replied. "It's Latin for 'silver.' "

"Hmmm." The Runner took a bite of the pastry and chewed thoughtfully.

"Why do you ask?"

A swallow. "There was a murder at Queen's Landing last night. The watchman who found the victim reported that he said the word *argentum*—several times, in fact—with his last dying breath."

"Who's the dead man?" inquired Wrexford.

"A clerk with the East India Company," answered the Runner. "With all the unloading of valuable cargoes, the Company wharves attract a criminal element," observed the earl. "Perhaps he witnessed the theft of a silver shipment, and that's why he was killed."

"Perhaps," replied Griffin as he studied the sultanas studding his muffin. "But . . ." He looked up. "Why say it in Latin?"

Wrexford shrugged. "I haven't a clue."

"Hmmm." The Runner sliced off a large chunk of ham and forked it into his mouth.

Griffin's slow movements and laconic style of speech often caused people to think he was dim witted. The earl, however, knew otherwise.

"What is it about the death that's caught your attention?" he asked. "Bow Street prefers that you investigate crimes involving the highest circles of Society. So, regrettable as it is, the murder of a clerk wouldn't normally be a case that concerns you."

"I can't say for sure." Griffin polished off a bite of eggs before adding, "At least not yet."

"Well, do take your time in thinking it over," quipped Wrexford. "You've still got a platter of deviled kidneys and a slice of pigeon pie to plow through." He rose. "But if you don't mind, I'll excuse myself. Unlike you and Tyler, I have work to do."

"Now, about the murder . . . Let us start from the beginning," said Charlotte, taking a seat in the armchair facing Skinny.

"It happened last night at Queen's Landing," replied the streetsweep. "The watchmen found the cove just before eleven bells in an alleyway near the gate leading out to Commercial Road." His eyes widened. "Word is, his throat was sliced open from ear te ear."

Her stomach gave a small lurch at the gruesome detail. "Is the victim's identity known?" she asked.

Skinny nodded. "Oiy, Alice the Eel Girl heard from Pudge that he was a . . . a clerk." His face scrunched in thought. "Wot's a clerk?"

"A man who keeps all the records organized for a company. He writes down all the business information and makes copies of all the letters sent and received," explained Charlotte.

"Sounds boring." Skinny rubbed at a gob of mud on his sleeve. "Are you and His Nibs gonna solve the murder?"

Charlotte felt a twinge of guilt. Much as she mourned the passing of any living being, she couldn't find justice for all of them.

London was a large city, and murders were a grim reality of its everyday life. The heartless truth was, only those that involved a prominent person or touched on a juicy scandal were of interest to the public who purchased her prints. Mr. Fores wouldn't publish something that everyone from the lowest pauper to the highest aristocrat knew was true—that countless nameless souls who inhabited the city would die as they had lived, with no one taking note of their existence.

"Alas, I'm not sure that Lord Wrexford and I can be of any help in this case," she said softly. "The man was likely killed for the few pence in his pocket, and the murderer has melted back into the stews, leaving no trail of his misdeed."

"Aye," agreed Skinny, with fatalism well beyond his years. "Bad things just happen. Not much ye can do about it when the Reaper decides te swing his blade at ye." His expression quickly brightened, however, as McClellan carried in a tray heaped with treats and moved a side table in front of his chair.

As he dug noisily into a jam tart, Charlotte leaned back, feeling troubled by the conversation.

*Am I losing my moral compass?*

Once she had made the momentous decision to step back into the splendor of the beau monde, she had vowed that she wouldn't lose her passion for fighting against the injustices of the world. But what if its seductive pleasures tempted her into losing her edge?

The thought squeezed the air from her lungs.

Lost in her brooding, Charlotte didn't hear the front door open or the patter of light-footed steps in the corridor. It was the sudden lush swirl of floral perfume tickling at her nose that caused her to sit up.

"Faawgh," exclaimed Skinny, making a face. "What happened? It smells like a French brothel in here."

"It's ungentlemanly to say the word *brothel* in front of a lady," called Hawk as he and his brother paused just outside the parlor.

Skinny grinned. "I ain't a gentlemun."

"No—you're an imp of Satan," called McClellan from the corridor. "I swear, you've left more horse droppings on the rug than a regiment of the King's Household cavalry!"

"Let us not tease Skinny," chided Charlotte as she turned in her chair. "I—"

Her words stuck in her throat as she caught sight of the massive bouquet of flowers the boys were carrying toward her. Pale pinks, creamy whites, and dusky lavenders, punctuated by curls of leafy greenery . . . and two dirt-streaked faces peering at her through the fronds.

The effect was breathtakingly beautiful.

A low whistle sounded. Even Skinny was rendered speechless.

"Mr. Tyler said that it's de-de . . . ," stuttered Hawk.

"De rigueur," prompted Raven.

"That it's de rigueur for a gentleman to show his admiration for a lady after a ball by sending her flowers the next day," finished Hawk.

"We know how well you waltz," added Raven. The boys had served as her practice partners while Tyler and McClellan had taught her the steps of the dance in preparation for the occasion. "And we saw how grand you looked in your ball gown . . ."

"Like a fairie princess!" chirped Hawk.

"So we wanted to present you with a token of our esteem." Raven then nudged his brother and waggled a brow.

"Oh. Right."

They both stepped forward and bowed in perfect unison.

Charlotte felt tears pearling on her lashes.

"Do you like them?" asked Hawk, looking up through his tangled curls.

"I love them."

They both smiled as she took the flowers, and suddenly the room seemed filled with a burst of warm light, chasing away the specter of Death and her own dark worries.

"Here, let me take those and put them in a vase." McClellan flashed a wink at the boys as she bustled by them. "Well done, Weasels."

"You knew," murmured Charlotte.

The maid assumed a look of innocence. "Knew what?"

"Owwff." Having polished off all the pastries, Skinny slid down from his chair. "I need te bobble my bones back te Piccadilly Street." He looked at the boys. "Ye wanna come along?"

"I can't. I have a lesson." Raven glanced at the mantel clock. "I'd better fetch my books and papers from upstairs."

"I'll go with you," said Hawk. "I wish to have a look around Covent Garden and see if there are any interesting new plants to sketch."

"Mebbe we'll hear something more about the murder," said Skinny as the two boys trooped out of the parlor.

"Thank heavens I don't have to turn my pen to the subject of violent death for my drawing," murmured Charlotte, though she still felt a little guilty that the poor man would go unremarked, save as a grim statistic. She turned and let out a startled huff.

"Forgive me for appearing unannounced, but the front door was open." Cordelia Mansfield paused in the doorway. "And McClellan waved at me to enter."

Charlotte quickly smiled. "As you know, we don't stand on ceremony in this house. Please come in. Raven is fetching his things from the aerie."

"What murder were the boys discussing?" asked Cordelia as she stepped into the sunlit parlor.

"A clerk was knifed to death."

"How terrible," replied her friend. "The city seems to be growing more perilous."

"I didn't mean to alarm you. The crime took place far from Mayfair, and the dockyards are known for being dangerous places."

The bag of books Cordelia was carrying slipped from her grasp and fell to the carpet with a thud. "How clumsy of me," she muttered, stooping to pick it up. "The crime occurred in the dockyards?"

"On Queen's Landing," explained Charlotte.

"Ah." Her friend tightened her hold on the books. "As you say, a world away."

"Indeed, a world away." Charlotte quickly cleared a jumble of skittles off the sofa table to make room for the sheets of equations and textbooks. "I'll ask McClellan to bring some tea and biscuits," she murmured after plucking the skull of a mouse from among the pillows and stuffing it into her pocket. "Sorry. Hawk was in here earlier, sketching from his collection of nature objects. But have no fear, there's nothing alive back there."

She checked a few more nooks, just to be sure. "At least I don't think so."

Cordelia gave a small smile, as she took a seat on the sofa. "As you know, I'm quite at home among eccentricities."

"No need for a summons." McClellan appeared with refreshments. "I took it upon myself to fix some hearty refreshments." She set down a tray loaded with savory tarts, fresh-baked bread, and a selection of cheeses. "You two were dancing until dawn, and that requires more than mere crumbs."

"Bless you," murmured Charlotte, surprised to find she was ravenous.

Cordelia, however, took only a tiny morsel of cheddar—and left it unnibbled on her plate.

In response to the maid's curiosity about the previous evening, the talk turned to the opulent decorations, the sumptuous refreshments, and the other guests.

"Though he claims otherwise, Mr. Sheffield dances quite well," observed Charlotte, having noticed that Cordelia had twice been his partner. In fact, she hadn't seen her on the dance floor with anyone else.

"Mr. Sheffield is more adept than he thinks at a great many things," replied her friend. "Perhaps it's the same with gentlemen as it is with ladies—if you possess beauty, it's presumed you don't possess a brain." Her brows rose in a sardonic arch. "Of course, I'm not speaking from personal experience."

Charlotte surreptitiously studied Cordelia with an artist's eye. It was true—her friend didn't fit the pattern card for feminine allure. There was nothing sweet or delicate about her looks. *Strong nose, wide mouth, angled cheekbones, eyes that blazed with a lively intelligence*—no doubt the aura of strength and vitality overpowered most people.

However, Charlotte found her face striking. "Beauty is in the eye of the beholder," she murmured. "The beau monde may currently favor delicate, doll-like features, devoid of any personality. But those who find pasteboard perfection boring prefer real individuality." She dusted the crumbs from her fingers. "I would love to draw you sometime, if you would be willing to sit for a portrait."

"I . . ." Cordelia appeared a little flustered. "I can't imagine that my face could be of any interest to you."

"Lady Charlotte sees nuances that most of us miss," said McClellan.

Despite the flush that had risen to her cheeks, Cordelia appeared to turn pale.

*We all have our own vulnerabilities and fears,* mused Charlotte. *No matter how silly they may seem to others.* "Ah, here is Raven," she announced, spotting the boy and looking to put an end to her friend's embarrassment.

"Did you work your way through all the assigned problems?" asked Cordelia.

"Yes," answered Raven. "Save for the last one, where I had a question about inverse functions."

"Well, come have a seat," she said, indicating a spot on the sofa next to her, "and let us see if we can figure out the answer together."

As McClellan cleared the refreshments, Charlotte took a few moments to gather up a few stray items lying around the parlor before heading up to her workroom. Cordelia was an excellent teacher, she noted, striking just the right note of encouragement and challenge. Raven, who tended to keep his feelings closely guarded, appeared to be flourishing under her tutelage.

The enthusiasm in his voice made Charlotte smile. To her, numbers were merely numbers, but to him, they were like her lines and colors—they could be formed into endlessly unique patterns that expressed something meaningful.

But enough philosophizing. She had a drawing to finish.

# CHAPTER 4

Charlotte added the last splash of color and leaned back, satisfied with the results. The humor was sharp but without a razored edge. Yes, the Duchess of York was eccentric.

*But so am I.*

The drawing was kind enough that people would laugh. But not in a vicious sort of way. Perhaps the talk of murder had softened her touch . . . though in truth, she liked to believe she was never deliberately cruel.

Angry and indignant when she uncovered hypocrisy, lies, and greed. But never gratuitously cruel.

"Or so I hope," she whispered. A commitment to honesty mattered, as did an unwavering belief in justice.

Once again, Charlotte felt her conscience begin to prickle. Now that she would be moving among the beau monde, there was a good chance that she would face the prospect of having to skewer someone with whom she had formed a friendship. It would be a moral dilemma she hadn't faced before.

*Truth and lies. Right and wrong.* Those were indelible concepts, written in black and white. To allow any shade of grey to creep in . . .

Would be the end of A. J. Quill.

Charlotte picked up a cloth and began to clean her pen. "I shall cross that ethical bridge when I come to it."

*And pray that I make the right decision.*

The simple task of putting away her paints and washing her brushes helped calm her uncertain thoughts. She was tired, and the act of murder always made her feel low.

As she rolled up the drawing and wrapped it in a length of oilskin for delivery to Mr. Fores, the murmur of voices downstairs in the parlor grew louder. Charlotte cocked an ear. It seemed Hawk had returned, bringing with him more news on the crime.

"And One-Eye Harry heard that the dead man was likely up to something havey-cavey."

The words seemed to stir a chill within the corridor's shadows as she approached the parlor.

"The guards at the gate said he worked in the big, fancy East India House on Leadenhall Street and was involved in accounting, not shipping, so had no reason to be around the docks," went on Hawk. "Especially at night."

"Are you saying the authorities think it's not simply a random robbery?" asked Charlotte.

Raven set down his pencil and looked up from the sheets of paper spread out across the sofa table. "Sounds like bad blood between thieves to me. You don't cut a cove's throat just to pick his pockets."

She nodded thoughtfully. "It does speak of anger or fear of betrayal."

Cordelia made a small sound of distress.

Distracted by the new facts about the crime, Charlotte had momentarily forgotten about her friend's presence. "Forgive us, Lady Cordelia," she said with an apologetic grimace. "We're interrupting the lesson with such ghoulish talk of murder."

"Oiy, but there's more," piped up Hawk. "Alice heard from one of the girls who sells eel pies at the wharves that Bow Street has been asking the supervisors what they know about something called ar . . . argentum."

"Argentum?" repeated Charlotte. Her brows pinched together. "I know that's the word for 'silver' in Latin," she mused. "But why would Bow Street be making inquiries in Latin? It must mean something else."

"Alice didn't know," replied Hawk.

"Perhaps it's a ship—" began Raven, but a sudden rustling of paper cut him off.

Cordelia quickly shuffled the sheets of equations into a neat pile and set them aside. Her hands seemed a little shaky as she closed the mathematics manual and stuffed it into her satchel.

Charlotte glanced at the clock. A routine had developed over the months since Cordelia had begun giving lessons to Raven. She always stayed for supper. He, too, looked aware that something was amiss.

"I'm sorry, I wasn't paying attention," he said in a tight voice. "I know we haven't finished—"

"It's me who needs to apologize," replied Cordelia. "I . . . I'm afraid I must be going."

To Charlotte's eye, her friend's face looked unnaturally pale. "Are you unwell?"

"Aye, you look a little green around the gills," offered Hawk.

"I must have eaten something last night that disagreed with me," answered Cordelia.

"McClellan makes a very good ginger tisane," said Charlotte. "I'll ring—"

"Thank you, but no." Cordelia rose. "I think it would be best for me to return home without delay."

"But of course," she answered. Argument would be churlish.

"Hawk, please go with Lady Cordelia and flag down a hackney for her."

Once the pair had left the room, Charlotte turned back to Raven. She had seen his eyes turn shadowed beneath the dark fringe of lashes. He didn't give of himself easily, and she worried that he would take Cordelia's abrupt departure too much to heart.

"She appeared uncomfortable before you came down for your lesson," she murmured. "It was a very long evening, with much wine and rich food." Not to speak of the confrontation with her brother. "So it's understandable if she's feeling a trifle out of sorts."

Raven didn't look up. "I s'pose." He carefully closed his book and placed the pile of equation-filled papers atop the cover. "I might as well put my books away. I'll finish the problems later."

Wrexford raised the brass knocker, but before he could let it fall, the painted portal flung open, nearly squashing his nose.

"Ho, what mischief are you Weasels about to wreak on the world?" he demanded, catching Hawk by the scruff of his collar as the boy tried to wriggle past him.

"Nothing as of yet," shot back Raven with a smirk. "But I'm sure we'll think of something by the time we're finished with our errand."

"And we mustn't be late, sir!" squeaked Hawk, holding Charlotte's well-wrapped drawing aloft. "Mr. Fores needs this delivered right away in order to have prints in his shop by tomorrow morning."

"*Tempus pecunia est,* " added Raven.

The earl chuckled. The older boy had begun to mimic Charlotte's habit of occasionally muttering Latin aphorisms. Where he learned them was as yet a mystery.

"Time is money," he translated. "Though not for indolent idlers like myself."

Raven made a rude sound.

"You know, some people are rather intimidated by my lordly title," drawled Wrexford. "You might want to show me a little more respect—especially as one of the many privileges of being a high-and-mighty aristocrat is having insolent little brats for breakfast."

"It's almost suppertime—" began Hawk, only to be interrupted by his brother.

"Ha! We would stick in your craw," retorted Raven.

Wrexford made a face. "True. You're all gristle and bone. I shall have to ask McClellan to fatten you up." The earl shifted, setting off a whispery crackle as he released his hold on Hawk.

"What's that?" demanded Raven, eyeing the cone of fancy wrapping paper he had tucked in the crook of his arm.

"Flowers for m'lady," the earl replied.

The boys looked at each other and burst out laughing.

"Pray, what's so amusing?"

Raven crinkled his nose. "That's a pretty puny bouquet."

"*Non multa, sed multum,*" retorted the earl.

"Do you know what that means?" whispered Hawk to his brother.

"Yes. He's telling us that because he learned a lot of habble-gabble at Oxford, he's smarter than we are."

Wrexford raised his brows. "It wasn't *me* who tossed down the habble-gabble gauntlet." He gave an airy wave. "Now run along, Weasels. Mr. Fores is waiting."

As they turned to go, the earl added, "And by the by, the habble-gabble means *Quality, not quantity, is what matters.*"

He watched them race away, moving like two dark flickers of quicksilver through the deepening shadows, before rapping a knock on the half-open door and entering into the small foyer.

"Ah. I thought I heard voices outside." Charlotte came out of the parlor, a small straw whisk broom and dustpan in her hands. "Do come in and make yourself comfortable, milord— though have a care not to sit in the armchair by the lamp table." Her nose crinkled as she glanced down. "Tyler would never forgive me if you ruined your expensive trousers."

Wrexford cleared his throat with a cough. He and his valet had recently given the Weasels an assortment of chemicals with which to experiment. They had been told to confine their explorations to the back garden. But mishaps did occur.

"Has there been some sort of accident?"

"Skinny isn't an accident—he's a force of Nature unto himself," she replied dryly. "Luckily, McClellan says she knows how to mix a cleaning solution for removing horse droppings from damask fabric."

"What brought Skinny here?" asked Wrexford, relieved to learn his conscience was clear.

"He—" Charlotte stopped abruptly. "What have you got in your hand?" She squinted. "It looks like a cone of pink and gold paper."

"My token offering isn't inspiring much enthusiasm in this household," he replied. "The Weasels were not impressed. They think it a very puny thing."

She appeared mystified. "Token offering?"

He held up the paper cone. "It's considered gentlemanly to bring a lady flowers after dancing with her."

Amusement lit in her eyes. "If you saw the massive bouquet they managed to put together, you would know why they were laughing. McClellan needed to locate a spare bucket, rather than a vase." She accepted the gift and carefully peeled back the edges of the paper. "Why, they're . . ."

Charlotte looked up. "They're beautiful."

"They're different." He had chosen a palette of subtle dusky blue and mauves instead of the traditional brighter hues. "I thought you might prefer something a little more interesting than roses."

The paper rustled. "They're beautiful," repeated Charlotte as she examined them more closely.

"And no bucket needed," he said lightly, though it pleased him that she seemed to like the bouquet. "But let us put aside the flowers for the moment . . ." He took the cone from her hands and set it on the side table, along with his hat. "And get back to Skinny. You were about to tell me why the lad was here."

"He had further news about a murder that took place last night." Her gaze turned clouded. "While we were dancing beneath myriad glittering candles and drinking fine French champagne."

"You know damnably well that Evil will walk the streets regardless of whether or not we dance until dawn."

"I . . ." Charlotte took a seat on the sofa. "I suppose you're right. But that doesn't make it any easier to accept."

"I don't know anyone who is less accepting of the fact that Evil exists," he said softly. "Few people have the courage and conviction to challenge it as you do."

A tight sigh was her only reply.

Wrexford settled himself in the armchair facing her. "I heard of the murder, as well, but it seemed to me that it wasn't the sort of crime to draw your attention. Did Skinny bring information that might alter that?"

Charlotte shifted her gaze to the windows. Rain clouds had blown in to block the sun, turning the light to a soggy grey haze. A few fat drops began to spatter against the glass.

"I'm not sure," she answered. "The victim was apparently a clerk involved in accounting at East India House and had no reason to be at the wharves."

"There are any number of reasons a man might go to a place where's he's not supposed to be," pointed out the earl.

Her expression turned even more troubled. "Yes, I'm all too aware of that."

He sensed she was wrestling with a conundrum. "Which means?"

A sigh. "I . . . I'm not sure it's right for me to say."

Wrexford waited. Charlotte rarely dithered in uncertainty, so it must be a decision fraught with complexities.

"But I confess . . . ," she said after a prolonged hesitation, "I would value your thoughts on the matter. Perhaps I am merely seeing specters where there is naught but harmless vapor."

"I think you know by now that I can be trusted to keep anything you tell me in strictest confidence."

A ghost of a smile flitted over her lips. "It goes without saying that I would trust you with my life." Another sigh, and then she quickly recounted the scene she had witnessed between Cordelia and her brother.

The earl carefully considered what he had heard before responding. "Granted, the river is not a usual haunt of the aristocracy, but there are reasonable explanations for why Woodbridge appeared to have strayed there. Gentlemen often hire a ferryman to cross over to the slums of Southwark or Rotherhithe for the dissolute pleasures available there."

Charlotte gave a rueful grimace. "I knew I could count on your logic to put my fanciful fears to rest."

Wrexford acknowledged the statement with a shrug. "It's merely one possibility out of many. But Woodbridge doesn't strike me as a fellow who would be involved in anything nefarious." He smiled. "His sister is far more clever. And as we know from recent experience, she's the one who possesses the imagination and daring to do something dangerous."

"True. However, Lady Cordelia is also very sensible as well

as clever. She calculated the risks of what she did very carefully and decided the odds were in her favor. And it was done out of necessity, not hubris or greed."

Charlotte thought for a moment before adding, "She has a strict code of honor. I don't think she's capable of wrongdoing."

"Given the right circumstances, anyone is capable of wrongdoing," he replied.

She bit her lip.

"But getting back to the murder, other than Woodbridge's suspicious appearance, is there any reason for you to think it might be a subject for your pen?"

"No," she admitted. "Though it seems Bow Street is asking some strange questions around the wharves. They seem very interested in the word *argentum*, though neither Skinny nor Alice knows why."

"Actually, I can provide an answer on that," said Wrexford. "The murdered clerk said, 'Argentum,' with his last dying breath."

"How on earth do you know that?"

"Griffin paid me a visit this morning to see whether my Oxford education might provide any insight as to what the word might refer to—other than 'silver,' of course." A pause. "Though I suspect his real reason was to see what my cook was serving for breakfast."

"And did you offer any suggestions?" asked Charlotte.

"No," he answered. "I haven't a clue as to why the fellow said it. And idle speculation seems pointless, unless one pens those ghastly horrid novels that seem to sell so well."

"Oh, come," murmured Charlotte. "*The Mysteries of Udolpho* is a very entertaining book."

"I have better things to do with my time."

She raised a brow. "Like teaching the boys how to make stink bombs?"

"Ah. So you *do* know about that." He cleared his throat.

"Actually, it's Tyler who deserves the credit for giving them the instructions. I merely supplied the chemicals."

Deciding it might be a good time to take his leave, Wrexford rose and retrieved his hat. "I mustn't keep you any longer, Lady Charlotte. Good day . . . and if I were you, I wouldn't fret about the murder. Whatever web of intrigue, if any, is involved, I can't see how its threads will entangle us."

# CHAPTER 5

Between mundane everyday chores, working on sketches for her next satire, and her new family demands—including a trip with the dowager and the boys to Gunter's Tea Shop for ice cream—the next few days were so filled with activity that concern over the Queen's Landing murder slowly receded from Charlotte's thoughts.

Bow Street seemed to have lost interest, as well. According to Raven and Hawk, none of their friends on the street had heard any further murmurings about an investigation. The clerk's death, like his life, was fast fading into oblivion.

"M'lady, m'lady!" A breathless Hawk hurried into her workroom, a pristine white note clutched in his muddy fist. "Aunt Alison's footman just delivered this for you."

The dowager had insisted that the boys call her "Aunt Alison." They in turn had explained that Wrexford called them "the Weasels"—which had greatly amused her, though thank heaven they had refrained from explaining why. Alison still didn't know the real story of how they had come to be Charlotte's wards.

And much to her credit, she hadn't asked.

Hawk placed the note on Charlotte's desk and looked expectantly at the ornate pink wax wafer. "Maybe it's another invitation to Gunter's."

"You mustn't pester her for sweets every time you see her. It's not polite," chided Charlotte as she cracked the seal. "Drat," she added under her breath. "I do hope she's not asking me to accompany her on a round of morning calls. I have work to do."

Sighing, she quickly unfolded the thick stationery and read over its contents.

"Is . . . is it bad news?" asked Hawk as he watched her face.

It took Charlotte a moment to react. "Hmm? No, no, it's not bad news." She read it again. "Just very unexpected."

After refolding the note and placing it in her desk drawer, she rinsed her brushes and put her paints away. "I have to pay a visit to Aunt Alison. Tell Raven that McClellan will have refreshments ready for when Lady Cordelia arrives for his lesson." A pause. "And I do hope that she will stay for supper."

"Shall I fetch you a hackney?" he asked.

"Thank you, yes." Charlotte tucked an errant curl behind her ear, a part of her wishing she could avoid the meeting. The changes in her life were already dizzying. To think of adding yet another spin was daunting.

*Especially this one.*

"What if . . . ," she whispered to the now-empty room.

A gust of air grazed against the windowpanes, the muted rattle mocking her fears. *Whatifwhatifwhatif.*

"Even if I'm knocked on my arse, I shall simply pick myself up." After all, she had long ago learned the art of survival.

The wheels clattered over the cobblestones, but the dowager's well-sprung carriage softened all the little bumps of Charlotte's return ride home. She leaned back against the soft leather squabs, still of two minds about Alison's unexpected proposal.

*Yes or no?*

The dowager had made it clear the decision was hers alone to make. Was she dithering out of pride? Or was it out of cowardice?

Uncertain of the true answer, Charlotte turned her gaze to the window and watched the fast-fading afternoon glow give way to twilight. Nothing ever stood still—or so the earl would tell her.

The thought brought a reluctant smile to her lips. Wrexford wouldn't allow her to turn in endless mental circles. He would force her to confront the conundrum with logic and come to a rational decision rather than cowering behind her conflicted emotions.

"Logic," she murmured as the dowager's coachman pulled the team to a halt in front of her residence. She suddenly found herself in need of the earl's counsel—and yes, his cajoling.

After hurrying up the entrance steps and through the front door, Charlotte quickly removed her bonnet and cloak, only to pause on seeing that the parlor was dark and deserted.

Puzzled, she headed for the kitchen, where a glimmer of light flickered beneath the closed door.

"McClellan?" she said on entering the warm, spice-scented room. The boys, she noted, were sitting at the worktable in the center of the space, quietly—too quietly—eating a stew of beef and potatoes. It took her a moment to spot the maid in the far corner by the stove, sliding a baking pan into the oven.

"Is something amiss?"

Raven answered before McClellan could respond. "Lady Cordelia never showed up for our lesson," he said.

"She was feeling poorly when she left here the other day, so whatever illness she has must be keeping her abed," reasoned Charlotte. Though it was odd that one of Woodbridge's servants had not brought word of it. "I do hope it's nothing—"

"She's not ill," interrupted Raven. He put his spoon down. "She's gone."

"Gone?" Charlotte shot a look at McClellan, who responded with a grim shrug.

"Aye," answered Raven. "When she didn't come, I went to Lord Woodbridge's townhouse to ask about her. The house was locked up, and no lights were showing in any of the windows."

Recalling the recent scene between brother and sister, Charlotte felt a frisson of alarm but was careful to mask it. "I imagine Lord Woodbridge was called away to his country manor and Lady Cordelia went with him. There are any number of things on an estate that can require immediate attention from the owner."

The boy shook his head. "The knocker was still up."

*Not a good sign*, she conceded. When a family left Town, it was customary to take down the brass knocker from the front door as a signal to all that the family wasn't in residence.

A glance showed McClellan's expression mirrored her concern.

Yet another reason to send word for the earl.

"When you're finished with supper, why don't you boys run around to Lord Wrexford's residence and ask if he might pay us a visit?"

Raven and Hawk slid down from their stools and were off in a flash.

McClellan set a fist on her hip as the front door banged shut. "Can you think of any reason for Lady Cordelia's absence, m'lady?"

"Unfortunately, yes." Charlotte repressed a sigh. "But I'm not at liberty to explain the details. I happened to witness a private scene between her and her brother. Suffice it to say, the family is wrestling with some demons."

"Aren't we all?" muttered the maid.

"Yes, well, misery may make welcome company," replied Charlotte wryly. "However, that doesn't help to solve one's problems."

"Perhaps Wrexford will have some ideas."

"Let us hope so," Charlotte replied. "For I fear that Raven will take it awfully hard if Lady Cordelia is caught up in some trouble."

Darkness had settled over the city by the time Wrexford arrived at Charlotte's residence. *Just as well,* he thought as he mounted the steps and rapped on the door. As a widow, Charlotte was allowed a good deal of leeway regarding the strictures of Society, especially as word had been discreetly passed to the neighbors that McClellan was a maiden relative, which allowed a gentleman to visit without stirring scandal.

Still, given her reintroduction to the beau monde, he didn't wish to provide the tabbies with grist for gossip by being too overt about his visits. That they could count on not being skewered by A. J. Quill helped quash any speculation. Given that Charlotte had attacked him before, the other satirical artists would assume that she would be the first to know of any indiscretion.

McClellan answered his knock and took his hat and coat.

"Halloo, Mac," he said. "The Weasels seemed rather blue deviled when they brought Lady Charlotte's message. Have you cut off their jam tarts for some misbehavior?" A pause. "If it has to do with some noxious odor, the fault lies with Tyler and me."

"I wish it were that simple, milord," replied the maid, a worried expression on her normally stoic face. "But I'll leave it for Lady Charlotte to explain."

He glanced at the parlor. An ominous silence hung heavy in the air, despite the cheery glow of lamplight spilling out through the half-open door.

"She's waiting for you," said McClellan. "Shall I bring you some tea?"

"It sounds like I may need a good Scottish malt instead."

"Aye," came the terse reply. "I put the bottle on the sideboard."

*Not a good omen.*

The maid retreated toward the kitchen, leaving him to enter the parlor on his own.

Charlotte looked up. "Thank you for coming so swiftly, Wrexford," she said, closing the notebook in her lap and setting it aside. "I'm very grateful."

He moved around the armchair, choosing instead to sit on the sofa beside her. "How can I help?"

She hesitated. "I'm not sure where to begin. I had intended to ask your advice on a personal matter. But on returning home from a meeting with Aunt Alison, I learned of an unsettling turn of events that's even more pressing."

"Go on," he encouraged, sensing her uncertainty.

"Lady Cordelia—and her brother—appear to have gone missing . . ." She explained about her friend's abrupt departure from the previous lesson and her failure to show up for the afternoon appointment.

"It's odd, but not overly alarming," responded Wrexford after taking a moment to think over what she had told him. Seeing she was about to speak, he quickly added, "Though what you saw and heard the night of the ball does add an element of concern."

"I wonder where they've gone," she murmured.

"They could very well be at their country estate. It's expensive to keep up the trappings of an earldom," he pointed out. "Wine merchants, tailors, bootmakers, carriages, servants . . . If Woodbridge is in financial straits, he may have decided to escape for a bit from the dunning of his creditors. And leaving the knocker up doesn't give away his flight."

"I suppose that makes some sense," said Charlotte. "And Lady Cordelia may have felt compelled to go with him, both as a measure of support and to counsel him on the dangers in . . ." Her mouth tightened for an instant. "In whatever havey-cavey business is going on."

"Let's be careful not to jump to conclusions." Speculations

had their own inherent dangers. "In my scientific experiments I've learned that one must follow the empirical evidence, rather than assume the result before it's happened."

"I—"

Charlotte's reply was interrupted by McClellan, whose brusque knock was followed by the click of the door latch. "Forgive me for interrupting, but Mr. Sheffield is here and asking to see you. He says it's urgent."

"Merciful heavens!" Charlotte rose, her look of alarm mirroring his own misgivings. Sheffield, for all his exaggerated quips, rarely indulged in true melodrama.

"Please have him come in," she went on.

Their friend pushed through the door an instant later, looking more agitated than Wrexford had ever seen him.

"Lady Cordelia!" he exclaimed without preamble. "Hell and damnation! Lady Cordelia has gone missing!"

# CHAPTER 6

A shiver snaked down Charlotte's spine as the lamplight played over Sheffield's pale face and the flicker of fear in his eyes. His attraction to the brilliant Bluestocking had been apparent since their first few encounters, but she hadn't realized how serious his feelings had become.

She looked to Wrexford, who was already up and moving to the sideboard. "Sit," he said, thrusting a glass of whisky into Sheffield's hand, "and drink, Kit. Then tell us what has you so worried."

Sheffield set it aside untouched and raked a hand through his hair, leaving it standing on end. "She's gone!" His boots beat an agitated tattoo on the carpet as he began to pace around the room. "I tell you, she's vanished into thin air!"

"Sit," repeated the earl. "We can't be of any help while you're babbling like Hamlet."

Expelling a ragged sigh, his friend dropped into one of the armchairs. "Right. Cold-blooded logic and precise order," he muttered, then took a moment to compose himself.

"Logic," murmured Wrexford, "is how one solves a problem. So, yes, let us try to apply it to this one."

The earl's dry tone seemed to soften Sheffield's distress.

"Sorry," he mumbled, pressing his palms to his temples. "It's just that . . . well, I'm worried."

"Understandably so," cut in Charlotte. "Lady Cordelia didn't show up for her tutoring session with Raven, which seemed decidedly odd. However, Wrexford has pointed out that there are any number of reasonable explanations for why she might have left London without informing her friends." She quickly recounted what the earl had mentioned, and repeating it made her feel more convinced he was right.

Sheffield, however, shook his head. "No. She wouldn't have left without telling me."

"Kit—" began Wrexford.

"She wouldn't have!"

The earl fixed him with a searching stare. "How can you be so sure?"

"Because we had a meeting scheduled, and she wouldn't have missed it unless something was wrong."

"What sort of meeting?" asked Wrexford.

As Sheffield averted his eyes, Charlotte saw a flush steal up to his cheeks. "I prefer not to say."

*Hell's teeth.* Her dismay deepened. Sheffield's charm and good looks made him a great favorite with the ladies, and he made no secret of his occasional dalliances—though in the past they had always been with married ladies, who knew the rules of the game. If he had seduced an innocent . . .

Affairs of the heart could unleash unpredictable and explosive emotions.

The earl must have read her thoughts, for he grimaced and uttered a scathing oath. "Damnation, Kit," he added, disappointment resonating in the gruff growl.

Sheffield flinched, as if struck. "You think . . ." A sputter. "No, no, I swear, it's nothing like that." He shifted uncomfortably. "I'm sworn to silence, so I can't reveal the reason."

His chest rose and fell. "But what I can say is that her brother has been acting erratically lately—all ebullience one moment and then plunging into the depths of despair in the blink of an eye. As the three of us know from our previous investigation, the family is facing financial difficulties because of the late earl's profligate spending, though they hide it well. And we also know Woodbridge allowed Cordelia to rescue him from the last crisis."

"And you fear he has done so again?" A note of skepticism colored the earl's question.

"Yes." Sheffield scrubbed a hand over his jaw. "Lady Cordelia has appeared increasingly distracted of late." His eyes narrowed. "And the last time I paid a visit to their townhouse, I was passing the drawing room—the doors were half-open— and saw Woodbridge with several other gentlemen. There were papers being signed, and when one of them caught sight of me, he quickly nudged the doors shut."

"Have you any proof that something unsavory is going on?" pressed Wrexford.

Sheffield remained silent—which to Charlotte was an eloquent enough answer.

Catching a quick warning glance from the earl, Charlotte agreed that for the moment it was best to make no mention of the scene she had witnessed between the brother and sister. Their friend's emotions were already too much on edge. "Sheffield, perhaps—"

"Something is wrong," he insisted. "I . . . I just know it in my bones."

"I'm sorry, Kit," responded the earl. "But we'll need more than that."

"Can't we ask Griffin to do some investigating?" asked Sheffield.

"And give him what to go on?" The earl made a face. "The only bones Griffin cares about are the ones on his supper plate.

Unless you can put more meat on the ones you're offering . . ." He lifted his shoulders in a shrug.

Their friend blinked. "So, you won't help me?"

"We didn't say that," answered Charlotte quickly. "Of course we'll make some inquiries. But without any clearer idea of where or why, I fear we'll be stumbling around in the dark. Is there nothing else you can tell us?"

Sheffield held himself very still for a long moment and then abruptly got to his feet. "Thank you. I won't take up any more of your time."

"Bloody hell," muttered Wrexford as their friend kicked the door shut on his way out.

Charlotte heard the hint of pain beneath his exasperation. His gruffness hid a deep loyalty to his friends, and she sensed that Sheffield's obvious disappointment had cut him to the quick.

"You mustn't feel guilty, Wrexford," she counseled. "Right now, he's caught up in a maelstrom of emotions. You were right to press him on the facts. Without some sort of solid information, it's hard to know how to help." The lamp flame shivered. "I, too, am very fond of Lady Cordelia. But we both know she's not afraid of taking risks—or of breaking whatever rules are necessary to achieve her goal."

"Lady Cordelia would *never* be involved in anything evil." Raven suddenly appeared in the doorway, a wraithlike shadow silhouetted against the darkness of the corridor. He lifted his chin. "I'm sure of it."

Charlotte felt her heart lurch, all thought of chiding him for eavesdropping chased away by the look on his face. "I fear it's not that simple, sweeting. There are times . . ." *Oh, how to explain it?* "There are times when a choice isn't a clear-cut one between good and evil."

Raven blinked, his sharp features pinching in disbelief as he shot a glare at Wrexford. "D'you think she's guilty?"

"You've grown up on the streets, lad," replied the earl, "and have seen that life rarely gives us the luxury of seeing the world in black and white. What m'lady means is that sometimes we're forced to find our way through a confusing muddle of greys."

*Thank you, Wrexford,* she thought, flashing him a grateful look.

"You heard Mr. Sheffield. He doesn't think her capable of evil," retorted Raven.

"Mr. Sheffield has certain feelings for Lady Cordelia," said Wrexford. "His judgment is colored by his emotions—"

"Love makes us see the best in those for whom we care," interjected Charlotte. "Even if circumstances have forced them to be less than we wish them to be."

Raven drew a shuddering breath. "So you're not going to try to prove her innocent?"

"Of course we'll look into her disappearance," said Charlotte. "But given the facts we know—"

"The facts all said your cousin was guilty as sin!" exclaimed Raven, his voice rising to a near shout. "But you refused to accept it could be true."

The accusation was like a knife stab to the heart. "You're right. I didn't give up, and nor shall any of us do so in this case." Two quick strides brought her close enough to enfold the boy in a fierce hug.

"We will do our best, sweeting, I promise you that." His bony shoulders felt sharp as knife blades against her chest. *So hard, and yet as fragile.* "But you must steel your heart for the fact that it might not be good enough."

He stepped back, looking very small and uncertain in the flitting shadows. "I think you're wrong. So . . . so . . ." Fisting his hands, he spun around and darted away into the darkness.

She stared at the ink-black shadows, wishing she could force them to surrender their secrets. "Lud, as if I needed life to become any more complicated," she whispered.

"Speaking of which," said the earl, "there was something else you wished to discuss with me."

"Never mind that now," replied Charlotte, suddenly feeling

too overwhelmed to think straight. "I fear Raven won't leave this alone. I must think about how to keep him—and Hawk—from getting into any real trouble."

"Leave the Weasels to me," said Wrexford.

She mustered a smile of thanks, but trepidation quickly squeezed it from her lips.

He sat in silence, and though she looked away, Charlotte felt his gaze probing, probing. *Damnation.* How was it that he always seemed to see more than she wished to reveal?

"You know, sharing worries helps to rob them of their power," he murmured. "I would hope that by now you would trust me to confide what else is troubling you."

"It's not a matter of trust, Wrexford," she replied. "It's . . ." A sigh. "It's just that I feel I burden you with enough of my problems as it is."

"Friendship isn't a burden."

Their eyes met, entangling her in a connection she didn't dare try to define.

"If you're wrestling with two conundrums," he added, "chances are you won't deal with either of them very well."

"Ever practical and logical," she murmured.

A flicker of amusement lit in his gaze. "Yes, well, you know me—my outlook on life is blessedly unclouded by feelings."

"Impossible man," she muttered.

Which made him laugh.

The rumbled sound somehow seemed to loosen the tightness in her chest.

"If you must know," conceded Charlotte, "Alison informed me this afternoon that my brother Hartley, the present Earl of Wolcott, now that my father and his first heir have shuffled off their mortal coils, reached out to her and would like to meet with me."

Pursing his lips, Wrexford considered the news. She didn't need to explain any further—he was well aware that her stiff-rumped family had disowned her years ago, when she had eloped with her drawing master.

"And you don't wish to do so?"

"The thought terrifies me," she admitted. "I've no idea what he'll think of me."

"Of course it terrifies you. The unknown is always frightening," he replied. "But you're no longer a green girl of seventeen. You've experienced life and conquered adversity, which has given you strength and courage, as well as the confidence to determine your own life."

Charlotte felt her a lump rise in her throat.

"He has no hold over you or what makes you happy," said Wrexford. "If he's unpleasant in any way, you can simply spit in his eye."

All at once, the conundrum seemed to unknot itself. "I can, can't I?" She considered the thought. "But Hartley was always kinder to me than my father or eldest brother."

He shrugged. "That wasn't so difficult. As I said, problems often untangle themselves when you attack them en masse."

"Thank you," she said. "Yet again."

"As I've said before, we're not keeping a ledger," replied Wrexford. "Though if it makes you feel any better, I would welcome your advice on what to do about Kit."

So he, too, had realized their earlier silence with Sheffield was fraught with profound consequences.

"We've kept him in the dark about what you witnessed between Lady Cordelia and her brother. And then there's the murder at Queen's Landing . . ." His brows rose in question.

"You must tell him about Lady Cordelia," she said without hesitation. "Otherwise he will see it as an elemental betrayal of your friendship—and the damage to your bond might not ever be repaired."

He gave a reluctant nod. "I know you're right."

"If it's any solace, I think we can in good conscience make no mention of the murder. It's likely nothing to do with her brother, so until there's any evidence to the contrary, there's no reason to say anything."

"Still, I fear Kit is liable to go off half-cocked and get into trouble. He hasn't our experience in how to conduct a discreet investigation." Wool rustled as he turned in profile, casting his features in shadow. "It's likely that the disappearance of Lady Cordelia and her brother is due to personal family travails. But if, perchance, it's part of a greater web of intrigue, then he could find himself ensnared in danger."

"I worry, too," answered Charlotte. "And yet he wouldn't thank us for trying to shield him from danger. So we'll just have to do our best to keep him from coming to grief."

"Pssst."

Sheffield whirled around and peered into the silvery swirls of mist ghosting through the deserted street. Too agitated to sit still in a hackney, he had decided to walk back to Mayfair from Charlotte's residence. But perhaps it hadn't been the wisest of ideas.

"Pssst." The sound came again, this time from within the muddled gloom to his left.

He slid his grip down on his walking stick, ready to brandish the brass knob.

The fog quivered as two shapes suddenly darted out and skidded to a stop.

"Put that away, Mr. Sheffield," cautioned Raven. "If you threaten a cove with a stick in this neighborhood, you better know how to use it."

"What makes you think I can't hold my own in a scrum?" he retorted.

"Cuz you'll fight like a gentleman," piped up Hawk. "And your opponent won't."

"What are you Weasels doing out this late at night?" grumbled Sheffield, letting his arm drop. "You should be home doing your schoolwork."

"Bugger schoolwork," retorted Raven. "I overheard you telling m'lady and His Nibs that Lady Cordelia is in trouble. What are you going to do about it?"

"Well, as to that . . ." Sheffield tapped the stick against his boot.

"His Nibs says you have to look at a problem with logic, so you need to have a plan," counseled Hawk. "Running around niffy-piffy won't do anyone any good."

"My brain may not be quite as sharp as that of Wrexford," replied Sheffield a little defensively. "But yes, that thought had occurred to me."

Raven fixed him with an unblinking stare. "Actually, Lady Cordelia says you're quite smart when you put your mind to it. So you just need to think on it."

"I—" Sheffield flinched as a shutter swung loose on a nearby building and banged against the sooty brick. "I *have* been thinking. And it seems to me that a first step would be to have a look around her brother's townhouse and see if there are any clues as to where they might have gone."

"Oiy, that makes some sense," replied Raven. "But how are you going to do that? I don't suppose you have a key to the front door?"

"No." Sheffield shifted his stance as a feral growl sounded from the alleyway. "However, I wasn't intending on going in through the main entrance."

The boys exchanged looks.

"I think," said Raven, "that we had better come with you."

"Oiy," agreed his brother.

"When?" demanded Raven.

"The sooner the better," responded Sheffield. "It's too late to try it tonight, so let's make it tomorrow."

Raven nodded. "We'll meet you in the center garden of Grosvenor Square at midnight."

"Don't wear those fancy boots," added Hawk. "You need soft-soled shoes so you don't sound like a cart horse galloping over cobblestones. And bring a dark knitted toque to hide that flaming gold hair."

"Anything else?" asked Sheffield.

The boys were already lost in the skittering shadows. "Oiy," answered Raven. "Don't tell m'lady, or she'll have all our heads on a platter."

Wrexford clicked open the door to his unlit workroom and stepped inside. It was late, and with the coals in the hearth having crumbled to ash, a chill pervaded the air. He paused for a moment to draw a deep breath, the familiar scents of vellum and leather from the bookshelves mingling with the faint tang of chemicals . . . and then released it in a low oath.

"Hell and damnation, what a coil," he added, shrugging out of his overcoat and letting it drop to the floor. It troubled him that he hadn't told Charlotte about his loan to Sheffield. The secret wasn't his to share, and yet it somehow felt wrong to have held it back. Stepping over the tangle of wool, he found a flint and steel on the work counter and struck a spark to an oil lamp.

A flame hissed to life.

"Ah, you're back." The flare of light showed Griffin seated in one of the armchairs by the hearth. "A pity. I was about to help myself to a second glass of your costliest brandy."

"Tyler may be looking for another position come morning," muttered the earl.

"Then please tell him to let Bow Street know. He would make an excellent Runner."

"You couldn't afford him. He has very expensive tastes." Wrexford moved to the sideboard and poured himself a whisky, then stalked over to refill Griffin's glass. "Given the hour, I take it this isn't a purely social call."

"Correct." Griffin savored a sip of the brandy before going on. "I've uncovered some further information about the clerk who was murdered at Queen's Landing. It seems he had a cousin, the Honorable David Mather, who's employed at C. Hoare & Co.—you know, the private bank. Mather is the son of a baron, so he moves in more exalted circles than his late relative. And yet they were apparently close friends."

"It's a heartening tale of family loyalty," interjected the earl as he returned the brandy bottle to the sideboard and took a seat. "But I don't see what it has to do with me."

"If you'll permit me, I'm getting there, milord," said the Runner dryly. "In my slow and plodding way."

Wrexford waved him to continue.

"Naturally, I paid Mather a visit, to see whether he might have any ideas of who might have wished his relative dead." Another leisurely sip. "His reply was that he couldn't imagine such a thing—the clerk hadn't an enemy in the world."

"It's bloody late, Griffin, and I'm in no mood for a bedtime story—"

"The trouble is," went on the Runner, "beef-witted as I can be at times, I have a good nose for sniffing an untruth. The fellow was lying through his teeth."

The earl stopped fidgeting in his chair.

"So I decided to take a closer look at Mr. Mather's activities. Interestingly enough, he's had some recent business dealings with the Earl of Woodbridge."

The Runner now had his full attention.

"As has Woodbridge's sister—though of course, not officially, as a female has few legal rights to manage money or own property in her own name." Griffin was now eyeing him over the rim of his glass. "Am I right to assume you're acquainted with Lord Woodbridge and Lady Cordelia?"

"Yes," answered Wrexford, aware of an uncomfortable prickling at the back of his neck. Until he had a chance to think through all that he had learned earlier in the evening, he wouldn't be ready to share the recent information he had learned about Woodbridge and his sister—especially the fact that they had gone missing. "But I don't see what that has to do with the murder."

"I'm not sure it does have any connection, milord," replied Griffin. "And yet . . ." The Runner paused. "I can't help but be curious about the fact that Lady Cordelia and your friend Mr. Sheffield recently opened an account at Hoare's for a newly formed company. The bank clerk who assisted them with the paperwork distinctly recalls the conversation between the lady and your friend. She was quite vocal about it being damnably unfair that she couldn't be listed a shareholder—because she was, in fact, part owner and running the company."

Wrexford kept his face expressionless.

"So Sheffield is listed on the official papers as one of the two stockholders. However, he holds only a small percentage of the shares." Griffin set down his glass. "The majority owner is you, milord."

A sound—something between a grunt and a growl—rose in his throat before the earl could stop it.

"Were you not aware of that?"

Wrexford was forced to shake his head. "I made him a loan, and he did insist that it was to be a business arrangement, so I would be given stock." He hesitated, but there seemed little point in further prevarication. "When I asked about his partners, he told me he wasn't at liberty to disclose that information for the time being."

"And you accepted the assertion without more probing?" The Runner lifted a shaggy brow. "You appear to have a very cavalier attitude toward your money. It was a rather large sum."

"Sheffield is a friend. I trust him without question."

"I see," murmured Griffin. "I'm aware that your friend likes to gamble." The Runner allowed a sliver of silence before adding, "I hope he's improved his skills, for past experience has shown he isn't very good at it."

*What the devil has Kit gotten himself into?*

Wrexford pushed aside the unsettling question. Until he had time to carefully consider the revelation and all its ramifications, he had no intention of discussing it with Griffin.

"Whatever business they are in, I don't see Sheffield and Lady Cordelia as cutthroat murderers," drawled the earl, though it wasn't quite the truth. Like Charlotte, Cordelia possessed a core strength and courage, but he wasn't entirely sure that her sense of right and wrong was forged from unbreakable steel.

Griffin didn't crack a smile.

"So I suggest we turn our attention back to Woodbridge and his dealings with the bank," he pressed. "What sort of business is he doing with the dead man's relative?"

"That I can't tell you, milord," answered the Runner. "I had no authority to interrogate the fellow about it, and the junior bank employees were tight lipped when I tried a few discreet questions."

"Couldn't you ask the Bow Street magistrates for official permission to pursue the matter?"

A snort. "You know as well as I do that the government starts breathing fire on Bow Street's collective arse when any of the Runners start sniffing around the aristocracy. So unless the magistrates decide there's a damnably good reason to suspect the bank business relates to the murder, I won't be allowed to ask any more questions." A shrug. "And there isn't a shred of evidence that it does."

"Be that as it may," mused the earl, "there's nothing to stop me from asking around about our highborn suspect and his activities."

"I was rather hoping you might suggest that, milord." Griffin finally allowed a glimmer of humor. "You have to admit, past investigations have proved that we make a very efficient team."

"Yes." Wrexford drained his whisky in one swallow. "I buy supper, and you eat it."

That drew a low chuckle. "I'll bid you good night, milord. Do keep me informed if you turn up anything interesting. Preferably over a beef and kidney pie." Griffin picked up his hat and rubbed at a grease stain on the brim. "And while you endeavor to learn more about Mather, you might also consider looking more closely at Mr. Sheffield, as well as Lord Woodbridge and his sister. As I said, my superiors won't allow me to question you lordly aristocrats without compelling evidence of wrongdoing. But simply because they are your friends doesn't mean their hands are lily white."

# CHAPTER 7

Releasing a harried sigh, Charlotte took a seat at her work-table and lit the lamp, grateful that supper was over. Dusk was fast giving way to night, and as darkness curtained the windows and the neighborhood settled into slumber, she finally had an interlude for quiet contemplation.

*Choices, choices.* She had struggled all day to keep her mind on household matters. The questions of how to deal with family and friends were demanding such difficult decisions. And yet . . .

"And yet I've no clue of what to do." Saying it aloud only exacerbated the sense of uncertainty churning inside her chest. Sheffield's hurt feelings, Cordelia's disappearance, her own brother's request for a family meeting . . .

Thank heavens that Raven hadn't added to her worries. She had feared that he might hare off on his own and attempt to learn more about Cordelia's mysterious absence. A dangerous undertaking for a boy, no matter how clever . . . God only knew what nefarious doings were afoot.

Charlotte dipped her pen in ink and began to draw the stark, sinuous outline of a slithering serpent. She had long ago learned that the aristocracy's glittering façade of civility hid a dark core writhing with fanged vipers. . . .

But to her relief, Raven had gone without protest to his afternoon lessons with Mr. Linsley, and he and his brother had retreated to their attic aerie after finishing supper, grumbling about how much work the tutor had assigned for their next session.

The soft creak of the floorboards overhead drew a fleeting smile to her lips. They seemed settled into their studies, and a shuffling across the corridor indicated McClellan had retired to her bedchamber. As for herself, Charlotte set her pen down, the act of sketching having helped to clarify her own thinking.

A complex conundrum often unknotted itself when one could find a thread to follow. And the more she pondered it, the more the murder at Queen's Landing seemed tied in some way to why Cordelia and her brother had disappeared.

"I'm good at unraveling secrets," she murmured, and as luck would have it, a tavernkeeper near the wharf was part of her extensive network of eyes and ears around London. "So perhaps it's time to do a little nocturnal sleuthing around the docklands."

A short while later, dressed in ragged male clothing and with her hair tucked up under a wide-brimmed slouched hat, Charlotte slipped out of the house and instinctively assumed the quick-footed lope of "Magpie," her street persona. She hurried through the back byways that led down to the river, carefully avoiding the rougher streets, where trouble often spilled out from the ramshackle gin houses pressed cheek by jowl among the rookeries.

On approaching the East India Company docks, Charlotte cut around to the rear of a small tavern that catered to the workers at the wharves and warehouses. A special knock, thumped on a side door, quickly drew a response.

"Oiy, ain't seen ye in a while, Magpie." The door cracked open, just enough for Charlotte to sidle inside a small room that was bare, save for two slat-back chairs and a small round table. "But I wondered whether the murder would bring ye flying."

"What do you know about it?" she asked, keeping her face hidden despite the fuzzed light.

"What'll ye pay for it?" countered the tavern owner, a portly fellow with dark hair greased back from a bulbous forehead. His breath reeked of fish and stale beer.

"Don't humbug me, Squid. You know I'm generous when it comes to accurate information. But feed me a farididdle and we won't be doing business together in the future."

"Oiy, it's true. Ye's always fair." Squid hitched up his canvas pants. "Wot's ye looking fer?"

"Did the murdered man meet regularly with anyone around here?" asked Charlotte.

Squid scratched at his unshaven chin. "He thought hisself high above our touch, but I happen te know he often had a chin-wag with a gentry cove over at Stubb's fancy Lantern."

Charlotte knew the place. The Ship's Lantern was a slightly more genteel tavern that catered to ship captains and merchants who traveled on the East India Company vessels.

"Do you know the name of the gentry cove?"

Squid leaned in closer. His fetid breath blew under the brim of her hat and tickled against her cheek. "Mather."

She kept herself from recoiling. "And does Mr. Mather have a Christian name?"

The tavernkeeper hesitated. Wondering, no doubt, whether he could squeeze a few extra pennies by playing it coy.

Charlotte took a few side steps and dropped a small purse on the table.

Squid cocked an ear. She imagined he could gauge the amount inside right down to the farthing just by the chink of the metal. It was a generous sum.

His smile revealed several missing teeth. "David. And he be the *Honorable* David Mather."

*So, not just gentry, but a member of the aristocracy.*

"That ain't all, Magpie. Word is, he works at a bank."

*A bank.* Her pulse kicked up a notch. "Which one?"

"Lemme think." The tavernkeeper rubbed at his jaw, anxious to keep any extra coins from slipping through his fingers. A moment later, he let out a guttural laugh. "Oiy—I remember it now! Whore's Bank." His jowls were now quivering with mirth. "Ye think they keep cunnies locked up in their vault?"

"No," she answered. "Too many places for a whore to hide away a handful of guineas."

Squid was now laughing so hard it brought tears to his eyes. Charlotte was smiling, as well. The clue was worth its weight in gold. C. Hoare & Co. was an old and respected private banking establishment, whose clients included Lord Byron and Eton College.

"My thanks. You've been a great help." She made a show of turning for the door. "Oh, one last thing." Charlotte slid her hand back into her pocket. "Is there anyone else I should know about?"

"Well, now that ye mention it, the murdered man was thick as thieves with a barmaid at the Lantern. A pretty blonde." He pantomimed a pair of buxom breasts. "I imagine that be valuable information. Bow Street don't know it, as Annie begged the others to keep mum about it. She must have a reason fer not wanting te draw the attention of the Runners. Anyone wid harf an eye can see she's got something te hide."

Charlotte withdrew another coin but kept her hand fisted. "Annie's full name?"

Squid licked his lips. "Annie Wright."

"What's she hiding?"

"Dunno," he muttered, shooting a greedy look at her fist.

"But you're a clever cully, Magpie, and are good at uncovering all the little secrets that people wish te keep hidden."

Satisfied that she had gotten all she could out of him, she tossed a guinea down beside the purse, setting off a glint of satisfaction in his eyes, and then shoved back the massive deadbolt on the inside of the door to let herself out.

"Always a pleasure doing business with ye, Magpie," he called softly as the age-black oak closed behind her with a thunk.

Yes, she had paid through the nose, but Charlotte felt she had gotten the best of the bargain. She now had two names.

Ones that only deepened the mystery surrounding the murder.

Raven let out a soft cry of a nightingale, then went very still. A moment later came the warble of a dove.

"Nobody's coming. Let's go," he murmured, rising from his crouch among the bushes rimming the back terrace of Woodbridge's townhouse and creeping toward the side window.

Sheffield followed, trying to mimic the boy's fluid stealth. "How—"

"Ssshhh," warned Raven as he pulled a knife from his boot and slid the blade between the iron-framed sashes. Hawk rejoined them an instant later.

"What's he doing?" whispered Sheffield.

"Feeling for the latch," answered Hawk. "Once you position the point of the knife just so, you can force it to release."

"How do you two know—"

"Ssshh!"

A breeze ruffled through the ivy framing the mullioned panes of glass. The twittering of a nightingale—a real one—floated out from the dark branches of a chestnut tree by the garden wall.

And then a tiny metallic *snick*.

Raven tucked the knife back in his boot and slowly eased

one of the window sashes open a crack. "Hawk, you go first and make sure there's nobody around."

His brother slithered up and in without a sound. Several moments later, he peeked up from the gloom, just long enough to give a quick nod.

"Now you, sir." Raven laced his hands together.

Sheffield hesitated, earning a muttered "Quickly!" Gingerly positioning his foot for a boost, he braced his palms on the sill, only to be catapulted up and into the slivered opening. His shoes scrabbled against the mortised stone, then Hawk seized his coat collar and hauled him inside.

Raven followed in a flash. After pulling the window shut, he dropped down to the carpet beside the others.

"Try to make a little less noise, sir," he counseled. "I really don't fancy being transported to the Antipodes for burglary."

"We're not planning on *stealing* anything," pointed out Sheffield.

The boys ignored the protest. It appeared they were in a small parlor, and after a glance around, Raven gestured to the door leading out to the corridor. "Follow me. We need to find Lord Woodbridge's study. And *do* try to stay light on your feet, Mr. Sheffield."

They crept along in single file, with Hawk bringing up the rear. After several halts for Raven to dart ahead and make a quick reconnaissance, they made their way to a wood-paneled room at the rear of the townhouse, a room redolent with the masculine scents of leather and cigar smoke.

Sheffield reached for a candle and struck a spark to the wick.

Hawk scrambled over to blow out the flame. "Not yet!" he whispered. "We need to draw the draperies first."

"Oh, er, right."

"You're not very good at this," observed Raven. "It's lucky we came with you."

"Pay attention, and we'll teach you how to keep your arse out of Newgate," chimed in Hawk.

"Dare I ask how you two Weasels acquired your expertise?" The boys exchanged sniggered laughs.

"You learn to be quick and nimble when you grow up on the street," explained Raven as he moved to the large oak desk and began testing the drawers. "Otherwise you don't survive—"

He gave a grunt when the bottom drawer didn't budge, and pulled a needle-thin steel probe from his pocket. It made quick work of the lock.

"*Now* you can light the candle, sir, and do a search of the papers here while we take a look around the rest of the room." After flint struck steel, Raven moved over to light a second candle from Sheffield's flame. "Try not to make too much of a mess."

"I think I can manage that," said Sheffield dryly.

"You know what you're looking for?" asked Hawk.

"I may be a bit bumbling on my feet, but yes, I'll know what's important when I see it. You two keep an eye out for any other papers or financial documents. But most importantly, look for any clue of where Woodbridge and Lady Cordelia might have gone. A letter, a guidebook, a map—"

"Right. Now let's get to work," urged Raven. "One of the keys to illegal entry, sir, is to be in and out as quickly as possible."

The three of them fell to their appointed tasks, working swiftly and silently in the dim light. Sheffield made a few low sounds in his throat as he sorted through some papers and shoved several sheets into his pocket. He shifted and was just reaching into the very back of the drawer when Raven froze and waved a frantic signal to blow out the candles and be still.

*Steps.* The sound was almost imperceptible. But someone was moving stealthily down the corridor. Raven darted a look at the curtained window, then shook his head at Hawk, indicating it was too late to flee. Instead, he grabbed up a heavy brass candlestick from the sideboard and rushed to take up a position atop the side table by the door.

Hawk signaled Sheffield to join him behind the sofa. "Be ready to run," he whispered just as the door latch rattled.

There was a moment of silence, and then the catch released.

Raven raised the candlestick and held his breath.

With a faint creak, the door slowly swung open. The shadows stirred as a tall, black-clad figure moved cautiously into the study.

Another half step would give Raven the perfect angle to strike.

The figure appeared to hesitate, then slid a booted foot forward. . . .

Charlotte followed the oily beacon of light across the cobbles and entered the smoke-swirled taproom of the Ship's Lantern. After squeezing through the crowd of sailors clustered by the barkeeper's counter, she found a stool in a shadowed nook and settled in to observe the activity around her.

The place was only moderately full—the tide was going out, so no ships would be arriving until well past sunrise. A handful of junior officers wearing the uniform of the East India Company were scattered around the tables near the hearth, while a group of Royal Marines were getting drunk on brandy in the center of the room. In an alcove at the rear of the establishment, stevedores were waging a game of darts, the low light from the wall sconces flickering over their sweat-sheened muscles. Judging by the snarls and mutters, the stakes were high.

Charlotte had no trouble picking out Annie Wright, at work clearing tables. Squid's description, while crass, was accurate. However, she made no attempt to attract the buxom blonde's attention. She was looking for a more roundabout route to her quarry.

A few minutes later, a lone man entered, earning a friendly nod from the dark-haired barmaid serving the tables near the door.

A *regular*, decided Charlotte. She studied him more carefully as he made his way toward one of the empty tables near her. A coat of decent quality but fraying around the edges . . . linen going grey with age . . . boots that had seen better days . . . A respectable fellow, but just barely—and slowly sliding into oblivion. The sort who could be made to feel important.

A quick wave drew the dark-haired barmaid. "A tankard of ale," said Charlotte, assuming the accent of the rookeries around the naval yards in Greenwich. "And one for 'im, too, as I don't wish to drink alone," she added, gesturing for the newcomer to join her.

"Much obliged," murmured the man. As Charlotte had suspected, he wasn't about to turn up his nose at the chance to keep his purse in his pocket. "You're not from around here," he remarked as he took a seat.

"From farther east along the river," replied Charlotte. "Did a job fer a friend over on the loading docks." She took a slurp of ale. "He warned me it was a dangerous place, but it don't seem so bad."

A grunt sounded in answer. Lifting his tankard to his lips, the man drained half of it in one prolonged swallow.

She scraped her stool closer to the table. "I heard talk that there was a murder on Queen's Landing just a few days ago, but I'll wager that's just argle-bargle."

"It's not," said the man, leaning in a little. He had a long, thin face, with sallow skin that reminded her of a cod's underbelly. His eyes were equally colorless, but they had an alertness that boded well for her purposes. "There *was* a murder."

"You're bamming me," she said with a note of skepticism. Men liked to gossip just as much as women. And knowing something that others didn't made a fellow feel important.

"I'm not. The fellow's throat was cut from ear to ear." Thin

Face smiled in satisfaction as she recoiled in shock. "I knew him. He came here often."

"You don't say!"

"Aye." Shaking his head, he took another long swallow of ale. "A dirty business," he said softly.

Charlotte signaled for another round of drinks. "What do you mean?"

His expression turned sly. "You would have to ask that Miss Nose in the Air over there." He jerked his head in the direction of Annie Wright. "She was thick as thieves with the dead man and yet was desperate to avoid talking to Bow Street about him." A nasty smile. "I can't help but wonder why."

"Why do you think?" she prompted once Thin Face had a fresh tankard of ale in his hands.

He savored a long swallow, prolonging the moment of being the center of attention. "She's hiding something, of course." After another swallow, he tapped at the side of his nose. "I know a rat when I smell it. And whatever it is, it just might get her killed, too."

As the intruder edged into range, Raven swung down hard with the brass candlestick, aiming a blow meant to stun. The air rippled—

But at the last instant, the figure spun around and with a careless flick of his hand caught the makeshift weapon hurtling at his head.

"Hell's teeth, I ought to birch your arse, Weasel," said Wrexford as he snagged the boy by his collar with his other hand and hauled him down from his perch.

"Don't ring a peal over the boys," said Sheffield, rising from his hiding place. "It's my fault—"

"Ssshhh," hushed Hawk. "You've got to keep your voice down when you're doing something illegal."

"*Non omne licitum honestum,*" retorted Raven.

"True. Not every lawful thing is honorable," said Wrexford. He cocked an ear to listen for any sign of movement in the rest of the house. Satisfied that their presence was still undetected, he marched Raven over to where the others were standing. "However, we'll discuss the morality of this little foray later. For now . . ."

He glanced at the desk and its still-open drawers. "Have you found anything useful?"

"A packet of financial papers hidden beneath a sheaf of bills from Woodbridge's wine merchant—which I've pocketed," answered Sheffield. "There's still another drawer to examine."

Wrexford pursed his lips. "Any incriminating evidence is likely tucked away in a less obvious hiding place." He took a moment to relight the candle on the desk. "A globe, a fancy curio . . ." His gaze returned to Raven. "Any sign of a safe?"

"I haven't finished checking the room, sir. But I noticed there's several blank spots on the walls where paintings recently hung."

"Woodbridge may be discreetly selling off some valuables," mused the earl. "We also must check Lady Cordelia's workroom for clues as to what's happened to her and her brother." A pause. "It's come to my attention that she's involved in some business interests that may have bearing on what dark mischief is afoot."

The weak light caught the flush of color rising to Sheffield's face. "Whatever you've heard . . . it's not what you think—"

"I have no idea what to think at this moment," snapped the earl. "But now isn't the time to discuss it. As the Weasels so sagely pointed out, we need search the place as quickly as possible and take our leave—preferably not in manacles."

"Lady Cordelia wouldn't do anything wrong—" began Raven.

"As a man of science, I come to my conclusions based on empirical evidence, not wishful thinking." He turned away. "Now let's get to work."

Woodbridge's study yielded no further clues, and the four of them quickly moved up the stairs to Lady Cordelia's workroom. On opening the door and seeing all the books and papers stacked atop the storage cabinets, Wrexford made a face.

"Well, at least there appeared to be some order to her arrangements."

Raven examined the nearest piles. "Most of it involves work on specific mathematical theorems," he explained.

"See if you can spot anything that strikes you as odd or out of place," replied the earl. To Sheffield and Hawk, he added, "And you two look for any correspondence."

While they began searching, the earl moved to the desk. More sheets of mathematical equations covered the blotter. But when he shifted the papers to set down his candle, something else caught his eye.

*Drawings.*

He carefully cleared away the mathematical calculations and began to page through a set of intricate mechanical drawings. Some showed a close-up of a specific part, while others appeared to depict sections of a complex assembly of gears, levers, and numbered disks. As for the margins, they were covered in a hodgepodge of complicated mathematical equations.

Frowning, he waved Raven over. "Any idea what these are?"

The boy appeared equally mystified. "No, sir. I've never seen them before." He leaned in to study the notations. "And I don't recognize the mathematics. The groupings appear to be a series of calculations, but"—he lifted his shoulders—"I don't know what they mean."

"Hmmph." Wrexford spread out the drawings and studied them for a moment longer. "It appears to be the plans for some sort of . . . machine."

"For adding and subtracting numbers?" said Sheffield after a long look. "Wouldn't *that* be a godsend."

"It's been done before, Kit," said the earl. "Several centuries ago, in fact." He continued to stare at the drawings for another long moment, then quickly shuffled them back into order and twirled them into a tight roll. "I'll take these with me. Maybe Tyler will have some ideas of what they are."

The call of the night watchman making his rounds on the nearby street floated in through the drawn draperies.

"Damnation," muttered Wrexford. "Let's be off. We've got plenty to puzzle through." He tucked the roll under his arm. "Though the devil only knows where it will lead us."

# CHAPTER 8

Charlotte patted back a yawn before taking a sip of her morning coffee. Dawn's first rays had been teasing at the horizon by the time she made her way home from the docklands. Footsore from the long trek—and headsore from the copious amounts of piss-poor ale she had been forced to drink with her informant—she would have much preferred to stay abed until well after noon.

Perhaps there were some benefits to rejoining the ranks of indolent aristocrats, she thought wryly. But alas, they didn't have deadlines hanging over their cosseted heads.

Wincing, she swallowed another mouthful of the scalding brew, hoping to jolt the muzziness from her head.

"A long night?" commented McClellan as she carried a platter of freshly fried gammon and shirred eggs to the table.

"Yes, I ended up working later than I intended." Charlotte touched her fingertips to her brow. "And will likely pay for it."

"And what's your excuse, Weasels?" demanded the maid. The boys, who were always ravenous, had been suspiciously unresponsive to the delicious smells wafting up from the stove.

"Hmmm?" Raven blinked as he looked up.

"Please take your elbows off the table," murmured Charlotte. "It's very ungentlemanly."

"I can't help but wonder . . ." McClellan's eyes narrowed as she served them each a generous helping of eggs. "What unholy mischief were you up to last night?"

"We did nuffink!" said Hawk.

Charlotte felt a skittering of unease. The boy's pronunciation tended to lapse only when he was nervous.

"We were looking at some difficult mathematical problems," said Raven.

The thought of numbers, and having to update her ledger with the monthly accounting of income and expenses, made her head hurt even more. "Better you than me," she muttered, breaking off a bite of toast. Though, numbers, she decided, were the least of her worries. "If you'll excuse me, I need to go work on the drawing that's due to Mr. Fores at the end of the day."

The boys didn't look up from their plates.

*Another unsettling sign.*

McClellan set down the empty frying pan. "I can brew a tisane if you're feeling poorly."

"I'm merely preoccupied," replied Charlotte. She would, of course, have to tell Wrexford what she had learned last night.

Once in her workroom, Charlotte quickly scribbled a note to the earl. Then she shifted a sheet of drawing paper onto her blotter and let out a guilty sigh. Of late, she hadn't been giving her work the thought it deserved.

"I know . . . I swore I wouldn't lose my edge," she whispered in response to the accusing glare of the blank page. If personal problems began to take precedence over keeping the public informed on the issues affecting their lives, then . . .

*Then I don't deserve to hold my pen.*

With that in mind, she pushed aside her own concerns and made herself focus. The price of bread had taken a recent upturn, and she had heard whispers that certain politicians might be profiting from it.

Charlotte quickly rose and called down to Raven and Hawk. After handing over the note for Wrexford, she took up a pencil and began to sketch.

"Interesting." Tyler slowly paged through the drawings, taking his time to study the details. "The draftsmanship is impressive, and the construction of interlocking gears and levers ingenious." He looked up. "However, I haven't a clue as to what is it."

"But the dials with the numbers, and the equations in the margins of the paper, must mean something," mused Wrexford. "Could it be a device for doing sums? Addition, subtraction, multiplication . . ."

The valet raised his brows. "The idea is certainly not a new one. It's been around for centuries." He thought for a moment. "Leonardo da Vinci did a sketch for such a device. Then, of course, there's Blaise Pascal's Pascaline and Gottfried Leibniz's Stepped Reckoner from the seventeenth century, though Leibniz's design never worked properly—"

"I simply asked for your humble opinion," muttered the earl, "not a history lesson."

"In that case," replied Tyler with an aggrieved sniff, "yes, it's a distinct possibility."

Turning his gaze back to the drawings, Wrexford frowned. "Be that as it may, it still begs the question of why Lady Cordelia had them in her possession."

The silence stretched out for several minutes before Tyler cleared his throat. "Some ladies have hobbies, like embroidery. Is she, perchance, mechanically minded?"

"Not that I know of." But clearly, he was ignorant about a great many things concerning his friends and acquaintances.

"You might ask Mr. Sheffield."

Wrexford gave a grim nod. Yes, but whether he would get a

straight answer was an entirely different question. For all his faults, Sheffield had always been unflinchingly honest, often to his own detriment. His new slyness was more worrisome than the earl cared to admit.

He knew Sheffield hated the helpless feeling of having no funds of his own. The prospect of making money was a powerful allure under any circumstances, and a force that could twist one's morality.

"Damnation," he muttered under his breath. There had been no time to discuss the discoveries with his friend last night. However, he fully expected a confrontation at any moment—

"Your pardon, milord." His butler's discreet cough drew him from his brooding. "But you have—"

"Show Sheffield in," he muttered with a resigned sigh.

"Actually, it's Master Thomas Ravenwood Sloane, milord," replied Riche, maintaining an expression of solemn formality. The Weasels, whose muck-flecked untidiness and guttersnipe language had greatly offended the butler on their first few encounters, now never passed up the opportunity to announce themselves with their high-and-mighty official monikers. "And his brother, Master Alexander Hawksley Sloane."

Feeling a spurt of relief—a coward's reaction, he conceded— Wrexford waved for the boys to enter.

"M'lady wants for you to pay her a visit this afternoon," announced Raven, handing over the note.

"You shouldn't read a missive that isn't meant for your eyes," he chided, unfolding the paper.

"We didn't!" protested Hawk. "That would have been ungentlemanly."

Tyler cleared his throat to smother a laugh.

"She told us to come here straightaway, because she hoped you would be free to come take tea with her," added Hawk in explanation.

"Tea," repeated the earl. The way the past few days had gone, he might prefer to be served hemlock. "Thank you. Please tell her I'll be there."

Raven had moved to the desk and was looking intently at the mechanical diagrams.

"Think hard, lad," said Wrexford. "Do you have any idea of why Lady Cordelia had these drawings in her desk?"

The boy shook his head.

"Does she perchance have a penchant for—"

"Making things?" suggested Tyler. "Could they be her own sketches for some whimsical apparatus that she intends to build for herself?"

Raven scrunched his face, carefully considering the questions. "She's never mentioned anything like that."

Frustrated, the earl kept pressing. "Then if they're not hers, have you any ideas of where she got them or what she's doing with them?"

"No, sir," answered Raven quickly.

*Too quickly.* And with a certainty belied by the flicker of doubt in his eyes.

Wrexford decided not to challenge him on it. Life had become much more complicated for the boys as well as for Charlotte. Loyalties were now interweaving and overlapping. He didn't want to risk snapping any of the fragile threads.

"Well, then, we must attack the conundrum from a different angle." Moving around his desk, the earl went to stand by the hearth. The day was warm, and the coals lay unlit in the grate, shadows dipping and darting through the dark chunks instead of flames.

Were the recent unsettling mysteries really linked? Or were they all seeing specters where there was naught but a simple ripple of air? It was tempting to see connections. But as Wrexford pondered all the evidence they had at hand, logic argued against it.

C. Hoare & Co. was a private bank of excellent repute and

handled money matters for a number of aristocratic families. That the dead man's cousin worked at the same establishment where Woodbridge had his finances was really not as much of a coincidence as it might seem at first blush. As for Woodbridge's muddy boots . . . Bloody hell, like moths drawn to a flame, a great many wealthy young men found the lure of London's less salubrious parts irresistible.

The voice of reason carried a knife-edge clarity. And yet the whisper in the shadows of his conscious thought refused to be silenced.

*Logic . . .*

As an idea suddenly leapt to mind, Wrexford turned abruptly and gathered up the drawings. "Tell Sheffield I'll meet him—"

"Meet me where?" His friend halted in the doorway, looking uncertain of whether he was welcome to join the others.

"A thought occurred to me on where I might learn more about the drawings we found," answered Wrexford. "I'll be back within an hour or two."

"Might I come with you?"

*Yes or no?* The earl sensed his reply would profoundly affect their friendship.

"Of course." He squeezed past Sheffield and gave a curt wave for him to follow. "But don't say I didn't warn you that the meeting will likely involve a lot of boring scientific habble-babble."

It was only a short walk to Albemarle Street and the Royal Institution, whose lecture hall and laboratories drew many of the leading scientific minds in Britain. The earl led the way up the stairs, bypassing the area devoted to chemistry and heading up to the workrooms housing the . . .

*Tinkerers.*

Wrexford knew that many of the traditional men of science who studied chemistry and physics looked down their noses at their colleagues who had a passion for engineering mechanical innovations, dismissing them as mere craftsmen rather than considering them erudite thinkers.

Wrexford suspected it was due in part from jealousy. The word *engineering* derived from the Latin *ingenium*, which meant "cleverness," and men like James Watt and his partner Matthew Boulton had earned great riches from the patents on their steam engines.

"What is that infernal racket?" asked Sheffield.

"You'll see in a moment," he answered. After turning down one of the side corridors, the earl paused at the first door and rapped loudly, hoping to be heard over the metallic *clack-clack* emanating from inside the laboratory.

"Come in, come in!" called a muffled voice. "But do watch your step."

Wrexford and Sheffield entered, both of them nearly tripping over an undulating oval formed by a pair of curving steel tracks that were fastened to the floor. They looped under a massive worktable, around a storage cabinet—

From behind it suddenly clattered a foot-high iron carriage belching steam from a smokestack rising up from its front as it raced through the curve.

Sheffield hopped out of the way and watched it speed back under the table, where a rumpled figure was crouched, peering at his pocket watch.

"Excellent, excellent!" exclaimed the fellow after the carriage gurgled to a stop. "Mark my words, we'll soon have goods and people moving smoothly along roads of rails, rather than bumping over ruts—and at far greater speed!"

"Quite impressive, Hedley," murmured the earl.

"Yes, Puffing Billy here is a model of my latest innovations—a locomotive with piston rods that extend upward to pivoting beams—"

"Fascinating," interrupted Wrexford. "But might I ask for a few moments of your time to look at something?"

"I've always time for a man of curiosity like yourself, milord." Hedley crawled out from under the table and tugged his coat into place, setting off a prodigious cloud of dust. "Pray, what is it?"

"Actually, that's why I'm here." Wrexford moved to the work desk and unrolled the drawings. "I'm hoping you might have some ideas."

The engineer patted at his pockets and fished out a pair of spectacles. "Let me have a look." He came to stand beside the earl and began to page through the drawings.

Sheffield remained where he was, and crouched down to make a closer inspection of the metal tracks and the still-steaming Puffing Billy.

"Hmmph," grunted Hedley, his brows tweaking up in surprise. "Differential equations."

"Which means?" asked the earl when the engineer didn't elaborate on the cryptic statement.

"Which means the man who scribbled in the margins has a very advanced understanding of mathematics."

*Or woman,* thought Wrexford.

More grunts followed as Hedley shuffled back and forth between several of the more detailed drawings, then ran a hand through his shaggy hair, leaving the strands standing in spiky tufts. "Ingenious."

He looked up. "Where did you get these?"

"At the moment, I'm not at liberty to say," replied the earl. "But I'm hoping to get some answers from you concerning its design."

"I'll do my best." The engineer traced a finger along a series of geared levers. "Though I confess, I've never seen anything quite like this." He blew out a breath. "The intricacy of the components rather boggles the mind. I'm not quite sure how one would actually fabricate all the parts . . . that is, assuming it's not just a pipe dream."

Perhaps it was merely an opium-induced hallucination, thought Wrexford. He had heard that the members of Lady Cordelia's intellectual salon included some very eccentric individuals.

But if it was real . . .

"Let's assume it's not a flight of fancy. Given all the numbered wheels, it looks to me like it might be a machine for doing advanced mathematical calculations. In your judgment, is that technically possible?"

Hedley made a face. "Up until seeing these drawings, I would have said that no mind could envision a design able to perform such complexities. But now . . ." He lifted his shoulders. "But now I'm not so sure."

The earl considered what he had just heard. "You're familiar with the best mathematicians in all of Great Britain. Who do you think is capable of such a feat?"

A wry laugh. "I can't say any of us mere mortals are that advanced in our thinking. But since you wish for a few names, allow me to think . . ." Pursing his lips, the engineer slowly shuffled through the papers again, studying both the technical diagrams and the equations written in the margins.

"At Oxford, there's an upstart American on a two-year fellowship to Merton College who's a brilliant theorist and has an expertise in the sort of functions shown here," he finally said. "But to my knowledge, he's never shown any sign of being mechanical minded."

"Nonetheless, I'd be grateful for his name," said Wrexford.

"I don't know it. He signs his scientific papers simply as JRE," answered Hedley. "However, I've heard he's related to a cadet branch of the Marlborough family, so it shouldn't be difficult to learn."

"Anyone else?"

"Sorry, but I really can't offer anyone else who might be capable of such advanced thinking."

"Thank you." The earl rerolled the drawings. "I appreciate your time."

Sheffield was still engrossed in studying the steam-powered engine. "You say you envision this machine moving people and goods, Hedley?"

"Yes!" The engineer's face took on a dreamy expression. "Mark my words, it will be the transportation of the future. I've already built a full-scale model prototype, and we're testing it at Wylam Colliery. Today I've just been tinkering with a slight modification."

Wrexford stepped carefully over the metal rails, ducking through a plume of steam that was wafting up from the water boiling over a large spirit lamp near the door. "Puffing Billy certainly looks to have great promise. I wish you good fortune with its development."

"I just need to make a few adjustments to the piston rods . . ."

"Come along, Kit. Let us leave Hedley to his work."

Sheffield reluctantly rose. But as Wrexford reached for the door latch, Hedley's murmurings suddenly trailed off. "Wait! A thought just occurred to me. There's one other name I can give you." The engineer made an uncertain face. "But I have to warn you, he's rather . . . odd."

The earl allowed a small smile. "I thought that was a given with those whose minds are immersed in a world of abstract numbers and what abstruse things they might mean."

"Just so," agreed Hedley. "But in a fellowship of thinkers known to be eccentric, Professor Isaac Newton Sudler is considered *exceedingly* odd."

Wrexford raised a questioning brow.

"No question that he's brilliant," added the engineer. "But alas, there's a fine line between genius and madness. I doubt . . ." A hesitation. "I don't wish to speak ill of a colleague."

"Please go on," he pressed. "It may be important."

Hedley shifted uncomfortably, a shimmering of dust motes

rising up from the shoulders of his coat. "For a number of years, he held an important position at Cambridge—in Trinity College, like his famous namesake. However, he's become a recluse and has given up his teaching duties in order to devote himself to research. And yet he's become fanatically secretive about what he's working on." A cough. "I thought of him not just because of his mathematical skills but also because he's an aficionado of automata."

Wrexford frowned in thought. *Automata* was the term used for complex mechanical devices that were made to amuse or entertain an audience through their technical sophistication. ""You mean . . . toys?"

"Some people call them that," admitted Hedley. "Though their technical sophistication transcends such a term. Some of the more well-known examples are quite astounding in their engineering. Why, an Indian sultan possesses a life-size model of a tiger that snarls and snaps its jaws at the fallen English soldier trapped within its paws."

"Tipu's Tiger," murmured Sheffield. "Yes, I've heard of it."

"Impressive, yes. But one of my favorites is a silver dancer designed by John Merlin." A laugh. "It's truly the work of a magician. When you wind it up, it spins around the floor, doing intricate dance steps. It even winks at you." Hedley rubbed at his jaw. "The point is, Sudler has been building automata since his undergraduate days. It began as a hobby, but then it became an obsession."

"Interesting," replied Wrexford softly. The information was tantalizing, but he reminded himself that it might only be sending him on a wild goose chase. "I take it Sudler can be found in his chambers at Trinity?"

"No, I heard that he moved out of the college to a private residence several years ago." Hedley held up his hands. "And before you ask, I can't tell you where. Nobody seems to know."

"Again, my thanks."

"Ha! You might wish to withdraw those words when—and if—you encounter Professor Sudler. But you did ask."

"So I did." For a moment, Wrexford silently cursed the sticky web of intrigue that had somehow come to entangle him and his friends. *Charlotte, Sheffield, Raven* . . . He hated to see them caught up in an impossible quest.

And yet he conceded, the bonds of friendship didn't give a devil's damn about what was reasonable or expedient.

So, no matter how far-fetched, he had no choice but to follow the clue.

# CHAPTER 9

"Thank heavens," muttered Charlotte on hearing a brusque knock and then the sound of voices in the entrance foyer. Shooting up from her work chair, she then hurried down the stairs.

"At last! You've finally arrived," she called to Wrexford.

"Had I realized that 'tea' was a precise time, I would have acted accordingly," drawled the earl as he shrugged out of his overcoat and handed it to McClellan. "If you were thirsty, you should have started without me."

"Please, sir, this is no time for jesting," she chided, gesturing for him to enter the parlor. "Given all that has occurred since last we met, we have some very serious matters to discuss."

A flicker of emotion—was it guilt?—seemed to darken his eyes, but he turned away too quickly for her to be sure.

"I assure you, it wasn't my idea," he responded. "Though I suppose I should have realized it was a possibility."

Charlotte felt a frisson of alarm. She had no idea what he meant. But she had a sinking suspicion that she wasn't going to like it when the truth was pried out of him.

After following him into the parlor, she shut the door behind her. "What the devil are you talking about?"

Wrexford settled himself in one of the armchairs and carefully crossed one booted leg over the other. "Never mind. It's not important—"

"Bollocks," she snapped, moving to the sofa and taking a seat facing him. "If we've learned one thing from our previous brushes with violent death, it's that holding back information is bloody dangerous."

Her words chased the trace of wry humor from the earl's chiseled features. "I wasn't intending on holding anything back," he replied, waggling the roll of papers he was carrying. "I was simply waiting for McClellan to bring in the refreshments so I could sweeten you up."

A clench of foreboding tightened her chest. "As you know, sir, I don't take sugar in my tea. So you might as well spit it out."

The earl shifted uncomfortably. "Are you sure you don't wish to have one of McClellan's ginger biscuits before we continue? They're remarkably good."

"I'm quite familiar with her cooking," replied Charlotte, finding it impossible to stay angry. They had been through too much together, she realized, for her to ever doubt the elemental bond of trust that twined them together. "Whatever you have to tell me, it can't be *that* bad. When I saw the boys at breakfast, they didn't appear to be missing any limbs."

He made a face. "Well, it's a good thing that *I* found the Weasels this past evening, rather than the night watchman. Else they, along with their partner in crime, might be locked up in Newgate, waiting for a ship to transport them to the penal colonies in the South Pacific for breaking into a private residence."

Charlotte closed her eyes for an instant. "Woodbridge's townhouse?"

"Yes."

"I should have guessed some mischief was afoot," she muttered. "They were far too eager to retire to their aerie and do their schoolwork."

"Instead, they and Sheffield decided to search for clues as to what troubles have ensnared Lady Cordelia and her brother," he said.

"And you found them—"

"I found them because the same thought had occurred to me," explained Wrexford. "Don't ring too sharp a peal over their heads. I think they did it in part to make sure Kit didn't make a mull of it. He doesn't have our experience in illegal activities."

That made her laugh.

"Be that as it may," he went on, "we did discover some intriguing clues in the townhouse. And that's only part of it. However, I think it best that I start at the beginning . . ."

A knock made him hesitate.

"Tea and biscuits," announced McClellan, shouldering the door open and bustling in to place the tray on the low table between Wrexford and Charlotte. "I took the liberty of not adding any knives to the tray."

"The earl and I have ceased cutting up at each other," said Charlotte, then added a sigh. "It seems I need to have a discussion with Raven and Hawk about deception, no matter that their recent actions broke no direct order."

"Hmmph. I feared as much," muttered McClellan as she poured two cups of tea and passed them around. "No ginger biscuits for the Weasels until further notice."

Charlotte cocked an ear. "I trust they're not hovering in the shadows. The earl and I have matters to discuss that I prefer they don't overhear."

The maid shook her head. "They went off a short while ago to take a crock of beef broth to Skinny, who has a touch of catarrh."

"Dear heavens! He's ill?" Charlotte felt a stab of guilt. Raven and Hawk's little band of urchin friends had become very dear to her. She had been meaning to think about their future, but her own life had been turning topsy-turvy of late. . . .

A poor excuse, and she knew it.

"I should go—"

"You and the earl concentrate on whatever conundrum you're facing," interrupted McClellan. "I'll make sure Skinny comes to no grief."

"Thank you," she said, though guilt still prickled at her conscience.

As the maid slipped from the room without further comment, Charlotte remained staring down at her lap, where her hands had knotted together. When she finally looked up, she found the earl watching her, his expression creased in concern.

"You can't save every homeless child in London, Lady Charlotte," he said softly.

"I know that." Their eyes met. "But they are our friends, Wrexford. I can't—"

"*We* can't," he corrected. "And we won't. I promise you that. But McClellan is right. We've got a daunting mystery to unravel that affects some of our other friends. Let us solve that one first while she keeps an eye on our raggle-taggle urchins."

In the face of Wrexford's steady calm, all her churning worries suddenly melted away.

*I promise.* Two simple words, and yet they resonated right down to the depth of her marrow. She knew that for all his faults, he would never break his pledge.

"Very well. Let's get back to the question of what unholy mayhem is afoot." She straightened her spine and smoothed out her skirts. "You were about to tell me there's more to your tale than the illegal entry into Woodbridge's townhouse."

"Much more." Wrexford proceeded to explain about Griffin's visit, the new information about the murder victim's connection to a private bank, and the surprising revelation of Sheffield and Cordelia's business partnership.

"Ye gods," she whispered. "I—"

"I haven't yet finished," he said quickly before she could go on. "During our search of Woodbridge's townhouse, we discovered some drawings in Lady Cordelia's study." Pushing the tray and unfinished cups of tea to one side, the earl unfurled the roll of papers.

Charlotte took her time in looking through them. "It looks like the design for a . . . a machine of some sort," she ventured once she was done.

"Yes," agreed Wrexford. "As to what it's for, Kit and I paid a visit earlier today to William Hedley, a scientific colleague at the Royal Institution whose specialty is engineering industrial innovations. He thinks there's a possibility it's meant to perform mathematical calculations."

Charlotte was suddenly aware of a throbbing at the back of her skull. None of this was making any sense. "But why would Lady Cordelia want a machine to calculate numbers? She does them so easily in her head."

Wrexford's expression turned grim. "At this point, I'd rather not speculate. I do wonder, however, whether you've ever heard her express an interest in anything mechanical."

"No, never," replied Charlotte.

"I know she's a member of a group of Bluestockings, who meet regularly to discuss intellectual topics. You've attended several of their soirees with Lady Peake. Have you ever heard any of the other ladies bring up the subject of mechanical innovation or the term *automata*?"

"Again, no. However, I'm not privy to every conversation that goes on during those evenings." She thought for a moment about what he had just said. "Doesn't *automata* refer to a type of fancy mechanical toy?"

"Mr. Hedley would chide you for calling them that," said Wrexford. "Granted, they are often constructed as entertainment for the wealthy. But advanced technical skills and innovative engineering are required to produce them. So, when I pressed Hedley on whether he knew any mathematician who also possessed mechanical expertise, he mentioned a reclusive Cambridge professor with a passion for automata."

Charlotte edged forward on the sofa. "You think Lady Cordelia and her brother may have taken refuge with him?"

"It seems possible, and right now, it's the only clue we have. I've asked Tyler to make some inquiries about the professor among certain friends of his. I should know more by tomorrow." He slowly released his breath in a harried sigh. "In the meantime, I'm meeting with Sheffield tonight to discuss what was in the documents he found in Woodbridge's desk."

A pause. "And to hear his explanation of why he felt compelled to hide the fact that he's involved in a business venture with Lady Cordelia."

Charlotte didn't blame him for sounding apprehensive. Much as she liked Cordelia, something about all of this felt wrong.

"I don't claim to have any expertise in mathematics, but to me, nothing is adding up right," she said. "And you've yet to hear what I've learned. You and the boys weren't the only ones doing some nocturnal sleuthing last night."

His expression turned even more troubled.

"I paid a visit to one of my sources around Queen's Landing—"

A growl rumbled in Wrexford's throat.

"Kindly refrain from comment until I'm finished, sir," she chided. "You need to hear this." His jaw tightened, and taking that as signal of surrender, she continued. "From my source, I, too, learned of the murder victim's connection to C. Hoare & Co. through his cousin, the Honorable David Mather, as well as the fact that the two men often met at a tavern near the dockyards. I paid it a visit and struck up a conversation with one of the regular denizens."

Another growl, which she ignored.

"From him I learned yet another interesting fact. The murder victim was apparently close to one of the barmaids there. And she was too frightened to speak to Bow Street when they came to make inquiries," explained Charlotte. "Her name is Annie Wright. I followed her to her lodgings in one of the rookeries off Tench Street, near Wapping Docks, and reconnoitered the area." She paused and then added, "However, I decided to speak with you first before I make contact with her."

To her surprise, Wrexford remained silent.

Charlotte waited, watching his face through her lowered lashes. She had learned to read the subtle signs of his moods. That his expression was undecipherable didn't bode well. Leaning back, she waited for whatever explosion was coming.

"The dockyards are a notoriously dangerous area." His voice was mild—another bad sign. "But, of course, you know that. Just as you know that asking questions pertaining to a murder makes it an even more dangerous place."

"I went in the guise of Magpie, who has a great deal of skill and experience at uncovering secrets in the worst hellholes of London."

"It takes only one tiny slip to get your bloody throat cut," he replied.

"I know the rules of stews, Wrexford," responded Charlotte. "Probably better than you do."

"Somehow, that's not overly comforting." He looked away to the shadows lurking beyond the mullioned windows. "If I thought it would do any good, I'd forbid you to seek out Annie Wright."

"Nothing about murder is comforting, milord. But as it seems likely this one is entangled with the troubles of our friends, you can't very well expect me to ignore it," she said. "So it's a good thing you have no authority to tell me what I may and may not do."

His gaze betrayed a flicker of emotion as he turned back to face her. It was gone in an instant, and yet its fire left a strange prickling on her flesh.

"I would hope you know me well enough to trust that I would never exercise such authority." Though his tone was carefully controlled, Charlotte heard the note of hurt shading his words. "Even if it were mine to wield."

"Forgive me, Wrexford," she whispered. "That was badly done of me." She drew in a shaky breath. "With all the recent changes in my life, I fear . . . I fear that I may lose a grip on who I really am."

A ghost of a smile tugged at his mouth. "I wouldn't worry about that. Your true self is woven into every fiber of your being—your conscience, your passions, your compassion, your sense of justice."

Her throat tightened as Charlotte sought for a reply. "I think you have more confidence in me than I have in myself," she finally managed to say.

This time, the silence between them had no sharp edges. A soft rustling stirred the air as they resettled themselves in their seats. When their eyes met again, they smiled.

"Well, I suppose we had better get back to the matter at hand," said Charlotte briskly. "And try to figure whether the pieces of information we've uncovered are all part of the same puzzle."

"Logic seems to dictate that there are two steps for us to take next," replied the earl. "We need to learn more about Professor Sudler, and whether Lady Cordelia and her brother have taken refuge with him. And we need to ascertain whether the murder at Queen's Landing and any information that Annie Wright possesses are connected to our friends."

"That makes sense," said Charlotte. "However, we must also face the question of what to tell Sheffield." A sigh. "The line between discretion and deception is, I fear, a very muddled one."

Wrexford's grunt signaled agreement.

She cleared her throat. "I have a thought . . ."

"Which I would greatly welcome," he responded.

"As we agreed the other night, we can't hold anything back about our efforts to find Lady Cordelia," she offered. "However, until we uncover evidence that she and her brother have any link to the murder, other than the fact that Hoare's Bank handles their finances, I think we can, in good conscience, leave that part of our investigation unmentioned."

"Some might say that we are parsing morality with a very sharp blade," observed Wrexford with a sardonic twitch of his brows. "But like you, I have a healthy regard for pragmatism."

"Excellent," murmured Charlotte. "Though I expect we will argue over how to deal with Annie Wright."

"I don't suppose I could convince you to let me accompany you?"

"You cut a very imposing figure, sir. Even disguised in shabby clothing, there's no way for you to go unnoticed in the stews."

He didn't argue.

"If it would put your mind at ease, I suppose I could ask Raven and Hawk to shadow me—"

"Let us leave the Weasels out of this part of the investigation," counseled Wrexford. "If even you and I are wrestling with the complexities of friendship and loyalty, imagine what Raven is feeling. We ought not to put him between a rock and a stone."

It was an astute observation, and one that showed softer sentiments lay hidden beneath his outward show of snaps and snarls.

Holding back a smile—she didn't wish to spoil the moment by making some teasing comment—Charlotte merely nodded. "Then you'll simply have to trust that I know what I'm doing."

She rose and began to reroll the mechanical drawings. "I have a dratted engagement to attend, an evening musical soiree at Lady Becton's residence with Alison. I would consider crying off, but she feels it's important for me to attend a few more social events to ensure my acceptance in the beau monde. And it may prove useful, as several of Lady Cordelia's friends from Lady Thirkell's Bluestocking salon will also be attending, which will allow me to probe as to her mechanical interests."

The papers crackled. "But after that, I shall go to the dockyards and make contact with Annie Wright," added Charlotte. "Whatever she is hiding, she'll soon learn that secrets, no matter how carefully guarded, have a way of slipping out."

*Secrets.* Wrexford watched as Charlotte deftly tucked the ends of the protective oilskin around the roll, masking what lay beneath the cloth.

She was, he mused, a master of the shadowy world of secrets. For years her survival had depended on her skills at hide-and-seek. No one was better at ferreting out the truth behind rumors and whispers. Just as no one was better at keeping others from knowing her own dark vulnerabilities.

Until lately.

And though the revelations had been voluntary, Wrexford sensed that she wasn't entirely at peace with herself over the momentous decision of stepping back into the beau monde. He worried that she might become reckless during the coming investigation to prove to herself that her passion for justice hadn't been smothered in the costly silks and satins of her new life.

It was absurd, of course. Charlotte was Charlotte. Steel would snap if it sought to bend her convictions.

*But we all have our inner demons,* he thought as he, too, got to his feet. *And they are what we see when we stare into the looking glass.*

"Is something wrong, Wrexford?" asked Charlotte as she offered him the wrapped drawings. "You have a very peculiar look on your face."

"Perhaps that's because you scare me to death."

Surprise spasmed across her features, followed by a flicker of emotion to which he couldn't give a name. "Oh, come, nothing scares you, least of all me." She said it lightly, though her gaze held a shadow of uncertainty. "I'm the one plagued by fears and self-doubts. It's your unshakable steadiness in the face of life's slings and arrows that gives me the courage to face the challenges."

"Steady?" Wrexford couldn't hold back a mocking laugh. "I'm the mercurial Moon—the cover of darkness hides a multitude of sins. While you're the Sun, who's not afraid to shine your light on every shadow, no matter how terrifying."

He heard her hitch in a breath. Was he making an utter fool of himself? Somehow he didn't care.

He put down the roll of papers. "Promise me you will be careful." Drawing her into his arms, he held himself very still, hardly daring to breathe as he brought her close and felt the beat of her heart thump against his chest. *I'm not sure how I would bear the darkness without your light*, he added to himself.

"Wrexford." Charlotte's voice was muffled as she pressed her cheek to his shoulder and slid her hands around his waist.

*Thump-thump.*

"So you see, my weaknesses far outweigh my strengths."

"As do mine," she said.

*Thump-thump.*

Charlotte shifted, just enough to angle her eyes up to meet his. Their smoke-blue hue shimmered like quicksilver in the deepening shadows. "Do you think I don't worry about you?" she asked. "You have come to be a rather . . . a rather large presence in my life."

"The past has proven that you manage extraordinarily well on your own," he said softly.

"That," said Charlotte, "doesn't mean that it would make me happy to do so in the future." She stepped back abruptly, her fingers twining with his for a fleeting moment before releasing them.

*The future.* He hesitated, but then, uncertain of how to reply, he simply said, "Now isn't the time to talk about the future. For the present, we need to concentrate on protecting our friends. So let us both promise to be careful. I fear this cursed web of intrigue will only turn more tangled, and God only knows what malicious spiders are lurking in its strands."

# CHAPTER 10

W rexford was still sorting through his feelings as he entered his townhouse. It felt as if something had changed between him and Charlotte. . . .

"Though I'm damned if I can say exactly how," he mused. Words didn't come easily when it came to articulating emotions.

They had both spoken—however obliquely—of the future. What that signified—

"Where the devil have you been?" demanded Sheffield, looking up from the sheaf of notes in his lap as the earl pushed through the door of the workroom. "And why is Tyler not here?"

"Because . . ."

*Because,* thought the earl, *he and I are running ourselves ragged trying to pull your cods out of the fire.*

Reminding himself that he wasn't the only one who was struggling with fear and worry, Wrexford drew a breath to quell his momentary ire. "Because he is pursuing a lead as to the location of Professor Sudler's private lair. As for my whereabouts, I was meeting with Lady Charlotte, who also undertook some sleuthing last night—in a very dangerous area, I might add."

"Forgive me." Sheffield pressed his palms to his brow. His face was pale and drawn, with ink-dark lines of anxiety etched at the corners of his eyes. "I feel so bloody useless." He grimaced. "Hell, mere children are more skilled than I am at breaking into a house and knowing how to conduct a clandestine search on their own."

"The Weasels aren't mere children," said the earl dryly. "They're afreets—demon spirits who possess unnatural powers for navigating the dark world of mischief and mayhem."

"Ha-ha." A weak laugh, but it seemed to break the tension in the air.

"When was the last time you slept?" asked Wrexford, feeling a bone-deep weariness as he slumped into his desk chair.

"Dunno." Sheffield blinked, looking like a startled owl as he turned away from the lamplight. "I can't remember."

"Exhaustion does no one any good." With his own nerves tied in knots, the earl was in no frame of mind to deal with his friend's emotions. "Go home and get some rest."

"But . . ." Sheffield held up the papers in his lap. "I've found something in Woodbridge's correspondence that may be another clue."

"The devil be damned, it can wait until morning, Kit."

Sheffield looked as if he had been punched in the gut. He sat for a moment in stunned silence, then rose and inclined a stiff nod. "Again, my apologies. I had no right to draw you and Lady Charlotte into this mess."

Wrexford expelled a harried sigh. "Sit."

His friend hesitated.

"Lady Charlotte is making another foray into the stews around the docklands tonight, after attending Lady Havemeyer's musical soiree." The earl's hands fisted. "Alone."

Sheffield pivoted and retreated into the shadows. A muted *clink*, a whispery splash. He returned and handed Wrexford a glass.

"It seems we both could use some liquid courage." The candlelight caught in a swirl of amber as he raised his own whisky to his lips. "*Slàinte.*"

The earl drew in a mouthful of the fiery malt. Would that it could melt the ice in his belly.

Sheffield returned to his chair. "Is there nothing we can do to . . . help?"

Wrexford shook his head. "She's meeting with another woman who she thinks may have some information that will help us." Reminding himself that Sheffield didn't yet know of the possible connection between the murder at Queen's Landing and Lady Cordelia's disappearance, he didn't elaborate. "And she told me in no uncertain terms that my presence might be noticed and might put her in danger."

"But why—"

Wrexford silenced him with grunt. "She said she'll explain it to me later."

Sheffield stared down into his glass and gave it a swirl. They both took another sip, savoring the comradely silence of long-time friends. "It seems we're both cursed with caring for ladies too smart and too fearless for their own good."

A mirthless laugh. "I'll drink to that."

"*Slàinte.*" Sheffield repeated the Gaelic toast and downed the rest of his whisky before rising and fetching the bottle to refill their glasses.

At this rate they would soon be four sheets to the wind, thought the earl. And perhaps that wasn't a bad thing, given where the conversation was headed.

"For now, let's focus our attention on finding our elusive Cambridge professor," he muttered after another swallow of spirits. "Though it may only be a wild goose chase."

"No, I think we're on the right trail." Sheffield's voice held a note of veiled excitement as he suddenly sat up straighter. "I've just recalled that Woodbridge attended Cambridge!"

"So did a great many other gentlemen," said Wrexford. "Granted, it's a connection, but a very tenuous one." He spun the glass between his palms. "We must also address Lady Cordelia's financial activities."

The sonorous notes of a string quartet swirled through the softly flickering candlelight, the graceful melody echoing the elegant furnishings and muted hues of the grand music room. Quelling her impatience, Charlotte sat amid the appreciative audience, hands folded primly in her silk-swathed lap, and made herself concentrate on the music. Mozart, not murder, ought to be the only thing on her mind. . . .

As if sensing her thoughts, Alison shifted slightly in the chair next to hers, the brush of skirts a subtle reminder that the guests would be watching Charlotte's performance, as well. The beau monde's polished manners and gilded smiles masked a darker side to its glitter. Those who didn't fit the pattern card of privilege and power would find themselves savaged by gossip and innuendo.

*Idleness and boredom beget bad behavior*, Charlotte reflected, noting the bejeweled ladies and faultlessly tailored gentlemen seated in the front row of chairs. She thought of Sheffield and Cordelia, and how they had to hide their involvement in business from Polite Society. Heaven forfend that aristocrats, no matter how smart or how hard pressed financially, sully their hands in trade. It was a bloody foolish stricture, like so many of the old rules. Perhaps the future would bring . . .

Another discreet nudge from Alison brought her back to the present moment. The music had ended, and the guests were beginning to rise and move into the main drawing room, where the clink of crystal goblets and the lilt of laughter and conversation would serve as the soiree's serenade.

*And gossip is the real reason I'm here.*

The dowager gathered her cane, and the two of them joined the festivities. Candlelight cast a mellow glow over the opulent furnishings, the myriad tiny flames catching the sparkle of the wine as liveried footmen moved through the crowd, ensuring that no one's glass was empty.

"Ah, there are Miss Greenfield and Miss Greeley, standing by that hideous painting of Lady Havemeyer's great-grandfather." Alison was aware of what sleuthing Charlotte wished to accomplish. "Come, let us go join them."

The two ladies welcomed them with friendly greetings, and Charlotte found it easy to respond with a genuine smile. When the dowager had first assured her that she would find kindred spirits within intellectually minded Bluestockings of the beau monde, she had been skeptical. But she had, in fact, made friends among the members of Lady Thirkell's weekly salon.

The talk quickly turned from the evening's musical performance to a recent essay on politics, and then, as several other ladies drifted over to join them, to a complex mathematical problem recently posed in the *Ladies' Diary*.

"I daresay Lady Cordelia will figure out the answer," mused Charlotte.

"I don't doubt it," replied Miss Greeley. "She finds such computations simple."

"Her mind," said Charlotte, "seems to run like a . . . a steam-powered engine. After allowing a tiny pause, she added, "Did I hear mention of her being interested in mechanical devices that can perform mathematical calculations?"

"Not that I know of." Miss Greeley raised her brows at the other members of the salon.

"I can't imagine it," said Miss Greenfield. "She can solve even the most complicated problems in her head."

The others in their group all nodded in agreement.

"Indeed, Lady Cordelia has often mentioned that she's all

thumbs when it comes to tasks requiring manual dexterity," continued Miss Greeley, "like embroidery or watercolors." A tiny furrow creased her brow. "Speaking of Lady Cordelia, she hasn't attended her usual meetings lately. Does anyone know why?"

The only reply was a puzzled silence.

"Ah, look. There is Miss Mather, and she's with her younger brother, Mister David Mather." After a moment, Lady Arabella Marquand, one of the younger and more outspoken members of the salon, gave a quick wave to a nearby couple. "They may know something."

Charlotte watched the young lady—a petite blonde whose pale features and cream-colored gown appeared to be made out of spun sugar—take hold of her brother's sleeve and hurry to join them. He, too, was fair haired, his golden curls artfully arranged in the latest à la Brutus style. An intricately tied cravat, an evening coat tailored to an impeccable fit, snug pantaloons festooned with an ornate watch fob . . . David Mather struck her as a fop who was trying a little too hard to appear a Tulip of the ton, an impression confirmed by the petulant curl of his well-shaped mouth.

"Mr. Mather," said Lady Arabella as soon as his sister had finished introducing him to the group, "you're a very good friend of Lord Woodbridge, so we were wondering if you happen to know if anything is amiss with Lady Cordelia."

Charlotte might have missed the subtle changes in his face if she hadn't been surreptitiously studying his features. His skin turned a bloodless color and tightened over his cheekbones, making them look sharp as knife blades.

"I've no idea why you think that," he replied curtly. "We are merely acquaintances. As for Lady Cordelia, I barely know her."

"Your sister . . . I-I must have misunderstood." Lady Arabella frowned but quickly recovered and attempted to smooth over the awkward moment. "I do hope you'll be accompanying your sister to more of these soirees, so we may all get to know each other better." She fluttered her lashes—David Mather was a very handsome man. "And do bring your raffish friend—the tall, dark-haired gentleman with the interesting scar on his cheek." A soft laugh. "Mama and I were in our carriage, returning home from a supper party the other evening, and I couldn't help but notice the two of you conversing near the corner of Hyde Park."

"You're mistaken." Mather's voice was as sharp as his cheekbones. "You've confused me with someone else."

Lady Arabella colored, but this time, she didn't back down. "I study botany, sir, and I have a very good eye for detail. The moonlight was quite bright—"

"Perhaps you also have a very vivid imagination," he suggested. "You ladies seem enamored of Mrs. Radcliffe's horrid novels."

"I don't read novels," replied Lady Arabella.

"Then perhaps you had imbibed too much champagne." On that nasty note, Mather turned to his sister. "I really must be going, Susanna. As I told you, I have an engagement for later, and it wouldn't do to be late."

Miss Mather appeared mortified as he muttered a barely civil good-bye to the group and stalked off. "Please forgive David's rudeness," she apologized. "He's been quite overset by the recent death of our cousin."

"My condolences," said Miss Greeley. "I wasn't aware of your loss."

"O-our families aren't close," stammered Miss Mather. "But David had formed a friendship with our cousin, and he's taken it hard."

Charlotte understood her reluctance to elaborate. Murder was something that touched the lower classes. It wasn't a subject to sully the sensibilities of the beau monde.

"I'm so sorry. Was it sudden?" inquired Miss Greenfield politely.

"Quite," answered Miss Mather, averting her gaze.

Silk rustled, the group's comfortable camaraderie broken by the ugly incident. Someone coughed.

Darting a look at the far end of the room, Miss Mather gathered her skirts. "If you'll excuse me, I must go pay my respects to the dowager Duchess of Wooster."

Her departure couldn't quite dispel the lingering pall of embarrassment, and after a few stilted pleasantries, the group drifted apart.

"One can't help but wonder what provoked such an ungentlemanly outburst," murmured Alison once they were alone. "Aside from grief."

Charlotte merely nodded. *Fear.* She hadn't missed the flash of fear in David Mather's eyes at the mention of the dark-haired gentleman.

The question was why.

"Now that I've played my part as a polished and proper lady of the *ton*, might we take our leave?" she asked.

There was yet another role to play before the night was over.

"I fear that I possess precious little patience." Sheffield paused as a guilty grimace tugged at his mouth. "And even less common sense."

Wrexford had closed his eyes, allowing the warmth of the whisky to mellow his mood. With great reluctance, he raised a lid. "We're all idiots, Kit." *Especially when it comes to love.*

His friend forced a wan smile. "Yes, but some of us are more so than others." He rose—a trifle unsteadily—and went to stand by the hearth. After staring for a long moment at the unlit coals, Sheffield turned and braced one arm on the mantel.

"I owe you an apology, Wrex. I let a recent promise take precedent over a longtime friendship. It was wrong—"

"Kit—" began the earl.

"No. Let me finish."

Wrexford's grudging sigh signaled him to go on.

"You trusted me, and I let you down," said Sheffield. "You deserved my loyalty, and my honesty." He shifted his stance. "I won't make the mistake of prevaricating again."

The mention of prevaricating caused Wrexford to feel a spasm of guilt. Keeping secrets, however well intentioned, was fraught with peril. Omissions tangled with misunderstandings, and suddenly trust, an oh-so-fragile bond to begin with, snapped.

"I owe you the truth, and if Lady Cordelia doesn't agree, then, well . . ." Sheffield squared his shoulders. "So be it."

"Since we are baring our souls," interjected the earl. "I haven't been entirely forthcoming with you, either." Charlotte would likely tease him for allowing emotion to overrule reason. But in this case, he would gladly be hoisted with his own petard.

"So," he added, "you may save your breath when it comes to explaining the business arrangements you've made with Lady Cordelia. I know about the account at Hoare's bank. Griffin learned about it during the course of investigating the murder at Queen's Landing and came to ask me some questions about it."

Sheffield appeared stunned. "But I . . . I can't imagine how the two things have anything—*anything!*—to do with each other."

*In for a farthing, in for a guinea.*

"Allow me to explain . . ." Wrexford gave a terse account of the murder victim's relationship to Woodbridge's banker, David Mather.

Sheffield turned pale as bleached muslin.

"That's not all." The earl forged on, determined to make a clean breast of it before he could change his mind. His friend deserved no less, no matter the consequences. "Lady Charlotte witnessed an incident at the ball . . ."

Sheffield listened in stark silence to the account of Cordelia's unsettling meeting with her brother.

"We made the decision not to mention this to you until there was solid evidence that the murder is connected in any way to Woodbridge," finished Wrexford. "We knew you were distraught about other things, and wished to protect you from further worry."

A few fat drops of rain spattered against the window glass. Somewhere in the distance, thunder rumbled.

The earl then went on. "But good intentions often pave the path to perdition. So I've concluded that painful though the truth may be, it's better than the alternatives."

His friend didn't react. He stared off into the shadows, seemingly lost in a fugue of his thoughts.

*Dark ones, by the look of it.* Perhaps he had made a mistake in being so brutally honest. Of late, his judgment had felt shaky.

"Kit?"

Roused from his reveries, Sheffield slowly turned and ran his fingers through his hair. "Ye gods. This changes everything."

"There's no need to sound so blue deviled. What we have are merely random bits of information. And as of yet, we've no reason to think that they all fit together."

Sheffield pulled a fistful of folded papers from his pocket. "That's because I haven't yet shown you the letters I found in Woodbridge's study."

Repressing a shiver, Charlotte turned up her coat collar. The wind had shifted, driving fitful gusts of damp air up from the tidal pools. The grit-flecked chill prickled like knifepoints against her skin as the stench swirled up to clog her nostrils.

She shifted her stance, sliding her sodden boots deeper into the recessed niche between two buildings. Like the others pressed cheek by jowl within the rookeries, they were a sorry jumble of drunken angles and crumbling walls. Time seemed to be mired in the same viscous mud that was seeping through her soles. Or perhaps it was merely the urgency of her own worries that had the minutes passing at a snail's pace.

Charlotte blew on her hands for warmth, watching her breath turn to silvery skeins of vapor, which quickly dissolved into the gloom.

Annie Wright would be coming. But whether she could shed any light on—

A scuffling of steps snapped her attention to full alert. She waited a moment, allowing whoever had entered the narrow cul-de-sac to pass her hiding place before venturing a peek.

*Swish-swish.* The lone figure was already gripped in the thick-fingered darkness of the narrow alley. It was the soft rustle of skirts that told Charlotte it was a woman.

After slipping out from her niche, Charlotte darted forward, quickly narrowing the distance between her and her quarry. With home just steps away, Annie Wright appeared to have re-laxed her guard. Head bent, the barmaid trudged around the corner leading to her own ramshackle building with nary a glance around to check her surroundings.

Charlotte came up behind her, close enough to reach out and grasp the fringe of the shawl wrapped around the barmaid's head and shoulders.

"Miss Wright."

Annie spun around and brandished a fist. A dribble of moon-light through the rotting shingles overhead showed she was holding a knife. "Get away from me," she warned. "Take a step closer and I'll gut ye."

Charlotte raised her hands to show she had no weapon. "I just want a word with you."

"Be off." The knife cut a menacing dance through the shadows. "I don't talk te strangers."

"It's important," pressed Charlotte. "A friend of yours is dead, and—"

Steel flashed as Annie lashed out a wild stab. Charlotte dodged the attack with a lightning-quick spin and thrust out an elbow, knocking Annie off-balance.

"Sorry," she muttered, seizing the barmaid's wrist and twisting it behind her back.

A yelp slipped through Annie's gritted teeth as her fingers spasmed, allowing Charlotte to wrest the weapon from her grip.

"Go ahead and kill me, ye bloody bastard." The barmaid ceased struggling, but defiance crackled in her voice. "I ain't saying nothing."

*A brave woman.* Naïve, but brave. If a hired cutthroat wished to extract information, she would soon be singing like a canary.

Releasing a small sigh, Charlotte stepped back and slid the knife into her pocket. "I've no intention of harming you." Dropping her deep-throated voice, she added, "As I said, a friend of yours is dead, and I'm trying to help ensure his murder doesn't go unpunished."

Annie rubbed at her wrist, her expression betraying both surprise and suspicion. "Ye're a . . . a . . ."

"Yes. A woman like you."

"Why . . . ?" The barmaid narrowed her eyes. "Why d'ye care?"

Charlotte glanced around. The surroundings were dark and silent as a crypt, but in the stews there were always unseen eyes and ears. "I'm happy to explain," she replied. "But not here."

A hesitation.

"If I wanted you dead, your blood would already be puddled in the mud. But given what happened to your friend, I daresay there are others who may wish you harm," continued Charlotte. "The choice is yours, of course. However, if I were you, I wouldn't want to face them on my own."

Annie's eyes betrayed a flicker of weary resignation. "I s'pose I'm damned if I do and damned if I don't." She gave a curt wave. "Follow me."

A short while later, Charlotte retraced her steps through the maze of alleyways leading away from the river. A long trek homeward lay ahead, while behind her lay . . .

More questions than answers. The first pearly hints of dawn were teasing at the horizon, and yet the mystery of the Queen's Landing murder remained tangled in fog and shadows.

Annie Wright had proved to be a conundrum—suspicious and secretive, as well she should be, given that violence had darkened her life. But Charlotte was adept at drawing out secrets, and the barmaid's story had slowly come to light around the guttering flicker of a single tallow candle.

It was her accent that had first given her away. Annie mimicked the slur of the stews very well, but Charlotte had caught the trace of a more cultured voice. When pressed, the barmaid had admitted to her the sad story of her past. A prosperous family, a disastrous marriage to a man beneath her station, who had turned out to be a violent lout. The murdered clerk—Charlotte had finally discovered the poor man's name was Henry Peabody—had been a childhood friend, and it was to him she had turned for help when the beatings had become unbearable.

Peabody had helped arrange for a job at the Ship's Lantern, allowing Annie to escape her marriage and melt away into the nameless swirl of the dockyard slums. Living in poverty was preferable to living in hell.

So that, mused Charlotte, explained why Annie had been

frightened of speaking with a Bow Street Runner, and why Henry Peabody had spent time around the wharves.

She darted across Ratcliff Highway and chose a path that would take her through Leadenhall Street, impelled by an inexplicable urge to see the grand East India Company headquarters, where Peabody had worked.

*Had his fellow clerks and employers mourned his passing?* she wondered.

However, the thought was quickly pushed aside by more pressing questions. While Annie Wright had appeared sincere in her grief, she had been evasive in answering questions about what motives might lie behind her friend's death. At one point, she had seemed on the verge of revealing something.

But then, when Charlotte had mentioned David Mather, fear had clamped Annie's teeth shut, and she had withdrawn into a sullen silence. Deciding further probing was pointless, Charlotte had contented herself with getting a grudging promise that the barmaid would think over things and meet with her again in a few days. She had also mentioned that if Annie wished to reach her sooner, she could send word through Alice the Eel Girl, who sold her wares near Limehouse Dock.

*Trust.* It was a bond fraught with complexities, even between friends. She understood Annie's reluctance to trust an utter stranger.

*And yet . . .*

Henry Peabody was dead, and Charlotte sensed the barmaid knew why.

Would the reason reveal that her own friends were in peril? It was, she determined, a question she couldn't afford to leave unanswered.

Sheffield set the papers on the desk blotter and carefully smoothed out the creases. "As you see, there are several letters expressing satisfaction that a mutually agreeable deal had been reached, and that all the official documents had been signed and the funds handed over," he explained.

"Kit, we're aware that Woodbridge is in need of money," murmured Wrexford after a cursory look. "It makes sense that he would seek a loan from one of the private banks that cater to the beau monde."

"Yes, yes, I'm aware that he wouldn't be the first aristocrat to mortgage future profits from his estate to cover pressing debts," replied his friend. "But now look at this." Sheffield shifted the letters, uncovering a scrawled list of four names, each with a small inked star beside it.

The earl picked up the list and subjected it to careful scrutiny.

"Hoare's, Gurney's, Barclays, Coutts . . . the names are all well-known private banks," said Sheffield.

The earl frowned. The list definitely stirred suspicions, but he kept himself from jumping to conclusions. "The stars could mean he visited them and tried to secure a loan—"

"That won't fadge, Wrex. We know he got money from Hoare's bank, and the letters I just showed you prove he also received loans from Gurney's and Barclays, which makes it likely that he did from Coutts, as well," retorted Sheffield. "You're always saying that we must look at empirical evidence, and this all seems to prove that Woodbridge is up to something havey-cavey."

Wrexford didn't disagree.

"Having done some research myself on the matter of bank loans," continued his friend, "I can assure you that the private banks on Woodbridge's list don't bother lending piddling sums of money. If he's convinced all four of them to given him a loan, he's secured—"

"A bloody big sack of blunt," murmured Wrexford.

Sheffield slapped his palm down on the desk. "I tell you, there's Satan's own mischief afoot here." He began to drum his fingers against the dark-grained wood. "The key question is,

How the devil did he borrow such a large sum of money? His estates aren't nearly enough collateral, and that's assuming they aren't already mortgaged to the hilt."

"Actually, there's perhaps an even more important question." The earl met his friend's gaze with a grim expression.

"Just how is he intending to pay it all back?"

# CHAPTER 11

A blade of sunlight pierced through the windowpane, its angled brightness a sharp reminder that the day was well past its zenith.

"Merciful heavens, I vowed that I wouldn't fall into the same slothful habits of the indolent rich," muttered Charlotte as she hurriedly shoved the last pins into her coiled hair and rose from her dressing table. "But at least I have a better excuse for my slumber than the frivolities of drinking and dancing until dawn."

*To the devil with champagne.* Smothering a yawn, she grabbed up a shawl and hurried downstairs. At this moment she would gladly sell her soul to Satan for a cup of steaming black coffee.

McClellan was busy kneading dough at the worktable and didn't look up as Charlotte slipped into the kitchen. "There's fresh coffee in the pot on the hob," murmured the maid, "and rolls warming in the oven."

"Bless you," replied Charlotte with a grateful sigh. She poured a cup, the rich burnt-spice aroma chasing the lingering smells of the stews from her nostrils as she quaffed a long swallow.

"A long night." It was more of a statement than a question.

After dusting the flour from her meaty hands, McClellan added, "I hope whatever you were doing proved worth the risk."

"We shall have to wait and see," said Charlotte. She fetched the warm rolls from the oven and took a seat at the table opposite the maid. "The earl and I have faced other wretchedly complicated investigations, but this one . . ." She broke off a bit of bread. "This one is proving difficult beyond words."

McClellan carefully wiped down the tabletop with a damp cloth. "Perhaps because it is your friends who are involved in possible misdeeds, and you fear that solving the mystery will bring heartache as well as justice."

Charlotte stopped crumbling the bread between her fingers. The maid, she knew, had some dark incident in her past. They had never discussed what it was. Charlotte was all too familiar with guarding painful personal secrets to have pressed for a revelation. However, she sensed McClellan understood that decisions were never black and white. And every shade of grey was tinged with consequences.

"Yes," she answered. "Right and wrong is a question that can cut one's heart in two."

"No, it isn't," replied McClellan. "Your heart knows what's right, and to act otherwise would be a betrayal of all you hold dear—a far worse crime than any of your friends may have committed."

"Thank you." She managed a wry smile. "For making the essence of a dilemma sound so simple."

The maid shrugged. "It usually is."

"*Errare humanum est,*" murmured Charlotte. *To err is human.* "If our friends have made mistakes, let us hope Wrexford and I can help them find a way to make things right."

Any further discussion on the subject was forestalled by the sound of steps racing down the corridor.

"Awake at last." Raven fixed her with an accusing stare as he skidded to a halt by the table.

"You never sleep late unless you've been up to something dangerous," added Hawk.

"Which means we should know about it." Raven scowled, mimicking the earl's expression of annoyance with frightening accuracy. "Where did you go?"

Charlotte raised a brow. "Do you really wish to pursue the subject of secretive nocturnal activities?"

It was almost comical how quickly their faces flushed with guilt.

"I thought not." She softened her words with a quick smile. "I know we are all trying to help our friends. But let us use prudence and good sense in how we do so." A pause. "Be assured that the earl knew what I was doing." Whether he agreed with it was another matter.

Raven gave a solemn nod, signaling an end to any further butting of heads. "Speaking of friends, we've just come from seeing Skinny. He's feeling much better, but he's still a bit quiffy-niffy." He looked to McClellan. "May we get some food and broth to bring to him?"

"Hmmph." The maid rose and turned to the larder. "Never mind that. I'm coming with you. I've some purchases to make in Covent Garden, so I'll have a look at him, just to be sure all is well."

"If you've any concerns about his well-being, bring him back here," said Charlotte. "I'll set up a cot in the aerie. The boys can go ask Wrexford for—"

"For what?" queried the earl, pausing at the kitchen's entrance. "Forgive me, but the front door was ajar, so I took the liberty of entering to ensure nothing was amiss."

Charlotte felt a rush of relief. Oddly enough, his deep-throated drawl had come to have a steadying effect on her.

"Skinny has been feeling poorly," answered McClellan. "I'm accompanying the boys to have a look at him. If need be, we may wish to borrow your carriage to bring him here."

"Take it now. It's right outside," said Wrexford. "I'll find a hackney for the trip home."

As the maid began assembling a basket of food, Charlotte flashed him a look of gratitude, then turned her attention to the boys.

"Don't fret about Skinny," she said. "We'll take care of him."

"Oiy," mumbled Raven, jamming his hands in his jacket pockets. But the assurance didn't dispel his troubled expression.

"Come, Weasels. Let's be off." McClellan shooed them toward the corridor.

A sigh slipped from Charlotte's lips.

"Rest easy. Skinny is in good hands." Wrexford took her arm. "As for our other friends . . ."

She allowed herself to be led to the parlor. He was right. They could solve only one conundrum at a time.

"Any luck with Annie Wright?" he asked once they were seated on the sofa.

"Annie was wary—understandably so." She explained the details of the encounter. "She clamped up tighter than an oyster when I mentioned David Mather. But whether it has any significance for our friends is impossible to tell." A sigh. "However, she promised to think about my request. I'll return in a day or two to press her further."

"Assuming she doesn't simply melt away into another one of the countless rookeries in London," mused the earl.

"Seeing as I'm morally opposed to using the stick, I chose to use the carrot instead," replied Charlotte. "I promised to help her find a situation more befitting to her station in life—a lady's maid or a seamstress—than that of a barmaid in a hellhole neighborhood."

"Clever," he conceded with a ghost of a smile.

"I can, on occasion, be as pragmatic as you are," she answered. "Speaking of Mather . . ." She recounted the unpleasant scene with the murdered clerk's cousin. "His reaction seemed odd."

Wrexford frowned. "Perhaps. But there are any number of reasons he might not have wanted his association with the dark-haired gentleman known."

Charlotte conceded the point. "What about you? Have you any news to report?"

"I do." He leaned back against the pillows. "Though it only casts more shadows rather than light on the situation."

She listened with a sinking heart as he described the banking list that Sheffield had found in Woodbridge's study.

"I suppose the stars could mean something other than a secured loan," she said, unable to muster any conviction for the assertion. "Perhaps they merely mean he had an acquaintance at the banks."

"And perhaps pigs have learned how to fly." A pause. "However, there's a glimmer of good news. Tyler is fairly certain he's uncovered Professor Sudler's location. It's an isolated cottage on the outskirts of Cambridge." He shifted. "An excellent spot in which to take refuge if one doesn't want to be found."

"I see." Charlotte bit her lip, taking a moment to think. "I think it's imperative for me to be part of the coming confrontation. I may have better luck at having a candid conversation with Lady Cordelia than you."

"Sheffield will insist on coming, too," said Wrexford. "By the by, I've told him everything. It . . ." He gave a wry grimace. "It felt like the right thing to do."

She couldn't help it. A laugh welled up in her throat.

"Yes, yes, I don't need your hilarity to grasp the irony of me acting on intuition."

"If it's any salve to your pride, I think you did the right thing," responded Charlotte. "He deserves our trust."

"The question of how to arrange the logistics of travel is an issue," mused Wrexford. "As you know, my estate is quite close to Cambridge, and Sheffield can stay with me. But propriety forbids you—"

"As to that, I have an idea," she interjected.

He raised a brow. "Dare I ask?"

"I'd rather not say just now." Just in case, thought Charlotte, the idea blew up in her face. "When do you plan to leave?"

"The sooner the better," he answered. "However, we can't ignore the other dangling threads in this case, so I wish to make an inquiry this evening and see where it leads before we make our next move."

It was still early in the evening, and White's had not yet come alive with the daily rituals of masculine revelries. The club's main reading room was empty, save for several elderly gentlemen asleep near the blazing fire, their snores punctuating the occasional rustle of the abandoned newspapers in their laps.

Wrexford moved into the main corridor and signaled to a passing porter. "Has Sir Charles arrived?"

"He's in the Blue Parlor, milord. It's Wednesday, so he's awaiting his usual backgammon partner."

The earl nodded his thanks. "Bring us a bottle of the club's best Madeira," he said and then headed for the stairs, grateful that the admiral—whose scientific papers on seashells had earned him a coveted membership in the Royal Society—was a creature of habit.

"Ah, Wrexford." The admiral looked up from the red and black draughts arranged on the game board as the earl entered the room. "How go your experiments with acids and quartz?"

"I've had some very interesting chemical results," answered the earl. "I'm working on a paper to submit to *Philosophical Transactions*."

"I'm delighted to hear it! The Royal Society's scientific journal needs modern thinking like yours to maintain its reputation for excellence in this new century."

"It may ruffle some feathers," murmured the earl.

Sir Charles let out a chortle. "Even better! Thinking outside the accepted boundaries is important. It's how discoveries are made."

Wrexford and the admiral attended many of the same scientific lectures and had developed a casual friendship. The British Navy was known as a bastion of traditional thinking, but despite his years of service and his crusty demeanor, Sir Charles had a very agile mind and held surprisingly progressive views on a variety of subjects.

"And how goes your book on conches of the West Indies?"

"Slowly." Sir Charles made a wry face. "I suppose at my age, I should feel some sense of urgency." He touched a finger to one of the painted points on the game board. "But after the years of discipline required by shipboard duties, I find myself enjoying the opportunity to explore a great many subjects and have allowed myself to be distracted from my writing."

"The opportunities have been well earned," murmured the earl. He turned as the porter arrived with the wine, and asked for it to be served.

"A very fine—and expensive—vintage." The admiral raised his glass in salute. "As a retired officer on half pay, I can't afford such luxuries." A wry smile curled at the corners of his mouth. "To what do I owe such generosity?"

"Professional and personal admiration," replied Wrexford with an answering smile as he took a seat next to his friend. Despite his silvery hair, Sir Charles still had the muscled physique of a much younger man. However, the Admiralty had been making room for younger officers to move up through the ranks. And so he had been removed from active duty after decades of military service around the globe . . . and naval pay was notoriously low. "I think it shameful that our government behaves so shabbily toward those who have devoted their lives to defending our country."

"I appreciate your words," said the admiral. "However, given your reputation, I doubt you've come here merely to spout heartfelt sentiments."

"Actually, you're correct," he answered. Clearly, retirement hadn't dulled the sharpness of his friend's mind. "I have several questions I'm hoping you'll be willing to answer."

Sir Charles took an appreciative swallow of the Madeira. "Fire away, milord."

"One of your cousins serves as a director of the East India Company, does he not?"

"Yes, yes, Copley. A fine fellow and a brilliant administrator. He was brought in several years ago to add, shall we say, a more progressive attitude to the Company's traditional views."

"And what is his opinion on the recent Charter Act passed by Parliament?" inquired the earl. "I've heard that the changes concerning the Company's trade monopoly have caused some dissension among the board of directors."

"As to that . . ." Sir Charles savored another sip of the wine. "You may ask him for yourself. He should be arriving at any moment."

Wrexford raised his brows in surprise. "But it's Wednesday."

A twinkle of amusement lit in the admiral's eyes. "I can, on occasion, improvise. Lord Ainsley is suffering from an attack of gout, so my cousin agreed to serve as a substitute for tonight's game."

"Though a poor one I may be," announced a voice from the corridor. "I prefer chess to backgammon."

Sir Charles made a rude sound. "My cousin dislikes that the luck of the dice comes into play. He favors a game where a player is allowed to make his own decisions on strategy."

"But chess still requires a player to react to his opponent's moves," said Wrexford.

"A very astute observation, sir," responded the admiral. "My dear Elgin, allow me to introduce Lord Wrexford, a gentleman known for his incisive intellect." He waggled a warning finger. "So if I were you, I'd have a care on crossing verbal swords with him." To the earl, he added, "My cousin, Elgin, Baron Copley."

Copley smiled and raised his hands in mock surrender. "Let us cry pax, Lord Wrexford. As I'm engaged in endeavors which require a pen, not a sword, I would never be so foolhardy as to challenge your steel."

"These days I'm a man of science, not war," replied the earl. "Though I do confess, I've been known to cut up something fierce with fellow members of the Royal Institution if I think their views on a subject are flawed."

"Ideas can certainly spark a war of words," said Copley.

"Speaking of which, Lord Wrexford was just asking how the board of directors has reacted to the Charter Act," interjected Sir Charles.

"Thank you." Copley accepted a glass of Madeira from the earl and took a sip. "That's a *very* fine wine," he murmured before addressing his cousin's comment. "As to the directors, there is, of course, some disagreement among them as to how to proceed. Old ways die hard, especially when they have proved profitable in the past."

"And you, Lord Copley?" asked Wrexford. "What is your opinion?"

"The world is changing. Our company must do so, too," replied the baron. "Yes, we will relinquish some past benefits, but new trading opportunities are opening up. Rather than bemoan our losses, we ought to be focused on taking advantage of them."

"A very practical and pragmatic viewpoint," replied Wrexford.

"Elgin is the leader of the forward-thinking directors who favor change," said Sir Charles.

"You exaggerate, Charles," murmured Copley. He cleared his throat. "Might I ask why you're so interested in the Charter Act, Lord Wrexford, and how it affects the East India Company?" A faint smile. "Are you perchance a stockholder?"

"No, my interest is purely personal." The earl had anticipated the question. "My valet was a good friend of your company clerk who was recently murdered at Queen's Landing," he lied. "He seems to have gotten it in his head that the reason might have to do with some turmoil within the Company brought on by the Charter Act."

Copley stared at him for a moment in mute disbelief before slowly shaking his head. "Merciful heavens, I can't imagine how he came to have that idea! We are a very respected trading company run by gentlemen, not a gang of murderous cutthroats."

*That is just as much a lie as my own farididdle*, thought the earl. The East India Company was the most powerful private enterprise in the world. A veritable empire unto itself, it had a monopoly on trade with the Indian subcontinent, along with its own private army of over 260,000 men to subjugate any local rulers who dared challenge its hegemony.

"That is yet another sad thing about murder," continued the baron. "It seems to stir all sorts of scurrilous rumors. Henry Peabody deserves better than that. He was a very valued employee—highly competent and totally trustworthy—and will be much missed."

"Did you know him personally?" asked Wrexford.

"I did," replied Copley. "He was the head clerk in one of the sections under my authority. His work was beyond reproach."

The baron set down his glass and drew a tight breath. "Bow Street is doing its best to keep the matter quiet and solve the murder without it coming into the public eye." He exhaled. "God forbid that scribbler A. J. Quill starts stirring ghoulish speculation about the East India Company simply to earn a few shillings from the poor man's death."

"Ha! If you ask me, the government ought to track down the fellow and have him arrested for libel," muttered Sir Charles. "Lord Almighty, you, of all people, Wrexford, ought to agree."

The earl shrugged at the mention of Charlotte's satirical

drawings concerning his own public quarrel with the late Reverend Holworthy. It was, in fact, the cleric's murder that had brought them together.

"On the contrary, I rather admire the scribbler," replied Wrexford. "A. J. Quill plays a role in keeping the high and mighty from abusing their power and privileges."

Copley plucked at his coat cuff. "I'm aware of your background in the military, and the fact that you've had some experience with Bow Street. Indeed, I've heard rumors that you helped them unravel some recent mysteries." He lowered his voice. "Are you perchance actively involved in helping the Runners solve Henry Peabody's murder?"

"As I said, my interest is purely personal," said Wrexford, carefully choosing his words.

"As is mine. Though, of course, I also have a professional interest," replied Copley with a heavy sigh. "So I pray that the crime is quickly solved. It's a sordid business, but I'm quite certain, it can have nothing to do with the East India Company." Looking uncomfortable, the baron shifted his stance. "Given your past association with Bow Street, I feel I can share some facts about Henry Peabody's murder that will let you put your valet's mind at ease—but I must ask that you keep what I tell you in strictest confidence."

The earl gave a small nod, deliberately saying nothing.

"At first, Bow Street assumed it was a random robbery," continued the baron. "But given the new developments, they are now of the opinion that it was likely a private quarrel over a woman that ended in blood being spilled."

"Indeed?" The earl was taken aback at the unexpected twist. Had he and his friends taken the pieces of the puzzle and fitted them together all wrong? "What new developments?"

"They've found witnesses who say they overheard heated arguments between Peabody and some . . . highborn gentleman."

"A highborn gentleman?" repeated Wrexford.

"Yes," answered Copley with obvious reluctance. "So you can understand why the authorities are anxious to keep it out of the newspapers. If the public starts to believe that the pillars of English society can't be trusted . . ." He let his words trail off.

The earl pondered over what he had just heard. In truth, the only real evidence in the case was the victim's corpse. All the rest was just swirls of fog and conjecture. "What makes them believe this highborn gentleman is guilty of the murder?"

"Apparently, the fellow has gone missing."

"I see," said Wrexford, careful to mask his dismay. "But they didn't mention his name?"

Copley shook his head. "No, not to me. But I suppose they wish to err on discretion until they make an arrest."

"Hmmph. Perhaps you need to run a tighter ship, Elgin," interjected the admiral. "No man under my command would dare do anything havey-cavey, knowing the punishment would be swift and severe."

Copley's face betrayed a momentary flicker of irritation before he forced a thin smile. "Alas, Charles, unlike the British Navy, the East India Company cannot exercise total control over the lives of our employees."

"Havey-cavey," repeated Sir Charles under his breath.

The baron ignored his cousin. "That is all I know, Wrexford," he said. "Let us hope Bow Street can quickly make an arrest and put an end to the sordid affair."

"Indeed." The earl rose. "Thank you for your time." He turned for the door and then paused. "Just one last question. Does the word *argentum* mean anything to you?"

"Other than as a painful reminder of how much I detested my Latin lessons at Eton?" quipped Copley. "I know it means 'silver,' but other than that . . ." Looking baffled, he shook his head. "Why do you ask? Is it important?"

"Quite likely not," replied the earl.

"Havey-cavey," repeated Sir Charles. "You may tell your

valet that his friend ought to have been more careful as to the company he kept."

"So it would seem," replied Wrexford. But like quicksilver, the facts of the case seemed to be constantly shifting their shape. A glimmer . . . a wink . . . and then they were gone.

"Thank you for your time, gentlemen," he added. "I'll not keep you any longer from your game."

"Yes, yes, do sit down, Elgin, and let us begin." After refilling his glass, the admiral winked at the earl. "Ha! There's nothing like a battle—even if it's just a battle of wits—to get the blood pulsing through my aged veins!"

# CHAPTER 12

Forcing her eyes away from the clock, Charlotte turned her attention back to her drawing. Darkness had settled over the city. And yet there were any number of reasonable explanations as to why the boys hadn't yet returned from the dowager's townhouse with a reply to her request.

Granted, what she had done was a risk.

"*Pericula ludus,*" she whispered. *Danger is my pleasure.* Many of her past actions seemed to give truth to the ancient Latin adage. Breaking the bars of a gilded cage had meant flying into the unknown.

After dipping her pen in the inkwell, Charlotte began to add cross-hatching to the dark outline of—

The sudden *clack* of the brass knocker nearly caused the quill to slip from her fingers. Cocking an ear, she listened as McClellan hurried from the kitchen to see who was calling.

"Lady Peake!" The maid's surprised voice floated up from below.

Her great-aunt had come to call at this hour? Charlotte felt a surge of panic. It was well after suppertime.

"Lady Charlotte requested a meeting, and as she said it was rather urgent, it occurred to me that the boys and I ought to all return together," came Alison's brisk reply. "Besides, I've been curious about where she lived."

*Ah, well.* Charlotte drew in a tight breath. *Two birds with one stone.* Another old adage, but her mind was too jumbled to recall the Latin phrase.

"Please allow me to show you to the parlor," said McClellan. "And then I'll let Lady Charlotte know you're here."

After tucking a loose curl behind her ear—she didn't care to contemplate what other strands had come free as she had worked—Charlotte rose and quickly shook out the creases from her work gown.

It was time for the dowager to see the sow's ear, not the silk purse.

On entering the parlor, she found Alison inspecting the books and paintings at the far end of the room.

"This is a wonderful landscape," said the dowager, turning from a large canvas of a Tuscan hillside and lowering her quizzing glass. "The light and colors are exquisitely rendered."

"It was done by my late husband," said Charlotte, finding her throat had gone very dry.

"He was very talented."

"Yes, very." She gestured to the sofa. "Won't you sit down?"

Shifting the cane to her other hand, Alison then crossed the carpet and settled herself against the sofa's thick pillows. All the lamps were lit, filling the room with a mellow glow.

"This is a very charming place," observed the dowager after another look around.

"It's nothing fancy, but it suits me," replied Charlotte, aware of how stilted she sounded. Despite her resolve, she was finding it hard to shake off her nervousness. Alison had always accepted— nay, encouraged—the fact that her grand-niece marched to a rebellious drumbeat.

*But what if the person I've become has crossed the line of no return?*

Charlotte looked up to find the dowager regarding her with an inscrutable stare.

"I gather there is something important that you wish to discuss with me?" said Alison.

"Yes," she answered. "But before I do so, I need to explain . . ."

"Tea," announced McClellan, carrying a tray into the parlor. "I thought refreshments might be welcome." Following behind her were Raven and Hawk, each bearing a platter of pastries.

Charlotte breathed a silent sigh of relief. She had sent the boys off with scrubbed faces and clean clothing, and by some miracles, they still appeared relatively tidy.

"Dundee cakes," announced Raven, setting his offering down on the table in front of Alison.

"And ginger biscuits," chirped Hawk. "They're my favorite," he confided to the dowager as he put down his plate.

"I'm *very* fond of ginger biscuits, too," replied Alison, her lips twitching upward. "However, I shall try to leave one or two for you."

"S'all right. Have as many as you like." He grinned, revealing a few molasses-flecked crumbs lodged between his teeth. "There's another pan in the oven."

McClellan cleared her throat. "Lady Charlotte has poured tea for Lady Peake. Be a gentleman and bring it to her, and then you may offer her a biscuit before fixing plates for you and your brother."

Raven had taken a perch on one of the facing armchairs, hands folded primly in his lap.

"Thank you," said the dowager once Hawk had finished serving her. She looked at Charlotte, her eyes alight with amusement. "The boys have such impeccable manners. I confess, I'm still trying to puzzle out why Wrexford calls them Weasels."

Charlotte had been struggling with how to broach the subject of her past—her real past, not the one gilded with half-truths and outright bouncers. And here, she decided, was a way to cut through all hemming and hawing in one fell swoop.

"It's because of our first encounter with the earl," she said. "Raven stuck a knife in Wrexford's leg, and Hawk flung a broken bottle at his head, when they thought that he was threatening me."

For a moment, the room was utterly still. Even the plume of steam rising from the teapot seemed to freeze in midair.

And then a tiny twitch as Hawk's eyes widened in shock. "I-I thought we were never, ever supposed to mention that," he whispered, his mouth quivering in confusion. "On account of . . . of . . ."

"On account of it giving away the truth," said Raven, turning to watch Alison intently through the fringe of his dark lashes. "The truth that we're orphan guttersnipes, not m'lady's respectable relatives."

The dowager blinked and took a moment to polish her quizzing glass before raising it to her eye.

"I found the boys—or rather, they found me—in my previous residence," explained Charlotte in a rush. Like peeling a bandage from a wound, it was best to get it over with quickly. "Which was on the fringes of St Giles, a far less pleasant neighborhood than this one. They had been abandoned, and Raven was doing his best to care for Hawk. They began doing odd errands in return for whatever scraps of food I could afford, and for shelter from . . ." She hesitated. "From all the evils than can befall children left to fend for themselves."

Alison sat pale and still as a statue carved from marble.

"It's true we're not bound by blood, but we *are* a family, one with bonds far more meaningful than a dribble of scarlet liquid." Charlotte crooked a smile. "As you know, I've always been a fool when it comes to love, whether it be my passions for art and ideas or for the people I wished to hold close to my heart."

Still no reaction from the dowager.

She closed her eyes for an instant. "There's more you need to know, assuming you're willing to hear it. But the boys need not stay."

Raven and Hawk quietly slid down from their seats and put their plates of untouched sweets on the table.

The muted *chink* seemed to unlock Alison's tongue. "Do you mean to say . . ." Light winked off the glass lens as she fixed her much-magnified eye on Raven. "You watched over your brother and fought to keep him safe?"

"Oiy." Raven lifted his bony shoulders in a shrug. "We're family. Ye take care of yer own," he added, letting his speech slur into the patter of the stews.

"Well, I think . . ." The dowager's voice stuck for an instant in her throat. "I think that's quite the bravest thing I've ever heard."

Catching the glint of a tear pearled on Alison's lashes, Charlotte dared to think the meeting might not end in utter disaster.

"Lord Wrexford says the mark of a true gentleman is that he protects the people he loves," murmured Hawk.

"Hmmph." Alison made a small sniff. "It seems His Lordship is not only a very handsome devil but also a very wise one."

Charlotte gave a small nod to Raven and Hawk. "You have your lessons to do, so off you go, while I finish my explanations . . ."

"Wait!" exclaimed the dowager as the boys turned for the doorway, punctuating the command with a thump of her cane. "How dare my little Weasels run off without giving their aunt a hug!"

An uncertain smile blossomed on Hawk's face as he took a tentative step toward the sofa. "But you're not really our aunt."

"The devil I'm not!" Alison seized him in a fierce embrace. "However, perhaps you've decided you don't want an old dragon as a relative."

"Of course we do," replied Raven, allowing a very un-

Raven-like grin. "Who else would ply us with ice cream and sweets at Gunter's?"

"That's very practical and pragmatic," said Alison with an approving nod. She released Hawk with a last fond ruffling of his unruly curls. "Now come take your leave of me properly, you young jackanapes. That is, unless you consider yourself too big for hugs."

Charlotte held her breath. Raven wasn't easy to reach.

The boy hesitated and then shuffled over and allowed the dowager to plant a peck on his cheek. He pulled away quickly, but not before Charlotte saw another grin tug at his lips.

"Weasels, the Dragon, and me—a strange bird Wrexford calls Phoenix," said Charlotte as they scampered off. "Lud, what an eccentric menagerie we make."

"Hmmph." Whether the sound was a snort or a laugh was impossible to discern.

"Thank you, Aunt Alison," she added. "For not falling into a swoon at the truth."

"Merciful heavens, did you think I believed for a moment your farididdle about the boys being orphaned relatives of your husband's family?" Alison reached for a ginger biscuit and took a bite before continuing. "They're far too clever and interesting to have been brought up in a respectable but boring gentry family."

"I'm very grateful that you're not easily shocked." Charlotte blew out her breath. "For I'm not yet done with the revelations."

The dowager finished her biscuit. After dusting the crumbs from her fingers, she once again lifted her quizzing glass. A Cyclops-like eye, widened in an unblinking stare, was admittedly a little unnerving, but Charlotte held herself steady.

"Well, do go on, gel," drawled Alison. "My delicate nerves can't stand the suspense."

\* \* \*

Feeling unaccountably chilled, Wrexford placed several chunks of coal in the hearth of his workroom and slowly coaxed a flame to life.

*Light and shadow.* He watched the two intertwine, recalling his words to Charlotte. It was true. The more they learned, the darker things looked for their friends. He now understood her wrenchingly visceral reaction to seeing her cousin charged with murder. He had sympathized, of course, but it had been an intellectual reaction, not this knife-sharp blade of fear jabbing at his gut.

If it turned out the clerk's murder was connected to Cordelia and her brother, that could mean Sheffield was entangled in something very dangerous. His worries would, of course, prove unfounded if it turned out Peabody's murder was a matter of personal passions gone awry. But somehow, he couldn't quite make himself believe that a love triangle lay at the heart of the conundrum. Woodbridge, Mather, Peabody . . . the connections seemed too much of a coincidence.

Feeling unsettled—he wasn't usually plagued by self-doubt— Wrexford rose and fetched the bank list that Sheffield had found in Woodbridge's desk before taking a seat in front of the dancing fire. He tried to make himself believe that the tiny stars drawn next to the bank names could mean something other than success in negotiating a loan.

But Reason refused to yield to Desire.

"Money," growled the earl, wondering what the devil Woodbridge was up to. "Money is the root of all evil."

"Actually, most people misquote the Bible." Tyler shouldered his way into the room and came to warm his hands by the fire. "The exact wording is 'For the love of money is the root of all evil.' Timothy, chapter six, verse ten."

"Please don't quote the Scriptures at me," said Wrexford. "I'm in a foul enough mood as it is." He glanced down at the list. "Did you learn anything new about the murder?"

Tyler shrugged out of his overcoat and placed it on the work counter before answering, "A bloody knife was found this afternoon, hidden in a stack of crates waiting for shipment on Queen's Landing. Bow Street thinks it may be the weapon used to murder the clerk."

"Does it provide a clue as to who the killer is?"

"Not exactly." His valet moved to the sideboard. "Would you care for a glass of brandy?"

In answer, Wrexford uttered a scalding oath.

"Lud, you really are in a foul mood." A muted *chink* of crystal. "If you don't mind, I'll help myself. I've been sleuthing for hours, and it was damnably cold down around the docks." After a quick swallow, Tyler took a seat in the other armchair.

The earl expelled a breath, trying to dispel the worst of his fears. "Forgive me for snapping. This investigation has turned very personal. Kit may be tangled in whatever trouble Woodbridge and Lady Cordelia have gotten themselves into, and I fear it may destroy him unless we can find a way to help."

"We will," said Tyler. The firelight winked off the faceted glass, setting off amber sparks. "Heaven help any villains who dare threaten our friends." His mouth twitched. "Lady Charlotte would cut out their livers with a rusty penknife."

A grudging smile ghosted over Wrexford's lips. It shouldn't be of moral comfort that Charlotte was his partner in mayhem. And yet it was. Yes, she was putting herself in danger. But Charlotte wouldn't be Charlotte without her fierce passions. He was learning to live with that.

"True," he murmured. "However, if I get to them first, they will already be chopped into mincemeat." He watched the flames lick up from the logs. "But at the moment, I feel like I'm wandering in the dark. I've just come from a meeting with Lord Copley, a director of the East India Company . . ."

Wrexford explained what he had been told. "The baron is under the impression that Bow Street thinks the murder may be a crime of passion and has nothing to do with money. But I'm finding that difficult to accept."

"I had better tell you about the knife." Tyler's expression turned troubled. "It's quite distinctive. The blade is Damascus steel, honed to a razor's edge," he explained. "And the hilt is made of chased silver."

"Argentum," mused Wrexford.

The valet nodded. "That's not all. On the butt is an ebony knob, inset with an ornate silver lion rampant."

*Lion rampant* was a heraldic term, signifying a lion standing on its hind legs, with its front paws raised.

The earl pursed his lips. "The majority of aristocratic families in Britain have a lion rampant as part of their coat of arms. Including the royal family."

"And including the Earl of Woodbridge," said the valet.

With a twitch to her skirts, Charlotte resettled herself against the pillows. "I haven't been entirely forthcoming with you about my artistic work and how I earn my bread."

Alison's expression turned even more owlish. "You mean to say you don't draw pictures of the latest fashions for publication?"

"Not precisely. Though I do occasionally highlight what people are wearing."

A chuckle. "By Jove, that reminds me of the wickedly sly caricatures you used to make of the pompous prigs among your father's friends. Perhaps I shouldn't have encouraged your drawings, but you had an uncanny knack for capturing their foibles."

The dowager gave another laugh. "You must enjoy A. J. Quill's satires as much as I do. The man has a razor-sharp eye and a cutting tongue. However, one cannot help but wonder . . ." She pursed her lips. "How on earth does he manage to uncover all those secrets?"

Charlotte fingered an ink stain on her cuff. "Through an extensive network of informants, no doubt."

Alison looked skeptical. "He would have to be rich as Croesus to buy that sort of information."

"Not necessarily," she replied. "You might be greatly surprised to discover just how intimately well servants know their employers, and how much is seen by the people on the streets—the streetsweeps and the flower girls, the costermongers and the urchins—who go unnoticed by their so-called betters."

"Hmmph. I confess, I hadn't considered that." The dowager furrowed her brow. "You think that's how he does it?"

"It's the most logical explanation." Charlotte allowed a small pause. "What makes you think A. J. Quill is a *he*?"

"Oh, pish. What woman would dare to lampoon the high and mighty? It would require..." Alison's voice suddenly trailed off.

It took another instant for the penny to do a last spinning somersault through the air and drop to the floor.

"Oh, no. No. Surely you're not saying..."

"You were asking how I came to know Wrexford," replied Charlotte. "If you recall, he was the prime suspect in a heinous murder—"

"Yes, of course," interrupted Alison. "And A. J. Quill was savaging his character, which fanned the flames of speculation."

"A. J. Quill was *satirizing* his character," Charlotte corrected. "The earl has conceded that it was a fair portrait, as he had been deliberating baiting the pompous Reverend Holworthy in the days leading up to his death."

"I believe that the authorities wondered how the artist depicted the murder scene with such accuracy," mused the dowager.

"As did Wrexford," replied Charlotte. "Which, to make a long story short, is how Raven and Hawk came to assault His Lordship."

Sitting back with a wry laugh, Alison shook her head. "Ye

heavens, how did I not see it? Now that I think of it, so many of the little details in A. J. Quill's caricatures should have struck me as familiar—the way of depicting curling hair, the exaggerated shape of a nose, a lady's scowl."

"One of the many lessons I've learned about human nature is that we tend to see what we expect to see," she murmured.

Alison nodded but maintained a pensive silence.

Charlotte stirred her now-cold tea, unwilling to intrude on the dowager's thoughts. Shock and surprise were likely some of the emotions swirling inside her head. Were disappointment and revulsion also among them?

As Alison's first reaction had indicated, there were boundaries past which a woman trespassed at her own peril. . . .

Courage was one thing. Foolhardiness was quite another. And unlike herself, Alison had never been a fool. Outspoken, yes, but aware of just how far she could step without putting her foot in forbidden territory.

The dowager cleared her throat, but only as a prelude to shifting in a whisper of silk.

As more seconds slid by, Charlotte realized how much the dowager's support meant to her. Alison had believed in her, had thought her dreams worthy.

"Please allow me to explain a bit more," she ventured. "It was Anthony who created A. J. Quill in order to make ends meet when he didn't get the painting commission he expected on returning to London from Italy. He was good at it."

A pause. "When he died, I decided to pick up his pen, as it offered the opportunity for more income than scrubbing floors or sewing piecework. As you know, I could never stitch a straight seam."

Charlotte didn't dare look up from her lap, for fear of what she might see in Alison's expression. "I was good at it, too. Not just the art, but the ideas behind the lines and colors. I felt I could help make sure that the rich and powerful were held accountable for their actions. I also wanted to be a voice for those who had no one else to speak for them, and focus attention on social injustices."

She knotted her hands together. "No doubt I've made more than my share of mistakes, but I have always tried to do what was right, not merely to pander to what the public might want to hear."

"Hmmph."

"I know what you're thinking," said Charlotte hastily. "But—"

"I doubt it," responded Alison, finally rousing herself to speech. "I am still searching for the words to articulate my . . . my . . ."

Charlotte steeled herself. A tongue-lashing from family had always been painful. But coming from the dowager, it would cut to the quick.

"My profound admiration and respect for your talents and passions," said Alison. "And how you have worked against all odds to use them for the Higher Good."

"I-I feared you might think I had no right to throw stones when I myself am so flawed."

"My dear Charley, none of us are perfect, but you . . . you have always demanded more of yourself than anyone else has." The dowager reached out and took her hand. "So strong, so capable," she murmured, brushing a soft caress to Charlotte's ink-stained fingers and palm. "I've never been prouder of you than I am at this moment."

A tear fell from Charlotte's lashes, and then another, and another. "Lud, I never cry," she murmured, blotting her cheeks with her sleeve.

After composing herself with a watery sniff, she quickly went on. "I was hoping you would accept me for who I am. Your unwavering support is the reason I dared to follow my heart all those years ago, no matter where it led. And now that we've come together again, I don't wish for there to be any secrets between us. You're too dear to me."

"I should hope you know you can trust me," replied Alison stoutly.

"I would trust you with my life." Charlotte gave a wry smile. "In fact, I just have—that is, my life as I know it. If I had to give up my pen . . ." A chill seized the nape of her neck at the thought of it.

"Thank you, my dear. I'm so glad you decided you could confide in me." An impish glint flashed in the dowager's sapphirine eyes. "I confess, I'm relieved to learn why I never drew A. J. Quill's notice. It made me feel quite low to think that I was losing my fire."

Alison regripped her cane. "But never mind that right now. You said that you wished to ask me a favor." She leaned forward. "How can I help?"

# CHAPTER 13

Paper crackled as Wrexford refolded the banking list Was the knife yet another black mark against Woodbridge? Or . . .

He drew in a pensive breath. And released it in a low snort. "Is it just me, or do you also smell a rat?"

Tyler took a sip of his brandy. "The odor is definitely teasing at the nostrils." He turned the glass in his hands. "But if it was planted, who did it? And why?"

"I don't know," admitted the earl. "And yet why would Woodbridge be so stupid as to leave such a distinctive weapon at the scene of the crime?"

"Perhaps he simply panicked."

"Perhaps," agreed Wrexford. "Especially if he didn't come to the rendezvous with the intention of committing murder. He and Peabody might have quarreled and it turned ugly, or the clerk might have threatened him." His brows drew together in thought. "Or perhaps the highborn gentleman seen arguing with the clerk is David Mather, not Woodbridge, and the knife belongs to him."

"You think Mather might have murdered his cousin?" Tyler raised a skeptical brow. "Over a woman?"

"Lady Charlotte witnessed an ugly incident involving Mather, which seems to indicate he has secrets to hide." The earl recounted what she had told him. "There are any number of reasons why two relatives—one born to aristocratic privilege and one born to modest means—might quarrel."

The valet pursed his lips, in thought. For several long moments, the only sound in the room was the muted hiss of the burning coals. "Very well. I'll check on whether Mather's family crest includes a lion rampant."

Wrexford closed his eyes, trying to force the amorphous clues into sharper focus. "Something just doesn't strike me as right about the murder being a matter of jealousy. I keep coming back to the connection between Woodbridge, Mather, Peabody. There has to be something other than a woman tying them together."

*Trust your intuition.* Charlotte's frequent exhortation teased at his conscious thought. And suddenly another idea popped to mind.

"Money," he muttered. "Perhaps Peabody had learned something from Mather about Woodbridge's finances and was using it to blackmail him."

Tyler's brows drew together. "An interesting possibility."

"Or perhaps the two of them were in league on the blackmail scheme and then quarreled over the money . . ." The earl rose and began to pace.

The coals crackled.

"I think you should track down Griffin and see if he'll consent to let us borrow the knife for a short time. Apparently, he had Henning look at Peabody's corpse right after the murder to see if the killer had left any telltale clues as to his identity." Basil Henning, an irascible surgeon and longtime friend, ran a clinic for the poor in the slums of Seven Dials. His skills at healing were matched by his uncanny ability to make the dead give up their secrets. "Now that we have a weapon, Henning may be able to tell us whether it was the one used to kill Peabody."

Tyler set down his glass with a martyred sigh. "Alas, no rest for the weary, I see."

"Indeed not." Wrexford turned abruptly to retrieve his coat. "Damnation, I need to pay a visit to Lady Charlotte and inform her of these latest twists. She sensed that Annie Wright was holding something back. If the barmaid knows something, be it the jealous rivalry or the blackmail scheme, we need to speak with her—and quickly."

"You think she might be in danger?" asked the valet softly. "From whom? Woodbridge?"

"The threat of having one's nefarious schemes exposed is certainly a motive for murder," he answered. "And one man is already dead."

A rush of gratitude welled up in Charlotte's throat. To once again have her great-aunt as a confidante made all the uncertainties she was facing seem a little less daunting. "Wrexford needs to visit Cambridge, and I wish to go as well," she explained. "And short of locking him in some deep, dark dungeon, Raven will likely find a way to follow us. You see, we fear that Lady Cordelia and her brother have become enmeshed in something dangerous . . ."

The dowager listened in rapt silence as Charlotte explained about her friend's disappearance and the unsettling clues discovered at Woodbridge's townhouse.

"Wrexford and Sheffield intend to stay at the earl's estate while they seek to locate the elusive professor," continued Charlotte. "It occurred to me that if the boys and I travel with you, it would be perfectly proper for us to pay them a visit. A country house party of sorts, though sleuthing would take precedence over frivolous entertainments."

"An excellent plan," said Alison. "The tabbies of the ton won't dare to gossip if I'm part of the party." She paused. "Though come to think of it, there has been some talk about Wrexford, and how attentive he's been to you." A cough. "Er, is he . . . that is, are you . . ."

Charlotte drew in a shaky breath. "We are . . ."

*Friends?* She couldn't bring herself to reduce their relationship to such a lame platitude. It was far more nuanced, with richly textured layers, shaded with subtle colors—and here and there a hint of shadow.

"We are special to each other, in ways that defy any words I can muster," she said softly. "For now, I'm afraid that's the best answer I can give you."

The dowager nodded sagely, but a hint of a smile curled at the corners of her lips. "Like the Weasels, the heart doesn't always choose to speak the King's English."

They sat for a long moment, holding hands in companionable silence. The universe, mused Charlotte, worked in mysterious ways. It was because of her cousin's shocking murder that she had been reunited with the dowager. Life was capricious. It was, she supposed, a stark reminder that things could change in the blink of an eye.

*Carpe diem. Seize the day.*

Perhaps she and Wrexford needed to—

An urgent knock on the parlor door chased the thought from her head. "Forgive me for interrupting," said McClellan. "But Lord Wrexford is here, and he says it's urgent."

The earl's dark silhouette was already looming behind the maid. "Well, don't just stand there, milord. Do come in," said Alison. "What dark mischief is afoot?"

Wrexford hesitated and darted a questioning look at Charlotte.

"There's no need for prevarication," she murmured. "Alison is now part of our inner circle. She knows all my secrets." A pause. "All of them."

"I see." His face was shrouded in shadows, making his expression impossible to read.

"And I can be trusted to keep them." The dowager fixed him with a challenging stare. "If you wish, I can write out a pledge in blood."

"I'll accept your word. Especially as the alternative would involve crossing canes with you." His mouth twitched. "I don't fancy having my shins bruised."

"Please, let's not waste time in sparring," interjected Charlotte, noting the tension beneath the earl's show of humor. "What's wrong, sir?"

Wrexford stepped into the room, and McClellan closed the parlor door behind him. Her steps echoed in the corridor as she discreetly withdrew.

"I've just come from White's," he answered, "where I had a discussion with one of the directors of the East India Company about the clerk's murder." Without further preamble, the earl recounted his meeting with the admiral and Copley and then went on to explain about his valet's discovery. "Peabody worked under Copley, and the baron had nothing but praise for his character and competence. He confided that Bow Street thinks the murder was a personal matter involving rivalry over a woman—"

"Annie Wright?" interjected Charlotte. "I can't believe that, given what she told me about her relationship with Peabody." She made herself think back over the encounter. "My sense is, she wasn't lying."

"I, too, feel this is about far more than jealousy," he replied. "After further thought, Tyler and I are of the opinion that black-mail might have been the motive."

Wrexford shifted closer to the sofa. "The connection between Woodbridge, Mather, and Peabody seems too strong to ignore. Our guess is, Peabody might have learned some unsavory secret about Woodbridge's finances from his cousin and decided to try to profit from it. I've asked Tyler to see if Griffin will allow us to have Henning look at the knife, to see whether he thinks it's the actual murder weapon."

"Mather," mused Charlotte. "His connection to Woodbridge is the bank, so perhaps the blackmail was his idea. He struck me as a fellow who yearns for more money than he has." She pondered the possibilities. "From what we've heard, Peabody was an honorable man. But I can understand how the temptation might have been too great. And it would explain Annie Wright's reluctance to talk. She may feel it's better for her friend's sins to remain buried with him."

"Forgive me for interrupting . . ." Alison cleared her throat. "But I find it hard to imagine Woodbridge being capable of killing another man."

"Fear and panic can push even the mildest of men to murder," replied Charlotte. "Self-preservation is a very primal emotion."

"Yes, I'm old enough to have witnessed the vagaries of human nature," replied the dowager. "Granted, he may not be as clever as his sister, but he's known as a very sober, solid fellow. If anything, his reputation is for being good hearted to a fault. There's no skeleton of scandal in his closet." She regripped her cane. "Trust me, even the slightest rattle of bones, and I would know about it."

A glint of amusement flashed in the earl's eyes. "It appears you've acquired yet another pair of very useful eyes and ears, Lady Charlotte," he said. "Speaking of bones locked away in closets, Lady Peake, what do you know about the Honorable David Mather?"

"Only that he holds a position at Hoare's Bank and is considered a modest catch on the marriage mart on account of being the second son of a baron," shot back the dowager. "However, I'm well acquainted with his grandmother. I can pay a morning call on her tomorrow, if that would help."

"Any information concerning Mather's personal life would be useful," he replied.

Charlotte nodded. "As for Annie Wright, perhaps I had better pay another visit to her tonight—"

"Alone?" exclaimed Alison. "And in such a dangerous, disreputable part of Town?"

"You will have to get used to it, Lady Peake," murmured the earl.

The comment earned him a horrified look.

"What Wrexford means is," said Charlotte, "I'm experienced in this sort of foray, and I go in disguise."

"In disguise?" Despite her obvious concern, the dowager couldn't help but sound a little intrigued.

"Lady Charlotte looks very fetching dressed in breeches," said the earl dryly. "However ill fitting."

"Enough teasing, Wrexford." Charlotte hesitated, suddenly aware that a choice had to be made. "I will need to go ready myself. But before I do so, we need to discuss Woodbridge and Lady Cordelia. One of the reasons for my revelations to Aunt Alison was to enlist her help and make it possible for me to journey to Cambridge."

"With me as a chaperone, sir," said the dowager, "it's perfectly proper for our party to stay at your estate."

"Raven and Hawk will demand to come, too," Charlotte quickly added. "If I try to leave them behind, Lord only knows what mischief they might wreak."

"It's an excellent solution," responded Wrexford. "As I said before, if we find Woodbridge and Lady Cordelia have taken refuge with Professor Sudler, your presence will be key, both in tempering Kit's emotions and in coaxing the truth out of Lady Cordelia. She trusts your judgment."

"I know it's important that we try to unravel the truth about Peabody's murder," mused Charlotte. "But it seems to me that it's even more critical to find Woodbridge. After all, he—and his sister—lies at the very heart of this mystery. If we hurry our preparations, Alison and I, along with the boys and McClellan, could leave early in the morning and reach your estate by evening. However, if I spend the night hoping to cajole Annie Wright into further revelations . . ." She hesitated.

But Wrexford merely waited, watching her intently. His silence was eloquent in its refusal to make the decision for her.

"It would mean delaying our departure," said Charlotte slowly. "And I don't think we should do that. Raven and Sheffield are depending on us. They asked for our help, and we can't let them down."

"Family and friends," murmured Alison. "There's a special loyalty that binds us together."

"I agree that it's the right decision," said Wrexford. "It's unlikely the barmaid is in any imminent danger."

Silk rustled as the dowager gathered her skirts. "I'll have my traveling carriage come around to fetch you at half past seven."

"I'll have my unmarked carriage meet you at your townhouse. You'll need a second vehicle for the baggage and your lady's maid. McClellan can ride with her," replied the earl. "Meanwhile, I'll alert Kit, and the two of us will leave at first light."

For an instant, his lips thinned to a grim line. "However, I'm not sure that any of us are going to be happy with what we find."

The dowager leaned forward, her eyes taking on a martial gleam. "Are we expecting trouble?"

"As Wrexford is so fond of saying," replied Charlotte, "even when we don't go looking for trouble, it seems intent on finding us."

# CHAPTER 14

Twilight had long since given way to night. And yet Charlotte couldn't help but venture a peek out the carriage window as the coachman called out that the journey was finally at an end and they were making the final turn through the gates of Wrexford's country estate.

Naught but shadows and amorphous shapes greeted her gaze as the graveled drive wound its way through a grove of ancient oaks.

It had been a long trip. Leaning back, she cast a guilty glance at the dowager, who had dozed off some miles ago. However comfortable the well-padded and well-sprung coach, the hour upon hour of bumping over the uneven roads had been grueling, even for the boys, who were also slumped back against the squabs.

*Crunch-crunch.* The carriage crested a gentle hill, and the wheels slowed, then lumbered to a halt. Light from the entrance lanterns illuminated a large courtyard. Several servants hurried out of the shadows to let down the carriage steps and open the door.

"Have we arrived?" asked Alison, her voice muzzy with sleep.

"You have, milady." Wrexford appeared in the doorway, his breeze-ruffled hair and broad shoulders a black silhouette against the flickering lantern flames. He held out a hand to help Alison. "Allow me to assist you."

The dowager winced as she descended the steps. "My old bones are a trifle stiff," she admitted.

"Perhaps a glass of sherry will soothe their complaints," he replied after helping Charlotte out of the carriage.

"I think I'd prefer brandy," said Alison, flexing her shoulders.

The boys scrambled out on their own and stared up at the stately façade of the massive mansion, its honey-colored limestone glowing bronze in the night light.

"Oiy!" said Hawk in a tone of awe as his gaze angled heavenward. "It's bigger than St. James's Palace."

Raven turned in a slow circle, sniffing the air. "It smells different here. And it's quiet as a crypt."

"The country is very different from the city in a great many ways," said Sheffield as he hurried down the front steps of the manor house to join them.

"We saw miles and miles of fields!" exclaimed Hawk. "And hills and hedgerows and—"

"Let us get settled inside, sweeting," murmured Charlotte, touching his shoulder. "And then we can recount all the wondrous things we saw on the journey."

"An excellent suggestion," said Wrexford, handing Alison her cane and then offering his arm.

Sheffield quickly made his greetings to everyone and came around to escort Charlotte.

"There's a warming fire lit in one of the side salons," added the earl. "Tea and a cold collation will be served as soon as we're seated." He led the way through a cavernous entrance hall—its age-dark paneled walls bristled with hunting tapestries, racks of antlers, and a bloodthirsty array of ancient weaponry—and turned down a side corridor, where a door stood half-open.

"The parlor is a bit cozier than the formal drawing room," he explained, guiding the dowager to the sofa set close to the blazing hearth. "Weasels!" he called as Alison seated herself on the plump pillows.

The boys had lingered in the entrance hall. *No doubt ogling the swords and other implements of war*, thought Charlotte. *And deciding the best way to scale the walls.*

Sure enough, the first words out of Raven's mouth were about the weaponry. "Will you show us how to shoot the crossbows?"

"That depends on whether you behave like little gentlemen or little savages," replied the earl.

Raven gave a rude snicker. "Behaving like little gentlemen is cursedly boring."

Wrexford shrugged. "The choice is yours." He let the statement hang between them for an instant before adding, "But be forewarned that any unauthorized high jinks with the weapons will have consequences. And don't imagine that I won't notice a minute shift in their position."

The boys exchanged a quick look.

"There are puppies in the stables," murmured the earl. "And ponies."

Hawk's eyes widened in alarm. "P-perhaps it would do no harm to practice being little gentlemen, at least for the next few days."

"A splendid idea," remarked Charlotte as two maids entered the parlor bearing a tea tray and a large platter heaped with food.

"Thank you," said the earl, indicating that the refreshments should be placed on the low table between the sofa and armchairs.

As he turned to the sideboard, Charlotte took a moment to

survey the room. Like the earl, it had an understated elegance highlighted by subtle touches of individuality. *A juxtaposition of tradition and whimsy.*

And the art on the walls was marvelous.

"Is this by Thomas Girtin?" she asked, moving to look more closely at an exquisite watercolor of an abbey ruin. "The light is ethereal."

"Yes." Wrexford came to stand beside her. "A prodigious talent. It's a pity he died at such a young age."

"Anthony was a great admirer of his work." She didn't add that her late husband had always voiced the sentiment with an undertone of resentment, as if the gods had somehow bestowed their gifts unfairly.

The earl offered her a brandy, and Charlotte found herself grateful for the heat of the spirits as she took a sip. She hadn't realized how chilled she was.

Sheffield carried a glass to the dowager, along with one for himself.

"Ah, that warms the cockles," murmured the dowager after a small swallow. She took another and then set it aside. "Hmmph. Now that we are all here, I imagine we're going to have a council of war." She eyed the boys. "Er, perhaps—"

Raven stiffened and lifted his chin. "We don't need protecting, Aunt Alison. Lady Cordelia is our friend, and we're already up to our necks in the investigation."

"It's true," conceded Charlotte with an apologetic shrug. "I did warn you that the Weasels aren't ordinary children."

"So I am learning," murmured Alison with a tiny smile. "Well, then, let us get on with it."

"Yes," agreed Wrexford, "but I suggest we don't do it on an empty stomach."

"We can both eat and talk," said Charlotte, impatient to hear any further discoveries. The earl and Sheffield had arrived several hours earlier. "Everyone please take a seat."

She waited for the settling-in to cease. "I shall fix some plates and pass them around while you tell us what you've learned. Has Tyler had a look at the professor's—"

"Tyler has been delayed in London," interrupted the earl. "I expect him to arrive sometime tomorrow. However, Sheffield and I rode out earlier today and did a quick reconnaissance of Professor Sudler's hideaway. It's nestled in a secluded spot, ringed by fallow fields and a glade of trees. There are several outbuildings abutting the main cottage, and the enclave is ringed by a high stone wall."

"The perfect place for someone wishing absolute privacy," observed Sheffield tightly. He looked down into his drink. "Whatever the reason."

He had been, noted Charlotte, uncharacteristically quiet since their arrival. Soft as the candlelight was, it illuminated the fine lines of worry—or was it fear?—etched at the corners of his eyes.

She wished to say something encouraging but couldn't muster any reply that didn't sound patronizing. The truth was, the evidence indicated that some very painful discoveries lay ahead.

And they all knew it.

Wrexford waited for Charlotte to be seated before breaking the uncomfortable silence. "My suggestion is that the three of us ride out very early in the morning. In my experience, a confrontation that comes when it's least expected gives the advantage to the interrogators."

Sheffield let out an unhappy sigh but merely nodded.

The earl looked to Charlotte. "I assume that you know how to handle a horse?"

"It's been some time since I've had my feet in the stirrups," she replied. "However, I'll manage."

"Pffft, you have nothing to fear, milord," announced the dowager. "Charley was a neck-and-leather rider in her youth."

Both boys looked up from their tarts.

"Will you teach us?" asked Hawk.

"M'lady will be busy with other concerns," called a voice from the corridor. McClellan appeared in the doorway a moment later. "*If* you behave, I'll show you the rudiments." She nodded a greeting to the others. "We've just arrived with the baggage. I've shown Lady Peake's maid to her room, and the footmen are bringing the trunks upstairs."

"Thank you, Mac," drawled the earl. "McClellan knows the estate and its workings better than I do, so if you have any questions, ask her."

"Come with me, Weasels," said McClellan, eyeing their empty plates and jam-smeared faces. "Let us leave your elders to finish their libations in peace. I'll show you to your quarters. And mind you, Polly, the upstairs maid, may look young, but she's under strict orders to brook no nonsense from the two of you. Disobey her at your peril."

"Puppies and ponies," murmured Charlotte.

Raven and Hawk rose without protest and hurried off.

Wrexford got up to pour himself another brandy. Sheffield waved off a refill and went to stand by the fire and warm his hands over the flames.

Sympathy tightened Charlotte's throat as she stared at Sheffield's back, noting the rigid set of his shoulders. She knew all too well the pain of discovering that someone for whom you cared deeply had feet of clay.

Her own late husband . . .

"Actually, unless there is anything else pressing to discuss, I suggest we all retire," said Wrexford. He, too, was watching his friend. "It's been a long day of travel, and we need to rise at dawn."


Mist swirled, casting a silvery sheen over the meadows beyond the stable paddocks. Wrexford handed the reins of his stallion to one of the grooms and crossed to where Charlotte was standing, awaiting the placid mare he had ordered saddled for her.

"Nervous?" he asked.

"Not about climbing atop a horse," she answered. Her gaze strayed to Sheffield, who had already mounted his dappled grey gelding, and she let out a tiny sigh. "Hearts are fragile things."

"But unlike fine porcelain, they can be mended well enough that the cracks don't show."

"That may be true," she replied. "And yet, in some cases, the damage is lasting."

Her words implied that Sheffield's devil-may-care demeanor hid a vulnerable soul. Wrexford wished he could sneer at the notion, but he knew his friend too well to make light of it.

"If Kit is shattered by what lies ahead, we must hope that our friendship and support will help him put the pieces back together again."

Charlotte touched his arm, and suddenly the morning's damp chill seemed to evaporate. "You're right, Wrexford. Love and friendship can work miracles."

His lips twitched. "As a man of science, I don't believe in miracles."

"And yet, as a man of science," she countered, "you must concede that there are forces of Nature you can't rationally explain."

"Granted, life is full of ticklish conundrums." A groom brought over the mare. Lacing his hands together, Wrexford offered her a boost into the saddle. "Let us hope we can solve at least one of them this morning."

Dawn's light was just touching the horizon as they rode out in silence, the earl leading the way through the sloping meadows to a country lane. After glancing back and seeing that

Charlotte looked at ease in the saddle, Wrexford spurred to an easy canter. The rhythmic thud of the hooves grew louder as the way wound through a swath of woodland. Shadows hung heavy in the leaves, mirroring the group's somber mood.

As a flicker of pale sunlight shone up ahead and the trees began to thin, the earl reined to halt.

"The cottage is close," he said to Charlotte once she and Sheffield had come abreast of him. "We'll dismount once we reach the hedgerow up ahead, and go on foot."

She nodded.

The gloom had brightened just enough to show that Sheffield's visage was pale as death.

"Kit," said Wrexford softly. "If you would prefer to wait—"

"No." Sheffield tightened his grip on his reins. "I'm not such a craven coward that I can't summon the backbone to have Lady Cordelia tell me to my face of her betrayal."

The earl released a silent sigh and spurred forward.

They dismounted, careful to keep their movements as quiet as possible, and then, once again, Wrexford took the lead. After squeezing through the narrow opening in the hedge, he led the way around a high ivy-covered wall. A wrought-iron gate guarded the opening facing the cart track. It wasn't locked. A soft *snick* allowed them to enter the inner yard.

The cottage windows were curtained, and no smoke rose from the chimney. The earl moved to the front door, hoping Sheffield didn't notice the weight of the pistol concealed in his coat pocket. He didn't expect trouble. But then again, desperate men were prone to doing desperate things, and despite the dowager's assessment, Woodbridge didn't strike him as the steadiest of fellows.

Wrexford tested the latch. It didn't budge, but it quickly yielded to the steel probe he had brought along. He motioned for the others to follow. What little light came in through the drawn draperies showed a small entrance foyer that opened into a center corridor. Ahead were stairs leading up to the second floor. He paused and then turned into the main parlor. Ashes lay in the hearth. Several empty glasses sat on the tea table.

"I'll have a look in the kitchen," whispered Charlotte.

The earl signaled her to go, then motioned for Sheffield to follow him through the door into what looked like the professor's study. Bookcases lined the walls, all crammed with leather-bound volumes and stacks of manuscript pages bound with twine. The desk was also covered with books and documents. As Wrexford approached it, he saw a pen on the blotter, its nib dark with dried ink.

He looked up and cocked an ear. No sounds from above. The inhabitants were either all asleep. Or . . .

He felt a tingle at the back of his neck. "You check the other rooms down here," he murmured to Sheffield. "I'm going to head upstairs."

His friend looked on the verge of protest, but after a tiny hesitation, he gave a grim nod and backtracked from the study to cross the corridor.

Slipping a hand into his pocket, Wrexford climbed the stairs, treading as softly as he could. There looked to be four chambers set along the narrow corridor, with two on each side. All the doors were shut, the age-dark oak looking black as Hades in the dim light. Holding his breath, he approached the nearest one and eased it open.

*Empty.*

Wrexford edged over to the next room. The hinges creaked as the door gave way to a light push. It, too, was empty, though the bedcovering looked a little rumpled, and a lady's lace fichu lay half-hidden behind the dressing table. Moving on, he found the other two rooms deserted, as well.

He hurried back down the stairs and met Charlotte, who had just left the kitchen.

"There's food in the larder, and dirty dishes on the worktable," she confided in a low voice. "Someone has been here recently, but—"

"But they've fled," he finished. "And God only knows where they've gone."

# CHAPTER 15

Charlotte turned as Sheffield came out of a side parlor, a wine-colored silk hair ribbon twined in his fingers.

"Lady Cordelia has been here." He held up the ribbon, its curling tail fluttering in the drafty gloom. "She's extremely fond of this particular shade of burgundy."

"It's not an uncommon color," pointed out Charlotte. "We mustn't jump to conclusions—"

"It has her scent," said Sheffield flatly. He looked down at his hands, the slight movement wreathing his face in shadow.

"There's other evidence that she and the others have been here recently," interjected the earl. "And it appears that they left in a hurry."

"I didn't warn them, if that's what you're thinking."

"I'm not, Kit," replied Wrexford. "I trust that you would have told me if you had."

Their friend released a pent-up breath. "Thank you for that. I know I've been a fool—"

"There's nothing foolish about friendship and loyalty," cut in Charlotte. "And until we find out what's going on, let us try not to assume the worst."

"The worst?" A mirthless snort. "What other possible explanation can there be?"

Her throat constricted. She wouldn't insult him with fairie tales.

"As I've said before, idle speculation is useless," announced Wrexford. "Let's take a closer look at Professor Sudler's study and then search the outbuildings to see if there's any tangible clue as to what they're up to." He turned on his heel. "Or where they might have gone."

*Ever logical*, thought Charlotte. *Thank heavens.* They mustn't allow Sheffield to fall into a chasm of blue-deviled brooding.

Sudler's desk yielded nothing but academic correspondence and page after page of incomprehensible formulas peppered with cryptic notes.

"The man is either a genius," muttered Sheffield as he thumbed through a notebook, "or stark raving mad."

"Sometimes the line between the two is razor thin," observed the earl. He slammed a drawer shut. "I think we've seen enough here. Perhaps we'll have better luck outside."

They made quick work of a shed, which held only a jumble of garden tools and broken terra-cotta pots, then moved on to the small stable. The three stalls and the tiny hayloft also told them naught but that a horse and cart had been housed there recently. The largest of the three structures, however, held a hint of promise. Its heavy iron-banded door was fastened with a massive padlock.

"Damnation," said Sheffield. "That's one of those newfangled German puzzle locks. I doubt you—"

"Oh, ye of little faith," murmured Wrexford as he once again pulled the steel probe from his boot. "Tyler and I . . ." *Click-click.* "Were rather curious as to how these mechanisms worked . . ." *Click-click.* "So we did a bit of study on the principles . . ." *Click-click.* "And disassembled several models in order to examine—"

The lock's shank released with a well-oiled snick.

"Ah, excellent." The earl allowed a grim smile. "Tyler will be delighted to hear that our surmise about the levers working the same way on all models is correct."

"You really must show me how to do that," said Charlotte.

"Ha! You find a way to winkle out enough secrets as it is," said Wrexford dryly. Taking up the lantern he had brought from the stable, he quickly struck a spark to the wick and beckoned them to follow him inside.

The still air had an oddly metallic chill to it, thought Charlotte as she stepped into the darkness. The windows were all tightly shuttered, which seemed to amplify the echo of their steps on the stone floor.

"Have a care," cautioned the earl as he felt his way forward. "There appears to be some rather large machinery in here."

She came to a halt on hearing him rustle around. A moment later, one of the shutters came open, revealing . . .

"Merciful heavens." Charlotte sucked in her breath.

Sheffield, too, was looking around the long and narrow room in wonder as Wrexford pried open several more of the window covers. "It looks like something out of Greek mythology. You know, the workshop of that fellow who served as blacksmith to the immortals of Olympus."

"Hephaestus," said the earl. "The god of fire and metalworking." He picked up a hammer from one of the work counters and tapped it against his palm. An array of intricate machinery made of iron, steel, and brass—lathes, drill presses, and fanciful assemblies that Charlotte couldn't begin to name—stretched down the entire length of the building. On the opposite wall hung a phalanx of hand tools and shelves above a work counter.

"He forged tools and weapons for the other gods," went on Wrexford. He put down the hammer and plucked a small brass object from a row arrayed atop a piece of felt on the corner of the counter. "The engineering of this is remarkable," he said after holding it up to the light.

Charlotte moved to a different section of the counter. "Look! There's a set of mechanical drawings here. And they appear to be duplicates of the ones we found."

Wrexford came over to examine them. "What the devil are they up to?" he muttered.

"It clearly involves numbers." She pointed to a large basket sitting on one of the shelves. It was filled with ivory wheels bearing the numerals zero through nine precisely spaced along the outer rim.

Sheffield had wandered off to explore behind the forge. Hearing his grunt of surprise, they rushed to join him.

"Why would Sudler have such a collection of . . . toys?" exclaimed their friend.

"Because," answered the earl as he approached the display table hidden in the alcove, "they're not toys. They're automata."

"Ah, right," murmured Sheffield. "That's the term Hedley used for . . ."

"For complex mechanical devices which are constructed with incredibly precise engineering," finished Wrexford, "allowing them to perform very sophisticated movements and functions."

He stepped closer to the collection and wound the key hidden at the back of one of the automata. It was the one mentioned by Hedley . . . the figure of a lady attired in an elegant ball gown, perhaps a foot tall and crafted entirely out of silver.

Charlotte gasped in amazement as the figure began to dance, spinning in circles upon its metal platform as it moved its arms and legs in harmony with the notes coming from a hidden music box beneath the platform.

"That's magical!" she said once the spring had unwound and the lady had come to a stop.

"An apt description, as Hedley told us it was made by John

Merlin." Wrexford looked up from examining the base of the automaton. "He also told Kit and me that Sudler has had a passion for automata since his university days. I would guess he's collected them in order to study their inner workings, which would help with the design for his own devices."

"And all this?" Sheffield gestured back at the machinery.

"It takes complex tools to craft complex parts," answered the earl. "I would guess that Sudler has to make all the pieces himself for his complicated designs."

"That makes sense." Charlotte frowned in thought. "However, I can't help but wonder . . . We've seen the plans lying on the counter and all the equipment for fabricating the individual parts. But where is the automaton that he's building?"

"Perhaps he hasn't yet started," said Sheffield. "Or perhaps he took it with him."

Wrexford remained silent for a moment, his expression turning troubled. "It seems to me there's an even more pressing question," he said. "Why does Sudler need Lady Cordelia?"

Charlotte felt a shiver snake down her spine. "Or vice versa," she whispered.

Sheffield stared at her in dismay. "You think it's Lady Cordelia who is spearheading a nefarious plot, rather than her brother?"

Charlotte hated to see the warring of hope and despair in his eyes. But it was becoming increasingly hard to see any other explanation for what was going on. "Woodbridge isn't nearly as clever as his sister," she pointed out. "I'm not sure he's capable of figuring out a complex financial plan to profit from all the money he has apparently borrowed. But . . ."

She paused to compose her thoughts, trying to find the words to express her fears as gently as possible.

Wrexford had no such compunction. "Lady Cordelia has both the brains and the sangfroid to come up with a plan to save her brother from financial ruin. We know that from past experience. And as for profit, you yourself know she has a head for business."

A tiny throat muscle jumped as Sheffield tightened his jaw.

"Perhaps what's going on is perfectly legal," continued the earl. "But when you add up the facts—a murder that connects, however tenuously, to Hoare's Bank, and the sudden flight of both brother and sister—the answer does seem to indicate that they're up to no good."

He paused. "I'm sorry, Kit, but it's nigh on impossible to imagine that it wasn't she who came up with the plan."

Touching a finger to the smoothly sculpted face of the silver dancer, Sheffield then traced the delicate planes of her face. "Much I as wish to disagree, I can't in good conscience offer any argument."

The glimmer of the precious metal suddenly stirred a question in Charlotte's mind.

"Silver," she said. "Or rather argentum. Have we given any more thought to the clerk's dying words and what he might have meant?"

Wrexford shook his head. "I can't begin to hazard a guess. The only metals I see in the workshop are brass, steel, and iron. Until we're able to speak with Lady Cordelia and her brother—"

"And Professor Sudler," she interjected. "He's involved for a reason."

"Yes, but until we know what that reason is, we're simply trying to grab at shadows—a mere trick of light." The earl grimaced. "Naught but thin air that slips through our fingers."

"So where do we start looking for them?" mused Charlotte.

"If I had any ideas, I would say so," said Sheffield, a note of defeat shading his voice.

"Wrexford?" she asked.

The earl took a moment to look at the hulking machinery. "I

need to think about it. But first, let's continue looking around and see if there's anything that might give us a more solid idea of what they're building."

They returned to the main work counters and began a methodical search, checking beneath the jumble of canvas coverings and inside the narrow cabinets set against the wall.

"Is this helpful?" asked Charlotte, holding out a box that contained an assembly of minute gears.

Wrexford took a look and shrugged. "Not particularly. Gears are used for a great many purposes, so it doesn't really tell us anything." He went back to his section of the counter and resumed his rummaging. "What we need is something that might indicate—"

A low whistle cut short his words as he shifted a large metal storage box and spotted a bulky object cloaked in a heavy oilskin cloth hidden behind it. He pulled off the cover, revealing a complex construction of rods and levers.

"Bring over the lantern, Kit."

Charlotte and Sheffield gathered around the earl as he took the light and angled it on the mechanical device.

"Look, there's a small wheel with a handle that must rotate," noted Sheffield.

Wrexford was already spinning it. They watched in wonder as the gleaming brass rods and levers moved, turning a complex construction of gears, which in turn spun and shifted a procession of the numbered ivory wheels that were attached to the rods.

"Ingenious," murmured Wrexford. "It looks to be a prototype of how a machine can do complex calculations. I don't pretend to know exactly how it works, but . . ." He thought for a long moment. "I recall hearing a lecture on Pascal's famous adding machine at the Royal Institution, and I saw a model of the device. It can't hold a candle to this in terms of sophisticated engineering."

"I think it's becoming clearer why Sudler needs Lady Cordelia," said Charlotte. "He would require a mathematical genius to complement his engineering genius."

"However they came together," said the earl, "it appears they've created . . ."

"A monster," intoned Sheffield.

# CHAPTER 16

The early morning mist had given way to a sun-bright sky. And yet the ride home felt overshadowed by a black cloud. Wrexford glanced at Sheffield's profile as they broke free of the trees, and felt a chill seep into his bones. To feel betrayed by a trusted friend cut to the quick.

And it was the sort of wound that could fester. . . .

The earl forced his thoughts back to a more immediate challenge. The machine was too big and too intricate to risk carrying on horseback, so he had decided to leave it. He and one of his grooms would return later with a cart and bring it back to the manor house. Perhaps Tyler, who was very mechanically minded, would have some ideas about its capabilities after examining it.

Still lost in thought as they entered his estate lands, Wrexford led the way down a bridle path that cut through a stretch of pastureland. But a sudden hail from Sheffield brought them all to a halt.

"If you don't mind, I shall leave you here and take the long way around to the stables."

"Of course, Kit," he replied.

With a gruff nod, Sheffield turned his mount and spurred off.

"Damnation," uttered Charlotte, her face wreathing in concern, as she watched him gallop away.

"Kit possesses more strength and resilience than he, or any of us, thinks. It seems to take adversity to bring his best qualities to the fore," said Wrexford, watching a plume of dust swirl up in their friend's wake. "Or so I tell myself."

The attempt at wry humor didn't draw a smile from Charlotte. Her worry seemed to deepen.

"I . . ." She blew out a sigh and fell silent.

"Go on," he urged.

Charlotte looked away. The breeze tugged at the ribbons of her bonnet, tangling them into a knot. Deciding the moment for her to confide her thoughts had passed, he shifted on the saddle and regripped his reins.

"The investigation has unsettled me, Wrexford." She turned to gaze out at the horizon. "In ways that are testing the very essence of who I am."

He waited.

Her eyes slowly came around to meet his. "Sorry. I know I'm not making any sense."

"You're making perfect sense," he replied. "I imagine what you mean is you feel torn between friendship and duty."

Her mare snorted and pulled at the reins.

"As Charlotte Sloane, you wish to help and protect those close to you," he went on. "But as A. J. Quill, you feel compelled to shine a light on the dark doings of those who think themselves above the law."

A ghost of a smile passed over her lips. "You seem to understand me better than I do myself."

Wrexford brought his stallion closer and reached out to touch his hand to hers. The chill air gave way to a mellow warmth. "I think we both know each other very well," he replied. "At times, too well. But that, I suppose, is the beauty of true friendship, where the bond runs deeper than we realize."

The breeze freshened, ruffling through the gold-flecked meadow grasses.

"I noted that you were carefully studying the workshop and its details, in case you decide it's necessary to draw the scene. But I don't think you should fret about what decisions lie ahead," he added. "When the time comes, you'll know in your heart what is right."

"Oh, Wrexford." The light that came to her eyes made his heart thump up against his ribs. "I don't know what I'd do without you and your logic to steady my doubts."

"There is, I grant you, an irony to me—a man cursed with mercurial moods—being a source of steadiness to anyone. But as you've often told me, intuition defies logic."

"Or they somehow work together in perfect tandem," murmured Charlotte. Lifting her cheeks to the sun, she inhaled deeply. "Perhaps Sheffield was right, and a good gallop is just the thing to clear the head."

The earl smiled. "Would you care to race to that far oak?" A wave indicated a distant tree at the edge of the pasture.

"You have an unfair advantage. It's been a long time since I've been in the saddle."

"I shall allow you a five-yard head start."

"Ha!" Sparks winked off her lashes. "Make that ten yards."

Wrexford realized with a jolt how much he loved the way she constantly challenged him. It wasn't always comfortable. . . .

She was already off, her mare's hooves pounding over the turf.

Wind whipped his face as he spurred to a gallop. All worries gave way to the moment . . . the sight of Charlotte crouched low over her horse's neck, the loosened strands of her hair dancing in the wind . . . the sheer exhilaration of just the two of them together, racing neck-and-leather across fields.

The mare had spirit and graceful speed, but his muscled stallion was quickly gaining ground. Tightening the reins, Wrexford pulled back. It seemed only right that they cross the finish line in perfect stride.

Breathless with laughter, Charlotte slowed her mount and circled back to meet him. Her cheeks were flushed, and her eyes were sparkling. "I had forgotten how glorious it is to fly over the fields!"

"Lady Peake wasn't exaggerating," he replied. "You're a very skilled rider."

"Yes, well, I spent a good deal of time in the saddle during my rebellious youth. It was one of the few places where I could exhale and feel free." Charlotte patted the mare's lathered neck. "Thank you, Wrexford. For not allowing me to stew in self-doubt."

"We all need occasional reminders that Darkness should never overpower Light."

She nodded, the very un-Charlotte-like uncertainty gone from her expression. "Speaking of darkness we should be getting back. Sheffield mustn't be allowed to brood. We need to regroup and plan our next steps."

They set off at a brisk canter, which soon brought them to the main carriage road.

"You go on to the stables," said Wrexford as they slowed to a walk. "I want to stop at the manor house first. Tyler should have arrived by now, and he may have learned something more about Professor Sudler before leaving London."

After handing over her mare to one of the grooms, Charlotte spotted Sheffield standing just inside the stable. As she moved to join him, she saw Raven was also there, on his hands and knees, playing with a large floppy-eared puppy whose ungainly legs seemed far too big for its body.

She was relieved to see Sheffield was smiling at the tug-and-pull antics involving a length of well-chewed rope.

He looked around at her approach. "I've just finished explaining to Raven about our discovery."

"May I see the mechanical device?" asked the boy, scrambling to his feet and brushing the worst of the muck from his knees.

"Wrexford plans to bring it back here later," she answered. "So yes, I'm sure you'll have ample opportunity to inspect it."

Raven's face scrunched in thought. "You say the rods go up and down, shifting the numbered wheels both vertically and horizontally?"

Sheffield grimaced. "Don't ask me how it works, lad. You'll have to see for yourself."

"By the by, where's your brother?" asked Charlotte as another puppy bounded down the stone walkway between the stalls and tripped over its own oversized paws.

Raven laughed, a carefree burble that reminded her all too sharply of how rarely he sounded like a child. Then, looking away from the dog, he answered, "Hawk went with the gardener to see the flower beds along the back terrace. He took his sketchbook, so he could do some drawings." Crouching down, the boy began wrestling with the newcomer. "But I'm going to find him now and see if he wants to play toss and fetch with these beasties."

"An excellent idea!" she encouraged. Gamboling in the fresh air and fields would do them good.

The puppies barked as he pulled a ball from his jacket pocket and scampered off, the animals following in hot pursuit.

Charlotte took Sheffield's arm. "Shall we go see if Tyler has arrived?"

They walked past the paddocks in silence as she debated whether to broach the subject of Lady Cordelia's betrayal and offer her support. She didn't wish to intrude, and a surreptitious glance at his profile did nothing to help her decide.

"Have I sprouted horns or purple spots?" he murmured.

"Sorry," stammered Charlotte.

"Don't be. I know my judgment in many things leaves much to be desired," he replied. "It's no wonder you have doubts—"

"You judge yourself far more harshly than Wrexford or I do," she said before he could go on.

Her words seemed to surprise him.

"But then," she continued, "I think our own faults are always far more glaring to us than they are to our friends."

"You're being kind, as always." A wry smile. "However, I did some thinking on the ride home . . ." Their steps crunched over gravel as they turned onto the walkway leading to the front of the house. "About how you and Wrexford have the strength and the courage to put truth and justice before personal sentiments, no matter how painful."

He drew in a breath. "I know I've made a mull of my recent choices. But I hope you and Wrex know where my true loyalty lies."

"We've never doubted that," said Charlotte. "But caring for someone is a strength, not a weakness."

A thoughtful silence lasted for several steps.

"Truth," murmured Sheffield, quickening his pace as they approached the entrance steps. "We need to follow the damnable twisted threads of this conundrum and find the truth." The stones rustled beneath his boots. "Wherever they may lead."

Charlotte heard the steel in his voice . . . along with a whisper of regret. "Let us keep in mind that we don't yet know for sure that Lady Cordelia has done anything wrong."

"I don't think either of us believes that's true," he murmured.

On entering the manor house, they were met by Higgins, the earl's country butler, who escorted them to Wrexford's study.

"Tyler has sent word that he's been delayed," announced the earl, a slight frown creasing his brow as he looked up from the note on his desk. "He won't be arriving until tomorrow."

"Is that bad news?" asked Charlotte.

"Not necessarily," replied Wrexford, his expression unreadable. "I asked him to see if he could learn more about the knife discovered at Queen's Landing."

"Shall the two of us go fetch the mechanical device from Sudler's hideaway?" asked Sheffield.

Wrexford considered the question. "On second thought, I've decided we should wait. I doubt that the fugitives are planning to return, so there's little risk in delaying." He had refastened the fancy lock on leaving the workshop. "I want Tyler to see all the machinery that was used to fabricate the device, in case it sparks any ideas."

Charlotte gingerly settled onto the sofa, suddenly aware of how the morning riding had required the exertion of long-unused muscles. "Where is Alison?"

"Higgins informed me that the dowager retired to take a nap after having nuncheon with the Weasels."

The mention of food made her realize she was famished, as well as sore. "Might we ring for tea?" she asked as Sheffield sat down beside her. "And then perhaps the three of us should discuss what to do next, before the boys finish being boys and Alison wakes from her slumber."

A maid was summoned and sent to fetch refreshments.

"Would that she could return with some facts for us to chew on," muttered the earl. "With what we know right now, there's not much to discuss. There seems little more we can learn here, so I see no choice but to return to Town."

He rose and began to pace. "We haven't a clue as to where Lady Cordelia and her two companions have gone, so it seems to me the logical step is to begin delving deeper into Woodbridge's mysterious bank loans."

"And the mysterious Annie Wright," added Charlotte.

Wrexford's grudging nod conceded the point. He then tapped his fingertips together. "And we need to see what develops regarding the bloody knife." A pause. "Though both Tyler and I find its discovery a little too convenient."

"Sometimes the very act of subterfuge can tell us more than the perpetrator realizes," mused Charlotte.

Sheffield looked a little puzzled. "What do you mean?"

"If someone is seeking to point a finger at Woodbridge, it indicates he's a threat to them," she explained. "Looking at it from that perspective may help us narrow down the possible suspects."

Their friend edged forward on his seat. "Who . . . ?"

"We need more information before we can begin drawing up a list," cut in the earl.

"Perhaps I can ferret out something useful," said Sheffield after a moment of thought. "Until now, I've felt beholden to keep my promise to Lady Cordelia not to reveal the other partners in our business. But I feel honor demands that my loyalty no longer be given to her lies. They may know more than I do about her current activities."

"And yet there were no other names listed as stockholders," observed Wrexford.

"That's because—" But before Sheffield could go on, an urgent knocking caused all three of them to turn to the door.

"Your pardon, milord," intoned the butler nervously after Wrexford hurried to click open the latch. "But there's a lady here demanding to see you."

A cough.

"And she says it's a matter of life and death."

# CHAPTER 17

"Thank you for agreeing to see me, milord." Lady Cordelia peeled off her kidskin gloves as she stepped out from behind the pale-faced Higgins and entered the study. "Please forgive the rather lurid exaggeration, but I had to make sure I wouldn't be turned away."

She wasn't quite so coolly composed as she wished to appear, noted Wrexford. Her hands were tremoring as she unknotted the strings of her bonnet and placed it on the side table.

Sheffield was staring in mute shock. Charlotte had settled back in her chair, schooling her expression to give nothing away.

"We've just ordered tea," said the earl. "Do have a seat. It should be here in a moment."

"Tea," repeated Cordelia, her voice hovering between horror and amusement. "Oh, quite right. What would we do without that lifeblood from the East to lubricate all the everyday lies and subterfuges of Polite Society?"

"An interesting choice of words," observed Wrexford.

She met his gaze without flinching. "I shall endeavor to explain them."

"Do sit," said Charlotte as the maid appeared with a large tray of refreshments. "There is something to be said for the power of rituals to break the ice, so to speak, and allow interactions to flow more smoothly."

Sheffield still hadn't taken his eyes off Cordelia. While she had studiously avoided any glance in his direction.

After a brief hesitation, Cordelia took a seat on the sofa.

The clink of porcelain punctuated soft splashes of liquid. Vapor curled up in silvery plumes as Charlotte passed around the cups. "By the by, how did you know we were here? We came to the professor's cottage early this morning, only to find you gone."

"I walked into the village last night to buy some bread and cheese and overheard a servant mention the earl was expecting guests. I added two and two together," replied Cordelia. "We left before dawn, as we were planning to return to London—"

"Enough of pleasantries," interrupted Sheffield, pushing aside his tea untasted. "What the devil are you doing here?"

Wrexford repressed a wince. The sparks crackling in his friend's gaze were fierce enough to burn Satan to a cinder.

"I imagine that's a rhetorical question, sir," replied Cordelia. "But in a nutshell, I've come to ask for your help."

"Why now?" demanded Sheffield

Cordelia carefully smoothed a section of her skirts into three equal pleats. "Because it's taken me this long to unravel the lies within lies and follow the money," she replied. "I'm now confident I know what evil is afoot, and Professor Sudler and I want to put an end to it. However, the men responsible for the scheme have threatened to ruin my brother and have him sent to prison unless we cooperate with them."

She hesitated. "So the professor and I have, for now, agreed to perform the tasks they demand of us. Not simply to save Jamie, but also to give us time to identify the men in charge and bring them to justice." Another tiny pause. "However, we can't do it on our own."

Sheffield narrowed his eyes. "How do we know you are not simply telling us more lies?"

Cordelia's face paled as all the blood rushed to her cheeks. "I never lied to you!"

"You . . ." He blinked. "You . . ."

"Yes?" she challenged.

"You and your brother left without any explanation," mumbled Sheffield. "When we discovered the bank loans he had secured, what else was I supposed to think other than that you had deceived me and used me as pawn to get money from Wrexford?"

Cordelia's indignation burned out just as quickly as it had flared. "I haven't ever lied to you in either word or deed, sir. Our business venture has *nothing* to do with my brother and the web of deceit in which he's become entangled. It's completely legitimate. You have my word on that." Her chin rose. "Assuming you'll believe me."

"Silence!" commanded the earl, before the discussion became impossibly confused. "If I'm to have any hope of understanding what's going on, we need to have an orderly explanation of this cursed mystery—"

"I shall try, milord." Cordelia pinched at the bridge of her nose. "Though I fear it's difficult to distill it into a simple explanation."

"Just start somewhere," Wrexford growled.

"Very well." She cleared her throat. "Jamie was approached by a friend and invited to invest in a financial venture that guaranteed a great profit. That, of course, seemed too good to be true. So I tried to warn him that there had to be something havey-cavey about it. However, Jamie wouldn't hear any caveats from me. Whose word do you think held the greater weight? That of his sister or that of the East India Company?"

"The East India Company?" Wrexford felt a chill touch the

top of his spine. A glance at Charlotte showed that she had experienced the same frisson of alarm. "To accuse them of impropriety is a very serious allegation to make, Lady Cordelia," he added softly.

"Nonetheless, it's true."

By virtue of its immense wealth and economic clout, the Company wielded great influence on politics and government affairs in Britain. Indeed, its tentacles reached into just about every aspect of society. The earl couldn't imagine a more dangerous enemy.

"Be that as it may, such statements could put you in grave peril if they reach the wrong ears," he pointed out.

"I'm safe enough for now, which I shall explain shortly," Cordelia replied. "But first let me finish explaining what is going on. I will be as clear as I can, but the threads twist and twine into a serpentine maze of deception that isn't always easy to unwind."

The earl nodded.

"Jamie was manipulated into taking out a number of bank loans in order to invest in the business venture. They fed him a number of clever lies about why the money couldn't appear to have come from the East India Company," she continued. "They then cobbled together a thick set of complicated legal documents, assuring him they all were simply formalities. My brother, alas, is an honest and trusting soul. He believed them and blithely penned his name everywhere they asked him to sign, and then turned over his personal loan documents for supposed safekeeping."

Cordelia took a moment to steady her voice. "And so Jamie is now the sole stockholder of a trading company whose only business is running a very sophisticated financial scheme involving fraud and morally reprehensible commerce. He can't withdraw or go to the authorities. The dastards hold all the funds necessary to repay the bank loans. And they cleverly left no trail to incriminate themselves, so he has no proof of his entrapment."

Sheffield uttered an oath. "Then how will you escape their clutches?"

She gave a tight smile. "I met with one of their henchmen and made a deal, which I'll explain shortly. Suffice it to say, it offers us a way to earn back the money and the legal papers."

"Assuming they'll keep their word," cut in Wrexford.

"I'm not as naïve as my brother, milord. I'm under no illusion that they'll ever release their hold on Jamie. Which is why I'm here." Cordelia shifted her gaze from him to Charlotte and then to Sheffield. "Knowing firsthand how skilled you are at solving diabolically clever crimes, I'm hoping you might help me discover the identity of the dastards and plan a way to bring them to justice."

"Is the murder of Henry Peabody part of this financial conspiracy?" asked Charlotte abruptly.

"Yes! But I swear to you that my brother didn't kill him. He's honorable to a fault and abhors violence!" responded Cordelia. "Jamie was summoned to a mysterious meeting at Queen's Landing. A man—he never identified himself, but it seems it must have been Mr. Peabody—somehow came to know that Jamie had become involved in the enterprise, and handed over papers that he claimed revealed it was a fraud. He also warned my brother of its evils and told him that it must be stopped. In leaving the dockyards, the two of them were attacked. Jamie managed to escape and assumed Peabody did, too. "

Cordelia bit her lower lip. "It was only later, when I arrived at your house for my lesson with Raven, that I learned otherwise."

"Go on with your story," urged Sheffield after several moments of silence had slid by.

The mention of murder appeared to have put Cordelia's nerves on edge. At the sound of steps coming down the corridor, she hesitated.

A discreet click sounded as the door to the study swung open.

"One of the maids mentioned that refreshments had just been served." The dowager paused to pat back a yawn. "I feel a bit peckish after my nap. Might I join you?"

"That depends on whether you care to digest a sordid tale of intrigue along with the freshly baked sultana muffins," said Cordelia from her seat in the shadows.

Alison turned and squinted through her spectacles. "Ye heavens! I saw the boys just now in the gardens, and Raven said you still hadn't been found."

"Yes, well, like the old adage says, 'A bad penny always turns up,'" came the sardonic reply.

"Do come in, Alison," murmured Charlotte. "You need to hear this, too, assuming you're not having second thoughts about getting involved in another murder investigation." A wry smile. "Wrexford and I seem to be making a habit of it."

The dowager quickly took a seat. "I wouldn't miss it for all the tea in China."

Cordelia huffed a grim laugh. "It's funny you should mention tea in China."

Charlotte tightened her fingers around her cup, the earl's expensive Imperial blend turning bitter on her tongue. The tea trade was worth a fortune, and while the East India Company had begun to cultivate their own plantations in India, most of the tea served around the world came from China.

And much to the Company's ire, China kept an iron-fisted control on its export.

"Lady Cordelia was just beginning to tell us that there's

something very rotten within the East India Company," said the earl.

Alison's expression turned grave. "Any trouble there could ripple out to the furthest reaches of society."

"Precisely." Wrexford steepled his hands and tapped the point against his chin. "So far, she's told us how her brother became entrapped in a fraudulent financial scheme being run by someone within the Company. And that the victim in the recent murder at Queen's Landing was a clerk who had discovered the financial irregularities in the company ledgers and had alerted Woodbridge of the fact."

"It began with a plot to make an obscene profit from tea," Cordelia said. "But as you'll see, the dastardly scheme has evolved considerably over time. The conspirators are malefactors of the worst sort, but they are supremely smart and sophisticated businessmen." Cordelia paused. "However, as I said, it all started with tea."

"But . . ." Alison looked troubled. "But that's impossible. I've heard the highest officials in government and the Company's board of directors say that not even a teaspoon of leaves can be exported, save through the Chinese emperor's consortium."

"It's difficult," allowed Cordelia. "But not impossible." She shifted in her chair. "It all has to do with silver."

"Argentum!" exclaimed Charlotte.

"Yes, Argentum is the name that the conspirators gave to their clever scheme." Cordelia pursed her lips and thought for a moment. "You see, the Chinese emperor will accept only silver as payment for tea and most other goods exported from his country. That has made silver a valuable commodity here in the West, which has driven up its price."

"That's simple economics. The law of supply and demand," observed the earl.

"Correct. And the situation is made even worse because the emperor will not allow his countrymen to buy British products in return. As a result, silver is flowing out of Britain to China, which has our Treasury extremely worried and further feeds into the increased price for us over here," said Cordelia. "But that's where the story begins to get complicated. When I said there was fraud going on within the Company, unfortunately, I can't tell you who is involved. Jamie and I have only met one of the henchmen, whom I call the Cobra, on account of his soulless reptilian gaze."

She took a moment to steady her voice. "Nor can I say whether the corruption is known to their superiors. But rot has a tendency to spread . . ."

Charlotte couldn't in good conscience disagree. Money was like a canker, eating away at even the strictest sense of morality.

"To get back to the details of the plan, the dastards originally came up with a scheme that allowed them to profit in multiple ways." Seeing that Wrexford was about to speak, Cordelia hurried on. "First of all, they set up a smuggling operation to bring opium from India into China, where only a very small amount is legally allowed to be imported. They make a large profit. As you say, milord, supply and demand."

"And they ask for the payment in silver," guessed Charlotte.

Sheffield's eyes widened. "Supply and demand! I'll wager they were able to demand a great deal of silver for their opium, due to its scarcity."

"Correct. You see, Mr. Sheffield, you have a very good head for business," said Cordelia. "They were, in effect, getting the silver at a very cheap price."

Sheffield again jumped in. "So I would guess they took the silver, used it to buy tea from the emperor's consortium, and brought the tea back to England, presumably using false accounts to make it all seem like legitimate East India Company business. And thereby they would make another healthy profit."

"Exactly," answered Cordelia, with an approving nod. "However, the dastards soon saw a way to improve on their scheme." She turned to the dowager. "To cut out the risk of shipping it back, they sold the tea to another foreign merchant—"

"Wait! I thought you said the Chinese controlled the trade in tea very strictly," protested Alison.

"They do. But all the foreign merchants are confined to a certain enclave at any Chinese port open to international trade. Canton, on the Pearl River, is the principle site used by foreigners. Within these enclaves are 'factories,' which is what the offices and the mercantile agents—"

"Actually, the mercantile agents are called 'supercargoes,' or *daban* in Chinese," interrupted Sheffield. When Cordelia raised her brows in surprise, he added, "As our company is planning to trade with China, I've been doing research on the subject."

She gave a small nod. "It is these supercargoes who help facilitate all the financial transactions. Once the official business with the Chinese officials is completed and the tea is moved to the export area, there are side deals to be made."

"On which, I assume, the Chinese choose to turn a blind eye," said the earl.

"A smart move," mused Sheffield. "Much better to leave it to the supercargoes, with their established trade routes and network of bribable officials, to disguise all this as a part of their legitimate trade."

"Yes, but then the laws of economics took over," Cordelia continued. "The emperor began demanding more and more silver for his tea. And it appears, based on what Jamie overheard a loose-lipped assistant to the Cobra say, that the conspirators began to worry, as they were paying out more and more bribes to men with whom it was dangerous to diddle."

"Whatever did they do then?" Sheffield asked.

"To make a long story short, they got out of the tea business, trading only enough to appear to be a legitimate trading operation," said Cordelia. "Instead, they concentrated on accumulating their silver."

"I think I can see where this is going," Wrexford interjected. "Because the silver was traded in the black market for opium, and because of the emperor's demands for payment in silver, the conspirators were accumulating silver at a much cheaper price than existed in the European markets."

"Yes, exactly, milord," Cordelia responded. "The dastards came to realize that the true potential source of profit was their ability to get cheap silver in China, since it had a much greater value in Europe."

Alison squinted in confusion. "So they began to trade in silver?"

"Well, for a time, yes," Cordelia responded. "But once again, the laws of market economics took over. They originally tried to have their partners—the supercargoes—bring the silver back to London to resell it at the higher price. But that, too, posed problems. The price of silver in Europe can be volatile, and this was a concern given the time it took to transport it back from China. In one of their earliest efforts, by the time they got the silver back to Europe, the price had dropped. That, plus all the bribes they had to pay to customs officials and co-conspirators within the Company for camouflaging the payments through East India Company accounts, meant they actually lost money on their trading."

"Shouldn't that have put an end to their machinations?" asked Alison.

Cordelia shook her head. "Alas, no. They are, as I said, very astute financially. They began to solve this last set of problems with bills of exchange."

"Bills of what?" exclaimed Alison. "Forgive me . . . but I thought they were exchanging opium and tea and silver."

"Bills of exchange have long been a common practice in the world of commerce," explained Cordelia, "They began in the Middle Ages, and are now becoming even more prevalent as trade expands around the globe."

"Ah! I've been studying these instruments, too!" Sheffield's face lit up. "They take a variety of forms. But I would think that what they did here was pay the opium suppliers in India with a bill of exchange, rather than cash in the form of either British pounds or the local Indian currency. Because of their international operations, the supercargoes had agents in most major cities along the trade routes. I won't go into the habble-babble about how the pieces of paper travel around the world and get converted back into actual currency by the billholders, but the system works."

"An excellent summary," said Cordelia approvingly. "There are a few other details, because of the various currencies involved and a few other technical aspects, but your description is bang on the mark."

Sheffield flashed a smile, but then his expression turned perplexed. "There's still one basic element that puzzles me. Didn't the supercargoes then have the same problem of bringing the silver back to Europe, with the same risks of fluctuations in the price of silver and of detection? After all, the conspirators still had to sell the silver in Europe to pay off the bills of exchange they had issued to their Indian suppliers."

"You're right, Mr. Sheffield. I'm just about to get to that part," said Cordelia.

"Perhaps we should order more tea before you begin," suggested Alison. Despite the warmth of the afternoon, Cordelia's words seemed to have caused a chill to settle over the room.

Feeling her head begin to throb, Charlotte pressed her fingertips to her temples. The case had unsettled her from the start, and she had a sense it was about to take an even darker turn.

The previous year she had done several satirical drawings that focused on a certain incident involving the East India Company. Her usual informants had been too terrified to talk to her, and though she had managed to cobble together enough facts to make a commentary, she had come away with the sense that the Company was utterly ruthless in protecting its reputation.

"I think we could all do with some sustenance," agreed Charlotte. She rose and moved to the diamond-paned windows while the parlormaid was summoned, hoping the sunlight slanting through the glass might warm the dread from her bones.

"Do you believe her?" murmured the earl as he came to stand beside her.

"I want to," she admitted. "But like you, I shall try to keep a healthy skepticism until I hear the whole story. As of yet, we've heard nothing about Professor Sudler's workshop, and I find it hard to imagine that those intricate gears and levers aren't in some way connected to . . ." A sigh. "To whatever evil Lady Cordelia is about to reveal."

"I confess to a morbid curiosity as to what that connection is," responded Wrexford. "On a purely intellectual plane, the scientific innovations of Sudler's mechanical device appear to hold revolutionary possibilities."

"Yes, but as we've seen in our previous cases, science is not a beautiful abstraction. Theories in themselves aren't good or evil. It's we who twist them to do our bidding."

He looked at her in concern. "You're usually not so pessimistic."

"I've become well enough acquainted with Lady Cordelia to know she doesn't frighten easily." Charlotte closed her eyes for an instant. "She's rattled, and I have to assume there's a good reason for it."

Clasping his hands behind his back, Wrexford turned to stare out over the back gardens and sloping lawns. A breeze ruffled the ivy twined around the windows, setting the dark leaves to whispering against the panes.

The sound drew her from her brooding, and she found herself gazing out at the pastoral scene.

"Hell and damnation," muttered Wrexford.

Charlotte suddenly saw it, too—a hulking grey shape stalking within the small glade of trees skirting the walled rose garden. "Good Lord, is that a *wolf*?"

"No." A pause. "It's Harper."

Harper appeared to be the size of a small pony. . . .

A flurry of fierce barks rumbled through the glass. "He's a Scottish deerhound," added the earl.

A gasp slipped from her lips as she spotted Raven and Hawk moving through the shadows close to the beast. "Is Harper dangerous?"

"Not usually," answered the earl. He hurriedly unlatched the window and let out a piercing whistle.

Harper pricked up his ears and then turned and came loping across the lawn. On reaching the window, he leaped up and planted his huge paws on the stone sill.

"Hallo," murmured Wrexford, curling his fingers in the hound's shaggy ruff and giving a vigorous rub.

With his lolling pink tongue and wagging tail, the animal didn't look quite so fearsome up close, decided Charlotte.

"He's quite good natured," explained the earl, "save for when he feels the estate is being threatened."

"What possible threat . . ." The words died in her throat as she saw the boys break free of the trees.

Hawk was brandishing an Elizabethan small sword, while Raven was cradling a medieval crossbow. And between them was the Earl of Woodbridge, his hands bound in front of him with a rather soggy-looking rope.

Cordelia must have spotted her brother from one of the side windows, because she rushed to join them. Elbowing Wrexford aside, she leaned out the window. "Raven! Dash it all, untie your prisoner this instant!"

As the dowager and Sheffield joined the commotion, Cordelia expelled an oath. "Damnation! Jamie was supposed to stay with the professor and his Engine."

"Well, well," observed Alison with an owlish blink. "The plot thickens."

# CHAPTER 18

Everyone quickly resettled in their seats as Wrexford poured a glass of brandy and thrust it into Woodbridge's hands.

"And now, Weasels," he intoned, turning to fix the boys with a gimlet gaze. "Kindly explain yourselves."

"We saw someone skulking in the trees," replied Raven, refusing to be intimidated. "And as we didn't know who it was, we decided it was better to be safe than sorry." He lifted his chin. "There's already been one murder. Hawk and I wanted to ensure there wouldn't be another."

The earl repressed a twitch of his lips. The little imps had cleverly seized the opportunity to handle the ancient weapons. But it was impossible to be angry, for he knew they would fight with tooth and nail if need be to protect Charlotte from harm.

"Trouble might be lurking anywhere," added Hawk. "We can't afford to let our guard down."

Harper, who was stretched out in front of the hearth, lifted his massive head and thumped his tail in agreement.

Woodbridge shivered and took a gulp of brandy. "I wasn't skulking. I was coming to take responsibility for my own cork-brained actions, rather than remain cowering like a lily-livered coward behind my sister's skirts."

"A noble sentiment," murmured Alison. "But then, I've never heard an ill word about your character, young man."

Woodbridge made a face. "Well, clearly, my intelligence deserves to be questioned."

Cordelia fixed him with a stern look. "You were supposed to stay in the carriage with Professor Sudler and help him keep guard over his invention."

"We both agreed it was unmanly to allow you to, er . . ." He glanced at Harper. "To face the wolves, as it were, on your own."

"As you see," murmured Charlotte, "no one has yet been eaten alive."

Cordelia's brother scrubbed a hand over his jaw. "The truth is, I deserve to be fed to the lions in the Tower Menagerie." The sunlight caught the faint glimmer of gold from the stubbled whiskers. He hadn't shaved this morning, and somehow that made him look younger and more vulnerable.

"I know I'm not as clever as Cordelia," he continued after expelling a ragged sigh. "I just want to take care of my estate and my tenants. A gentleman has a duty to be a good steward of the land and pass it on to future generations."

Wrexford felt an unexpected twinge of sympathy. In truth, he found Woodbridge a likable fellow who didn't appear to have an ounce of guile or cunning to his nature.

Charlotte seemed to have the same reaction, for she flashed him a sympathetic smile. "We all have our strengths, Lord Woodbridge. Yours are equally important as those of your sister."

"But I made a mull of it." He looked stricken. "What a gudgeon I was to believe—"

The rest of his words were suddenly swallowed in a deep-throated bark from Harper.

The earl spun around. He, too, had heard the faint *click-click* in the adjoining room, where a door led out to the back terrace.

The hound was by his side in a flash, and the two of them hurried into the corridor.

A yelp sounded. Ignoring Charlotte's whispered warning, Raven snatched up the Elizabethan small sword. But before he could move, Wrexford and Harper returned. And between them was a rotund little man with bushy brows and long silver hair tied back in an old-fashioned queue. He was wearing a shapeless brown coat with oil stains around the cuffs.

"I take it," said Charlotte, "that we are about to meet the elusive Professor Sudler."

Cordelia chuffed an exasperated sigh. "Isaac, you're supposed to be standing guard over your Engine."

"It seemed rather pointless, as I have no idea how to aim and fire a pistol." Sudler's brow furrowed. "Such a primitive mechanism. The engineering could be greatly improved. If one made a cartridge that contained both the bullet and—"

"Let us leave ballistics aside for now," she gently chided. "We need to talk about numbers."

"Yes, numbers," said Wrexford. "Lady Cordelia was just about to tell us why they are adding up to murder and mayhem."

"That's because greed became the most important part of the equation for the miscreants." Sudler tugged at his cuff. "I know what the numbers tell me. But alas, my tongue tends to be clumsy. Lady Cordelia is much better with words, so she had better explain it."

"Your tongue may be clumsy, but your hands aren't," said the earl. "Your workshop is a marvel. As is your prototype."

The professor's expression clouded. "The Computing Engine is meant to be used as a force for progress, not manipulated for personal greed."

"That's why we're here. To ask for help to ensure that it's not used to do evil," said Cordelia.

Sudler nodded, but shadows hovered beneath his lashes.

After a moment of hesitation, she knotted her hands together in her lap and resumed her explanation. "Before I return to the dastards and their scheme, I should first explain how Isaac and I came to be friends and mathematical collaborators. We met when Jamie was studying at Cambridge and attended the professor's lectures on mathematics. I confess, I occasionally dressed as a man so I could sneak in and hear them, too."

"Brilliant gel," said Sudler with a fond smile. "Far smarter than any of the young fribbles at the university."

"We met at several soirees and became close. Since then, we've corresponded regularly, and he's often visited our estate," she went on. "I've been helping him for several years on thinking through the concept of his mechanical Computing Engine and what mathematical operations it could possibly perform. When I began planning to start my own business, we designed some practical tests on how to put its power into practice."

Cordelia cleared her throat with a cough. "For now, suffice it to say, we can run certain basic computations at a speed that provides an edge in making certain business transactions. However, the full capabilities of the Computing Engine are still theoretical. It will take years to figure out the final design."

Alison gave a curt wave. "I doubt I would understand it even if you tried to explain. So I'm happy to have you skip over a more detailed explanation."

Raven appeared about to protest, but a look from Charlotte warned him to stay silent.

"Never fear, lad," murmured Wrexford. "You'll have a chance to learn the details."

"And now," said Cordelia, "I'll recount exactly how Jamie became involved in Argentum."

"*Credula est spes improba,*" murmured the professor.

"He who lives on hope dances without music," translated Charlotte. "Alas, very true."

"Actually, it should be me who explains my folly," said Woodbridge. "I foolishly talked among my friends about how brilliant and clever my sister is." He darted a fond smile at Cordelia. "I'm proud of her intellect, and I mentioned her wondrous mathematical talent and her work on a revolutionary Computing Engine. Shortly after that, I was approached by a friend, who asked if I might be interested in working on a hush-hush enterprise created by the East India Company. He gave me some Canterbury tale about the need for secrecy. It had something to do with not letting a trading consortium on the Continent get wind of the idea."

"And you naturally believed him," mused Charlotte.

"Yes. One assumes one's friends are telling the truth," replied Woodbridge. "And the fact that I was guaranteed a large profit made me even more gullible."

"But why you in particular?" asked the earl.

"Because they said they needed a titled gentleman to secure bank loans so no one would know the money was being raised for the East India Company."

"But why did the East India Company need to raise outside money?" asked Charlotte. "From what I've heard, their coffers are overflowing."

"I know, I know. I should have smelled a rat." His voice took on a bitter edge. "Cordelia did, but the henchman—the Cobra—had another Canterbury tale to explain the reason."

Wrexford was suddenly beginning to see the pieces of the puzzle and how they fit together. "Actually, I would venture to guess that the board of directors doesn't know about this enterprise. The conspirators are operating a private business within the Company."

"Yes, that's my surmise, though I have to believe it's being run by someone in a very senior position," said Cordelia. "Whoever put together the idea is using Company assets, like ships and trad-

ing partners, as part of their illicit scheme. And they've set up
fraudulent trading accounts on the Company's ledgers to keep
track of the profits and pay out the bribes to the various partners, making them appear to be legitimate Company business.
Henry Peabody somehow stumbled across the truth and tried
to stop the scheme by giving us copies of the ledgers."

"Who is the friend who approached you?" Wrexford asked,
finally feeling they were getting somewhere.

"The Honorable David Mather," answered Woodbridge.
"But my sense is they have some hold over him, too, and forced
him to find a likely pigeon."

"It seems the dastards have been very careful to shroud
themselves in secrecy," mused the earl. "And clever. They had
Mather find a respectable aristocrat with lands to guarantee any
loan. Only Mather and Hoare's bank knew of Woodbridge's financial troubles, and they keep mum about such things. There's
a code of silence and discretion within the banking world."

Sheffield looked at Cordelia's brother. "Which meant the
other banks willing to do business with you also kept the information private. And with one hand not knowing what the
other was doing, you were able to borrow far more than your
actual assets should have allowed."

Woodbridge's grimace confirmed the surmise.

"So, now we know the background," intoned the earl.
"What went wrong?"

The echo of the words seemed to linger, reverberating again
and again against the dark wood paneling.

Leaning forward, Woodbridge took his head in his hands.

Charlotte felt a surge of sympathy. Her late husband had
fallen prey to the unscrupulous scheming of so-called friends.
He had been too desperate for an easy way out of his troubles
to see through the lies and fraud that had quickly ensnared him.

Until it had been too late.

"As you can imagine, the dastards aren't telling us anything, so for much of this, I'm making guesses and conjectures." Cordelia looked up. Her face was ashen, save for the bruise-dark hollows beneath her eyes. "Are you all familiar with the term *arbitrage?*"

Alison and Sheffield looked utterly mystified, but Wrexford's eyes narrowed. "Hell's teeth, so that's what they're up to."

Charlotte had done a drawing some time ago on a scandal involving government bonds, so she grasped the basic concept of how such trading worked. But she couldn't quite imagine. . . .

"It would take hours, if not days, to explain the complexities of arbitrage," announced the earl. "But for now, let's just say that arbitrage is the *simultaneous* purchase and sale of an asset or related assets to profit from differentials in price."

He frowned. "We've already established why the cost of silver in China was so much lower for the conspirators than the price for which they could sell the same silver in European markets. So I assume that as the conspirators acquired the cheap silver in China through their opium operations, at exactly the same time, they sold a similar amount in European markets, making a trade that was both profitable and entirely riskless. Even if the price of silver went up or down, they still made a profit as long as the difference in price prevailed."

"Yes, exactly!" exclaimed Cordelia. "The miscreants would sell the opium on the fifteenth of every month in China, thus in effect *buying* the silver at a very low price. As we just discussed, they would pay by issuing a bill of exchange, payable in London in pounds. Meanwhile, on the same day they would *sell* that same amount of silver in Amsterdam, Hamburg, or Antwerp at the much higher European price, promising future delivery and taking in payment a bill of exchange payable in pounds."

"But how did they know exactly how the prices compared in Europe and China?" demanded Charlotte.

"A very astute question," replied Cordelia. "They didn't know exactly. But there are ships coming into Canton every day. They have the latest information on gold and silver prices, as well as exchange rates. As long as the conspirators could be reasonably certain that some significant price differential remained, they knew that by buying and selling at the same time, they were earning a riskless profit. The calculation of their exact profit would be worked out later."

"Oh, dear," murmured Alison. "I fear I don't follow all this money and bills going around in circles. But I get the sense that the miscreants negotiated an agreement with someone to pay them a large amount of profits in British pounds, which is exactly what they wanted."

"Precisely," agreed Cordelia. "The conspirators set up a joint account within the East India Company, one disguised as a legitimate trading account, to keep track of the profits, which they then divided among the conspirators and their partners at the supercargoes, along with the many people they bribed in connection with their scheme. They made the exact calculation of their profits, adjusted for movements in exchange rates through these accounts, and all the conspirators were happy."

She made a face. "Thievery by double-entry accounting rather than pistols."

"Interesting," muttered the earl. "They are unfortunately fiendishly skilled at financing."

"Indeed. The bills of exchange even minimized the amount of silver which had to be physically transported," explained Cordelia, now struggling somewhat to control tears. "No need to go into the details here, but it's much like when I write a cheque on my bank and give it to you to deposit in your bank. The banks don't ship the actual precious metal for each check back and forth. They merely net out the transactions at regular intervals and move only a small amount of actual currency to balance accounts."

She paused. "And just the same way, the various agents in the cities receiving or paying the bills of exchange deal regularly with each other and simply net out all the transactions. As a result, very little silver has to be transported in any direction."

Wrexford grimaced. "Clever. And fascinating that, as the late economist and philosopher Adam Smith wrote, the 'invisible hand' of the market is what shapes the nature of all commerce. Even in crime, capital flows to where it can earn the highest return with the least amount of risk."

"Yes," agreed Cordelia. "Fiendishly clever."

The group fell silent, pondering the elaborately sophisticated machinations that Cordelia had just described.

Cordelia fisted her hands together. "It's taken me some time to piece together all the information I've just told you. Please bear with me while I finish explaining how the professor and I were forced to become part of their nefarious scheme."

Sheffield nodded. "Go on."

"Jamie had mentioned my mathematical skills and the wonders of the professor's machine to his friends, including Mather. Apparently, the conspirators got wind of it. Having tricked Jamie into borrowing money for the venture and signing his name to the official company documents, they have threatened to ruin him and make the machination appear to be all his doing unless the professor and I use the Computing Engine—based on principles of arbitrage—to buy and sell silver in different markets to maximum advantage."

Cordelia drew in a shaky breath. "The best trading strategies depend on the wide range of variables—the price of silver, the interest on money borrowed, the exchange rate for the various currencies involved, the transport costs, to name just a few. The Computing Engine, however, when properly programmed by the mechanical instructions that my mathematical skills allow me to devise, can work the math required in a fraction of the time, and much more accurately than a roomful of accounting clerks."

"I've heard," the earl mused, "that an understanding of the mathematics of the arbitrage trade has been the subject of considerable study in the past fifty years. Most recently, a Mr. William Tate believes he has worked out a general analysis of the relevant mathematics. Or so my friends at the Exchange tell me."

"Mr. Tate has done exactly that," agreed Cordelia. "I'm acquainted with him, and I know that he hopes to publish his writing on the subject soon. But in the meantime, he shared a draft with me. The calculations are laborious and often require prodigious amounts of human labor. Moreover, given all the variables, the most potentially profitable trading arrangements may not be immediately apparent to the human eye. For example, we've seen over the past ten years a staggering growth in the 'forward markets' as compared with the 'cash market,' further complicating the exact calculations . . ."

Her voice trailed off as she realized that the others were reaching the end of their understanding.

And their patience.

"In any event," she said hurriedly, "now that the professor and I have identified some long-term strategies for profit, I've demanded that they let us all withdraw from the wicked scheme. So, Cobra and the ringleaders have promised that if we make enough profit for them in the next arbitrage cycle, they will give Jamie the money he needs to repay the loans taken in his name and will return the corporate documents necessary to allow him to quietly disband Argentum Trading Company. But . . ." Her voice cracked.

"But you don't believe them," said Charlotte softly.

"And quite rightly," growled Wrexford. "This won't end until we identify the ringleaders and see that they are brought to justice for their crimes."

Charlotte was of the same opinion. Blackmailers rarely let

their victims walk away when there was still money to be squeezed out of them.

"There's one last thing," said Cordelia. "In addition to the arbitrage numbers, they've also given the professor and me a very complex set of equations to calculate as part of the deal for getting back Jamie's papers. I don't know why. I've not yet had a chance to examine the required work carefully, so I can't hazard a guess on what it's for."

"I've not yet had a look at it, either, but it can be nothing good," muttered Sudler. "Of that you can be sure."

Cordelia sucked in a breath. "So, now you know all that we know. And while I have no right to ask for your help . . ."

"Of course m'lady will help," piped up Raven. As the boy turned to her, Charlotte saw the ripple of mute appeal in his eyes. "Won't you?"

"That goes without saying," she replied softly.

"Well, then," said Sheffield quickly, "we need to make a plan."

"All in good time," counseled Wrexford. "First, you and Woodbridge should go retrieve the Computing Engine. We need to keep it safe."

Raven shot to his feet, pulling his brother up with him. "We'll go with you."

Harper gave a canine stretch and padded over to join them.

"I'll go, too," said Cordelia.

"Leave the crossbow and sword here, Weasels," said the earl before the boys could slip away with the weapons.

"Speaking of swords . . ." The mention of blades suddenly reminded Charlotte of another mystery within the mystery. "The Runners recovered a silver-handled knife with a lion rampant inset on the hilt at Queen's Landing. Have you any idea to whom it might belong?"

"Ah, so it has been found." Woodbridge blew out his cheeks with a wry sigh. "It's mine. The Cobra told us he had it stolen from my townhouse and hidden there as a warning of how easily the conspirators can make me look guilty of any crime. He said that I won't be in danger of being arrested, as the authorities wouldn't accuse an earl of the crime unless there was ironclad proof that I murdered Mr. Peabody."

"Like an eyewitness," interjected Cordelia. "Which they could also produce if they so chose."

"As I said, the East India Company—or those who are cloaked in its aura of power and prestige—is a very dangerous enemy," responded Wrexford. "We would all do well never to forget that."

# CHAPTER 19

The echo of the words hung heavy over the room as the rescue party took a solemn leave from the room.

"Ye heavens, with all the excitement, I could use another nap," murmured Alison as she watched the group disappear into the corridor.

"And I," said Sudler, "could use another brandy."

Wrexford refilled the professor's glass and then came to take Charlotte's arm. "Come, let's take a stroll outside. Perhaps the sunshine will shed some clarity on how to untangle this coil of vipers," he muttered. "But I fear we'll need more than light." They crossed the corridor and passed through the door leading out to the back terrace. "We'll need a bloody miracle."

"We've faced daunting situations before," pointed out Charlotte. "And daunting foes."

"Yes, but this mystery, I fear, is a web that's woven far wider than any we've faced before."

The breeze slipped beneath the neckline of her gown and, like an icy finger, stirred a shiver along the length of her spine. "I believe Lady Cordelia is telling us the truth."

"The truth as she knows it," agreed the earl. "But if there's this level of corruption within the East India Company, I have to believe that someone in a very senior position is behind it."

Charlotte understood enough about the world of power and privilege to know that he was likely right. "As I make my living uncovering the secrets and scandals of Polite Society, I'm aware of how a thin veneer of perfectly polished respectability can hide a core of rot."

She thought of the murdered Henry Peabody, an ordinary man who believed that the rules should apply to everyone. "But no matter how deeply that rot goes, or whom it touches, I intend to expose it."

Wrexford heaved a long-suffering sigh. "I was afraid you were going to say that."

"Don't pretend that my sentiments surprise you."

His mouth curled up at the corners.

"And besides," she added, "you hate hypocrisy as much as I do."

The smile grew more pronounced. Tucking her hand in the crook of his elbow, Wrexford led her down a set of stairs to a low stone wall that looked out over a distant lake. He sat and patted the spot beside him. "We shall have to plan our next steps very carefully. With all our well-meaning friends running around, trying to help, it's imperative that we don't let them stray into trouble."

"I was thinking much the same thing," said Charlotte. "We need to be methodical. You have entrée into the world of banking, and into the clubs to which the senior officials of the East India Company belong, so I suggest that is where you begin your investigations."

"Yes, I'll certainly need to have a word with Mather. And another chat with Copley."

"What's your impression of him?" asked Charlotte. She knew the man only by reputation.

"Smooth and polished as one of the classical marble statues in the British Museum," said the earl. "But as we keep reminding each other, appearances can be deceiving." He considered the question for a moment longer. "That said, I've not heard a whisper about any flaws. We shall have to ask Lady Peake—"

"Ask me what?" The *tap-tap* of Alison's cane quickened over the flagstones. "Forgive me for interrupting, but something came to mind that I thought you ought to know."

"We were just wondering what you know about Lord Elgin Copley," replied Charlotte as Wrexford quickly rose and assisted the dowager in taking a seat beside her.

"His reputation is as pristine as virgin snow. Though that in itself might stir suspicions," came Alison's tart reply. "For no one is perfect." A pause. "However, from all that I have heard since he arrived back in England, Copley comes close to deserving a pedestal. Not only is he said to be a brilliant administrator, but he's also very generous in his support of a variety of worthy charities and champions sensible reforms in Parliament."

"Yes," mused the earl after resuming his perch on the wall. "He seems a paragon of progressive thinking."

"While you're looking for someone whose past contains some unpleasant little secrets that might relate to our investigation," responded the dowager. "And that's why I sought you out. I suddenly remembered some rumors regarding the youngest son of Sir Joseph Alston. He left Oxford abruptly to take a position in the East India Company's civil service . . . a post in one of the regional headquarters, if memory serves me right. That was perhaps twenty years ago, and he apparently served there without incident until four or five years ago. The details never came out at the time, but the gossip in the drawing rooms implied that he was forced out because of financial improprieties."

Charlotte tried to recollect any recent scandal involving the name Alston. She caught the earl's inquiring look and shook her head. "Nothing concerning the family comes to mind. But given the youngest son's past, we have to consider him a suspect."

Alison looked pleased.

"Do you perchance know his given name?" Charlotte pressed.

The dowager's brow furrowed. "Frederick . . . no, Fenwick! Fenwick Alston. However, I've heard no mention of him since the incident in India."

"Sheffield may be able to dig up some information on him and his current whereabouts in the gambling hells of Southwark and Seven Dials," murmured Wrexford. "Knaves and scoundrels have a sixth sense for knowing all the fiddle-faddles of their fellow sinners."

"Well, that's all I have to offer for the moment," said Alison. "I shall keep digging in the nether regions of my memory for any other buried scandals. And I'll also make some discreet inquiries about Copley and the other directors." Waving off any assistance, the dowager rose. "Now, I shall toddle off for my nap and leave you to your plotting—though I must say, sleuthing is an even better tonic for these old bones than sleep."

The cane's *tap-tap* faded into the twitter of birdsong and the sound of the breeze ruffling through the ivy. Wrexford watched the sunlight skitter over the dark-hued leaves. A glimmer of hope? Or merely taunting flickers? As of yet, they were still grasping at specters.

"I'll seek out another meeting with Annie Wright as soon as we return to London." Charlotte's voice drew him back from his brooding. "And see what I can learn from my informants around the docks about any suspicious activity within the East India Company wharves."

He shook off his pessimism. "As I said, it's time to confront

David Mather. And I'll now need to speak with Sir Joseph Alston, as well as Copley."

"I was also thinking of Jeremy," offered Charlotte. "He's become very involved in Mrs. Ashmun's mills and has been investing in their expansion, so he knows a good deal about the world of commerce. He may have some ideas on how to find the evidence we need . . ." Her words trailed off. Squinting into the sun, she raised a hand to shade her eyes. "Is that a horse and rider coming up the drive?"

Wrexford shot to his feet for a better look. "It's Tyler." He waved his arms.

Spotting the signal, the valet swerved off the road and cantered over to join them. He had been riding hard. Dust coated his clothing, and sweat lathered his horse's flanks.

"I managed to get what you asked for," Tyler announced without preamble. "Though I'm not sure whether you're going to be pleased." He pulled an oilskin packet from his pocket and handed it to the earl. "By the by, that cost me a *very* expensive meal. And Griffin will have your guts for garters if he doesn't get it back by tomorrow."

As the earl plucked a knife from the folds, a mote of light danced down the steel blade.

"Griffin can't say for sure that it's the murder weapon," began the valet. "What he does know is that it definitely belongs to Woodbridge."

"Yes, Woodbridge is here and has told us as much," cut in Wrexford, "along with a good deal more." He gave a terse explanation of the situation.

"Damnation. Then you're not going to be happy with the other bit of news I've learned," replied Tyler. "Mather appears to have left Town. Word is, he's taken a leave of absence from the bank to make a trip to Ireland with some friends."

"Damnation, the banker looks blacker by the moment." Wrexford kicked himself for not having sought out the fellow sooner. "Go on to the stables and have your horse rubbed down. Then have McClellan fix you a hot meal." He rewrapped the knife. "And tell Jenkins to have my stallion saddled. I mean to leave for London within the hour."

Tyler removed his hat and slapped the dust from the crown before settling it back on his head. "If you're hell-bent on returning to Town this afternoon, I'll come with you."

"I'd rather you stay and accompany the rest of our party tomorrow."

The valet stiffened. "Has there been trouble?"

"Not as of yet." Wrexford's expression turned grim. "But we're about to poke a stick into a nest of very dangerous vipers within the East India Company. Until we've pulled their fangs, we need to be on guard."

Charlotte touched his sleeve. "You've seen that I can ride well enough not to slow you down. Allow me to come with you. I, too, ought to begin my inquiries as quickly as possible."

"I don't doubt your fortitude. But it's been years since you've been in the saddle, and you're experienced enough in equestrian matters to know that after such an ordeal, you wouldn't be able to walk for the next week."

When she made no retort, Wrexford added, "An even more pressing practicality is the damage it would do to your reputation. As Lady Charlotte Sloane . . ."

"Yes, yes," she snapped. "Of course, you're right to remind me that my life has changed." A sigh. "And not all of it has been for the better."

"It's a matter of compromise," he murmured. "You've gained advantages, as well as given them up."

"That's true," she conceded. "I'm being churlish."

"And besides, I would feel more at ease if you travel with the others and help Tyler keep an eye on things." He touched her hand, a fleeting caress that lasted only an instant, but the warmth seemed to linger on his fingertips. "Just promise me you won't do something appallingly brave and try to beat the devil on your own."

"Even I'm not that appallingly foolish," she replied with a twitch of her lips. "I'm well aware that the dastards we face likely wield more influence and power than any of the villains we've faced in the past."

And yet the steely glint in her eyes gave her words a suspiciously hollow ring.

# CHAPTER 20

Wrexford cursed as a brewer's wagon clattered through a turn, splashing his boots with muck. "Oh, to be an indolent aristocrat," he grumbled, dodging a dray cart to cross the street, "whose only thoughts are of earthly pleasures, rather than bloody abstractions like right and wrong."

It had been past midnight by the time he arrived back in London, and though he had managed a few hours of sleep, a sense of urgency had roused him from his bed to seek out first Griffin and then Henning.

Alas, the note he had dispatched to Bow Street had come back with the unwelcome news that the Runner was presently occupied with a robbery on the south side of the river. Which accounted for his current foul mood. Deciding that there was time for a quick visit to the surgeon before seeking out Griffin, he had left his townhouse without breakfast.

After turning down a muddy lane, he followed it to the end, where a ramshackle dwelling stood beside a fenced-in patch of bare ground, with a small stone outbuilding pressed up against its far end. The wooden stairs groaned as he took them two at a time, and then began thumping a fist on the front door.

"The devil take it! Stop that infernal pounding!" came a querulous cry from inside after a minute or two had passed. The door flung open, revealing the bleary-eyed surgeon, who looked even more disheveled than usual. "Are you trying to wake the bloody dead?"

"Apparently yes." Wrexford stepped inside and eyed his friend's unshaven face and rumpled attire. "You look like a corpse—save that a dead man is usually laid out in relatively clean clothing."

"Stubble the witticisms. I'm in no mood for humor at this hour of the morning," said Henning, gesturing for the earl to take a seat in the small parlor off the entrance foyer. "It *is* morning, isn't it?"

Seeing the satchel filled with medical instruments that had been dropped by the doorway, Wrexford asked, "A long night?"

"An outbreak of influenza in one of the rookeries near Monmouth Street. Three children are dead, as well as their mother." The surgeon ran a hand through his tangled hair and slouched into one of the chairs by the unlit hearth. "It's decent food they need, not medicine. I've had a batch of nourishing broth sent to the sufferers. Perhaps that will send the Grim Reaper looking elsewhere."

Wrexford nodded grimly, making a mental note to increase his donation to his friend's clinic for the poor. "I'm sorry."

Henning made a wry face. "I'm assuming death must have crossed your path, too, else you wouldn't be here at such a god-benighted hour."

"Correct." He took the knife from his pocket and unwrapped it. "Any chance you might remember the corpse Griffin sent to you last week? I'm curious whether this blade might have been used to slit the poor fellow's throat."

"It would have helped to have this when I had the body at my disposal," groused Henning.

"It was discovered only recently."

Expelling a snort, Henning examined the fancy hilt and then had a close look at the blade.

"There's a bit of dried blood embedded in the silver chasing," offered the earl.

"I have eyes, laddie." The surgeon tested the knife's sharpness against his thumb. "No, this isn't the murder weapon. The death slash cut cleanly through muscle and sinew. This blade is far too dull. It feels to me like it's been used as a letter opener. Paper has a certain way of taking the edge off of steel."

"Thank you." Wrexford rewrapped the weapon. "I thought as much, but I wished to have you confirm it."

"I can't help but wonder why both you and Griffin are interested in the murder of a clerk. From what I've heard, he was an ordinary fellow."

"An ordinary fellow who happened to work in accounting for one of the directors of the East India Company," replied the earl.

The surgeon's jaw tightened as he ran a hand over his bristled chin. "Is there mischief afoot among those pompous prigs?" Henning had very revolutionary ideas about wealth and the ruling class.

"More than mischief, Baz. Lady Charlotte and I have reason to believe there's a diabolical scheme of financial fraud and currency manipulation that reaches the very top. We're looking for proof—"

"And if you find it, the scandal would rock the very foundations of Britain's economy. And that would in turn have political repercussions." An unholy glint lit in Henning's eyes as he smoothed at a wrinkle in his cuff. "How can I help?"

"Let us not set up a guillotine in your yard just yet," said the earl. "There are other ways to bring the miscreants to justice." He thought for a moment. "If you truly wish to help, see what you can learn about a barmaid named Annie Wright, who works at the Ship's Lantern in the dockyards."

"I'll make some inquiries," replied the surgeon. "I have a number of friends in the area who owe me favors."

"You might also ask around among your acquaintances as to whether any of the smaller private banks in Town are known for not asking too many questions about the movement of money in and out of a client's account."

A rusty chuckle. "Are you implying that I consort with the wrong sort of people?"

"I devoutly hope that you do." The earl rose. "I must be off and see if I can find Griffin. If you discover anything, send word, or come around yourself. Tyler has recently purchased some very fine Scottish malt."

The wind was gusting as he made his way back to the main thoroughfare and flagged down a hackney. As it crossed Black-friars Bridge and dropped him off several streets east of Astley's Amphitheatre, the leaden clouds turned even more ominous, promising rain at any moment.

After consulting the note from Bow Street, he turned down Mason Street, hoping he wasn't wasting his time on a wild goose chase. But thankfully, he spotted his quarry up ahead.

Quickening his steps, the earl caught up with Griffin just as the Runner was climbing into a waiting hackney.

"Milord," said Griffin, his shrewd eyes narrowing in interest. "Tyler said you were out of Town. And yet here you are."

A spattering of drops began to fall. The earl turned up the collar of his coat. "Might I have a word with you?"

"I'm on a case and need to report to the magistrate on my progress. However, you're welcome to join me for the ride back to Bow Street."

Wrexford slid onto the well-worn seat and slammed the door shut.

"A pity I don't have more time," added Griffin. "Otherwise I'd invite you to breakfast."

The earl uttered a rude word.

A chuckle rumbled in reply.

Before going on, Wrexford took the cloth-wrapped knife from his pocket and passed it over.

Leather whispered as the Runner sat up a little straighter. "Have you learned whether Lord Woodbridge did indeed kill Henry Peabody?" he demanded. "Granted, my superiors dislike it when a member of the aristocracy is guilty of a heinous crime. Be that as it may, I think you know I'll do my best to see that justice is served."

"Actually, I'm quite certain he's innocent of murder. Henning has confirmed the knife is far too dull to have been the murder weapon," replied the earl. "However, your superiors are going to dislike the alternative even more." He took a moment to carefully consider his next words. "Tell me, have you or any of your men heard any whispers around the wharves or from Mr. Peabody's fellow clerks in accounting about any . . . irregularities concerning the East India Company's finances?"

Griffin remained silent, but all of a sudden, the still air within the hackney seemed to be crackling with unseen electricity.

"Perhaps concerning the movement of funds between departmental accounts, or the bookkeeping methods used for the financial ledgers," added Wrexford.

More silence, amplified by the hackney's rattling as it turned onto Westminster Bridge.

When the reply came, it was barely audible. "No, I have not." Griffin shifted, and his beefy bulk blocked out what little light oozed in through the tiny window. "Have I missed something, milord?"

"It's a pity you don't have time for me to fill your gullet with an expensive breakfast," drawled the earl. "But even then, I fear you'll find that my answer will stick in your craw."

The Runner let out an unhappy sigh. "Bloody hell. Have you any idea what a dangerous accusation you're making?"

"I haven't made any accusations," replied Wrexford. "Not yet."

The gallows humor drew no smile. "I can keep my ears open, milord. But I can't make any inquiries into the Company's business unless you can give me compelling evidence that there is a reason to do so. And even then, my superiors would be . . ."

"Would be terrified to approve any official action," finished Wrexford. "Yes, I know that."

"When I said it was dangerous, I didn't use the word lightly," said Griffin. "Your title and your money won't protect you if it's decided you represent a threat."

"Then I shall just have to rely on my wits."

"I'm serious, milord. This is no jesting matter."

"Indeed not. To think that you might go hungry if I were to stick my spoon into the wall is nothing to laugh about."

A snort.

"I've no desire to meet my Maker quite yet, so I intend to be careful," said Wrexford. "I can, on occasion, exercise discretion."

"You'll need more than discretion." Griffin pursed his lips. "I'll do what I can to help, but I must tread very carefully. It would help if I knew what you're looking for."

"For one thing, I'm interested in knowing of any private banks here in Town that might be willing to work with a client who needs to bend the rules to suit his needs."

"There are some small establishments around the Exchange who are said to be less than scrupulous about their paperwork. I can compile a list."

"Please do," replied the earl. "I had intended to press the Honorable David Mather about certain loans Hoare's Bank has made. But he has apparently left Town."

"Your friend Sheffield—"

"Sheffield is not involved in any wrongdoing. I give you my word on that," interrupted Wrexford. "I have reason to believe that Lord Woodbridge may have been used as a pawn in certain fraudulent financial transactions, of which Mather was a part. And that Henry Peabody, conscientious clerk that he was, may have stumbled across a business within a business going on at the East India Company, which is why he was murdered."

"And you think the perpetrators of this business within a business sought to frame Woodbridge for the murder?"

"Woodbridge believed what he was told when he agreed to be part of a clandestine consortium. When he learned that he had been misled about the nature of the business and why it must be kept secret, he demanded to withdraw," explained the earl. "I think the planting of the knife is a warning. Right now, it's just circumstantial evidence. You don't have enough proof to bring charges against a peer of the realm."

He let the words hang in the air for a moment before adding, "However, they're sending the message that they are powerful enough to destroy him with a few well-placed words to the right person."

"I won't ask you how you know all this," muttered Griffin.

"It's best you don't," agreed the earl. "I've some ideas on how to begin gathering the evidence I need to expose the dastards."

"You know, if there's a whisper of scandal stirring within the world of the wealthy and powerful . . ." The Runner leaned back against the squabs. "Then I imagine A. J. Quill will hear of it. I swear, a flea can't fart in this city without that infernal scribbler getting wind of it."

Griffin made a face. "So perhaps you should find a way to learn his identity and see if he'll share his sources with you." A humorless laugh. "And convince him to help you root out the dastards. God knows, he seems to share your abhorrence of the high and mighty misusing their power. A few of his satirical drawings hinting at malfeasance within the almighty East India Company would work in your favor by stirring up a buzzing of hornets."

*Or a slithering of serpents.*

A gust of rain-soaked wind slapped against the window glass, and Wrexford was suddenly aware of the chill seeping into the hackney.

*Charlotte's pen could put her in grave peril. . . .*

The wheels clattered to a halt. "I must attend to my current duties," said Griffin as he grasped the latch and swung the door open. "A word of caution . . . think carefully on just how far you're willing to go for the truth, milord. I admire your passion for justice. But not if it costs you your life."

His hobnailed boots scraped over the cobblestones. "And my beefsteak suppers."

The journey back to London had passed without incident, and on entering the city just after nightfall, Tyler and Sheffield had headed for Mayfair with their companions, while Alison's carriage had turned east to drop Charlotte, McClellan, and the boys at her residence.

Despite the jolts and jostling of travel, Charlotte had managed to doze off for part of the journey. The other hours had been spent in thinking, thinking. . . .

*Time is of the essence, but how to attack an enemy who is still just an unseen specter flitting through the shadows?*

McClellan unlocked the front door and bustled the boys into the kitchen for a simple supper. "It won't take long to fix a pot of hot porridge," she said to Charlotte after lighting the stove and setting the kettle on the hob. "Sit and I'll brew a cup of tea."

"Tea would be lovely," answered Charlotte. "But I'll just have some cheese and bread from the larder."

Raven leaned forward on his stool and set his elbows on the worktable. "You're going out, aren't you?"

"Yes, I am." Her skirts whispered over the flagged floor as

she took a seat and met his gaze. "And we need to establish some rules as to the comings and goings of this household."

The muted chink of pots ceased as McClellan went very still.

A mutinous flicker lit in Raven's eyes. "You've never sought to clip our wings before."

That wasn't entirely true. But Charlotte understood the elemental challenge he was making and prayed that she could handle it without breaking the bonds of trust that tied their little family together.

"You've become older and more involved in adult affairs," she began carefully. "Which are more complicated and fraught with consequences, both for you and for your friends."

Hawk shot an uncertain look at his brother.

"Decisions must be weighed with great care, and the scales are often very hard to balance. Sometimes you must tip them against your inclinations because it's the right thing to do."

Charlotte paused, watching Raven closely.

The war of emotions was writ plainly on his face. He was on the cusp of adolescence—not quite a child, but not yet an adult. Rebellion was natural, as she knew all too well. His eyes narrowed. . . .

And then a tiny twitch curled the corners of his mouth upward. "So you're saying that Lord Wrexford is right, and that there are times you have to look at a problem with logic and act on reason, not emotion?"

"Yes, that's precisely what I'm saying."

The smile became more pronounced. "You don't always listen to His Lordship's requests."

"On the contrary. I always listen very carefully and give his words great weight," responded Charlotte. That didn't mean she always did exactly as he wished. But she left that thought unsaid.

Raven appeared to be mulling over her reply.

"In past investigations, we were up against a small group of individuals. This time, we're facing a powerful institution with ties to the highest circles of government. The dangers are great. In fact, they're terrifying." She drew in a measured breath. "Or should be."

"How can we help?" asked Hawk in a small voice.

"By accepting that there will be times, like tonight, when I will need to ask you to do as I say, even though you might not like it," said Charlotte. She thought for a moment and allowed a small smile. "You saw Professor's Sudler's amazing Computing Engine before we left Wrexford's estate. Well, with the number of our friends involved in this investigation, we are like the Engine, in that we have complicated parts which must all work together. If one piece comes unhinged, it can wreck all the others."

Raven nodded solemnly. "Oiy, I see what you're saying."

She released an inward sigh of relief.

"But if you must go out alone," he added, "you need to tell us where you're going. In case . . ."

*In case I don't return.*

"Fair enough," said Charlotte.

"In fact," piped up McClellan as she tapped a cooking spoon against her palm, "I suggest that for the time being, the house rule is none of us go out without the others knowing where we're headed."

"Agreed," answered Charlotte.

"Agreed," echoed the boys.

"Excellent," murmured the maid. "I shall make a batch of ginger biscuits to seal the pledge."

Charlotte rose. "I need to go to the docklands tonight and have a word with Annie Wright. I expect to be back before dawn."

"The porridge should be ready by the time you've changed your plumage to become Magpie," said McClellan. "One should never square off against the enemy on an empty stomach."

*    *    *

The Great Fog, which had gripped the city since the beginning of the year, seemed to hang heavy over the deserted warehouses, despite the fitful breeze blowing in from the river. Slowing her steps, Charlotte moved cautiously through the gloom, searching for a glimmer of light in the surrounding darkness. Perhaps it was the talk of knives and murder that had her nerves on edge. A prickling of foreboding teased at the nape of her neck, and every little skitter and rattle from alleyways set her heart to thudding against her ribs.

At last, a creeping turn brought her down to the wharves, and she spotted the glow of the Ship's Lantern up ahead.

Charlotte pushed through the tavern's door and was immediately enveloped in the sweaty fugue of stale ale and unwashed bodies. A merchant ship must have sailed in on the earlier flood tide, for the taproom was packed with a raucous crowd of warrant officers, who were drinking, laughing . . . and groping at the passing serving wenches.

Slipping into a shadowed niche, she squinted through the haze of smoke, watching and waiting. . . .

The minutes slid by, but with no sign of Annie Wright.

Charlotte waited until one of the kitchen girls cut toward the kitchen with a tray of empty mugs, and darted out to block her path.

"I'm looking for Annie," she murmured.

The girl paused to rebalance her load. "Annie musta done a runner. She ain't shown up fer work in three days."

"Any idea where she might have gone?"

"Naw." The girl scowled. "Why ye asking?"

"I'm a friend. It's important that I find her."

"Yeah?" A frown pinched the girl's flushed face. "Annie suddenly seems te have friends crawling like rats outta the sewers."

A frisson of alarm slithered down Charlotte's spine. "Have there been others asking for her?"

The girl retreated a step. "Like I said, I dunno nuffink."

Charlotte muttered a thanks and turned away, but not before she saw the girl sidle over to the bar counter and exchange a hurried whisper with the man behind it.

*Damnation.* She ducked out into the night, cursing her own stupidity in letting Annie slip through her fingers without pressing her for answers regarding the murder. The barmaid had scarpered, and Charlotte didn't need a mathematical Engine to compute the chances of finding her again.

They were virtually nil.

Overhead, the scrim of clouds had blown off to reveal a crescent moon, but the here-and-there glimmer of stars did little to lighten the skeins of vapor swirling in the alleyway. Charlotte turned up her coat collar to ward off the damp-fingered gusts. It was low tide, and the stench of decay deepened her sense of failure.

*Mather, and now Annie . . .*

Shallowing her breathing, she hesitated as the narrow passageway opened onto a lane leading over to Ratcliff Highway. Turning left would take her home, while turning right . . .

She decided there was nothing to lose by paying a call on Squid, her dockland informant. His tavern was a squalid hellhole, but despite his untidy habits, he was surprisingly observant and his information was usually accurate.

Her special knock drew a quick answer.

"Come in, Magpie. What shiny little baubles of dirt are ye seeking tonight?" A flash of yellowed teeth and a rumbled laugh at his own witticism. "Whatever yer seeking, I'm always happy te oblige." He leered. "Including me."

In no mood to banter, Charlotte stepped inside and jingled the purse in her pocket. "Annie Wright seems to have disappeared. Any idea of where she's gone?"

The clink of coins brought Squid to full alert. "Oiy, I heard she's scarpered." He thought for a moment. "Kat thought she mitta seen her get into a hackney wiv a fancy cove, but she couldn't say fer sure it was Annie. Ye want me te ask around?"

*Could it have been Mather who had taken Annie away?* she wondered.

"Ask Kat if she can describe the cove she saw," replied Charlotte. "But do it *very* quietly. And don't share the information with anyone else."

Squid mimed locking his lips.

Preoccupied with her own brooding, she gave a wordless nod and turned to let herself out.

"Wait, I just remembered sommink!"

Charlotte looked around.

"Alice the Eel Girl stopped by here looking fer ye yesterday afternoon. Said te tell ye if I saw ye." He grimaced. "But she wouldn't tell me why."

She reached into her purse and pulled out a coin. Candlelight winked off the shiny metal as it spun through the air. "That's because, like you, Alice knows on which side her bread is buttered."

The door fell shut on his rusty chuckle, stirring a quiver of the thick fog. Swearing under her breath, Charlotte punched in frustration at the silvery vapor. Alice wouldn't be at her post until after dawn.

Yet another precious few hours for the trail of Annie Wright to grow colder.

It appeared that Mather had indeed left Town, for he couldn't be found at any of his usual haunts. Wrexford and Sheffield left a gaming hell off St. James's Square known for its deep play—which might explain why the young banker was willing to sell Woodbridge and Peabody to the devil—and split up to try a few other possibilities. Sheffield headed to the stews of St. Giles, while Wrexford decided to check the cardroom at White's.

But no luck. The only gamesters were a group of elderly members playing whist for a penny a point.

Frustration quickening his steps, the earl cut through the main reading room, where the crackling coals in the massive hearth cast a whisky-gold glow over the dark leather armchairs arrayed near the fire. They were empty, save for a lone figure studying the sheaf of papers in his lap.

Light winked off his spectacles as the gentleman looked up. "Ah, Wrexford." A flick of his fingers indicated a bottle on the drinks table. "You appear in a hurry. Otherwise, I'd invite you to help me polish off a very fine port."

The earl paused and pivoted. "There's always time to savor the good things in life, Copley."

"A sentiment not always associated with you," said the baron as Wrexford took a seat beside him. "You've a reputation for having little patience, especially for those who can't keep pace with your way of thinking."

"True. I don't suffer fools gladly," he agreed, accepting a glass of the spirits from the baron. "But I like to think I appreciate excellence and creativity, no matter what form they take."

Copley cocked a small salute. "Then let us drink to the times in which we live. There is much excellence and creativity taking shape around us. It is an exciting era, and one that will shape a very different world in the years to come, as old ways are eclipsed by new ones."

Wrexford took a sip of his wine. "I, too, can't help but remark that your sentiments might surprise many. As someone who runs a very large and profitable company that is facing changes to its way of doing business, I would expect you to favor old ways over new ones."

"One must innovate—and sometimes improvise—if one wants to stay ahead of the competition. The world is going to change, whether we like it or not. I prefer not to be left in the dust."

Copley clearly possessed a sharp intellect and an analytical mind unafraid of assessing challenging ideas. Which begged the question . . .

*Is he* too *clever?*

A chuffed laugh sounded in response to the earl's silence. "Forgive my odd musings. I've been immersed in my papers for the past few hours, which has put me in a reflective mood."

Catching a glimpse of numbers on the top page of the baron's pile, Wrexford replied, "It can't be easy trying to navigate through the new waters created by the Charter Act."

A smile. "One must stay constantly alert to which way the winds are blowing." The baron refilled his glass and offered the bottle to the earl.

He declined, and then replied, "Innovation and the ability to improvise are admirable traits. Unless, of course, they tempt one to bend the rules to stay ahead of the competition."

Copley took a long swallow of his wine. "Are you still concerned about Henry Peabody's murder?"

"No," Wrexford answered. "It's just that I heard a curious rumor recently about another past employee of the East India Company. Were you acquainted with a gentleman by the name of Fenwick Alston while you were in India?"

"Indeed. I worked with him in Calcutta." Copley let out a mournful sigh. "He was extremely talented, but alas, he allowed greed to cloud his judgment."

"So, the rumors of financial irregularities are true?"

"Yes. He began altering cargo manifests in order to take some of the goods to sell for himself. The discrepancies were discovered," explained the baron. "Alston was allowed to quietly resign and leave the country. A public scandal was not in the interest of the Company or the family."

"Have you any idea where Alston is now?"

"I haven't a clue." Copley made a face. "To be honest, it's an incident I preferred to forget. I consider it a failing that I didn't spot the problem sooner."

"We all make mistakes," said Wrexford. He fingered his empty glass, feeling even more unsettled.

*Hero or villain? Or simply a clever man of business taking advantage of the opportunities in a changing world?*

"Thank you for your candor. And for the excellent wine." The earl rose. "I'll leave you to your numbers. May they all add up correctly."

# CHAPTER 21

"You look fagged." Hands fisted on his hips, Raven stood in the doorway of the kitchen, Hawk hovering just behind him. "We think we should come with you."

Charlotte swallowed a mouthful of coffee, willing it to scald the muzziness from her head. It was early morning, and she had managed only an hour or two of sleep. Fatigue, she conceded, felt as if it had seeped right into the very marrow of her bones. Not a good sign when she needed her wits on full alert.

"He's right," agreed McClellan as she refilled Charlotte's cup.

"I'm simply going to fetch a message from Alice the Eel Girl," Charlotte replied.

"Which means you might need us to inform His Nibs of what it says," countered Raven. "Or spread the word to our other friends to keep their peepers open for something havey-cavey."

"It's a sensible suggestion," murmured McClellan

A plume of steam rose from the devil-dark brew. "It is," she replied. So why it stirred a frisson of unease eluded her. But then, she clearly wasn't thinking straight.

"Very well." Charlotte quickly finished the last bite of her muffin and rose. The sooner she accomplished the task, the sooner she could crawl back under the covers for some blissful hours of sleep.

Outside, the fog still lingered, the dawn's gossamer glow doing little to lighten the pewter-grey vapor cloaking the streets. She and the boys moved quickly, wraithlike shapes flitting dark on dark through the chill morning.

Through the windblown mist, the river gleamed like a ribbon of polished steel as they made their way down to the docklands. The loading areas were just coming to life, the rattle of barrows and the shouts of the stevedores twining with the groaning timbers and the thrumming rigging of the ships tied at the wharves.

Alice the Eel Girl was doing a brisk business selling her still-warm pasties to the workers. Charlotte waited for a pair of blacksmiths to make their purchases and drift away before approaching her.

"Oiy!" Alice's eyes came alight. She shifted her tray and angled a little deeper into the shadows of the brick warehouse fronting the docks before going on. "A woman by the name o' Annie gave me a message fer ye. I'm te tell ye she's sorry, an' that she expects ye'll get the answer ye want soon enuff."

Charlotte huffed in frustration. *Damnation!* What the devil did that mean? They didn't have time to spin in circles.

Alice, however, still had the odd gleam in her eyes. "I figgered ye were expecting something more, so I waited a bit and then followed her."

*Oh, you clever, clever girl,* thought Charlotte. "And did you discover her hidey-hole?"

The girl's face fell. "Naw. Up near Ratcliff Highway, a fancy gennelmun stopped her, and after a bit o' chin-wagging, she got in his carriage and they drove off."

*Mather.* Who else could it be but Mather?

"He didn't force her," added Alice. "Looked te me like she wuz happy te go wiv him."

Could it be that the barmaid had betrayed her childhood friend to his cousin? Annie was, by her own admission, struggling to survive in a world that gave no quarter to sentiment.

"Does that help?" asked the girl.

"Yes, it does," answered Charlotte, all at once unsure of whether she could trust her own judgment, given how easily Annie had humbugged her.

Feeling a little light headed, she handed Alice another coin and looked around for the boys, who had darted off to greet their urchin friends who made a living along the waterfront.

"Confound it," she muttered. They were nowhere to be seen.

The breeze had freshened, setting the signal flags on a nearby merchant ship to snapping in the swirling air. She gazed up at the dancing colors strung from the main halyard, noting the private ensign of the East India Company flying from the top of the mainmast. Sailors were already aloft, preparing the furled sails for the journey east. The tide was about to turn. No doubt, they would soon be casting off the mooring lines.

For an instant, the idea of simply sailing away from all the frightening conundrums teased at her consciousness. The vast ocean, Charlotte knew from experience, had a way of simplifying the world. It stripped away all artifice, leaving only the purely elemental forces of Nature.

Lifting her chin, she watched the clouds scud through the muddled sky, and found her momentary doubts flittering off into the gloom. Strangely enough, a simple world held no allure. It would mean leaving all she loved . . .

"Oiy, oiy!" The sounds of Raven and Hawk larking through one of the alleyways cut through her thoughts. As the boys broke free of the shadows, they waved.

Hunching her shoulders, she let out a low whistle in reply,

just another urchin intent on joining in with a raggle-taggle band of friends. It wasn't until they were well away from the wharves and hidden in the confines of a narrow passageway between warehouses that Raven spun around and drew in a quick breath.

"M'lady, m'lady, we just saw one of the dastards! I'm sure of it!"

Sheffield accepted a cup of coffee from Tyler and slouched back in his seat. "Now what are we going to do? Mather was our only link to learning the identities of the ringleaders."

"There's never just one way to skin a snake," replied Wrexford. "You forget that Lady Cordelia has seen the Cobra. And while she mentioned he swathed his face in black silk, she may have noticed other things about him that will prove useful."

"Hmmm." Sheffield puffed out his cheeks. "I see I have a great deal to learn about how to conduct clandestine investigations."

"Don't worry," quipped Tyler, setting a plate heaped with breakfast on the side table by Sheffield's armchair. "Your mind will soon be working along the same devious lines as ours."

There was a momentary clatter of cutlery. "So, what do we do next?" asked Sheffield through a mouthful of shirred eggs.

"I suggest we leave the matter of the Cobra until this evening, when Lady Cordelia comes to work on the daily mathematical computations with the professor," said Wrexford.

It had been decided that Sudler and his Engine should be kept hidden from the consortium, so they had been installed in a downstairs workroom of the earl's townhouse, next to the kitchens. Cordelia and her brother had returned to their own residence. Given her experience in masquerading as a man, she slipped out each night after dark and made her way through the alleyways to the back gate of the earl's garden.

"Speaking of which," muttered Sheffield, "what if the dastards have Woodbridge's townhouse under surveillance? Shouldn't we worry about whether she's being followed?"

"We've thought of that," offered Tyler. "Raven and Hawk have their band of urchins keeping watch on whether there are predators on the prowl."

Sheffield chewed thoughtfully on a piece of gammon, then suddenly sat up straighter. "What about Fenwick Alston?"

"Tyler was right," drawled Wrexford. "You're beginning to understand the art of sleuthing."

"Ha!" His friend made a face. "I won't consider myself anything but a callow novice until I can earn praise from the Weasels."

"Fetch your hat and coat," said the earl. "As it happens, we're going to pay a call now on the current baronet. Sir Joseph passed away several years ago. His eldest son, Bentley, inherited the title."

"But it's not yet noon," protested Sheffield, darting a longing look at his untouched muffins. "The butler won't admit visitors at such an ungodly hour."

"Yes, but Sir Bentley has his weekly fencing lesson this morning at Angelo's Academy." Wrexford rose. "And with the great Harry Angelo himself, so he'll be there."

They made the short walk to Bond Street and entered the academy. The earthy scent of sweat and masculine musk wafted through the air as they crossed the foyer and paused in the doorway leading to the fencing salons. The cavernous main room echoed with the ring of clashing steel and the huffed snorts of male exertion.

"No, no, no!" A slender gentleman, his hair drawn back from his high forehead in an old-fashioned queue, danced to a halt and waggled his rapier. "You must hold your hand higher and balance on the balls of your feet." He demonstrated the move with a cat-like quickness. "Like so!"

His pupil blinked and dabbed a soaked shirtsleeve to his brow.

"Now try it by yourself, slowly, and repeat it several times."

"You're a hard taskmaster, Harry," called Wrexford as the legendary fencing master stepped back from the center of the room.

"Ah, Wrexford." Henry Charles Angelo cut a quick flourish through the air with his blade. "You must come around for a session with me soon, so my students can see a good example of a swordsman who understands the principles of control and precision." He cocked his brow. "I trust your skills have stayed sharp, milord?"

"Scientific experimentation demands precision," the earl answered. "I try to keep myself honed to a razor's edge."

"Excellent! As I said, this gentleman here would benefit from seeing some proper swordplay." Angelo grinned before turning back to his panting student. "That's enough for today, Sir Bentley. Try to practice your footwork for our next session." He patted his flat abdomen and added, "Oh, and it appears you're getting a bit *por-tly*." A chuckle. "So you might consider limiting your intake of wine."

Sir Bentley's face turned even redder at the teasing. Shoulders slumping, the baronet blew out his breath and slunk away to towel off in one of the changing salons.

"Don't take it to heart. Harry isn't easy to please," murmured Wrexford as he and Sheffield followed him into the room.

"That's kind of you, milord," answered Sir Bentley after another wheeze. "I'm under no illusion as to my prowess with a sword. But a gentleman ought to know the rudiments of wielding a blade, so I make an effort, however paltry."

"Which is all to your credit."

Sir Bentley looked a little puzzled at having attracted Wrexford's attention. He flashed an uncertain smile and was about to retreat to the washbasins when the earl shifted slightly to block his way.

"Might we have a private word with you, sir?"

"Y-yes, er, of course . . ." The baronet's expression turned wary, but he shrugged and stepped back into one of the changing alcoves. "But I can't imagine why."

"It's about your youngest brother."

The baronet's gaze turned clouded. "It's not a subject I enjoy discussing."

"I understand," replied Wrexford. "I'd simply like to ask if you know his current whereabouts."

A hesitation, punctuated by an unhappy exhale. "Some graveyard in Jamaica, though I couldn't tell you which one. As far as the family is concerned, his memory is best left buried in oblivion, along with his corpse."

Wrexford gritted his teeth. *Damnation. Yet another dead end.*

Seeing the earl's reaction, Sir Bentley added, "Fenwick was killed several years ago. An altercation over business matters."

"Might I ask exactly when?" inquired Sheffield.

The baronet pursed his lips. "Three . . . no, less than that . . . It was the summer of eleven."

"And in what sort of business was he engaged?" pressed Sheffield.

Another awkward silence.

"We're not asking out of prurient interest, sir," said Wrexford. "We're aware of your brother's trouble in India and are trying to discern whether he might have been part of a current trading enterprise."

"An illicit one, I take it," said the baronet tightly. "Perhaps he was." A pause. "Since I'm aware of your reputation for solving crimes, I'm willing to tell you the sordid details, milord. But I ask for your word of honor in keeping it confidential."

"That goes without saying."

"Very well." Sir Bentley blew out his breath. "A well-placed friend in the governor-general's office in Jamaica let me know that Fenwick was suspected of trading goods with the French on Martinique. That would, of course, be not only illegal, but . . ."

"Treasonous," said the earl softly.

"So, you understand why I wish to leave my brother dead and buried," responded the baronet. "I trust that answers your questions. If you are looking to punish those responsible for a current crime, you may rest assured that Fenwick is already roasting in hell for his sins."

The devil seemed to be taking malicious delight in tangling the Argentum conundrum into a proverbial Gordian knot. Wrexford glanced at the rack of practice weapons hanging on the wall. *Perhaps I need to borrow Angelo's rapier to slice through it.*

But even then, would it cut to the truth?

"Thank you for your candor, Sir Bentley. Be assured that you can count on our discretion," he replied. "We won't detain you any longer."

Once out on the street, the earl gave vent to his frustration with a muttered oath. "Hell's teeth, we're not a damnable step closer to finding the dastards." He hated feeling so lost. "Let us hope Lady Charlotte has had better luck with Annie Wright."

Though that was a two-edged sword, as she would insist on following any lead. Which would likely put her in danger.

"Come, we had better return to my townhouse and see if the Weasels have brought any message," Wrexford added.

"You go on," said Sheffield. "I have a few things I wish to do first. I'll meet up with you later."

Silk rustled against silk as Charlotte shifted against the sofa pillows. And then shifted again. She put down her teacup and fluffed her skirts, then rose and moved to the bowfront window overlooking the street.

"Do stop skittering around like a cat on a hot griddle," counseled Alison. "I'm sure Wrexford will come as soon as he gets your note."

Charlotte knew her impatience was irrational. The ship had sailed. And even if it hadn't, they would never have been permitted to board an East India Company vessel and interrogate its passengers.

"Sorry." She flicked at the draperies. "I was naïve to think Annie Wright would trust me. If only—"

"If only there were winged unicorns, we could fly to the heavens and take tea with the Man in the Moon," drawled the dowager. "If only I were forty years younger, I would . . ." A pause. "Oh, pish. I would likely do not a thing differently."

Charlotte laughed in spite of her jangling nerves. "Do you think the Man in the Moon prefers Bohea or Hyson tea?"

"Being the ruler of his realm, I daresay he would choose Imperial," replied Alison.

"While I," cut in a voice from the doorway, "would welcome a wee dram of good Scottish malt, if given my druthers." Wrexford moved past the dowager's butler before the fellow had a chance to announce him. He favored Alison with a smile, but Charlotte knew him well enough to read the underlying tension in his face.

"What's wrong?" she asked, quelling her own impatience to tell him what she had just discovered.

"Alas, the lead on Alston led nowhere." He explained about his meeting with the baronet.

She heard the frustration in his voice—a mirror of her own—though he sought to temper it as he finished with a wry observation. "Kit is acquiring a knack for sleuthing. He asked some astute questions, though they came to naught."

"There's a bottle of malt on the sideboard," said Alison. "As well as an excellent French brandy—from before the Revolution, I might add, so it's not smuggled goods."

"Thank you," replied Wrexford. "Much as it's tempting, I prefer to keep a clear head." He looked to Charlotte. "Dare I hope you've learned something?"

"Yes," warned Charlotte. "But it only adds more urgency to the mystery we're trying to unravel."

"Sit," ordered Alison.

Wrexford perched a hip on the arm of the facing chair. "Go on."

"As you suspected, Annie Wright scarpered . . ." Charlotte recounted her conversation with Squid and the cryptic message the barmaid had left with Alice the Eel Girl.

"But that's not the worst of it," she added, seeing his mouth tighten to a grim line. "Raven and Hawk accompanied me to the docklands and made the rounds of their friends to gather the latest scuttlebutt while I met with Alice. While they were talking with Strings, the boy who picks apart old rope to make oakum for caulking, two gentlemen passed close by on their way to an East India merchant ship about to depart."

Alison edged forward expectantly, having not yet heard this part of the story.

"They paused behind a stack of crates, and the boys overheard their conversation," continued Charlotte. "The older of the two was adamant that his companion had to leave the country immediately for his own safety."

Wrexford looked about to speak.

"And yes," she went on quickly, "the boys caught a name. The man being ordered to sail on the ship was Mather. As you know, they have sharp ears and sharp memories and recalled it from our councils of war." Her voice tightened. "And the two gentlemen were then joined by a woman who fits Annie's description, and she accompanied Mather onto the ship. It seems she was in league with the dastards, after all, and betrayed her old friend."

Charlotte paused for just an instant. "Clearly, the conspirators are aware that their activities have come under scrutiny. Which will make the ringleaders even more difficult to discover."

"Damnation." However, the earl didn't waste time in recriminations. "What about the other man's name?" he demanded.

"Unfortunately, Mather didn't say it," she answered. "But the boys did get a description of both gentlemen." Charlotte quickly described the one called Mather, and the earl nodded a confirmation that it fit the banker.

"As for the other gentleman," she went on, "he was older, with dark hair silvering at the temples and combed à la Brutus. Medium height, average build, and dressed in expensive clothing, fashioned by Weston or Stutz, guessed Hawk." The boy had developed a frightfully discerning eye for detail. "Though the muted shades of navy and charcoal grey offer no distinctive clue that either tailor might use to identify the man."

Charlotte shifted her stance. "He did, however, have one unusual item—a walking stick covered with an exotic-looking black leather. Hawk got close enough to see the pattern—you know how interested he is in the natural world—and identified it as snakeskin. And he saw that the knob was carved from a dark reddish translucent stone, which he thinks might be carnelian."

Wrexford was suddenly on his feet.

"Does that help?" asked Charlotte.

"I shall have a better idea later this evening," he answered. Their eyes met.

"After I have a private word with Lord Copley."

# CHAPTER 22

Twilight was fading to darkness by the time Wrexford returned to his townhouse. He had spent the afternoon making inquiries, including confirming with the head porter at White's that the admiral's regular backgammon partner was still ill.

Copley would likely serve again as a surrogate, he thought, a smile touching his lips, as he crossed the black-and-white checked tiles of the entrance foyer. The board game was considered by many to be a metaphor for war, but the real battle would begin in earnest once the dice and the counters were put away.

Laughter—along with a series of deep-throated rumbles—interrupted his thoughts as he approached his workroom. It seemed his sacrosanct study space had become . . . a playground.

"What the devil is going on in here?"

"Harper was getting bored," said Raven, looking up from playing tug-of-war with the hound over a disgusting-looking bone.

"And lonely," chirped Hawk, who was sprawled atop

Harper's shaggy iron-grey flank. "So we decided to come over early, before Lady Cordelia arrives, to keep him company."

Wrexford made a pained face at Tyler. "What were you thinking to bring along that big hairy beast to the city?"

Harper let go of the bone and pricked up his ears.

"The Weasels suggested that he would make an excellent guard for the professor," replied the valet. " Any intruder will think twice before challenging those fearsome teeth."

To Raven's and Hawk's chortling delight, the hound responded with a monstrous yawn.

"It would serve you right if he bites *you*," growled the earl.

Tyler smirked. "He won't. He's Scottish." A pause. "As you're a Sassenach, it's far more likely that he'll snap at you."

"He had better not bite the hand that feeds him," warned the earl, "or he'll find himself exiled to the Outer Hebrides."

Harper, his pink tongue lolling out of his massive jaws, rolled onto his back and let out a whuffle of contentment as Hawk scratched his belly.

"Lud, just look at you." Wrexford shook his head in censure. "You heard Tyler. You're supposed to be a fierce guard dog, ready to tear an intruder limb from limb."

The hound flopped onto his side and bared his teeth in a canine smile.

"You're an embarrassment to your wolfly ancestors," muttered the earl, though the corners of his mouth twitched upward.

"*Woof.*"

More laughter.

"Out, you little beasts," ordered the earl. "And take Harper with you."

"May we take him for a run in Hyde Park?" asked Raven.

"Absolutely not. Two lads running wild with a large animal might attract undue attention, even at this hour. He gets his exercise with me on my morning ride. I'm known to be eccentric, so nobody questions it."

Seeing the two crestfallen faces, Wrexford added, "You'll have ample opportunity to take him on runs when we return him to the country."

"We're invited for another visit?" asked Hawk.

"Yes, but it's up to Lady Charlotte and Lady Peake," the earl replied. "So I suggest you follow orders. I would hate to have to say a bad word about your behavior."

They scampered for the door, Raven turning to let out a low whistle. Harper rose and padded off after them.

"Don't scowl at me," said Tyler as he picked up the bone and placed it in one of the workroom waste pails. "You said yourself we're up against a very dangerous enemy. The hound is an extra measure of protection."

"Enough jesting." Waving off the offer of a drink, Wrexford sat down at his desk. "I need you to make some inquiries about Lord Elgin Copley."

"For what am I looking?"

"Whether his saintly appearance masks some very dark sins," replied the earl.

The valet went very still. He was no longer smiling. "You think the corruption runs that high? Copley is the most powerful and respected member of the board of directors."

"It's quite possible." The earl passed on what Charlotte had told him, then explained, "I noticed that he carried just such a snakeskin walking stick when he came to play backgammon with his cousin at White's. He was a trifle late and hurried upstairs without passing over his coat and hat to the porters."

Silence.

Wrexford continued sorting through some papers, looking for some notes he had made on the case. But after several moments, he looked up. It wasn't like Tyler to refrain from comment.

"Are you troubled by this?"

"Yes," said Tyler without hesitation. "And if he's the one running the scheme, so should you be."

"I may be stubborn, but I like to think I'm not a fool. If you have concerns, I would like to hear them."

Normally quick with his wit and his tongue, the valet took his time in composing a reply. "When circumstances first forced you to take up sleuthing to solve a crime, you were the only person at risk if you failed."

"Lady Charlotte and the Weasels—"

"Yes, yes, they were soon entwined," said Tyler. "Then in the Ashton affair, Sheffield and McClellan were drawn into the heart of the mystery." Rain had just begun to fall, the first hesitant drops pattering softly against the windowpanes. "And now Lady Peake . . ."

Wrexford watched the dark silhouettes of ivy shudder in the swirling breeze. It was true. Being alone gave one the luxury of a devil-be-damned attitude toward life. "You think I should back away to keep them out of trouble?"

A measured exhale.

He waited, using the moment to marshal his own thoughts.

And then, thankfully, a very Tyler-like laugh. "I'm neither a bloody idiot nor a bloody hypocrite. Of course I don't expect you to slink away when you know something is wrong. I just want to remind you to exercise caution in confronting Copley."

The valet moved to the hearth and warmed his hands over the fire. "Unlike our previous opponents, the East India Company has both the resources and the power to crush anyone who stands in the way of their plans."

Wrexford nodded. "I'm very aware of that. I've spent the afternoon speaking with friends who are more intimately acquainted with the workings of the Company than I am. The recent Charter Act has created factions within the board of directors, so the more I think about it, the more I'm convinced that the Argentum scheme is not some secret official endeavor of the East India Company, but rather a purely private financial manipulation."

"Even so, the men involved are powerful and possess the means to eliminate any threat to their objectives."

"Which is all the more reason to knock those who seek to abuse such responsibilities on their arse," responded the earl. "Yes, in the past, I might have recognized wrongdoing but have felt cynical enough to dismiss it as the way of the world. But friendships change one's perspective."

In ways that defied mere words.

"It matters deeply to fight wrongdoing. Not just for friends, but also for those who can't fight for themselves." Charlotte, he knew, had always understood that. It was, he realized, one of the things he loved best about her.

Tyler struggled to smother a smile. "It seems the cynic may be turning into a sentimentalist."

"Don't hold your breath waiting," retorted Wrexford.

"Quite right. I'll need it for trudging through the rain and muck to dig up whatever dirt I can find on Copley." The valet fetched his hat and coat from the corner of the room. "Still, let us both tread carefully, so we don't end up falling down some deep and dark chasm . . ."

Tyler's words were still echoing in his ears as the earl entered White's an hour later and made his way upstairs to wait in the parlor adjoining the game room. He flipped open his pocket watch and watched the hands slowly move to mark the hour.

*Tread carefully.* Wrexford had been mulling over the admonition on his walk to the club. It was good advice, given the situation. But sometimes a bold step was necessary to force an enemy into making a fatal mistake. . . .

The scrape of chairs sounded from next door as Sir Charles, true to his military precision, announced that time was up and they would continue the game at the next session. Wrexford moved into the corridor and contrived to pass by just as the admiral and his cousin were quitting the room.

"Ah, Copley." He stopped and turned. "Actually, might I have a quick word with you?"

The admiral gave a curt wave. "Don't rush on my account. I'm toddling home to finish a section of my writing that simply must get done."

The earl gestured to the empty parlor. "In that case, shall I have a porter bring up a bottle of port so we can enjoy an unrushed interlude of quiet conversation?"

"By all means," answered Copley with a gracious nod. "A tête-à-tête with a man of your wide-ranging interests is always a thought-provoking way to pass the evening."

A gust tugged at Charlotte's hat, sending another drizzle of windblown rain snaking down her spine. Hunching deeper into the collar of her coat, she darted through the unlocked gate in the garden wall and hurried to the scullery door. Too unsettled to sit still in her workroom, she had abandoned her sketching and decided to pay a visit to the earl's townhouse.

At this hour, Cordelia and the professor would be hard at work running their calculations, and the boys had left their aerie earlier in order to watch. Raven was especially fascinated by the Computing Engine. And while she acknowledged that the mechanical complexities were a technical wonder, it was the flesh-and-blood warmth of friends that Charlotte sought, rather than the solitude of waiting alone to hear from Wrexford about the confrontation.

The earl's implication that Copley might be the mastermind of Argentum had chilled her to the marrow. She had no illusions on how often the better angels of human nature were seduced into falling from grace. Still, she hadn't wanted to believe that the evildoing could emanate from the East India Company's directors. The power, the privileges, the money they received legitimately should be enough to satisfy anyone.

"Why?" she whispered, making her way through the damp gloom of the darkened scullery, even though she had long ago learned the answer. For some people, lust—for money, for power, for control—was never satiated.

The thought stirred a pebbling of gooseflesh on her flesh. Another reminder of how dangerous an enemy they were facing.

As she slipped out into the corridor, a glimmer of light up ahead helped banish her brooding. The *clack-clack* of the machine grew louder as she entered the room. The professor was turning the hand crank, setting off a wink of gold sparks from the spinning gears and rotating brass rods. Cordelia was sitting beside him, working furiously with pencil and paper, while Raven watched the proceeding over her shoulder.

With all the noise, they didn't hear her come in. Harper, however, awoke from his slumber and woofed a friendly greeting. He no longer looked quite so intimidating. Perhaps that was because Hawk was curled up against the hound's middle, head pillowed on his shoulder.

The boy sat up and yawned. "Mathematics is boring," he confided as Charlotte crouched down to give him a hug.

"Not as boring or filthy as mouse skulls!" called his brother.

That didn't appear to be entirely true. Raven's shirtfront was smeared with oil and grease.

Charlotte held up a parcel. "I brought a batch of McClellan's ginger biscuits for refreshments."

Cordelia waggled her finger as she continued to write. "One moment . . ." The rods clack-clacked through another cycle and then came to rest. The professor read off a final sequence of numbers from a set of ivory wheels.

"Excellent." Cordelia then looked up. "I'm famished. Biscuits would be very welcome. Let's also order some tea and take a brief respite from work."

The boys helped her clear the piles of paper from a round table at the far end of the room, and they all took their seats as one of the kitchen maids carried in a massive tray with the steaming pot and a cold collation of meats, cheese, and bread to supplement the biscuits.

"I've a question, Professor," said Raven after noisily gobbling down several of the sweets.

"Yes?" replied Sudler.

"You've mentioned that your Computing Engine will be key in creating tables, but what are tables for?" replied Raven. "And why do you need a machine when you and Lady Cordelia do mathematics so easily in your head?"

A grin quivered on Cordelia's lips. "I trust you're ready for a rather long lecture."

Charlotte had been wondering much the same thing. "I, too, am interested in hearing the explanation."

In answer, Sudler rose and fetched a book from one of the worktables pushed up against the wall.

With everyone momentarily distracted, Hawk quietly filched a piece of ham from the platter and slid off his seat to join Harper.

Charlotte pretended not to notice.

Clearing his throat, the professor shifted the tray and slapped the book down on the center of the table, then opened it to display two facing pages.

"What do you see?" he asked.

"Numbers," murmured Charlotte dryly. "A lot of them."

"It's a *table*," corrected Cordelia. "And while most people haven't a clue as to the importance of mathematical tables—that is, logarithm tables—without them, a number of our fundamental institutions of society, like finance, insurance, and the military, couldn't function."

Raven took a closer look at the pages. "How so?"

"This book is compilation of tables made for banks. They are constantly lending money and must calculate the interest rates over various periods of time," explained Sudler. "A task made even more complicated when they have to compound the interest. To work out the numbers every time they make a loan would require countless hours of work. So standard tables have been created over the years. Say the interest rate is two percent a year, and a banker is making a loan for five years. Well, he can find the table for two percent . . ." The professor tapped a finger on the table displayed on the open pages. "Then scroll down to find the line showing five years and read off the correct amount of interest to charge his client."

"The military depends on tables for ballistics. Artillery officers use logarithm tables to calculate the variables for distance and trajectory, which allows them to hit their targets," added Cordelia. "The country couldn't finance itself without issuing government bonds. And all those complicated computations couldn't be done without logarithm tables."

"But . . ." Raven's face scrunched in thought. ""But if you already have them, why—"

"Ah! An excellent question, young man!" exclaimed Sudler. "It's because every printed table I've checked is riddled—*riddled*—with mistakes!"

"Human error," murmured Cordelia.

"Quite right!" The professor bounced in his chair, his voice growing more animated. "And the mistakes get compounded because the tables are calculated through polynomial functions that require several steps of precise calculation—"

"Polynomial functions?" interrupted Charlotte in bewilderment.

"What that means is that there are complicated formulas that require several steps to reach a final answer," explained Cordelia. "You do one calculation, then use the result to perform another calculation. When they are done by hand, there is a lot of room for error. Whereas a Computing Engine . . ." A smile. "The professor has been working on the concept for years. Together we've been striving to find a mechanical design that will be able to perform such complicated mathematics."

"And?" prompted Charlotte, fascinated in spite of herself.

"And this present model . . ." Sudler cast a fond look at the massive brass and steel contraption bathed in the glow of the bright lamps. "Is able to run simple calculations with absolute accuracy! Once I figure out a way to store the results of the first calculation, then shift them to a new set of rods and run the second set of calculations . . ." A look of transcendent joy came over his face. "Then I can envision creating a series of punch cards, like they use in Jacquard looms, to run a program by itself."

"That is theoretical, and years away from reality," said Cordelia softly. "If ever."

"Yes, but a man can dream!"

"Why, sir . . ." Raven sucked in his breath. "Such a machine could revolutionize the world."

"Indeed, indeed." The professor flashed a smile that mingled regret and hope. "I won't live to see it built. It will require young men like you to pick up the torch of knowledge and carry it forward."

A pensive silence settled over the table.

Raven turned to contemplate the Computing Engine. "You know," he mused after several moments, "it might be able to run even faster if a small steam engine were to power the hand crank."

"What a splendid idea! Come, let us have a look at how that might be done."

"Professor." Cordelia's voice held a note of gentle chiding. "Much as it's a good idea for the future, we need to complete our nightly calculations. I must deliver another sample table by the end of the week to the consortium."

Sudler's face darkened. "Knaves and scoundrels! Mark my

words! They mean to use the Engine's power for their own selfish plans, rather than use it to better the world for all."

"And we intend to stop them," countered Cordelia. "But for the time being, we must appear to be cooperating."

Grumbling under his breath, Sudler stalked over to the Engine. "Come help me set the numbered wheels for the next calculations, lad."

Charlotte began to gather the empty teacups and return them to the tray. Cordelia lingered to help.

"Have you figured out why the consortium wants the sample mathematical tables they've demanded from you?" Charlotte asked.

"No," answered her friend. A hesitation. "That is, I have an idea, but I wish to consult with a friend before coming to any conclusions."

Charlotte was about to respond when the sound of approaching footsteps drew a low *woof* from Harper.

Her heart leapt into her throat. Was it the earl coming with some new information that might bring them closer to unmasking the enemy? After dropping the cups with a clatter, she turned to the door.

"Where's Wrexford?" demanded Sheffield after a quick look around.

"He left several hours ago," volunteered Hawk. "And hasn't returned."

"And Tyler?"

"He's out, as well," called Raven. "We don't know where."

"What is it?" asked Charlotte, trying to read Sheffield's face through the pearls of rain dripping from his hat brim. "Is something wrong?"

"I'm not sure," he answered. "But I took it upon myself to do a little sleuthing earlier today and have discovered something that just isn't adding up right."

# CHAPTER 23

The cork slid out of the bottle with a silky sigh, releasing a tantalizing sweetness, which quickly perfumed the air.

Copley gave an appreciative sniff. "You know your wine, sir."

"I make it my business to know as much as I can about the subjects which interest me." Wrexford poured two glasses of the garnet-dark port and passed one to the baron. "You'll find this one quite different from the one we shared the other evening."

"But no less enjoyable, I'm sure."

"Let us see how it reacts," said the earl slowly, "once its secrets are exposed to light and air."

The baron raised a brow in response but said nothing. Lifting his glass up to the branch of candles, he set the wine to swirling in a slow vortex. Glints of red flickered against the cream-colored plaster wall.

Wrexford took a small sip. He preferred the sharp heat of whisky to the syrupy seductiveness of port. The sticky richness was like a spider's web, wrapping round and round one's tongue.

"You seem in a philosophical mood," observed Copley after several moments of silence had slipped by.

"Does philosophy interest you, Copley?"

"I'm afraid not." The baron drank deeply before adding, "I'm a man who thrives on practical challenges. I like analyzing a problem and figuring out how to fix it."

"Indeed?" The earl toyed with his own glass. "Then perhaps you wouldn't mind advising me on a rather delicate matter."

"Considering your generosity in serving such superb spirits, I would be happy to offer any help I can." The candle flames caught the genial curl of Copley's lips. "What is the problem?"

"It's a complicated matter." Wrexford shifted in his chair and refilled the baron's glass. "Bear with me while I sketch out the crux of the conundrum. A friend—you may know him, Lord Woodbridge—has found himself caught up in a nasty coil. It seems an acquaintance he trusted took advantage of his integrity and honesty to humbug him. A trading venture was presented to him under false pretenses . . ."

Copley maintained a polite smile, but his flesh paled as the earl explained about the bank loans and the unscrupulous documents.

"If I might offer a comment," said the baron as Wrexford paused to pour more wine. "I'm acquainted with Lord Woodbridge, and much as I dislike speaking ill of a gentleman, he's known for being an unstable young man, and rumor has it that his profligate father, a man of shabby character, left the family in desperate financial straits. So I counsel you to take his story with a healthy grain of salt. It sounds like a complete hum to me." A pause. "There is an old adage, 'Like father, like son.'"

"On the contrary," said Wrexford. "Woodbridge has the reputation of being a very sober, steady fellow. His only fault seems to be that his own unflinching sense of honor blinded him to the possibility that other so-called gentlemen might not have the same scruples."

Copley smoothed a hand over the folds of his faultlessly tied cravat, a glint of gold flashing from his signet ring. He was no longer looking so amiable.

"As if such deviousness and deceit weren't enough," continued the earl, "the conspirators also forced Woodbridge's sister into playing a part in their scheme, in order for him to earn back the documents and his original investment—"

A harsh laugh cut off his words. "Good God, Wrexford. Have you taken temporary leave of your senses? What possible role would a lady play in this . . . this fairie-tale business you've been describing?"

"Lady Cordelia Mansfield is a brilliant mathematician. And she's been working with a professor from Cambridge on a revolutionary Computing Engine."

A sputter as the baron nearly choked on a swallow of port.

"Using this new technology, the two of them have designed a system for doing arbitrage. As a man intimately involved in commerce, I'm assuming you're familiar with the term."

"I can't fathom how a man of your intelligence is giving credence to outrageous lies," exclaimed Copley. "The lady is an odd, unstable spinster. Clearly, her eccentricities have descended into mental instability." He drew in a shaky breath. "Women are by nature flighty and prone to delusional fantasies. I pity the poor lady, but that's a far cry from believing such noxious farididdles. I'm shocked beyond words that you would be so gullible, sir."

Wrexford fixed him with an unblinking stare. The baron held steady for a moment, then averted his eyes.

"Believe what you wish, Wrexford, but I can't help you. Indeed, I find myself unable to listen any further to such madness."

"I haven't finished," said the earl as Copley started to rise. "I suggest you sit down and hear the rest of what I have to say."

A telltale quiver of flesh at the baron's temples betrayed the quickening of his pulse. He was nervous.

Wrexford waited.

A faint hiss, like the air leaking out of a balloon . . . Copley sank back into his chair.

"It's all very well to dismiss what I've said as a flight of fancy," the earl went on. "But how does that explain the fact that David Mather, the banker in question, was seen boarding an East India Company merchant ship this morning? He was accompanied by a gentleman carrying a distinctive walking stick."

The baron was now white as a ghost.

"A silly mistake," murmured the earl. "But I imagine hubris eventually convinces a criminal that he's too clever to ever get caught." He leaned back in his chair and folded his arms across his chest. "Be that as it may, it occurred to me that you, as a director of the Company, have a vested interested in ensuring that your august institution is above reproach. So, I'm wondering whether you have any thoughts on how such corruption could have taken root within the many legitimate businesses you run. And more importantly, how it can be cut away before it does irreparable damage."

Copley reached for his wine with a tremoring hand and raised it to wet his lips. "Let me answer your tale of conjectures with one of my own."

He put the glass down. "Here is how I imagine such a thing could have happened. A young and able administrator is asked to bend the rules for someone he felt obliged to help, only to find that the fellow had deliberately kept proof of the indiscretion, and used it to force him to continue aiding an illicit scheme for several years. The blackmail then stopped, and over the years, the administrator earned a reputation for skill, savvy, and integrity. He rises in position, the company thrives, and he takes pride in all that he has accomplished."

Wrexford tapped his fingertips together. "And then?"

"And then the blackmailer returns, forcing the administrator to make a decision. He can lose everything because of a mistake in the distant past. Or he can continue his good work . . ."

"All he has to do is sell his soul to the devil," interjected the earl.

"It's not quite so black and white, Wrexford. A bit of embezzlement balanced against all the innovations that contribute to the country's economic strength? The Company doesn't miss the money, and the administrator is now a wealthy man who doesn't need the money. He uses his share of the illicit profits to support socially progressive programs. He gives to orphans and war widows." Copley paused for breath. "What real harm is it doing?"

"What harm?" Wrexford felt a spurt of fury rise in his gorge. "What about the smuggled opium, which destroys countless lives?"

"China has a very different attitude toward life than we Westerners," responded the baron. "They don't value—"

"And what about Henry Peabody? Does he, too, count for nothing?"

A tiny muscle jumped in Copley's jaw.

"I think Mr. Peabody deserves that justice be done," said the earl. "The question is how to rip out this evil from the East India Company."

"As to that . . ." The baron twisted at his ring. "I have a suggestion."

"I'm listening."

"Let us assume the administrator is willing to help identify the culprits who are guilty of putting the venture into motion, in return for having his name not dragged through the mud. Wouldn't justice be served?"

The earl said nothing.

"My guess is," said Copley in a rush, "the administrator abhors violence and never condoned murder. The other men went too far."

"So you're saying the administrator claims that his hands aren't dirty, because he left it to his partners to slit Henry Peabody's throat?" The sarcasm in Wrexford's voice made the baron flinch. "Ah yes. 'It wasn't my fault'—the refuge of sanctimonious cowards throughout the ages. And yet he still took the money. So don't you dare try to tell me he's a victim in this." A pause. "If you are asking that he escape with no punishment whatsoever, the answer is no."

Copley straightened and somehow regained his composure. "Business, as well as life, is all about compromises, Wrexford. You've told a riveting story, but where are the facts to back it up? You think the authorities will take the word of Woodbridge? As for his sister, a lady's testimony would be dismissed as unreliable, even if she weren't an eccentric Bluestocking. If I were you, I'd make a deal."

"Unlike your saintly administrator, I don't do deals with the devil and his minions."

"Then you'll never catch the Satan you're after," replied Copley. "He and his cohorts will ruin your friends and quite likely hurt other people in the process."

Wrexford flattened his palms on the table and leaned in closer to the candlelight. "I'm a bit of a devil myself. Bet against me in a match with your Satan and, trust me, you'll regret it."

He rose and kicked back his chair. "Think on what I've said and pass on my offer to the administrator. Assuming, of course, that you know who he is. If he decides to cooperate, he can come to me anytime. What I will promise is that I'll inform Bow Street that he's been instrumental in helping to catch the culprits. That will likely soften his punishment—but he will be punished."

Wrexford took two quick steps and stopped abruptly, his fluttering coat brushing up against the baron's thigh. "One last thing . . ." Would a bluff work? He decided there was no harm in trying. "If you think I have no proof of the misdeeds, you may wish to think again."

A whoosh of wool stirred the air as the earl turned for the door without waiting for a reply. Still, he caught Copley's parting whisper.

"Threaten all you wish, Wrexford. But I'm telling you— you're not quite as clever as you think, for you're hounding the wrong man."

Taking the stairs two at a time, the earl hurried down to the main corridor and quit the club. A fine mist was falling, and skeins of silvery fog were flitting through the light and shadows of St. James's Street. It wasn't until he had crossed Piccadilly Street that he slowed his pace. The cobbles were slippery beneath his boots, making the footing a bit treacherous.

It was quiet, the darkness muffling the sounds of the city, as he walked deeper into the gloom. So quiet that the voice of his own misgivings was thrumming in his ears. Skidding to a sudden stop beneath the entrance portico of a slumbering townhouse, Wrexford blew out his breath and watched the vapor dissolve into nothingness.

Frustration welled up in his throat. He fisted his hand, then hit the marble column. Again, and again, willing the pain to overpower his uncertainty.

"Damn. I was so bloody sure I was right about him being the dastard behind all this." Was Copley lying about his culpability? Something in the baron's eyes had told him no. But now . . .

But now he couldn't help but wonder whether he had, in fact, been barking up the wrong tree.

# CHAPTER 24

Spotting the tray of food, Sheffield helped himself to a slab of bread and topped it with ham and cheese. "Sleuthing works up a devil of an appetite," he said through a mouthful of cheddar.

Cordelia watched him with ill-concealed impatience. "Ye heavens, sir. The hound has better table manners than you do."

"May Harper have another slice of ham?" asked Hawk, choosing his moment well.

"Sheffield . . . ," murmured Charlotte, knowing Cordelia was on edge and not wanting his penchant for drawing out a dramatic moment to spark a quarrel between them.

"Yes, yes." He wolfed down the last bite of his bread. "I couldn't help but be curious about a few small details mentioned by Sir Bentley at this morning's meeting. So, I decided to do a little digging." A glance at Charlotte. "I've learned from you that a seemingly insignificant thing can be the key to unlocking a conundrum."

"And?" snapped Cordelia.

"And I'll have you know it's cursedly unpleasant to sit for hours reading through old newspapers," he replied. "Not to speak of dealing with John Debrett, the very prickly and officious editor of *Debrett's Correct Peerage of England, Scotland, and Ireland.*"

The Computing Engine's gears began to whirr, stirring a symphony of low-pitched metallic clicks.

"Nonetheless, the ordeal proved enlightening," he went on. "I checked through every edition of the *Weekly Aristocrat* from the relevant time—as you know, they are sticklers for reporting the births and deaths of the ton—and there's no mention of Fenwick Alston's demise. Nor does *Debrett's* have any record of it."

Charlotte took a moment to consider the news. "Wrexford mentioned that Sir Bentley wished to bury the whole sordid affair. It's understandable that he might have wished for his brother to be forgotten. After all, he hadn't been in England for years, and as the youngest son, there are no inheritance issues."

"But *Debrett's* is the bible of the aristocracy," countered Sheffield. "It's simply not done to omit informing them of a death."

"That's true," mused Cordelia.

"Still, I wouldn't be so sure that their information is accurate," argued Charlotte. "We were just speaking earlier of human error. Even those who possess an expertise in a subject are prone to making mistakes."

Sheffield smiled. "Which is why I spent the evening making inquiries in several gaming hells that cater to rascals and rogues, in order to follow up on my suspicions. A few of the regular patrons are fellows who've spent time recently in the West Indies."

He shifted and flicked another morsel of ham to Harper, who caught it with one quick snap of his jaws. "As you know, Jamaica is a field in which the black sheep of the beau monde are wont to graze. And from what I've uncovered, Fenwick Alston is as black as they come. His family took pains to hush it up, but he left Oxford on account of cheating at cards and then thrashing his accuser to within an inch of his life."

*A thoroughly dirty dish*, thought Charlotte. *And yet . . .*

"Be that as it may, according to my friends," continued Sheffield, "Fenwick Alston didn't perish in a quarrel with his business associates. On the contrary, they say he's far too clever and ruthless to have given up the ghost that way, and if anyone had been killed, it would have been the others. Word is, he absconded to Martinique with French smugglers to avoid arrest."

*Rumors and conjectures*, Charlotte reminded herself. "Even if Fenwick Alston is alive," she pointed out, "there's nothing to connect him to our current conundrum save for the fact that he was in India."

*And our own wishful thinking.*

"Lady Charlotte is right," said Cordelia. "Without evidence, we're just spitting into the wind."

"Yes, I'm aware of that, which is why I didn't come straight here after leaving the gaming hells. As luck would have it, I was able to track down an old friend. Whenever he's in Town, which isn't often, I might add, he always stays at the Sun and Sextant Club."

Cordelia appeared about to interrupt, but he continued on in a rush. "According to Sir Darius Roy, Fenwick Alston was involved in opium smuggling while based in Calcutta."

"That still doesn't prove—" began Cordelia.

"*And*," announced Sheffield, "he happens to know that Alston is currently here in London."

Wrexford halted in the doorway. Despite his marrow-deep worries, the sight of his friends warmed some of the dread from his bones.

*Perhaps Tyler is right and I'm becoming a sentimental fool in my old age.*

In the past, the thought would have horrified him. He shifted, bracing his shoulder against the molding, and took a moment to observe the scene. What with the clatter of the Engine and the apparently fraught gathering around the refreshment table, his presence was still unremarked.

*And now?* A smile crept, unbidden, to his lips as he watched the conversation.

Charlotte moved back a step as Sheffield and Cordelia began a more animated exchange. Limned in the glow of the Argand lamps, her profile—all the familiar little shapes and angles of her face—looked even more lovely in contrast to her ragged urchin's garb.

He must have moved, for she turned her head. . . .

And the spark that came alight in her eyes lifted the worst of the darkness from his spirits.

"Wrexford!"

Everyone turned. Harper looked up guiltily, still chewing on another piece of ham that Hawk had filched while no one was paying attention.

"Thank goodness you're here," continued Charlotte. "Sheffield has made an important discovery."

"As have I." The earl came into the room and shrugged off his sodden coat. After eyeing the teapot for an instant, he blew out his cheeks. "But the information might go down a bit easier if accompanied by a swallow of whisky."

"I'll go fetch the bottle, sir," offered Hawk, shooting to his feet.

"Thank you," replied Wrexford. To Harper, he added, "You! Stay where you are. It's bad enough that you're getting fat. I'd rather not have you get foxed, as well."

The hound responded with an aggrieved whuffle.

"Sit," ordered Charlotte as she fixed the earl a slice of bread topped with cheddar and the last morsel of meat. "You look dead on your feet. Eat, while Sheffield tells you what he's un-covered."

"It was exceedingly clever of him," said Cordelia. "It showed both imagination and initiative to see the trail of clues and follow them."

Sheffield's face altered . . . though Wrexford found his ex-pression impossible to read.

"Now get on with it, Mr. Sheffield," chided Cordelia. "Don't keep His Lordship in suspense."

As Wrexford wolfed down his food, Sheffield explained about his hunch concerning Fenwick Alston and his peregrina-tions in following up on it.

"Sir Darius Roy?" the earl interrupted when their friend came to that part of the story. "Why does that name ring a bell?"

"We knew him at Oxford. A very interesting fellow and, like you, curious about a great many subjects. He left his studies early to accompany a diplomatic mission to the Far East. Since then, he's made quite a name for himself as an intrepid adven-turer and explorer," replied Sheffield. "Less well known is the fact that he works with the Foreign Office in dealing with sen-sitive diplomatic matters in exotic parts of the world." A pause. "It turns out he has excellent connections with both India and China."

Before he could go on, a call from the professor rose up from behind the Computing Engine. "Lady Cordelia! Come, we're ready to run the calculations!"

"Drat." Cordelia made a face. "We must get the numbers done tonight, so I had better go help him."

"I'm sure Sheffield will be happy to give you a full report once you're done," said Charlotte.

His quick nod confirmed the offer.

As Cordelia moved away to join Sudler and Raven amid the

clack-clacking of the moving rods and gears, Hawk returned with the whisky, and Wrexford poured three healthy measures into the empty cups.

Charlotte accepted the spirits without protest. She, too, looked tired and tense. Wrexford felt a frisson of guilt. His own actions may have added to their troubles.

After warming his innards with a quick swallow of the amber-hued malt, the earl signaled for Sheffield to resume his report.

"As I was saying, Sir Darius has spent time in India and China and has forged a network of friendships outside the expatriate communities in those countries. I asked him a few discreet questions about China's unhappiness with the illegal opium flowing into the country," explained Sheffield. "It turns out he knows of Fenwick Alston and confided to me that the fellow was involved in opium smuggling while working for the East India Company in Calcutta."

"That seems to prove he's part of Argentum," said Charlotte. "It's difficult to believe that there are two separate illegal enterprises."

Wrexford nodded thoughtfully. "I wonder what other details Sir Darius might know about the venture."

"The same thought occurred to me," answered Sheffield. "Which is why you're invited to meet with him at the Sun and Sextant Club tomorrow at noon."

"Well done, Sheffield." Charlotte's smile softened the lines of worry etched around her mouth.

The praise made him blush. "Am I getting a little better at sleuthing?"

"Much," she replied. "Indeed, it may lead us—"

"Before you go on," interrupted Wrexford, "you had better hear about my evening. I, too, had a private meeting that elicited some surprising revelations."

"Did Copley have information that can help us?" asked Charlotte. "Did he know the identity of the gentleman with the snakeskin walking stick?"

He averted his eyes, her look of hope making him feel even more wretched. "Yes and no."

"What kind of answer is that?" responded Sheffield.

"A damnably complicated one," answered the earl. Unwilling to add cowardice to his earlier missteps, he forced himself to meet Charlotte's gaze. "I recognized your description of the stick. It belongs to Copley, and it appears that the baron is not quite the shining light that Society thinks he is. There's a dark side to his business talents and his benevolent generosity . . ."

Wrexford quickly recounted the meeting, stripping it down to the bare bones of the dilemma. "I took a calculated risk, assuming I was right in my conclusion before having proved it. Which, of course, broke the cardinal rule of scientific inquiry." He spun his cup between his palms. "Forgive me for being such a bloody fool. I fear I've put all of us in danger."

"There's a good chance he's lying," pointed out Sheffield.

"He's certainly mastered the art of deception." Wrexford thought back on the conversation and the subtle flickers in Copley's eyes. "But I don't think so. And if he's just another fly caught in this malicious web . . ." He paused for breath.

Sheffield's expression turned uncertain.

As for Charlotte, she was staring down at her hands, her lowered lashes making it impossible to read her thoughts.

"Then the master spider who's weaving it now has the advantage over us," Wrexford finished. "We have to assume Copley will warn him."

Harper shifted in his sleep, a growl rumbling deep in his throat.

"On the contrary." Charlotte lifted her chin, steel flashing in her gaze. "We've seen in the past that poking a stick at predators can force them to improvise. And that's when mistakes can happen. I say we continue the offensive."

Wrexford guessed what she meant. "I don't like it."

"I don't imagine you do," she countered. "But if A. J. Quill stirs some questions about the East India Company's business practices, that will breathe added fire on the dastards."

"Making them determined that it's A. J. Quill who gets burned to a crisp."

"I know how to take care of myself."

He bit back a retort. An argument would only flare into a war of words, and that might only goad her into doing something even more damnably brave. As he wrestled with how to reply, Charlotte rose and found paper and pencil among Cordelia's notebooks.

*Bloody hell.* One of her infernal lists was in the making. Wrexford wasn't sure whether to laugh or howl at the heavens.

"We need to be clear about our objectives," said Charlotte. "It seems to me we have two of them. First of all, we must save Lord Woodbridge from ruin. And secondly, we must see that the men who created Argentum are unmasked and punished for their misdeeds."

"Is that all?" asked the earl. "While we're at it, shall we also find a way to defeat Napoleon and end the war ravaging half the world?"

Charlotte resumed her seat at the table. "Sarcasm isn't constructive, sir."

"Neither is flinging a flaming arrow into the devil's eye."

Her brow furrowed. And then she began to laugh. "Oh, Wrexford, I shall keep that image in mind for one of my drawings when we're ready to deliver the coup de grâce."

He couldn't help surrendering a smile. "You're incorrigible."

"That little fact should have long ago ceased to surprise you."

That Charlotte was a source of endless surprises spurred a wry chuckle. "Though I'll likely regret asking, I'm assuming you have a plan."

She squared the paper and tapped the pencil in a slow, steady rhythm against the tip of her chin. An unconscious habit, no doubt, to summon inspiration.

*Tap, tap.*

"If that's some arcane pagan ritual for summoning divine intervention," he said softly, "I devoutly hope that blood sacrifices aren't required."

"I'm glad to see you haven't lost your sense of humor," she replied. *Tap, tap.* "I'm thinking . . ." *Tap, tap.*

The sound struck him as a distinctly human echo of the steel-and-brass brain churning away on the other side of the room. *Man versus machine.* As someone dedicated to the pursuit of knowledge, he couldn't help but applaud the momentous advances that curious minds like his own were making. But he wasn't blind to the pitfalls of Progress, and its potential for bringing out the worst as well as the best in mankind. *Good versus Evil.* Those two opposing forces seemed to be woven into the very flesh and blood of humanity.

*Forcing us to fight a never-ending war between the light and dark sides of our nature.*

It made Charlotte and her courage seem even more extraordinary.

After another moment, she paused and cocked an ear. The Computing Engine was slowing, the noise dying away to a series of clicks and chirps. "Lady Cordelia, if you and the professor have finished your work, it would be best if you both join in our council of war. There is, as you've shown, strength in numbers."

"Nothing would give me greater pleasure than to kick those dastards in the . . ." Cordelia paused, realizing that Raven was right beside her. "In a spot that will hurt like hell."

"Aim for the bollocks," counseled the boy. "A man drops like a sack of stones when you hit his privies."

Sheffield gave an involuntary wince.

"I shall keep that tidbit in mind, should the occasion arise," replied Cordelia. "Come, Professor," she added on hearing a loud thump from behind the Engine. "Lady Charlotte is summoning us to plan a strategy to beat the devils at their own game."

Sudler extracted himself from the machinery and made his way to the table, blinking owlishly. As he took a seat, Cordelia plucked the grease-smeared spectacles from his nose, cleaned them with a napkin, and returned them to their perch.

"By Jove." More blinks. "The dratted dog has eaten all the ham."

"There's more in the kitchen. Shall I go get it?" volunteered Hawk.

"Please do," answered Wrexford. "But if I see one more sliver of it going down Harper's gullet, you'll both be banished to the mews."

Charlotte's tapping had ceased. "Let us turn our thoughts from filling our stomachs to something even more elementally important—ensuring that the high and mighty don't gorge themselves on greed because no one will hold them accountable for their misdeeds."

Sheffield shifted his chair and in a hushed murmur quickly explained to Cordelia and Sudler what they had missed.

The professor adjusted his spectacles. "I don't see how we, a small band of individuals, can bring them to justice. Lady Cordelia is of the opinion that she and I might be able to buy her brother's release from their clutches. But to be honest, I fear that is wishful thinking."

"It won't be easy," replied Charlotte. "But it can be done."

Wrexford was aware of all eyes turning to him. "I concur," he said without hesitation.

For the look of gratitude that flickered beneath her lashes, he would have gladly agreed to journey to hell and back.

"It will require boldness and courage," he continued, "but we have that in spades."

"Thank you, Wrexford." Pencil poised above the paper, Charlotte pursed her lips. "Let's first address freeing Woodbridge from Argentum's control. To do that we need two things—the money to repay the loans and the official documents that he signed making him the sole owner of Argentum Trading Company."

A cough from Sudler. "That's only making me feel even more pessimistic."

"It shouldn't," remarked Sheffield. "I have a feeling that Lady Charlotte has a plan, and in my experience, that bodes ill for any miscreant."

"I do," Charlotte said. "As Wrexford is fond of saying, one merely needs to apply logic to a problem, and it usually becomes simpler. To wit, let's take the money. All the arbitrage trading Lady Cordelia and the professor are running for Argentum is generating a constant source of it. And my guess is that it's being deposited into a bank account somewhere, until it's time to purchase a bill of exchange to sail with a corrupt ship captain for the next round of buying opium in India."

"A bank account set up for Argentum Trading Company in order to have Woodbridge take the blame if anything goes awry," mused Sheffield.

"Our thinking aligns, Lady Charlotte," said Wrexford. "I've already begun making inquiries into which of the smaller private banks cater to a less than scrupulous clientele."

"And I plan to meet with Jeremy in the morning, sir. He'll likely have some ideas, as well," Charlotte replied. To Cordelia and Sudler, she explained, "Lord Sterling is an old friend, and his recent involvement in expansion plans for Mrs. Ashton's mills has given him experience in financing commercial enterprises."

"Excellent, excellent," said Sudler.

The earl wasn't sure whether the professor was referring to banking matters or Hawk's arrival with a platter of freshly sliced ham and a loaf of crusty bread.

Cordelia, however, appeared less certain. "Even if we do discover where the dastards are stashing the money, I don't see how it will do us much good. Without the official documents to prove he's the legal owner, Jamie won't be able to touch it." A humorless smile thinned her lips. "So unless you possess a magical scrying glass to tell us where the dratted papers might be . . ."

"Magic is beyond my power," cut in Charlotte. "However, I do have an idea." She didn't elaborate. "I'm hoping you have one key piece of information that may help indicate the spot. Have the dastards given you a date for completing your arbitrage trading?"

"They have," replied Cordelia. "It's Friday."

*Four days,* thought Wrexford. *We have four days to piece together the puzzle before the money sails for India. Likely taking with it all proof of the evils done to possess it.*

A prodigious yawn from Sudler forestalled any further questions. The elderly professor's shoulders had slumped, and his eyelids were beginning to droop.

Cordelia patted his arm. "Come, let me take you up to your bedchamber. It's been a long night, and you need your rest."

"As do you," observed Sheffield. "However ungentlemanly it may be to remark on it, you look exhausted. And fatigue makes one prone to making mistakes." He eyed her urchin's garb. "The Weasels will escort you home."

Cordelia opened her mouth as if to argue, but whatever words she was intending surrendered to a sigh.

"We'll meet you in the scullery," said Raven.

She nodded. "I'll just be a moment in seeing the professor to his quarters."

Sheffield waited for the boys to follow her and Sudler out of the workroom before clearing his throat and looking to Wrexford and Charlotte. "So, now that's it's just the three of us, tell me—do you really have an idea on where the documents Woodbridge signed are being kept?"

His gaze shifted to Charlotte's paper, on which she had been scribbling some notes. "And even more importantly, does that mean you have a plan for getting them back?"

"My intuition tells me there's one logical place for them to be," she replied. "The dastards will be keeping them somewhere safe. And what better place than East India House, the Company's headquarters on Leadenhall Street? Its imposing stone façade gives it an aura of invincibility, and it's well guarded at all hours of the day."

Wrexford saw that she had done a quick scribble of the massive Doric columns of East India House's main entrance portico as she spoke.

"And now that we know Lord Copley is involved, however reluctantly, I would guess that it's in his private office," Charlotte added.

"But what if he's telling the truth and someone else is in charge?" asked Sheffield. "Then it could be anywhere."

"I think Lady Charlotte is right," interjected Wrexford. "These men have shown themselves to be clever in avoiding any personal connection to the illicit activities. A place like East India House provides ironclad security, but it also offers a perfect alibi if the documents somehow come to light. They could easily claim they were hidden in Copley's files by someone else. After all, clerks and junior administrators must come and go constantly through that section of the building."

"Very well, let's assume the surmise is correct." Sheffield frowned. "I'm not sure why you're looking like a cat who knocked over the cream pot. We haven't got a snowball's chance in hell of getting those papers out of the devil's own lair."

"Oh, ye of little faith," said Charlotte. "As a matter of fact, I *do* have a plan, and I am quite confident it will work. Here's what I have in mind . . ."

"Ye gods." Sheffield let out a low whistle once she had finished. "You're either mad or brilliant."

"Sometimes the difference between the two is less than a hairsbreadth," murmured Wrexford.

"It's bold, I give you that," said Sheffield. "But there are so many things that can go wrong."

"That can be said for most endeavors," pointed out Charlotte. "If we wish to save Lord Woodbridge and Lady Cordelia from ruin, we must strike quickly. Time is growing short, and we can't afford to be fainthearted."

"No one would ever accuse you of being fainthearted, m'lady." Henning paused in the doorway to slap the raindrops from his hat. "Thank heavens you weren't jesting about the whisky," he added, heading straight to the bottle and pouring himself a glass.

"Ah." The surgeon let out a blissful sigh after quaffing a long swallow. "That warms the cockles."

"There's food here, as well, though the choices are rather limited," said Charlotte with a rueful look at the nearly empty platter. "The boys are like locusts."

"As is the hound," groused Wrexford.

Harper continued his gusty snores.

"Malt is sustenance enough," replied Henning as he refilled his glass. Turning, he caught sight of the massive machine. "What the devil is *that*?"

"Professor Sudler's Computing Engine," replied the earl.

"Hell's teeth. It's . . ." The surgeon approached the behemoth and studied the intricate assembly of polished metal. "It's extraordinary." After another few moments of scrutiny, he shuffled over to join them at the table. "I imagine it's connected to whatever devilry you're investigating."

"Yes," answered Wrexford.

Henning's gaze was still on the Engine. Like the earl, he had a great interest in scientific innovations. "How does it work?"

"We haven't a clue," confessed Charlotte. "You would have to ask Lady Cordelia."

"Never mind the mechanics," snapped Wrexford. "We have more important problems to solve."

"Perhaps this will help." The surgeon fished a soggy piece of paper from his pocket and placed it on the table. "You asked for a list of banks willing to work with scoundrels."

Wrexford read it and then passed it to Charlotte, who quickly copied the names onto her notes before pushing it on to Sheffield.

"As for Annie Wright," continued Henning, "no one has seen hide nor hair of her."

"With good reason," replied the earl. "She's one of the enemy and has fled London." A pause. "No doubt with her purse bulging with blood money."

Charlotte bowed her head.

It was Sheffield who ventured to speak after several moments of heavy silence. "As to money . . ." He looked up from Henning's list. "If these establishments are in league with criminals, what makes you think they will hand over the money, even if you're successful in recovering the documents that show Woodbridge is the owner of Argentum Trading Company?"

"Because," answered Wrexford, "I can be very persuasive when I put my mind to it."

Charlotte folded her notes. "I suggest we all get some sleep, as we mean to put our plan into action tomorrow." She glanced at Sheffield. "I know you wish to help, but—"

He cut her off with a dismissive wave. "I'm aware that my

skills, such as they are, aren't nearly polished enough to be of aid in what you have in mind. Still, I shall try to be useful. I've been tasked by Lady Cordelia to take charge of overseeing our legitimate business while she's occupied with the professor and his Engine."

Wrexford's brows twitched upward, but he caught himself before making a caustic quip.

"I wish you all luck." Henning lifted his near-empty glass in salute. "Here's to kicking the bastards where it hurts."

# CHAPTER 25

"Thank you for coming." Charlotte greeted her old friend at the entrance to the parlor and gestured for him to take a seat on the sofa. Much had changed since their childhood. Jeremy was now Lord Sterling, having unexpectedly inherited his cousin's title and wealth. And she . . .

Well, her life had undergone even more momentous changes. But the bond between them had survived all the twists and turns of life.

"You've made this a very comfortable place," he observed, looking around with approval at the paintings by her late husband and at all the other little touches of individuality that made a house a home.

"I owe you a debt of gratitude for finding this house." It was Jeremy who had encouraged her to move from her first residence in London—a cramped, shabby place barely clinging to respectability—in order to put the past behind her and look to the future.

"I merely helped you with the paperwork. It's you who made it come to life," he replied. He shifted and reached behind his back to pluck a chunk of sharp-edged quartz and a shark's tooth from among the pillows. "The Weasels appear to be thriving."

She laughed and put the objects on the side table. "Hawk is enamored with the natural world and is showing great aptitude in sketching the specimens he collects. And Raven has a special gift for mathematics. Who would have guessed . . . ?"

They sat for a moment in companionable silence, the morning sunlight dancing in through the diamond-paned windows, filling the room with a buttery warmth.

"Life is certainly unpredictable," said Jeremy softly. "And while there are many who believe that mere Chance is what shapes our fate, I like to think we have a say in our destiny, if we dare to believe in ourselves."

Dust motes shimmered as they spun in a whisper of air.

"I'm glad you've reconnected with Lady Peake," he added. "Family is important." An only child, Jeremy had lost his parents to an influenza epidemic while he was attending university.

"Hartley has reached out, as well," she said. "Though I confess I'm a trifle nervous about the prospect."

"Don't be, Charley. He was always the best of your brothers." A pause. "He'll be very proud of the brave, compassionate, and principled lady his sister has become."

Charlotte felt a lump form in her throat.

He patted her arm. "But I have a feeling you didn't invite me here to discuss philosophy. Are you perchance involved in solving another murder?"

She surrendered a sigh. "As it so happens, I am. And I'm hoping you might be able to answer some questions about banking and bills of exchange."

"Finance, eh? Dare I ask . . ."

"It would be best if you didn't," she replied.

Having been involved in several of her previous investigations, he accepted the statement without argument. "What is it you want to know?"

Charlotte tucked a loose lock of hair behind her ear. "I'm looking for the names of any banks here in London which have a reputation for being lax in their business practices."

His brows drew together. "Lax in what way?"

"As in asking no questions when opening an account for a business consortium, such as who owns it and who is legally entitled to order transactions. And as in facilitating the movement of money in and out of the account with a minimum of official paperwork."

Jeremy took a long moment to ponder her answer. She could see he was both intrigued and uneasy by its ramifications.

"That would," he said carefully, "rule out the well-established banks, like Coutts, Hoare's, Barclays, and Gurney's." It was half statement, half question.

"Yes. We're looking for smaller establishments that cater to facilitating more shadowy dealings. I've been given a list by our friend Henning. I'm hoping you might help us narrow the choices."

"Ah." Jeremy appeared relieved. For all his radical views on certain things, he was a traditionalist when it came to respect for the pillars of Society. "I'm aware of several banks around the Exchange that are rumored to bend the rules if their palms are greased."

"Have you any names?" asked Charlotte, taking up a small notebook and pencil from the side table.

He gave her three.

She wrote them down. "Thank you." One was a match with Henning's names.

"Do be careful, Charley." Jeremy pinched at the pleat of his finely tailored trousers. "Much as I admire your passion for justice, it sometimes frightens me half to death."

"Actually, I'm far more cautious than I used to be." She thought of the Weasels and Wrexford and her ever-widening circle of friends. *Perhaps that's because I have far more to lose than I did in the past.*

He let out a skeptical snort, but then softened it with a smile. "Since we've brought up the subject of change, I have something on a personal note to tell you, now that we have finished with business."

"Oh?"

"Yes." Jeremy hesitated. "Isobel—that is, Mrs. Ashton—and I are to be married."

For a moment, Charlotte could do no more than stare in mute shock. But she quickly gathered her wits. "Why, that's wonderful news. I'm . . ."

"Astonished?" he suggested.

"Very happy for you," she finished in a rush.

Amusement pooled in his azure eyes. "It's not like you to fiddle-faddle around a subject."

She blew out her breath and then couldn't help but laugh. "Very well, I confess you caught me by surprise, and my first reaction was, indeed, astonishment." The two of them had forged a close-knit friendship during childhood—a closeness akin to that of brother and sister—and had shared their most intimate secrets and longings with each other. "But now that I think on it, the match is perfect."

The widow had, for a time, been a suspect in one of their previous murder investigations because of her intelligence and business acumen—and because of a sordid secret in her past.

"Mrs. Ashton is not only smart and steady, but she possesses just the right sort of dry humor to rub along well with yours," she added.

"Working together on her late husband's weaving mills has given us a common purpose," said Jeremy. "And we have come to like each other very much." His voice didn't alter, but Charlotte sensed the depth of feeling that those simple words held. "Our partnership may not blaze with passion, but we have a very special friendship."

"Friendship," said Charlotte, "is perhaps the very best foundation on which to build a marriage."

"I knew you would understand." Jeremy brushed a light caress to her cheek. "What about you? Have you any friendships that may result in matrimony?"

She felt heat rise to her cheeks. "Unless the beau monde's rules have turned upside down while I haven't been looking, it's not up to me to make a proposal."

He held her gaze with a searching stare, making her flush turn prickly. Flustered, she looked away.

"Again, I wish you happy."

Flashing another smile, Jeremy rose. "Alas, I must be off to a business engagement. But I shall stop by again before I return to the North next week. In the meantime, please promise me to be careful."

As the first part of their plan couldn't begin until later in the afternoon, Wrexford decided he had time to keep his appointment with Sir Darius Roy. He found the explorer perusing the Royal Society's latest scientific journal in the reading room of his club.

The firelight caught the gleam in Sir Darius's eye as he looked up at the sound of the earl's approach. "It's quite fascinating the advances we're making in botany and geology. Perhaps one day we'll understand all the working of the world around us."

"Not in our lifetime," said Wrexford. "Nor in a hundred lifetimes."

"Quite right," agreed Sir Darius. "Like the star-dotted heavens, the breadth and depth of Knowledge seem unfathomable. And I suppose that's a good thing. It keeps us inquisitive."

"Indeed."

"Questions, questions." The explorer flashed a wry smile. "Kit says you have a few pressing questions that I may be able to answer."

"I do." Wrexford glanced around. "Might we go somewhere more private?"

"I've reserved one of the private parlors." Sir Darius tucked the journal under his arm and rose. "I've asked several friends to join us, as they may also have information you'll find helpful." He led the way to the central stairs and started up them two at a time. "I don't suppose you speak Mandarin?"

"Not a word."

"No matter. Their English is excellent."

On reaching the top landing, they turned down one of the narrow corridors and passed the club's library, which was crammed with large curiosity cabinets as well as floor-to-ceiling bookcases.

"In here," said Sir Darius, clicking open a door and standing aside to allow the earl to enter.

Two men were seated at a rectangular table by the window, drinking tea and playing some sort of game involving ivory tiles covered with a variety of Chinese symbols. They stood as Wrexford crossed onto the carpet, both of them looking every inch the proper English gentleman with their faultless tailored coats and impeccably tied cravats. It was only the shape and taper of their dark, watchful eyes that gave them an exotic aura.

"Wrexford, allow me to introduce Mr. Jiang and Mr. Gu." To his friends, Sir Darius said, "This is Lord Wrexford."

"The chemist," said Gu, the shorter of the two. "Your paper challenging the results of Benjamin Silliman's experiment in fusing chalcedony was quite convincing."

"Are you a man of science, Mr. Gu?" asked the earl.

"The subject interests me. As do a great many others." A

shrug. "However, I've not devoted enough time to any of them to claim any mastery."

"Alas, we are what you Westerners call dilettantes," said Jiang.

"Rather, you are well-traveled men of the world," corrected Sir Darius. "The three of us met a number of years ago in the Forbidden City, while I was on a diplomatic mission for the Foreign Office. We have since journeyed together through parts of the ancient Silk Road trade routes, exploring India and the Levant."

"One learns much by experiencing other cultures," observed Jiang. "And gains new perspectives, which our emperor finds useful in dealing with the world beyond our realm."

"You have a very enlightened outlook, Mr. Jiang," replied Wrexford. "Would that more of mankind would possess such an open mind."

"True. And yet it seems human nature is ruled by self-interest, regardless of where one travels," said Gu.

*Kindred spirits?* The earl didn't often meet men whose curiosity and slightly sardonic view of the world's foibles matched his own. He found himself wishing he had the luxury of engaging in lengthy conversation with Sir Darius and his friends. However . . .

"Our thoughts align, Mr. Gu. And it so happens that a matter of self-interest is what brings me here." Wrexford looked to Sir Darius. "And much as I'd prefer to speak of other things, it's a matter of some urgency."

"Yes, yes." Sir Darius gestured for them all to be seated. "It is for us, as well. It so happens that Mr. Jiang and Mr. Gu are here in London for private talks with the Foreign Office over a grave concern to their country—and to ours. It concerns opium."

"Opium is a scourge. The emperor has forbidden its import

into our country," said Jiang. "And yet it's being smuggled into our country from India."

"Which greatly concerns our king, as our country wishes to maintain cordial relations with the Dragon Throne," added Sir Darius.

"Cordial relations," murmured Gu, "are in the self-interest of both rulers, as our empires look to expand trading opportunities."

"My concern is opium, too," said Wrexford.

"So Kit told me," replied Sir Darius. "A fortuitous conversation, as our government would be happy to see the problem solved discreetly." He picked up a portfolio of papers from beside the box of ivory tiles. "Are you familiar with mah-jongg, Wrexford? It's a game of skill and strategy developed in China during the Qing dynasty."

"I've heard of it but have never seen the tiles. It sounds similar to backgammon," observed the earl.

"And chess, all of which were created in the East," said Jiang. A mere ghost of a smile seemed to flit across his lips. "But then, here in the West, we Orientals are said to have sly and devious minds."

"Those traits, I fear, are evenly spread throughout mankind." Sir Darius opened the portfolio and passed a sheaf of documents to Wrexford. "Mr. Jiang and Mr. Gu have a network of contacts both in India and here in the dockyards of London. They've compiled a report that indicates the opium problem lies somewhere with the East India Company."

"My inquiries have suggested the same thing." Wrexford began skimming the pages. "Though I've still not confirmed to my satisfaction that I've identified the leaders of the illicit consortium."

"We can be of some help there," said Gu. "A man named Fenwick Alston created the smuggling enterprise some years ago. And though he's no longer in Calcutta, we suspect that he still has a hand in running the trade."

"According to his older brother, Fenwick Alston was killed in the West Indies," replied Wrexford.

"How convenient, seeing as he was about to be apprehended for trading with Britain's enemy," cut in Jiang before the earl could continue. "But it seems the gentleman possesses not only the slipperiness of an eel but also the supernatural powers of returning from the dead. For he's here in London. We've confirmed that for ourselves."

Gu nodded. "Nobody notices two humble Chinese laborers working around the East India docks, as many of the stevedores are foreigners. We met the fellow in Calcutta during our visit with Sir Darius, so we're familiar with his face. He was overseeing the loading of cargo into one of the storage warehouses just several days ago."

"You're sure of this?" asked Wrexford.

"Positive," replied Jiang and then tapped a finger to the outer ridge of his left cheekbone. "He has a crescent-shaped knife scar here."

The earl thought about Cordelia's description of the Cobra. "Would he perchance have cold, snakelike eyes?"

"A perfect description," answered Gu. "You've seen him, too?"

"No, but a friend has." Wrexford looked up from the papers. "What about Lord Elgin Copley? Have you any proof of his involvement?"

"Ah, Copley." Sir Darius pursed his lips. "A very careful fellow. Try as we might, we've found no proof to connect him to any wrongdoing. Though it's hard to believe he's not aware of what's going on."

"As to that, I have an idea as to why . . ." Wrexford quickly summarized his conversation with the baron.

"Blackmail, eh?" Sir Darius let out an unhappy sigh. "The

road to perdition starts with such small steps, and one thinks one can halt at any time. But suddenly the slope turns steep and slippery. I confess, Copley has done much good over the years, but the scales of justice aren't about simply balancing good and evil."

"The question is, who's blackmailing him?" mused Wrexford.

"My guess is that it's Alston," replied Jiang. "This is a complex operation, involving complicated logistics and a network of corrupt operatives. Copley is an able administrator, but his expertise isn't in moving goods or paying bribes."

The statement drew a confirming nod from Gu. "Alston has run two successful smuggling operations. One can't help but believe he's doing the same thing here in London."

"His methods are becoming even more sophisticated," continued Jiang. "He's involved a very reputable private bank in helping to obscure the movement of the consortium's illegal money. One of the staff is apparently no stranger to smuggling."

Wrexford felt his innards turn to ice. "Hoare's?"

"How did you know?" asked Sir Darius.

"I became aware of this whole scheme because an acquaintance was humbugged into putting money into the consortium by David Mather."

Sir Darius made a moue of distaste. "He's one of those fellows who yearns for more than he has. He's apparently very clever with finances, and while at Oxford, he became involved with some childhood friends in a smuggling operation involving French brandy. Because of his age and the intercession of his mother's uncle, a prominent member of the House of Lords, it was all hushed up."

"Surely he's not one of the leaders," said Wrexford.

Sir Darius pursed his lips. "He has charm and guile."

Wrexford took a moment to absorb what he had just heard. "I still say he's not one of the leaders. I have witnesses who say Copley put him on an East India merchant ship, and I would guess it was to keep his mouth shut."

Sir Darius raised a questioning brow. "Are you sure Mather actually departed?"

A grim silence was his only answer.

"Whoever is heading it, this illicit consortium needs to be stopped," pressed Jiang. "Else it threatens the relations between our two empires, and at a very delicate time, considering Parliament's recent Charter Act."

"I think I have a way of accomplishing that," replied the earl. He shuffled the documents back in order and slid them across to Sir Darius. "However, I may have to bend a few legalities to do so."

"There are times when it's necessary for legalities to be flexible," came Sir Darius's measured answer. "The Foreign Office is aware of your previous help in eliminating a betrayal that would have greatly embarrassed the government, and would welcome your assistance once again." A cough. "But this time, do try to avoid burning down half of London."

Raven squirmed as Charlotte tucked an unruly tangle of hair behind his ear. "I'm not going to take tea with His Majesty, m'lady. I'm simply acting as the errand boy."

"Nonetheless, you must look like a proper servant of an earl," she retorted. "Show me your hands—and they had better be well scrubbed."

He mumbled a word that earned him a sharp rebuke from McClellan. "Say that again in m'lady's presence and you'll be eating soap for supper for the next month."

Their nerves were all on edge, thought Charlotte, forcing herself to draw a steadying breath. It was Raven who was tasked with putting their plan in motion. And while she conceded that the idea was clever and posed little risk for the boy, she couldn't entirely put aside the knowledge that a man lay dead for daring to oppose their enemy.

"Sorry," said Raven, holding out his hands for inspection. His fingernails were shockingly clean, considering what unmentionable substances were usually embedded beneath them.

Charlotte smiled. "Excellent. Do try to arrive at the earl's townhouse without them coming to grief."

He rolled his eyes, impatient to be off.

Death had been a frequent visitor to the slums in which the boys had spent their early childhood, and they possessed an unruffled acceptance that his shadow was part of everyday life. To Raven, this was an exciting adventure, but she felt as if she was sending him into the maw of a monster.

She pulled him into a fierce hug. "Be careful."

McClellan flashed her a sympathetic look. "Aye, Weasel. You are *not* to stray a step from His Lordship's orders. Let us hear them once again before you go."

The boy made a pained face. "Be assured, every word is chiseled into my skull."

The maid crossed her arms. "Then it will only take you a moment to recite them."

A sigh. "When I arrive at Lord Wrexford's townhouse, I will dress in the bootboy's fancy livery—no matter that I'll look like a street fiddler's monkey—and then His Lordship's carriage will take me to East India House . . ."

Charlotte repressed a shudder.

"Where I'll wave a note festooned with the earl's impressive wax seals under the nose of the head porter and demand to be taken to Lord Copley's office, as His Lordship has given me strict orders that it must be handed to the director's private secretary."

That would get the boy into the bowels of the building. And then . . .

"And then?" prompted McClellan.

"And then, as the minion starts to escort me back to the entrance hall," recited Raven, "I'll begin to squirm and whine that I desperately need a pisspot, else I might have to relieve myself on one of the precious marble statues lining the corridors."

Wrexford had come up with a clever ruse, admitted Charlotte. She doubted any of the attendants would dare risk the wrath of a superior by allowing the boy to befoul the Company's decorative art.

"Once I'm directed down to the basement . . ." Tyler's inquiries among his various friends had provided them with an accurate layout of East India House. "I'll find the first storage room that faces out on Lime Street, unlock the window, and put a wooden wedge under the frame, so that the earl can get inside the building later tonight."

"What if the attendant insists on escorting you to the basement?" asked Charlotte.

"Pffft. Mr. Tyler says they'll all think it beneath their dignity to serve as a guide for a boy."

"And what if you're spotted wandering around where you shouldn't be?" demanded McClellan.

"I'll say I'm lost, and if pressed, I'll burst into tears."

Raven's recital of the plan steadied Charlotte's fluttery nerves. As Wrexford had assured, there wasn't any danger to this part of it.

"I need to scarper, m'lady," he added in a rush. "I can't be late." The timing called for Raven to arrive right before the end of the working day, in order to lessen the chances of a clerk entering the storage room and noticing the window wasn't locked.

"Go," she said after giving him another quick hug.

"Don't worry," counseled McClellan as Raven raced out to the back garden, where Hawk was waiting by the loose board in the back fence. "This is child's play for Raven. He won't have any trouble doing his part." The maid's expression betrayed a tiny flicker of concern. "It's Wrexford who may face trouble. I imagine there are guards patrolling the building at night. And given what the enemy has to protect, I imagine they won't hesitate to use violence—"

Charlotte turned from watching the shadows flitting through the corridor, her expression causing the maid to fall silent.

"In which case, they'll be in for a rude surprise."

# CHAPTER 26

Squeezing himself deeper into the narrow gap between the warehouses, Wrexford cast a look at the darkened windows of East India House's rear façade. The last light had gone out perhaps a quarter hour ago, but he had decided to err on caution and wait a little longer, just to be sure the inner offices had settled into slumber.

However, the ominous clouds blowing in from the east stirred a prickling of uncertainty. A trail of telltale raindrops would make his intended foray even more dangerous.

He had only himself to blame for that. *I was so bloody sure Copley would agree to a deal.*

Now that Copley knew his illicit activities were no longer a secret, would he have arranged for additional security in his own area of the building? Guards who wouldn't hesitate to shed blood to keep any proof of the misdeeds from slipping out?

Cursing himself for a fool, Wrexford fingered the pocket pistol inside his coat. He had broken his own cardinal rule in leaping to conclusions. Hubris was not without a price. However, it was of some solace that breaking into the building put only himself at risk,

A sound, a mere whisper among the other night rustlings, snapped his attention back to the moment. Wrexford noiselessly shifted his stance and flattened his back against the bricks. As of yet, he had seen no sign of guards patrolling the building's perimeter. With luck . . .

A wraithlike shadow, a swirl of vapor within the gun smoke-grey mist, flitted past the opening to his hiding place. The night was always alive with denizens of the dark, intent on no good.

All was still again. He slowly let out his breath. . . .

"Wrexford." The wraith slipped into the slivered space, the brush of wool against his shoulder an unwelcome assurance that it wasn't a figment of his brooding.

"What the devil are you doing here?"

"I assume that's a rhetorical question." Like him, Charlotte was dressed all in black, with a silk mask hiding her face. The eyes slits, however, revealed an all-too-familiar steely gaze.

"I—"

"Ssshhh. Keep your voice down," she whispered. "Two can search quicker than one. And I've even more experience than you do in this sort of endeavor."

He couldn't argue on that point. "But the risk—"

"Is the same for you."

A fraught silence quivered between them. Wrexford tried to maintain his righteous anger. It was wrong to feel a warmth steal through his bones. Duty demanded that a gentleman protect the weaker sex—

*The weaker sex—ha!*

He surrendered a grudging smile. "Two conditions—I lead the way, and if I order you to fly, you don't argue."

Charlotte hesitated. Debating, no doubt, how finely she could parse the definition of *order*.

"Very well," came her answer. She looked across the walkway to East India House, its pale Portland stone rising from the fog like a massive ship under full sail. "After you, sir."

Wrexford led the way to the ground-floor storage room where Raven had wedged open the window. A quick tug raised the sash, and he slithered inside. Charlotte was right behind him and pushed it back into place. After taking a thick piece of felt from his pocket, he cleaned the bottoms of his soft-soled shoes and wordlessly passed the cloth to her.

The storage room's door had been locked for the night. Wrexford eased the bolt open and checked the corridor. Upon finding all was still, he crept into the gloom.

Tyler had procured a floor plan of the interior, and the earl had memorized the way to Copley's set of offices. A small folding lantern was in his pocket, but he didn't wish to risk a light until they reached the baron's inner lair. Navigating by touch and feel, he followed the wall to a side stairwell. Their steps padded noiselessly over the smooth stone.

Another door, which opened to reveal an unblinking darkness.

Charlotte grasped his sleeve just as he started forward, and cocked an ear. Wrexford heard it, too—the click of steps echoing from the front of the building.

They waited. The sound quickly faded away. There was, he knew, a night porter on duty at the main entrance. The logbooks and company correspondence that sailed with every East India merchant ship could arrive at any hour.

He signaled for them to continue. Copley's offices were to the left, behind an ornately carved set of locked teak doors.

*Snick, snick.* The steel probe jiggled, and the tumblers released with a discreet sigh.

A bank of windows on the wall facing Leadenhall Street allowed in just enough illumination to show a large room filled with long rows of wooden desks and stools on either side of a center walkway. In daytime, a regiment of scriveners would be busy with pen and ink . . . fifty tiny hearts beating in tune, compiling the leather-bound ledgers that recorded the Company's lifeblood flowing in and out.

Straight ahead was another set of teak doors, ornamented with inlaid ivory. These, too, were locked.

"You really *must* show me how to do that," said Charlotte, crouching down beside him to watch.

"You're dangerous enough as it is," he replied. "I shudder . . ." *Snick, snick.* "To think what mischief . . ." *Snick, snick.* This mechanism was more complicated than the first one.

"Ah, finally," he said. The doors swung open on well-oiled hinges.

Wrexford gestured for her to enter the inner office, then carefully reset the lock.

The large room was tastefully furnished in dark woods, with brass accents on the document storage cabinets adding a nautical look to the well-ordered space. Two desks sat side by side. A glance at the open appointment book on the nearest one seemed to indicate this was where Copley's personal secretaries toiled. A small side office looked to belong to a senior administrative assistant. After a cursory glance at the stack of ledgers, he returned to the main room.

Up ahead, an archway opened into a short corridor. Charlotte was already wreathed in its shadows, moving lightly on the balls of her feet.

She returned a moment later and gestured for him to come along.

"This must be Copley's private lair," she said once he had joined her. "The door has two locks." A grimace. "I feel as though I'm inside one of those elaborate Russian wooden dolls. You know, the ones that nest inside one another."

"*Matryoshka* dolls." He set to work with his steel probe. *Secrets within secrets.* Logic said that Woodbridge's documents, if they were indeed here in East India House, would be kept where an underling wouldn't inadvertently come across them.

And Copley struck him as a logical gentleman. If he wasn't . . .

Charlotte seemed to be thinking along the same lines. She looked back over her shoulder at the outer offices. "We won't have time to search everywhere. What would you suggest we do? We can either both search the baron's lair, or you can concentrate on his room, while I use my intuition to guess where in the outer rooms he might have hidden the banking papers."

Wrexford found himself wavering, but only for a moment. "Blackmail . . . Even if the story Copley told me was a humbug, it shows his concern with blackmail. I think he will be keeping them close."

A nod signaled her agreement.

He took hold of the door latch and eased it open. "Then let's get to work."

Charlotte heard a soft hiss escape from his lungs as he stepped into the office. In the next instant she saw why.

Along with the array of bookcases and storage cabinets, the room held a number of display shelves showcasing exotic curios, many of which were quite large and ornate. In addition, there were a number of carved wooden statues—they looked to be Hindu deities—painted in jewel-tone colors, with bits of gaudy glass adding extra glitter and texture.

All of which could contain hidden compartments, perfect for hiding a sheaf of paper.

"Hell and damnation," she agreed as he reset the locks.

"Let's not waste our breath feeling sorry for ourselves," he muttered. "I'll start with the desk." He took out the folding lantern and set the candle and shutters in place, then indicated the small oil lamp on the tea table. "We'll have to chance a second light."

The clouds had thickened, and a few windblown raindrops were spattering the window glass.

"You've the more artistic eye," he said, easing open one of the drawers. "See if you spot any signs of a hidey-hole within the statues. Then move on to the storage cabinets."

They worked in methodical silence, with naught but the sigh of paper and the whisper of opening and closing drawers joining the patter of the rain.

Charlotte decided not to spend much of their precious time on the statues. The elaborate carving and inlaid glass made it difficult to discern any telltale seams of a secret compartment. After circling the room, she returned to the storage cabinets, which each contained multiple drawers filled with neatly filed folders.

*Luck.* They would have to be extraordinarily lucky to find the dratted papers.

She finished with one row of financial reports—Ye heavens, it seemed that half the wealth of the world must pass through the Company—and moved on to the next one. Halfway through it, she paused to flex a crick from her neck. . . .

And froze.

*Footsteps.* Beating a hurried tattoo on the marble floor and coming closer.

"Someone's coming," she hissed and quickly blew out her own flame. *A night watchman making his rounds?* Then perhaps he would simply turn away at the first locked doors.

Wrexford wasn't counting on that. "There's no time to flee," he responded, batting the air to disperse the tiny curls of smoke. "We need to hide."

Charlotte was already moving for the massive elephant-headed deity standing in the far corner, flanking the tall bank of mullioned windows. Having made a careful inspection, she knew there was room behind it. Better still, heavy damask draperies hung within the deep shadows.

"In here," she urged, finding an opening within the folds.

He squeezed in, and she followed, then flattened her back against his chest and twitched the fabric back in place.

The scrape of key sounded in one of the locks.

To her horror, she felt the earl move . . . but it was only to make a tiny peephole.

More scraping . . . the brush of boots over the woven carpet . . . the strike of flint against steel.

And then the tiny sputter of a candle coming to life.

Charlotte held her breath, hoping the darkness muddled the shape of the draperies enough to hide their presence.

A cabinet opened. Rustling . . . and then a metallic *thunk*. She leaned back, just enough to see through the slivered opening. The flickering flame revealed a lone figure in a caped coat, but she couldn't see his face. He had just placed a brass box on the counter and was hurriedly unfastening the lid.

She felt Wrexford fist his hands in frustration as the gentleman pulled out a set of folded documents and clicked the lid shut. After a quick look at the papers, he tucked them inside his coat and quickly returned the box to the cabinet.

He turned and, with a quick puff, blew out the candle and stepped out of view.

It seemed like an eternity before the sounds of his retreat faded, leaving only the spit of rain to keep them company.

Chuffing an oath, the earl pushed through the fabric.

"Was it Copley?" she asked.

He nodded. "How is it the bloody dastards keep staying one step ahead of us?"

"Perhaps because they're impelled by panic," she replied. "We're breathing down their necks."

"Always the optimist," growled Wrexford. After glancing around the room, he gave a shrug. "Come, there's no point in lingering here."

She followed him to the outer office and paused while he reset the locks. The papers had slipped through their fingers tonight, but perhaps all was not lost. An idea was beginning to form. . . .

Her mind on their next move, Charlotte trailed the earl into the main workroom. Halfway down the center aisle, she slipped on a patch of wetness and bumped into one of the long work desks.

Wrexford turned and speared her with a silent rebuke.

*How odd,* she thought. Copley's coat hadn't looked dripping wet, and yet there seemed to be a large puddle on the marble. Her shoe was soaked. Looking down to avoid another mishap, she took a careful step. . . .

Only to see her sole leave a streak of blood on the pale marble.

"Don't dawdle," chided Wrexford in a taut whisper, but as his gaze followed hers, he fell silent.

Charlotte dropped to a crouch and immediately spotted the body shoved up against the wooden back of one of the desks. The man was lying facedown.

"The killer knew what he was doing," said Wrexford, after avoiding a dark rivulet of blood that snaked across the tiles and making a quick examination of the body. "The thrust was precisely aimed. It's not easy to avoid a rib." He fingered the rent in the victim's coat. "The blade looks to have been a rather wide one . . . but never mind that now."

She watched as he gingerly turned the man over. The sightless eyes were open, the white gleaming bright despite the gloom.

Wrexford leaned in closer and let out a grunt of surprise. "It's Fenwick Alston."

"H-how do you know that?"

"The scar on his cheek. It's exactly as Sir Darius's friends described it."

"Fenwick Alston. But . . ." Charlotte shook her head. "But

that makes no sense. Surely he's one of the ringleaders, so why—"

He pulled her to her feet. "Never mind that now. We need to leave, and quickly. Strip off your bloody shoes until we're outside. I'd rather that the body isn't found until morning."

They retraced their route to the lower storage room without incident and were soon deep within the maze of alleyways leading back toward Mayfair.

Wrexford appeared in no mood for conversation, and Charlotte didn't press him. At the moment, there was naught but a single question echoing inside her head.

*What the devil is going on?*

# CHAPTER 27

"Griffin wasn't at all happy at being informed that he and his men will find a dead man within the inner sanctum of East India House—and that you suggested he have the corpse taken to Henning," announced Tyler as he entered the breakfast room. He peeled off his gloves and poured himself a cup of coffee before adding, "Though judging from his querulous tone, my guess is he hadn't yet had his breakfast."

"Nor have I," said Wrexford. It was only an hour or two past dawn, and his mind was a little muzzy. He gulped down another long swallow of his own dark brew, hoping to scald his senses to full alert. "Shirred eggs and toast will be out in a moment."

"Griffin asks that you send him a note explaining what happened."

The earl refilled his cup and blew away a plume of steam. "He will have to be patient. I'm not prepared to tell him anything for now."

Tyler took a seat at the table. "Do you think Copley killed Fenwick Alston? By your account, there wasn't much time for him to do it after he left you."

"He could have done it on his way in. The two of them could have quarreled over strategy, and Copley decided his partner had become a liability," mused Wrexford. "But it does seem out of character."

"Then perhaps we need to think more about David Mather," said the valet. "Given what Sir Darius and his friends told you, the fellow may not be an underling, after all."

Wrexford pursed his lips. "That occurred to me, as well. In retrospect, he, of all people, was in a position to know that his cousin had discovered the fraudulent accounting going on within the East India Company. In fact, Henry Peabody might well have confided in him."

"And then, suspecting that Annie Wright knew about it, too, he lured her to take refuge on an East India merchant ship with a promise of escaping danger," suggested Tyler.

Finally, the pieces of the puzzle were beginning to fit together.

"It makes sense," he agreed. "Mather has gained an expertise in finance, which makes him very useful to an illegal consortium. More than that, handling money for the wealthy and privileged has likely made him both jealous and ambitious to enjoy the same luxuries. I doubt that it would have been difficult to seduce him."

Breakfast arrived, and the earl leaned back as Tyler helped himself. "Once you've filled your gullet, head down to the dockyards and see what other information you can gather on the merchant ship's departure. It would be helpful if someone can confirm that Mather wasn't on it."

Tyler sighed through a mouthful of broiled kidney. "No rest for the weary."

"I don't pay you to sleep."

Another mumbled comment, which Wrexford pretended not to hear. He reached for a piece of toast.

"Your pardon, milord." His butler appeared in the doorway. "But a message has arrived from—"

"From Lady Charlotte," announced Raven, darting past Riche and slapping a folded missive on the table. Hawk was right behind him.

The earl eyed the muddy fingerprints—or were they paw prints?—on the once-pristine paper. "If your hands were cleaner, I'd invite you to have a muffin."

Raven wiped his filthy palms on the seat of his pants, drawing a muffled laugh from Tyler. "*Consuetudinis magna vis est,*" he replied with a shrug.

*Old habits die hard.* Wrexford's mouth twitched. "Be that as it may, whatever is smeared on your fingers is robbing me of my appetite."

"But it's only—" Hawk swallowed the rest of his words as his brother kicked his shin.

The earl unfolded the note and skimmed the contents. "As luck would have it, Lady Charlotte is taking tea with Lady Peake this morning and requests my presence. That will allow me to tell her of our thoughts concerning Mather." He looked up. "Weasels, kindly fetch paper and pencil from my workroom. I need to write a response, and then I also want to send a message to—"

"Your pardon, milord." The butler reappeared in the doorway. "But another missive has arrived." This one, a fancy piece of folded stationery fixed with an ornate wax seal, he passed to the earl himself.

"The devil be damned," muttered Wrexford as he read the note.

Tyler came alert. "What is it?"

"Lord Copley is requesting a meeting with me at White's on a matter of utmost urgency."

"When?"

"At noon," replied the earl.

"Hmmph, in broad daylight on St. James's Street," mused the valet. "I daresay it's not a trap. Still . . ."

"Weasels!" The earl snapped his fingers. "Paper and pencil, along with some sealing wax!"

The boys were back in a flash. He quickly scribbled out two notes and used his signet ring to add his official imprimatur. "Leave this for Mr. Griffin at the Bow Street magistrates' office," he said, handing one of them to Hawk. "But first, go tell Lady Charlotte I will meet her at Lady Peake's residence at eleven. Then head to Sheffield's room and ask him to meet me there, as well."

The earl turned to Raven. "And you—you take this to Lord Copley. But listen carefully, lad . . ." He leaned in closer, coming nearly nose to nose with the boy. "I want you to linger around his residence, and when he leaves, stick to him like a cocklebur until he arrives at White's. I wish to know whether he makes any stops or meets anyone else. However, do it carefully, understand? He may be a murderer."

Raven gave a solemn nod. "Oiy, sir. I won't let you down."

"Then off you go, Weasels." He watched them dart away and disappear into the corridor. Raven's task wasn't dangerous, he told himself, and the boy was too clever and agile to come to any grief. Still, he couldn't help but feel a twinge of worry.

"He'll be fine," counseled Tyler. "Urchins are invisible to men like Copley."

It was true. The raggle-taggle children who roamed the streets were beneath the notice of the beau monde—save when they weren't there on the street corners to sweep the manure aside so the fancy aristocrats didn't soil their elegant footwear.

Wrexford pushed back his chair. "Let us fetch our coats. We both have much to do before the clock strikes twelve bells."

Alison's brow furrowed in concern as Charlotte entered the parlor and took a seat beside her. Light winked off the lens of her quizzing glass as she raised it to her eye. "My dear, you look like death warmed over."

Charlotte winced, finding both the word *death* and the scrutiny of a much-magnified sapphirine orb unnerving. "It's rather unpleasant to stumble over a man who has just had his heart pierced by a knife."

"Another murder?" The dowager gave her hand a sympathetic squeeze. "What a ghastly shock for you."

Charlotte refrained from enumerating all the dead bodies she had tripped over since taking up A. J. Quill's pen from her late husband. Some secrets were better left unsaid. Instead, she quickly explained about the foray to East India House.

"However uncharitable it is of me," said Alison, "I find it hard to muster any sympathy for Fenwick Alston. He was a scoundrel who dedicated his life to corrupting good into evil."

"He'll foment no more trouble in the world," said Charlotte. She, too, found it hard to feel any pity. *Vives in gladio in gladio mori. Live by the sword, die by the sword.* "But let us leave off speaking ill of the dead. It's the living who concern me."

"Copley," said the dowager, her expression grim. "It seems there's no chance now of getting the documents Woodbridge signed."

"As to that . . ." Charlotte hesitated. An idea had come to her as she had tossed and turned in the hours of darkness just before dawn. But it would require the help of their friends and was not without risk.

"Yes?" urged Alison, her eyes alight with curiosity.

"I will wait until Wrexford arrives to explain," she said. "Though I have a feeling he won't agree to the idea."

"What idea?" asked the earl as the dowager's butler led him into the parlor.

Charlotte waited for his escort to withdraw before replying, "One that concerns retrieving the Argentum documents from Lord Copley."

"The situation has changed," announced Wrexford.

She edged forward in her seat. "How so?"

"Copley just sent me a note requesting a meeting at noon."
Her eyes widened. "What do you think he wants?"

"It seems pointless to speculate," he replied. "From the very beginning of all these intertwining mysteries, nothing has been what it seems. So, we shall just have to wait and see."

With steady, light-footed steps—not too fast, not too slow—Raven wove in and out of the sun and shadows dappling the street, just another tiny flicker of movement in the vast tapestry of London's unruly daily life. Up ahead, his quarry marched along at a purposeful pace, head down, preoccupied with his own thoughts.

Like all the highborn aristocrats, Lord Copley appeared oblivious to the world around him, observed the boy. Never a wise decision. Trouble didn't give a rat's arse as to whether one possessed pedigree and privilege.

The way grew more crowded as Copley turned onto Piccadilly Street, heading for St. James's Street. Fancy carriages and high-perch phaetons clattered over the cobbles, cheek by jowl with drab dray carts and hackneys. Up ahead at the corner, people were clustered at the curb, waiting for a brewery wagon filled with barrels to squeeze past a barouche. Through the press of bodies, Raven caught a glimpse of Skinny holding his broom in readiness. This was his regular street-sweeping spot, and business looked to be good.

Tapping his stick to his boot in impatience, Copley maneuvered his way to the edge of the street. Ducking and dodging elbows, Raven quickened his steps, not wishing to be caught up in the crush of people waiting to cross when the way cleared.

Out of the corner of his eye, the boy saw someone else start to move. . . .

The two drivers began to shout at each other, sparking the pedestrians to add their own voices to the curses. A whip cracked. The agitated ring of iron-shod hooves echoed off the stones. And all at once, the wagon broke free.

Seizing the opening, a curricle pulled by a matched pair of muscled chestnuts shot forward.

Copley hesitated. . . .

Raven saw the pearly-white flash of a gloved hand—

And then suddenly a blur of well-tailored wool was tumbling into the path of the oncoming horses.

A scream rose above the sickening crunch of bone and splintering wood. Wheels skittering, the vehicle swerved drunkenly and came to a halt halfway up the street.

As the onlookers jostled in shock and confusion, a gentleman waved them away from the gruesome sight.

"Stand back, stand back!" he ordered, taking care to avoid the puddles of blood as he approached the unmoving body.

Raven wriggled through the press of bodies, his eyes locking for an instant with Skinny's before shifting to the dark-clad figure who had taken charge.

Crouching down, the gentleman flexed his long fingers—another flash of pearly white—before turning Copley face up.

The boy crept across the cobbles, close enough to hear the breath rattle in Copley's throat.

"Blue Peter." It was hardly more than a whispery rasp. Copley's eyes fluttered open for an instant and then fell shut. A shudder racked his broken body. "T-tell Wrexford to watch for Blue Peter."

Shifting slightly, the gentleman pressed a palm to the baron's windpipe and then calmly crushed the life out of him. Without batting an eye, he slipped his fingers inside Copley's coat.

*Searching, searching . . .*

Raven inched closer. Spotting a papery flicker as the gentleman withdrew a packet of folded documents, the boy darted forward and snatched it from his grasp.

Snarling an oath, the gentleman grabbed Raven's jacket, but as he fell to his knees, the boy twisted and kicked free. Scrambling to his feet, he skidded on the blood-slick stones, teetering off-balance for an instant, and then broke into a run.

Quick as a snake, the gentleman was up and after him. A lunge, and his fingers hooked in Raven's collar.

"Oiy, oiy!"

His feet suddenly entangled in a dung-encrusted broom, the gentleman went sprawling. He was up in a flash, but Raven had already disappeared down one of the side streets.

"You miserable little piece of filth." Spinning around, he lashed out a blow that caught Skinny flush on his bony shoulder.

"Oiy, oiy!" he howled. "I wuz jest tryin' te help!"

Fixing the urchin with a venomous look, the gentleman cocked his fist to strike again.

"Here, here, sirrah!" A portly fellow dressed in a navy coat and biscuit-colored pantaloons stepped between them. "Shame on you. No man of honor should ever beat a helpless little child."

The gentleman spat out another oath.

"Are you hurt, lad?" asked the portly fellow.

Skinny, tears rolling down his face, gave a theatrical wince.

Spotting two officers from Horse Guards striding from Whitehall, the portly fellow let out a sigh of relief. "Ah, here come the authorities ! We shall let them sort this all out, eh?"

But the pearly-white-gloved gentleman had already melted away into the crowd.

Wrexford left the dowager's townhouse early, intent on arriving at White's with time to spare. Sheffield hadn't shown up, but as the earl's note had explained about the foray to East India House and Alston's murder, he suspected that his friend had chosen to stop first at Woodbridge's residence to inform Lady Cordelia and her brother of the death blow to their plans.

For without the official documents showing Woodbridge as the owner of Argentum Trading Company, there was no chance of recovering the money held in the company's bank account before the dastards withdrew it as a bill of exchange.

Copley, he admitted, had outmaneuvered them and now held the upper hand. Which begged the question of why he had asked for a meeting.

Unless it was to gloat.

A sense of profound failure shook him to the bone. For all his so-called reason and logic, he had done naught but chase after shadows, only to be left lost in the dark. His friends had looked to him for help.

*And I let them down.*

Wrexford quickened his steps, trying to shake off his self-loathing and concentrate on what bargaining chips he might have to play in the coming meeting.

"Wrex!"

The earl looked up and felt a spasm of fear on seeing Sheffield's face.

His friend took his arm and drew him into the shade of a bookshop's bowfront window. "There's been an accident on Piccadilly Street."

*Raven.* His heart leapt into his throat.

"A gentleman somehow stumbled into the path of an oncoming carriage and was crushed to death." Sheffield's voice dropped to an even lower pitch. "I couldn't get close enough for a look, but word is, it's Copley, though that may be mere crowd rumor."

The earl spun around. "I had Raven following him. If anything . . ." No, he refused to contemplate the worst. "If anything has happened, the boy will fly back to Berkeley Square."

# CHAPTER 28

Lungs burning, pulse pounding, Wrexford raced up the front steps of his townhouse and flung the door open, Sheffield right on his heels. The sound of their boots echoed like gunfire as they crossed the entrance hall's marble tiles and skidded into the main corridor.

"Milord!" Riche's hail went unheard.

Wrexford's palms were clammy as he fumbled with the brass latch to his workroom.

"Sorry, sir." Hands shoved in his jacket pockets, Raven was standing with his back to the banked fire. "I bolloxed the job. But—"

After crossing the carpet in three swift steps, Wrexford swept the boy into a fierce hug.

"Oiy, oiy! You're cracking my ribs!"

*Be damned with appearing a sentimental fool.* He held tight, reveling in every little jab and jut of the boy's bony body.

Sheffield cleared his throat with a cough—or perhaps it was a laugh. Wrexford didn't care. Raven's warmth was melting the ice from his blood.

"What happened to your face, lad?" queried his friend.

"I slipped on the cobblestones . . ."

Wrexford reluctantly allowed Raven to wriggle free. The boy's cheek was scraped, and the bruise spreading over his jaw made his grin look a little lopsided.

"But thanks to Skinny, the smarmy dastard couldn't catch me!"

"What dastard? And why Skinny—" began the earl, only to have the rest of his question die on his lips as Raven plucked a packet of papers out of his pocket.

"The dastard who pushed Copley under the wheels of a curricle—it was horrible—tried to steal these documents from inside his coat," explained the boy in a rush. "I figured they must be important, so I snatched them for you."

The thick papers were speckled with blood, noted the earl, as he accepted them from Raven. "Well done, lad."

"That isn't all, sir."

His hands tightened, setting off a faint crackling.

"Lord Copley whispered something just before the dastard crushed his throat," continued Raven. "He said, 'Blue Peter. Watch for Blue Peter.'"

Wrexford frowned in thought. "Who would be called by such a moniker?"

"Someone at the docks?" suggested Sheffield. "There are all manner of exotic foreigners working as stevedores or warehouse workers. Perhaps *blue* refers to a tattoo?"

"Excellent thinking, Kit. That makes sense. Sir Darius and his friends might know of him."

"There's another thing, sir," said Raven. "The dastard who pushed Copley was wearing white gloves. Seemed odd to me."

The boy was right. It *was* odd. However, that little detail could wait. The earl moved to his desk. "Never mind that now. Before anything else, we need to look at these papers."

Raven and Sheffield hurried to join him as Wrexford unfolded the sheaf of documents. The top sheet was a letter, written in a tiny, cramped script. But before he read it, he took a quick look beneath it.

A smile touched his lips, mingling both surprise and satisfaction. He passed several of the pages to Sheffield.

"By Jove," murmured his friend as he quickly scanned the contents. He paused for a moment to touch the thick wax seals affixed to one page, next to the signature of Jameson Thirkell Mansfield, Earl of Woodbridge, before looking up. "I thought it a lost cause, but you did it, Wrex."

"*We* did it," murmured Wrexford, reaching out to ruffle Raven's hair.

In addition to the legal papers naming Woodbridge as sole proprietor of Argentum Trading Company, Copley had included all the bank promissory notes that Woodbridge had entrusted to the consortium. While the others chortled in celebration, the earl quickly returned to the letter, anxious to know what had caused Copley to have a crisis of conscience.

"Bloody hell," he whispered after reading through the long and detailed explanation. It didn't excuse the baron's choices. But perhaps his final act was an atonement of sorts for his past sins.

"What?" demanded Sheffield.

"Copley has given me all the pieces of the Argentum puzzle." A grunt. "Save for the name of the real ringleader, which he wanted to tell me in person, rather than commit to paper."

The earl refolded the letter and put it in his pocket. "But never mind that now. We must move quickly. You need to rush to Woodbridge's residence. I'll be by shortly with my carriage to fetch both of you." He explained why. "But say nothing to Lady Cordelia. I don't wish for her to get her hopes up, in case things don't go well."

Turning to Raven, he touched the boy's scraped cheek. "My apologies, lad, but might I ask you to run several more errands?"

Raven let out a snigger. "Just because I agreed to a fancy new name doesn't mean I've gone soft as a prancing popinjay. What do you need me to do?"

Wrexford scribbled out two short notes and handed them over. "Run to Bow Street and hand the first one to Griffin, who should be waiting for it. Then head to the Sun and Sextant Club and leave the other for Sir Darius Roy," he replied. "After that, return to Lady Charlotte and ask her to don her urchin's garb and come to my townhouse as soon as it's dark."

By then, he hoped to have some good news. "Oh, and you may tell McClellan that she has orders to make you and Hawk as many ginger biscuits as you can eat."

A whoop echoed in the corridor as the boy raced off.

"Ah, to possess the resilience of youth," said Sheffield, flexing his shoulders as he picked up his hat from the work counter. "It's a sad commentary on my advancing age when the prospect of a full night of sleep seems far more desirable than a great many other pleasures."

The earl opened his desk drawer and took out several items, which he quickly shoved into his pockets. Given what the rest of Copley's letter had spelled out, the final moves of the games within games were about to play out.

"If Luck falls our way, we will all soon be resting easy."

Charlotte paused in her pacing to take a look out the window of her workroom. *No sign of the boys.* But a grudging glance at the mantel clock was a stark reminder that sheer force of will couldn't force the hands to turn any faster.

"Then again," she muttered, "perhaps Professor Sudler could design an intricate machine to make time fly." A sigh. "His Engine certainly makes numbers do things that astound the imagination."

The street below was quiet, with naught but a stray dog

sniffing through the bushes. A breeze ruffled the ivy growing outside the mullioned glass, setting the dark, glossy leaves to chattering against the panes. Twitching the draperies back in place, Charlotte returned to her desk and picked up her pen.

The half-finished sketch was a clever composition. A caricature of Copley peered out from behind an ornate tea chest, its lid open to reveal a pile of silver coins. In pencil, she had lettered a large caption that read WHAT IS LORD COPLEY HIDING?

But instead of dipping the nib in the inkwell, Charlotte set her pen down in frustration. Until Wrexford returned from his meeting with the baron, it was pointless to continue. Satire was most effective when one knew a subject's weaknesses. And given the events of last night, it was she and her friends who were most vulnerable.

Copley was no fool. She shuddered to think of how he meant to leverage his advantage.

Another glance at the clock. Surely by now, the meeting was over.

Realizing that her hands were shaking, she curled her fingers into fists and pressed them to her temples.

*Where the devil is Wrexford?*

A muted jingle of bells sounded as Wrexford pushed open the door to J. F. Stockton & Co. Despite the windows looking out on the narrow side street, the reception area was dark, and the air fusty with the scent of stale smoke and sour cabbage. A lone clerk was at work at the desk behind the reception counter, a massive fortresslike hulk of age-black oak that looked deliberately designed to repel intruders. He rose reluctantly, his eyes narrowing to a suspicious squint as he peered out at the earl.

"Yes?"

Wrexford assumed his most imperious stare. "I wish to speak with Mr. Stockton." He placed a pristine calling card on the dusty wood and slid it toward the fellow. "I need to conduct some financial transactions, and I have it from reliable sources that this establishment is capable of handling them in a discreet manner."

The clerk's expression turned decidedly less hostile. "Please have a seat for a moment . . ." He waved at two straight-backed chairs sitting in the shadow of the reception counter. "While I see whether Mr. Stockton is free to see you, sir."

He disappeared through a paneled door leading to the back of the building. Ignoring the chairs, the earl moved to the window and flashed a quick signal.

A moment later, the clerk returned, followed by a tall, beefy man with a fringe of greying hair circling his bald pate. His face was unremarkable, save for the ferret-like eyes that gleamed through the round glass of his gold-rimmed spectacles.

"Lord Wrexford, I am Stockton." He rubbed his plump hands together. "How may I be of service?"

"I understand you are an establishment that can be trusted to do its business discreetly."

"Quite right, quite right. Discretion is our motto, milord," replied Stockton with an oily smile. "We pride ourselves on performing our tasks so efficiently and quietly that no one even notices we're here."

Wrexford pursed his lips.

"Does that satisfy your needs, sir?"

"I believe it does."

"Excellent, excellent." Stockton stepped aside with an unctuous bow and gestured for Wrexford to proceed into the inner sanctum. "Let us go into my private office, where we may discuss your needs with all due privacy."

The earl took several steps and then turned, making sure to

block the opening in the counter so the banker couldn't slip past him. "Just a moment." A wave to the window. "My partners in this transaction are joining me."

Stockton wet his lips. "W-wouldn't d-discretion be better served by a more intimate discussion . . ."

He fell silent as the bells jangled.

"Not at all," said Wrexford. "I trust them wholeheartedly."

The banker's throat constricted in a sickly swallow as he eyed the untidy bulk of Griffin, flanked by Sheffield and Woodbridge, squeeze through the front door.

"Come." The earl took Stockton's arm. "Lead the way."

The thud of their steps sounded unnaturally loud as they made their way through the dimly lit corridor. Wrexford could smell fear wafting off the banker as the man pushed open the door to his private lair.

"We needn't take up much of your time, Stockton," he said. "What we have in mind is actually a simple transaction. We simply need to close an account that we have with you."

Stockton had scuttled behind his desk as soon as Wrexford had released his arm. He was now staring at the earl in confusion. "I fear there has been some m-mistake. You gentlemen have no—"

"Ah, did I neglect to mention the name of our enterprise?" interrupted the earl. "It's Argentum Trading Company. Of which Lord Woodbridge is the sole proprietor."

Woodbridge stepped forward and placed the official company documents on the desk, along with the account statement provided by Copley.

"B-but I've always dealt with someone else from Argentum," stammered the banker. "He gave strict orders—"

"Never mind his orders," snapped Sheffield. "He no longer works for the company."

"B-but . . ."

"Be assured, you won't be seeing the fellow again," said Sheffield with a wolfish grin. "He's dead."

Wrexford gave Stockton a moment to digest the news. "As you see, the papers are all in perfect order. In fact, to ensure that all the legalities are followed to the letter, we've brought along our friend Mr. Griffin, the head Runner with the Bow Street magistrates."

Griffin shifted his unbuttoned coat just enough to show a flash of his red vest and badge.

The flickering lamplight showed that Stockton's face was now the same sickly shade of white as the underbelly of a dead codfish.

"Once this particular transaction goes smoothly, we'll all be on our way." The earl tapped the account statement. "We wish to withdraw these funds and receive a document, signed and witnessed by the present company, acknowledging that Argentum's account is closed."

"I-I haven't anywhere near that amount of money here, milord. It will take—"

In one swift motion, Wrexford seized the banker by his soiled cravat and hauled him up from his chair. "On the contrary, you expected to turn the funds over tomorrow. So, you've conveniently converted all the various bills of exchange made out to Argentum that have been deposited here over the past three months into standard Bank of England letters of credit, which are negotiable anywhere."

Stockton's eyes were bulging.

"Yes, I know exactly how you do business with Argentum. Now, make your decision. Head to your safe now, and we'll overlook your part in this scheme. Or head to Newgate Prison."

A whimper as the earl released his hold, followed by a hurried scrabbling as Stockton unlocked his desk drawer and snatched up a ring of keys.

"And you will, of course, add the additional funds that have come in over this week from the daily arbitrage trades," Wrexford called as the banker scurried from the room.

Woodbridge expelled a pent-up breath. "Thank you, Wrexford."

"You're welcome. But next time you're tempted to make an investment, kindly consult your sister. She has a better head for business than you do." He passed over a second packet of papers to Lady Cordelia's brother. "I'll leave the three of you to finish up here. Once you have the letters of credit, Woodbridge, go to the banks from whom you've borrowed and pay off your loans. Once you're done, I imagine you'll have a tidy sum left over for putting your estate back in order."

Cocking a small salute, Wrexford moved for the door. "Now it's time to put an end to the rest of this sordid scheme."

"Copley is *dead*?" Charlotte had risen from her chair when Raven rushed into her workroom, but now sat down again rather heavily.

"Oiy!" The boy explained about the shove that had sent the baron to his death, and the ensuing struggle for the documents.

A horrified hiss slipped from her lips as he described his escape from the man's clutches. "Thank heavens for Skinny's quick thinking."

Raven grinned, accentuating the purpling bruise spreading over his jaw. "Us guttersnipes stick together."

"That scrape needs to be cleaned, and a cold compress put on the swelling," she said, forcing herself not to think of what else might have happened. As for Skinny . . ."

"No need to fuss!" Raven danced out of arm's reach. "McClellan said she'll have a piece of beefsteak ready to put on the bruise by the time the batch of ginger biscuits comes out of the oven."

Charlotte surrendered a sigh. For the boys, sweets were panacea for every ailment. "Very well. But let us go to the kitchen now."

McClellan had just set the hot pan of pastries on the hob as they entered the sugar-scented room. A moment later, Hawk flew in through the back door.

"Biscuits!" he chirped. "Huzzah! I'm famished."

A telltale smudge of jam on his chin belied the assertion. And it explained why he had taken so long to return from delivering a note to Alison.

"After you've gobbled down your share," said his brother, "we need to go down to the docks and ask around for a man by the name of Blue Peter."

"Blue Peter?" pressed Charlotte.

"Oiy." Raven told her about Copley's last words. "His Lordship and Mr. Sheffield think the cove must know something important."

"Perhaps he's privy to the identity of the man who's manipulating all this mayhem," suggested McClellan.

Charlotte shook her head. Raven had dodged enough danger for one day. One did not spit in the face of Luck. "No, I think it best not to stir up suspicions on the wharves until Wrexford has decided what to do."

The boy made a face, but he didn't argue. "*Optimam partem exercitus discretio,*" he murmured. *Discretion is the better part of valor.* "I suppose that makes sense. His Lordship wants us all to gather at his townhouse right after dark, so we can draw up a plan for crushing these bastards."

"Don't say 'bastard,'" whispered Hawk. "It's very ungentlemanly."

Raven crammed a biscuit in his mouth. "Those bastards ain't gentlemen."

\* \* \*

"Well, well." Sir Darius steepled his fingers and stared pensively at the fire burning in the private parlor's hearth. "Both Alston and Copley are dead?"

Wrexford nodded. "Within hours of each other."

His friends Jiang and Gu exchanged troubled looks.

"Our informants have passed on no other names," said Jiang. "That means whoever is in charge is—"

"Diabolically clever and cunning," finished Sir Darius.

"There's Mather," pointed out Gu. "Though it would surprise me. He's ambitious enough but doesn't strike me as having the cold-blooded imagination for such actions."

For a long moment the only sound in the room was the hissing of the undulating flames.

"Copley said the name Blue Peter with his dying breath." Wrexford raised a brow at the two Chinese diplomats. "Have any of your informants mentioned a man by that name?"

They shook their heads.

"The only other clue is that the assassin was wearing white gloves," the earl added.

Jiang tapped his fingertips together. "But all you English gentlemen wear gloves when you go out, and in a wide assortment of colors."

"Yes, but never white," replied Wrexford. "It must mean something."

The echo of his words seemed to crackle through the air, along with the sound of the crumbling coals.

"By Jove, of course!" Sir Darius suddenly sat up straighter, nearly tipping over his chair. "Blue Peter! It's not a person. It's a nautical flag! One that's flown from the topmast to signal all hands must return to the ship because the vessel is about to set sail. The thing is . . ."

Wrexford went very still, waiting for him to go on.

"The thing is, it's mostly used by the Royal Navy. And it's British military officers who wear white gloves."

"We saw a naval frigate moored at one of the East India Company docks yesterday," said Jiang.

"And were told that it's rare to see one there," added Gu.

"Which wharf?" demanded the earl.

"The one nearest Old Dock," replied Jiang.

"The devil be damned." The earl snatched up his hat and bolted for the door.

"Wait! Where are you going?" called Sir Darius.

"To beat a dastard at his own cunning little game."

# CHAPTER 29

Tyler looked up as Wrexford slipped into the workroom. "The others are all gathered downstairs. I'm just gathering some papers Lady Cord—"

"Ssshh." The earl quietly closed the door. "I prefer to come and go without them knowing I've been here."

"Trouble?" asked the valet, watching the earl take down the pearwood case holding his pistols from one of the shelves.

"Perhaps." He checked the priming and then shrugged out of his snugly tailored dress coat. "Kindly fetch my black overcoat."

The valet returned in a moment from the adjoining storeroom. Wrexford slid the weapons into the deep pockets, along with a pouch of extra bullets.

"I need you to do one other task for me," he said. "Once you've taken the papers to Lady Cordelia, leave quietly, and then go to Bow Street and ask Griffin to come meet me at Old Dock, within the East India Company complex. Have him bring several of his men and find a place to hide and wait for my signal."

Wrexford added a vial of gunpowder to his pocket. "I'd ask the Weasels to do it, but I fear that Lady Charlotte would feel compelled to follow me." The idea of her crossing swords with a man for whom violent death was a way of life made the burn of bile rise in his gorge. "And that would be too bloody dangerous."

"You know who's behind all this?" asked Tyler, passing over a thin-bladed knife for the earl to slide into the hidden sheath inside his boot.

"I do."

"The question is, can you prove it?" The valet's expression was grim. "I've heard that Copley passed on a number of incriminating documents, but these dastards have been awfully clever in leaving no tangible clues. And with the other conspirators dead . . ."

"You're right. The man who's been manipulating all the pieces on the game board has been exceedingly clever. However, there is one telling piece of evidence, and I expect to find it tonight. That, along with the confessions in Copley's note, will be enough to prove the dastard's guilt."

Wrexford reached up and adjusted his hat, pulling it low on his brow. "You see, I now understand what those mathematical calculations that Lady Cordelia and the professor have been running are for. Our adversary isn't just interested in buying and selling silver. He's got an even more lucrative plan in mind."

Tyler, never one to dither in his thoughts, hesitated in answering. "Which makes him even more bloody dangerous." Their eyes met. "You shouldn't go alone. I'll come—"

"No," he said flatly. "Copley's murder proves the ringleader has at least one ruthless henchman on the loose. Lady Cordelia and the professor may be at risk, so I need you and Kit to remain on guard here."

The valet's nostrils flared in frustration.

"There's no need to worry. Griffin and his men are reliable."

After a last pat to his pockets, Wrexford turned without further word and moved noiselessly into the corridor.

A muffled laugh floated up from the stairs leading down to the kitchen and workroom.

*Charlotte.* However faint, her voice had a way of wrapping itself around his heart.

He paused for just an instant and then quickly retraced his steps to the front of the townhouse, taking care to stay light on his feet as he crossed the marble tiles of the entrance hall. Silence shrouded the unlit space. He reached for the door latch— only to freeze as a muted *click-click* caught his ear.

A long moment slid by, and then it came again. *Click-click.* He turned to see a large shaggy shape materialize from the gloom.

*Click-click.* Harper padded across checkered tiles, his long claws trailing tiny sounds across the stone.

"Go back," growled the earl, punctuating the order with a brusque wave.

The hound stopped and wagged his tail.

"Back!" he repeated. "Stay with the Weasels."

A whuffle. Which sounded suspiciously similar to a human sigh. Wrexford held his breath, silently cursing Tyler's soft-headedness in bringing the big beast to London simply to amuse the boys. But to his relief, Harper turned, head drooping in disappointment, and retreated back the way he had come.

He waited until silence had once again settled over the house, then eased the door open and slipped out into the night.

The tide was at low ebb, the stink of decay rising up to foul the mist-chilled air.

The earl crept down Robin Hood Lane and let himself into the East India docklands through the locked gate by Leicester Street. A cluster of squat warehouses stood huddled dark on dark within the gloom. After following the narrow walkway around to the front of the complex, he found a recessed niche and took shelter in order to survey the surroundings.

Up ahead, past the cluttered shipyard, a glimmer of moonlight on the wind-rippled water showed the silhouette of the naval frigate moored in the protected pool of Old Dock. Flickers of lantern light showed the ship wasn't sleeping.

Was that a flutter of a naval flag atop the mainmast? Wrexford squinted, but the distance was too great to tell for sure.

Swiveling his gaze to the row of windowless brick buildings to his left, he saw a dull hint of light skitter through the fog. One of the far doors appeared slightly ajar. Easing a pistol from his pocket, Wrexford picked his way through the shadows toward the glow.

A muttering of voices floated out from behind the half-open door. After inching a step closer, he ventured a peek through the narrow gap between the heavy hinges.

"All is in readiness?" Despite its low pitch, the voice was instantly recognizable.

"Aye, sir," came the reply. "Pass me the cargo by noon, and I'll sail on the afternoon tide."

A ghost of a laugh. "Never fear, Barton. You'll have the precious letter of credit. And once you pass it off to our East India captain in Tenerife, this voyage will be the most profitable one ever." A pause. "But not nearly as profitable as our other venture."

Wrexford allowed a small smile. His guess had been right about the ringleader. *You rolled the dice and chose to move the wrong pieces on the game board.*

Barton cleared his throat. "I apologize again for Lieutenant Waltham's mishandling of his mission."

"An unfortunate bungling. But Copley's crisis of conscience has come to naught. Thankfully, we need not fret over a filthy little urchin who was hoping to snatch money. I'll wager that the documents have already been tossed away in some stinking alleyway, which serves our purposes just as well," replied the ringleader. "However, incompetence in our underlings can't be tolerated. See to it that Waltham is lost at sea before you reach Tenerife."

"Aye, sir." The scuff of leather on stone. "If you've no further orders—"

"Actually, I wish to borrow your book of navigation tables until morning." A whisper of shuffling papers. "I'll come with you to the ship. There are times when I miss the feel of a deck beneath my feet."

Wrexford quickly drew back and slipped into the narrow gap between buildings.

The two men came out. A scudding of starlight sparked in the ringleader's silvery hair as he closed the door behind him. The earl watched them turn onto one of the walkways leading through the warren of smaller storage sheds down to the wharves.

*Hubris.* There had been no snick of the lock and no sign of papers in the ringleader's hands. *A fatal flaw in men who think themselves so much cleverer than other mere mortals.*

Holding himself in check, Wrexford remained in his hiding place, watching and waiting to be sure the area was deserted. There was no hurry. He merely needed to retrieve the sample calculations run by Lady Cordelia and the professor—he was now sure the whispery flutter had been made by the incriminating papers—and show them to Griffin.

The evidence, along with Copley's letter explaining the scheme and his own testimony, should convince the Runner to arrest the three conspirators.

As the shadows suddenly deepened, he looked up and saw the clouds were thickening. All the better for making his move.

It took only a moment to dart around the corner of the building and enter the warehouse. The oil lamp had been left alight, and there on the small table were the mathematical tables created by the Computing Engine.

*Numbers calculated in blood.* Three men lay dead.

The earl reached out to pick them up. . . .

Only to feel the prick of a sword point between his shoulder blades.

"Tsk, tsk, Lord Wrexford. You've been alarmingly clever about a good many things. But, alas, you failed to realize that a man who's spent his life at sea becomes attuned to every tiny sound around him, no matter how nuanced. I thought I heard a whisper of wool." The blade dug in a little deeper. "So I decided to come back. And lo and behold, look what I've found."

*Hubris.* Wrexford cursed himself for being such a bloody, bloody fool. "Do try not to put a hole in my coat, Sir Charles. My valet would be greatly distressed. It pains him when I injure my clothing."

"An injury to your clothing is the least of your concerns," replied the admiral. "Now kindly raise your hands above your head." One by one, he removed the pistols from the earl's coat pockets and tucked them in his own. "And now turn around. Slowly, if you will. I would hate to cut your throat now, but be assured I'll do so if necessary."

Wrexford did as he was ordered.

"Well, well, here we are, with the last roll of the dice about to be made." The admiral's smile was coolly unemotional. He might have been merely sliding the black-and-white backgammon markers across the game board. "You played well, milord, with a bold and imaginative strategy. I like that in a man."

"But clearly, my imagination wasn't quite a match for yours." The earl wanted to keep Sir Charles talking while he assessed his options. Which, at the moment, appeared rather limited. "I'm curious. I've worked out most of the puzzle, but there are a few missing pieces. How did you first come to have a hold on Copley?"

"I commanded a squadron of frigates escorting troop ships to India during the Mysore uprising in ninety-nine. As the French were supporting Tipu Sultan, I had orders to remain in the area and keep the oceans under British control," replied the admiral. "As you know, the navy pays its officers a pittance. While I was based in Calcutta, there was an opportunity to acquire some exotic and expensive merchandise for my trip home. My cousin Elgin owed me a great favor from his youth, and so he signed certain papers that allowed me access to the restricted warehouse, pretending, of course, that he didn't really know that I meant to steal the items."

Sir Charles shrugged. "The saintly Lord Copley was like that. He took great care to ensure that no dirt could cling to his pristine reputation."

"And once you had him in your clutches—" began Wrexford.

"I saw the opportunity for building a smuggling network," interjected the admiral, appearing happy to have an audience. "Like Elgin, I had a very good mind for business. And ample opportunity to think during the endless hours at sea. A fortuitous meeting with Fenwick Alston provided me with an excellent partner on shore. Together we built a very profitable enterprise."

"But then his corruption was discovered."

"Yes, Elgin wasn't able to cover that up. But it turned out it opened up other opportunities."

Wrexford thought over what he knew about Alston and suddenly fitted in another missing piece of the puzzle. "So Alston went to the West Indies. As did you."

"Very good, milord. You've an agile mind. Yes, I asked the Admiralty for a chance to do my duty in the Caribbean. Which offered a great many smuggling possibilities between the French- and British-held islands, as well as America."

"It didn't bother you that you were conspiring with the enemy?"

"Oh, come, Wrexford. I've heard you're a man who has little patience for the silly strictures of conventional morality."

*I have even less for selfish greed and cold-blooded murder.* The earl managed to hold back the retort. There were still things he wished to clarify, so quickly he changed the subject.

"So, once Copley returned to England, you decided to move your base of operations to London?"

"Opium was growing more and more profitable, and we still had a network of partners in India. We simply had to make some logistical adjustments," explained Sir Charles.

His expression darkened. "And as the need for our naval presence in the West Indies was lessening, the Admiralty decided to put me ashore at half pay."

Greed and hubris, thought the earl, were always a dangerous combination.

"As so," said Wrexford, "the idea for Argentum Trading Company was conceived."

"Yes, but as the logistics for shipping tea became increasingly complicated, and the bribes involved increasingly expensive, I saw a new opportunity. I'm very good at mathematics, and during the long voyages, I read extensively on stock trading and bills of exchange. The system of arbitrage was intriguing. And then I heard about Woodbridge and his brilliant sister, who had access to a wondrous machine."

"That explains all your commercial ventures," mused Wrexford. "But tell, when did you realize you could make a fortune from creating truly accurate navigational tables?"

"Ah." The admiral looked surprised. "You're even cleverer than I thought. Pray, how did you figure that out?"

"It doesn't matter," he replied, not wishing to risk putting Lady Cordelia and the professor in peril before Sir Charles and his conspirators were arrested. He took some grim solace in the fact that his own death would hasten their demise. "Suffice it to say, I simply began adding up a number of clues—complex calculations, shipping, your expertise in navigation—and came up with the answer."

Wrexford paused and then sought to confirm one other piece of the puzzle that Copley had revealed in his letter. "It was you who murdered Fenwick Alston, wasn't it? I assume it's because he realized you were going to cut him out of the new venture, and he was seeking to blackmail you over the Argentum business."

"You *are* astute." Sir Charles gave a mournful shake of his head. "It's a pity you have to die."

Wrexford eyed the naval cutlass, gauging whether he could knock it aside before it slit his throat. However, the admiral, despite his age, was quick to catch the flicker of his gaze.

The steel point flashed in the lamplight and pressed at a point just below the earl's chin. A bead of blood welled up.

"I'm very, very good at the game of war, Lord Wrexford, be it on the backgammon board or in the flesh. As I said, I regret that I can't let you live. But die you must. However, I'll do you the courtesy of answering your last question. Yes, accurate navigation tables will make me rich beyond my wildest dreams. As you know, they are a key compendium of numbers that allow sailors to determine their exact position in the ocean after using a sextant to triangulate the ship's position relative to the sun. And the current ones are riddled with errors. The British government will pay an astronomical amount of money to possess a perfect version, as it gives both naval and commercial ships an advantage over those who don't have them."

The admiral smiled. "Or I could provoke a bidding war. America would likely be willing to make a handsome offer."

"A pox on your traitorous hide," replied Wrexford.

"Curse me all you like but it's you who are going to your Maker." Another prick, another drop of blood. "Now we're going to take a stroll down to the frigate," said Sir Charles as he carefully shifted to stand behind Wrexford, circling the sword around the base of the earl's throat as he moved.

A walk that would take him through the shipyard, thought Wrexford, where Griffin and his men would be waiting.

Perhaps all was not lost.

However, that hope died a quick death, as the admiral prodded him toward a different footpath as soon as they left the warehouse. "We'll take a more roundabout way to the wharf. One that's more hidden. We wouldn't want to be spotted, would we?"

Wrexford said nothing but kept moving, as demanded by the bite of steel. Somehow, he would have to find a way to make an unholy racket—knocking over some crates or barrels came to mind—and hope that Griffin would come running.

"Halt."

Lost in his thoughts, it took Wrexford an instant to obey. Then he heard it, too—a low raspy sound, like iron reverberating against iron, coming from somewhere close by.

The admiral peered all around, trying to see through the serpentine swirls of fog. "What the devil—"

The rasp suddenly turned into a roar. . . .

And then all hell broke loose.

As the sword fell away from the back of his neck, Wrexford spun around just in time to see a huge dark shape come hurtling out of the shadows and knock Sir Charles to the ground. A scream rose above the bloodcurdling snaps and snarls as the blade went flying.

"Get off me! Get off me!" howled Sir Charles, scrabbling at his coat and trying to draw the pistols. He managed to pull one of them free, but as he tried to take aim, a hairy paw batted the barrel away.

A deafening explosion rent the air, the shower of sparks momentarily illuminating Harper's bared fangs, mere inches from the admiral's terrified face. Claw marks cut across both of his cheeks, and his cravat was torn to shreds.

Wrexford grabbed at the hound's leather collar and fought to pull him off his prey. "Harper! Harper, enough!"

The sound of running feet echoed off the sooty brick.

"Wrexford!"

"Over here, Griffin!" he called. Releasing his hold on Harper, he pointed to one of the side alleys. "Go!" he said in a low voice. "Sit and stay quiet."

The admiral was still curled in a fetal position, moaning as if Cerberus, the mythical hound of hell, were gnawing on his leg.

A moment later the Runner broke free of the fog and skidded to a halt, several men right behind him.

"Lord Almighty," muttered Griffin after eyeing the admiral's bleeding hands and mangled clothing. "What happened to him?"

"Divine retribution?" suggested Wrexford.

Griffin didn't smile. "Holy hell," he said, crouching down for a closer look.

"Looks like one of the guard dogs broke loose from the kennel," offered one of the Runner's men. "Those big mastiffs are nasty, ill-tempered brutes."

Griffin looked up in question at the earl. And received a shrug in reply.

"Yes, so it would seem." Wrexford rubbed at his neck. "Never mind the beast. You need to round up the rest of the dastards. Have your men board the frigate and arrest Captain Barton and Lieutenant Waltham. You'll also find a sheaf of documents in an open warehouse just up this footpath. Retrieve them. They'll be important evidence in proving the admiral's perfidy in one of his many crimes."

Griffin barked at his men, and they raced off.

Sir Charles had recovered his composure and slowly sat up. "Evidence?" He laughed. "A sheaf of mathematical calculations isn't evidence of a crime. You've got no proof of anything."

"On the contrary, Sir Charles," said Wrexford. "Lord Copley wrote a very detailed confession on your various ventures."

"But that . . ." began the admiral, and then he abruptly fell silent.

"But that disappeared?" The earl smiled. "Unfortunately for you, there are some street urchins who know how to read."

The admiral paled.

"And by the by . . ." Wrexford couldn't resist a last little jab. "You would have found Argentum Trading Company's bank account empty when you visited Stockton's bank tomorrow— including not only the original funds but also all the additional profits generated by Lady Cordelia Mansfield. Like you, she's very, very good at mathematics and business."

Griffin frowned. "What in the devil are you talking about?"

"I'll explain later about Lord Woodbridge's sister," replied the earl.

Sir Charles was shaking with fury. "The bloody bitch! She'll go down with me. I'll make public her financial machinations. Her reputation will be ruined, and she'll go to prison!"

Wrexford laughed. "She did nothing illegal. As for ruining her reputation, what man in his right mind will believe such a story! A lady being smarter than all the male stockbrokers in London?" He shook his head. "I'm afraid she outwitted you, Sir Charles. You lost that game, as well as this one."

Snarling an oath, the admiral drew the second pistol, but Griffin kicked it from his hand.

"Get up, you mangy cur." The Runner seized the admiral by his collar and hauled him to his feet. To Wrexford, he added, "I wish to ensure that my men and I tie up all the loose ends here, so I'd prefer to put off hearing your full explanation until later." His mouth twitched. "Let us meet at your townhouse in the morning, say, around breakfast time?"

The earl watched Griffin lead his prisoner toward the wharves and waited until the two figures were swallowed in the sea of vaporous mist before turning away to the alleyway behind him.

"You can come out now, Weasels."

A gust of wind rattled the iron padlocks of the nearby ware-houses. And then in the hazy silence that followed, he heard the light-footed patter of steps on the hard-packed ground.

"I gave strict orders that you weren't to follow me," he said as he spotted two—or was it three?—wraithlike shapes flitting within the shadows of the alleyway's opening.

"We weren't following you." Raven's disembodied voice floated out from the darkness. "We were following Harper."

"We were worried about him," added Hawk. "He's new to London and doesn't know his way around."

The earl felt his lips twitch. "I should birch your bottoms—all three of you."

"Oiy, well," retorted Raven, "I s'pose a sore bum is worth not having to tell m'lady that your head was severed from your neck and rolled into the River Thames."

"Spare the rod, spoil the child," the earl countered.

Hawk chortled. "We're not children. We're Weasels."

"In that case—"

"Oh, do stop ringing a peal over their heads, Wrexford." Charlotte slipped out from her hiding place just as a blade of moonlight cut through the clouds. The pale light was lost for a moment in the dirty brim of her urchin's cap, but she looked up, and in that instant, her face came alive with a luminous glow.

His heart skittered and skipped a beat.

"We all know your bark is worse than your bite . . . ,"

A low *woof* punctuated her words.

"By now," she went on, "you should know better than to think we were going to let you sneak away and confront the devils on your own."

It took him a moment to find his voice. "I suppose I keep hoping that Reason will triumph over . . ."

*Emotion?* He wished he could give a name to the rippling he saw in the depth of her eyes.

They stood, gazes locked, as another phalanx of iron-dark clouds stormed in from the west and shrouded the moon. Wrexford blinked, and suddenly he felt her arms come around him and the warmth of her body press against his.

"The definition of *insanity* is 'to keep repeating the same experiment...'" Charlotte leaned back and traced her palm along the line of his jaw. "'And think that you'll get a different result.'"

He laughed. *Insanity.* Perhaps that explained the fizzy heat bubbling through his blood. "An interesting concept to ponder." He caught her hand and twined his fingers with hers. "However, right now, I'm too exhausted to think about anything but making our way home."

Charlotte tightened her hold.

"Weasels," called Wrexford. "Hold on to Harper. We wouldn't want the beast to get lost on his way back to Mayfair. And kindly refrain from any further mischief."

"Indeed," murmured Charlotte as they turned to make their way out of the dockyard. "I think we've all had enough mischief for one night."

# CHAPTER 30

Dropping the playing cards in his hand, Sheffield jumped up from his chair as the door bumped open.

"Thank heaven," he said, a smile chasing the pinch of worry from his face.

Lady Cordelia was on her feet, as well. Darting around the table, she hurried to Charlotte and clasped her in a quick hug, then flashed a grateful look at Wrexford. "Yes, thank heaven you're both safe." Her breath caught in her throat. "And the boys—"

"The boys are fine," assured Charlotte, though a chill touched her spine on thinking about what a razor-thin line had separated life from death for Wrexford. She had taken aim with her pistol when the admiral had forced him toward the wharves, but the angle had made it a dangerous shot. . . .

The scrabbling of the boys and their companion on the stairs drew her back from brooding over what might have been. Wrexford had exercised his lordly prerogative and commandeered one of Griffin's waiting carriages to carry all of them back to his townhouse.

They burst into the room, the boys nearly tripping over the hound's long legs in their rush to tell the others about the events of the evening.

"Harper saved the day!" announced Raven.

Much to Hawk's hilarity, Harper padded over to the hearth and, after a gusty canine stretch, dropped to the floor and promptly fell asleep.

"Hold your fire, lad," ordered Tyler from the corridor. "And wait until we're all assembled before you begin." He appeared a moment later, followed by Woodbridge.

Charlotte knew the two of them had been standing guard at the front and the rear of the townhouse, in case the enemy had discovered where the professor and his Computing Engine were hidden. She smiled to see they had set aside their weapons and were now each carrying a bottle of the earl's finest whisky.

Wrexford made an appreciative sound deep in his throat. "Remind me to raise your wages." After taking the spirits from his valet, he moved to the tray of glasses on the sideboard. Flickers of amber danced through the candlelight as he poured out six measures.

Raven's face fell.

The earl cast a look at Charlotte, who answered with a tiny nod. He drizzled a small taste of the spirits into the two remaining glasses and handed them to the boys while Tyler passed around the other libations.

"*Slàinte.*" Cocking a salute, Wrexford swirled the spirits and drained his drink in one swift swallow.

Closing her eyes, Charlotte chose to savor the whisky, slowly allowing its fire to melt the last bit of ice in her blood and form a mellow pool of warmth deep inside her.

*Fire and ice.* For a moment, the happy chatter of voices around her blurred to an indistinct babble as the spirits stirred the strangest thoughts. She had left England as a giddy, rebellious schoolgirl, oh-so sure that Love would smooth all of

Life's rough edges. Those innocent illusions hadn't lasted long. She had returned to London as a practical, pragmatic woman of the world, wary of foolish fantasies and youthful hubris.

Survival demanded strength. Emotions made one vulnerable.

The sounds grew a little louder, provoking an odd little flutter inside her rib cage. So it was, Charlotte admitted, an irony that emotion had—against all reason—somehow found its way back into her heart.

It was frightening. *I know the pain and heartache of disappointed dreams.*

And yet . . .

*And yet Love in all its glorious permutations has taken hold of me.*

Her lashes lifted, and Charlotte found Wrexford was watching her with a Sphinxlike stare.

*In ways I can't begin to define.*

"A penny for your thoughts?" he murmured after coming to stand beside her.

"I'm not sure they're worth a farthing," she said lightly.

A tiny crease formed between his brows, but before he could reply, Cordelia set down her glass and cleared her throat.

"Is the evil really over?" she asked, placing a hand on her brother's arm.

"It is," replied Wrexford. "The ringleader and his henchmen have been apprehended. They won't harm anyone else."

Woodbridge let out a shuddering sigh. "I can't begin to express my thanks." He looked around. "To all of you, who risked your lives to save me from my own bloody foolishness." His gaze dropped to the toes of his boots. "There aren't words for what you did."

"Actually, there's a simple one," said Charlotte. "Friendship. A bond that brings out strengths that we sometimes don't even know we possess."

Cordelia gave her brother a quick hug. "Your intentions

were all for the good, Jamie. You were trying to save the estate from our father's folly and ensure that our tenants wouldn't suffer because of his spendthrift ways. That you trusted your friend David Mather is only to your credit—"

"Speaking of Mather," interrupted Sheffield. "He's on the ship, so perhaps the evil isn't yet over."

"Copley explained about Mather in his note," said Wrexford. "Along with a number of other things." He blew out his breath. "The details can all be parsed at a later time. For now, I shall try to explain it all in a nutshell."

Tyler moved over and wordlessly refilled the earl's glass.

"Like many younger sons, Mather had little money and was jealous of his wealthy friends within the beau monde. So he swallowed his scruples when Copley recruited him to find someone to draw into the scheme for Argentum Trading Company."

"Which proved to be me, a gullible lackwit," muttered Woodbridge in self-disgust.

"But it wasn't just greed. Copley also used a bit of blackmail himself, forcing Mather to cooperate because of his past smuggling adventure, which was more of a youthful lark than any real malfeasance. However, Mather was never a real part of the conspirators," continued Wrexford. "He was horrified by his cousin's murder and realized that Annie Wright might also be in danger because of her friendship with Henry Peabody. And so he appealed to Copley for help."

He paused for a sip of whisky. "Copley, as we now know, was being blackmailed by Sir Charles and was a reluctant part of Argentum. The murder also shocked him, and in his note, he said that he had begun to take steps to stop the whole scheme."

"So, Copley did have a vestige of conscience left," mused Charlotte.

"Not enough to admit that his façade of being a paragon of perfection was a fraud," replied Wrexford. "But in the end, he did atone for some of his sins. When he learned that Sir Charles intended to murder Mather and Annie Wright, he arranged for them to take passage on an East India merchant ship. Right now, they are on their way to Calcutta, and Mather would do well to stay there and begin a new life. And given Annie Wright's abusive marriage, I imagine she'll welcome the opportunity to shed her old skin."

"Perhaps not as happy an ending as the one for Lady Cordelia and Lord Woodbridge," observed Sheffield. "But as Mather showed a concern for Annie Wright, I don't begrudge him a second chance."

"Most people," said Charlotte softly, "deserve a second chance."

"Thanks to all of you, that includes me." Woodbridge drew Cordelia into a heartfelt hug. "I know how fortunate I am to have a sister who's not only brilliant but also kind and compassionate to those who aren't blessed with intelligence."

Sheffield nodded. "Yes, you are indeed lucky, Woodbridge."

Charlotte saw a faint blush steal over Cordelia's face.

"As am I," said Cordelia. "You didn't lose faith in me, even when the evidence gave you reason to do so."

"I think," answered Sheffield, "that we all had faith in each other."

Wrexford kept a stoic face, but Charlotte discerned a glimmer of emotion in his eyes.

He shifted his stance before continuing. "That explains the basic machinations surrounding Argentum Trading Company. The last—and perhaps most important—part of Sir Charles's nefarious scheming involved Professor Sudler's Computing Engine. He—"

"Hmmph!"

They all turned to see the professor shuffle into the doorway. He was wearing a dressing gown over his nightshirt, and the flicker of the single candle clutched in his fist showed his grey hair was sticking out in spiky tufts from beneath his knitted nightcap.

"I knew they were rotten to the core," added Sudler darkly. "What the devil were they up to?"

"You should be getting your rest, sir," chided Cordelia, clearly concerned for her elderly friend. "We can explain everything in the morning."

"Be damned with rest," grumbled the professor. "I couldn't sleep, and then I heard your voices. I want to know whether we prevented them from achieving whatever evil they had in mind."

"That we did," answered Wrexford. "Sir Charles had lived most of his life at sea, which gave his extraordinarily gifted mind much free time in which to think. Some of his endeavors were worthy ones, like his scientific book on seashells. But greed quickly came to dominate his thoughts. He devised some lucrative trading schemes, but as sea captains must have skill in mathematics for navigation, it was the rumor of your Engine that sparked his most ambitious plan—"

"Navigation tables!" Sudler slapped his palm to his brow. "Good Lord, how did I not see it?"

"I missed it, as well." Cordelia grimaced. "I saw only numbers and couldn't put two and two together."

"None of us knew that the admiral was involved," pointed out Wrexford. "It is easy to see what a puzzle represents when all the pieces have been fitted together."

"True." The professor shook his head and fixed Cordelia with an apologetic look. "Much as it may pain you to hear this, my dear friend, this ordeal has taught me that I don't wish to continue to run computations for monetary gain. I intend to return to my cottage and continue to work on improving my Engine's capabilities. It will be years before it's fully functional. And then . . ."

A beatific smile lit up his wrinkled face. "And then I shall

create accurate tables for all to use freely—things like navigation tables, which will save countless lives by helping eliminate
shipwrecks. The only reward I want is seeing all our new scientific innovations contribute to making the world a better place."

"I couldn't agree more," said Cordelia. "I prefer the challenge
of using my own head for calculations rather than a machine.
And I like thinking about the human aspects of my business
ventures, and how to create value and not just profits."

Charlotte considered her friend's words. Like herself, Cordelia kept her feelings well guarded. It was easy to see her as
ruled by cold logic. But her stalwart support of her brother,
along with her progressive views on business, revealed her heart
was not made of steel rods and brass gears.

A glance at Sheffield showed he appeared to be thinking
much the same thing.

"But as to making our partnership profitable, I owe you an
apology, Mr. Sheffield." Cordelia sat down rather heavily in
one of the empty chairs around the table. "With all the pressures of running the arbitrage calculations and the tables for Sir
Charles, I've neglected our own business venture. I've paid no
attention to our investments, which was horribly unfair." A
pause. "As I was asking you to oversee the operation before
you had an opportunity to gain some experience in commerce."

Sheffield's expression went through a series of odd little con-
tortions. "Actually, no apologies are necessary, Lady Cordelia.
Miss Winchester and Miss Howe are extremely clever . . ."

He paused and turned to Wrexford. "Miss Winchester and
Miss Howe are our other two business partners. The fact that
they are women is why I couldn't reveal their names to you in
the first place."

The earl nodded. "I understand. And given the circumstances, you needn't worry about my investment. I don't expect—"

The sudden crackle of papers caused him to fall silent.

Sheffield extracted a packet from his pocket. To Charlotte, he looked a little sheepish as he offered it to Wrexford, whose eyes flared in surprise when he peeled back the covering to reveal a sheaf of banknotes.

"It so happens I can return your initial investment now," explained Sheffield. "It goes without saying that you retain your stock in the company, and I expect that we'll be paying handsome quarterly dividends going forward."

Cordelia stared at him in mute shock.

Woodbridge let out a low whistle. "How did you manage to make all that money? I . . . I thought you weren't very good at numbers."

"I'm not," answered Sheffield with a wry shrug. "I simply added up other variables in my head."

"W-what variables?" stammered Cordelia.

Sheffield pursed his lips. "Well, it all started when Wrexford took me with him to see Hedley, the engineering fellow who invented Puffing Billy."

"Yes, I remember," mused the earl. "You seemed awfully intrigued with his model locomotive."

"Well, the Ashton affair made it very clear that innovations in steam engines were very profitable, and the idea of moving engines seemed like a very revolutionary idea that would change transportation forever. So, as Lady Cordelia left the temporary running of the business to me, I made the decision to invest your money in Hedley's idea. And then . . ."

"And then?" pressed Cordelia when Sheffield paused for breath.

"And then it turned out the owners of Wylam Colliery offered to buy me out at triple what I paid after the test model ran so well. I considered holding the investment, but when I had a chat with Lady Charlotte's good friend Lord Sterling about the future of steam, he made a very interesting proposal."

With an owlish blink, the professor braced himself against

the door molding. "Steam is a marvelous thing, is it not? A small steam engine would be enormously useful in turning the crank to my Computing Engine . . ."

"Quite marvelous," agreed Sheffield. "As it turns out, Sterling and Mrs. Ashton have designed a new range of fabrics which are proving highly popular in the Netherlands and Prussia. Their mill is running at full capacity, so he suggested our company invest in building a second mill. What with Miss Winchester's contacts in the shipping world and Miss Howe's connections in America, I believe that as soon as this dratted war is over with our former colonies, we have the potential to open up a whole lucrative new market."

Sheffield clasped his hands behind his back. "So, I sold half the shares in Puffing Billy—we can sell the rest at a later date, when they are even more valuable—and invested the funds with Sterling. Not only will we make money on the venture, but as you recall, Mrs. Ashton puts aside part of the mill's profits for schooling and medical clinics for her workers, as well as generous bonuses."

"Brilliant," murmured Cordelia. "Absolutely brilliant."

A tentative smile blossomed on Sheffield's face. "You mean I actually did something right?"

As the others fell into a lively discussion of the new business revelations, Wrexford took Charlotte's arm and led her to a quiet nook next to the professor's Computing Engine.

"It's been quite an evening of revelations," he murmured.

The brass and steel machinery cast hard-edged shadows over the painted plaster wall, but the earl's presence seemed to soften all the stark angles, his flesh-and-blood warmth dispelling the metallic chill within the cramped space. And yet she wished she could see his expression. Flitting swirls of darkness lingered around his face.

"Indeed," she said, attempting to match his drawl. "Let us

hope that mayhem and murder—" To her dismay, her voice trembled and died, the words sticking like knife blades in her throat.

Wrexford slowly turned to face her and set his hands on the jut of her shoulders. "Come, come, the danger is over, Lady Charlotte."

*But what about the next threat?*

This was the second time she had witnessed the earl come within a hairsbreadth of death. The thought of ever facing such a horror again threatened to squeeze the very marrow from her bones.

She was dimly aware of sounds in the room . . . the gentle jostling as Woodbridge and Tyler linked arms with the professor and convinced him to return to his bed . . . the murmur of Sheffield and Cordelia in private conversation . . . the mingled sleep-soft breaths of boys and hound curled up in front of the fire. . . .

But it was the skittery thump of her heart against her rib cage that filled her ears. Charlotte felt as if her chest might explode.

"Lady Charlotte?"

He sounded so very far away.

*"Charlotte?"* The whisper twined with her tangled hair.

She slid her hands inside his coat, her palms feeling the heat of his skin through the light layer of linen as she fumbled to draw him into her arms.

*Thump, thump.*

Wrexford went very still, save for a tiny pulsing beneath the left lapel of his coat.

A moment passed—or was it an hour? Charlotte tightened her hold. *Be damned with abstractions.* Let the minutes slip through her fingers. All that mattered was Wrexford was here.

And achingly, joyfully alive.

He shifted, his hands moving to frame her face and tilt it upward.

Candlelight flickered off the Engine's brass rods, the muted gold sparks catching the curl of his lips as he said her name again. "Charlotte."

"A-Alexander," she murmured.

Silent laughter lit his eyes. "Are you sure that's my given name? I think it may be Agamemnon."

Charlotte smiled. "We've been over this before. I'm fairly certain it's Alexander."

"Hmmm." His mouth feathered against her cheek. "Well, perhaps it's time we settled the matter once and for all—"

A sudden wood-against-wood thud jarred them apart.

"Ah, I was hoping you would all still be awake!" Henning kicked the door shut behind him. "Thank God there's still a bit of whisky left."

Wrexford's sigh—along with a wry oath—tickled against her flesh as he released his hold. "Is there a reason you're here at this hour?" he called to the surgeon. "Other than to drain my wine cellar?"

"Yes." A noisy slurp. "Kindly tell Griffin to stop sending your dead bodies to my mortuary." Another splash, another slurp. "By the by, who killed Lord Copley?"

"It's a lengthy story," replied the earl, moving out from behind the Engine. "Suffice it to say, the culprits have been caught, and the murders involving us are over."

Henning chuffed a skeptical sound. "For now."

Bereft of Wrexford's touch, Charlotte hugged her arms to her chest, feeling the shadows darken and turn cold as ice as they swirled around her, squeezing the air from her lungs. She took a moment to shake off the sensation, then followed him out into the light.

Only to find the intensity of her emotions had left her utterly spent.

"I-it's late . . . and there's much to be done in the coming hours, so I had better take my leave," she announced. "Mr.

Fores needs a drawing from me, and first thing in the morning, Alison must be informed of all that has happened."

The note in her voice roused the others. The boys came instantly awake and scrambled to their feet. Sheffield edged back from his tête-à-tête with Cordelia and cleared his throat.

"Indeed, I ought to be going, as well," he said, retrieving his hat from the side table.

"So should I," added Cordelia hastily. "I'll find Jamie and we'll make our way home."

Wrexford said nothing, and his face was impossible to read.

"Hmmph, I seem to have blown in like a storm cloud and cast a shadow over the celebration," observed Henning. "But before you all go, allow me to offer a toast."

He picked up the near-empty bottle and splashed the rest of its contents into his glass. "To peace and quiet . . ." A whisper of amber-gold liquid swirled in a slow spinning vortex. "Though with this group, that's likely wishful thinking. But you never know. Miracles do happen."

# CHAPTER 31

"*P*eace and quiet . . .

"Ha!" muttered Wrexford, wincing at the clatter of traveling trunks being maneuvered down the curved staircase and carried out to the waiting carriage.

The previous day had passed in a whirlwind of activity—breakfast with Griffin . . . a meeting with Sir Darius to put together a story for the public that would minimize embarrassment for the good of the country . . . logistics arranged to transport the professor and his precious Engine back to the cottage in Cambridge. . . .

And now dawn had barely tinged the horizon with its rosy glow and already the morning was alive with the well-oiled bustle of his staff preparing for a journey.

Sheffield came out of the breakfast room, a cup of steaming coffee in one hand, a roll of thick paper in the other. "Why did Tyler just leave the mews with your unmarked carriage? I thought Lady Charlotte, along with the Weasels and McClellan, are going to travel with Lady Peake."

Mention of Charlotte stirred a silent oath of frustration.

What with all the humble-jumble, Wrexford hadn't had a moment alone with her since the night of nearly losing his head to the admiral's naval cutlass. Granted, the dowager had deserved a detailed account of how good had triumphed over evil.

But much as he cared for all his friends, at the moment, he wished them all to the devil.

"They are," he answered through gritted teeth. "As for Tyler, he is handling a few errands for me before heading north."

"Woodbridge and Lady Cordelia are accompanying the professor," mused Sheffield through a sip of coffee. "So, it seems we shall have a jolly little gathering at your estate come evening."

The thought didn't improve Wrexford's mood.

"By the by, I stopped by Fores's printshop on the way here. Charlotte's latest drawing was published this morning." Sheffield set aside his empty cup and unrolled the paper.

Despite his foul temper, Wrexford couldn't hold back a bark of laughter.

The drawing depicted Sir Charles, dressed in full naval regalia, down on all fours, sinking in an ugly ooze of muck, with a demonic black hellhound biting his arse. The bold headline read—DOGGED BY FORCES OF JUSTICE, A TRAITOROUS ADMIRAL IS BROUGHT TO HIS KNEES!

"The Home Office should be pleased," said Sheffield with a grin. "For once, A. J. Quill is making the government look halfway clever."

"Lady Charlotte felt she owed it to Griffin for trusting us about Woodbridge," Wrexford answered.

"A fair resolution for all involved," responded his friend, and the earl didn't disagree.

Harper ambled by, a meaty bone protruding from his jaws.

"That," said Wrexford, "had better be finished before you try to take a spot in the baggage coach."

The hound didn't dignify the remark with a reaction.

"Your pardon, milord." Riche had been trailing the hound at a discreet distance. "The last of the trunks have been loaded, and the carriages are ready to depart."

Charlotte stopped on the garden path and drew in a lungful of the country air. An early morning sweetness filled her nostrils, a delicate perfume of dew-damp flowers unfolding to the warming rays of sunlight.

The quiet—just a soft rustling of leaves serenaded by the faint twitter of birdsong and the gentle hum of honeybees— was very welcome after the raucous revelry of the previous evening, as the earl's manor house had filled with the invited guests.

As well as a few unexpected surprises.

A lump slowly formed in her throat as she recalled the sight of Raven and Hawk pelting into the formal drawing room— followed by Skinny, Alice the Eel Girl, Pudge, and One-Eye Harry. Wrexford had revealed yet another facet of his complexities and conundrums. Polite Society would be agog to learn the sardonic, sharp-tongued earl—a man known for his hair-trigger temper and lack of patience—had sent his private carriage to collect a raggle-taggle band of street urchins for a stay at his country estate.

The children had gorged themselves on sweets and fruit punch, while the adults had enjoyed an excess of effervescent champagne, along with a sumptuous feast of delicacies. Charlotte doubted that Alison would wake before teatime.

Her own head was still a little worse for the wine, but the prospect of a solitary walk as the simple beauties of a new day came to life had drawn her from a fitful slumber. Lifting her cheeks to the breeze, she was glad of it. The demands of the past few days had allowed her to avoid contemplating the tangled state of her emotions.

But cowardice offered only a fool's gold glitter of comfort. It quickly lost its shine.

"What am I afraid of?" she wondered aloud.

The warble of a dove hidden in the long grasses offered no easy answer. Yes, in the past, Love had cut her to the quick, and the folly of youthful illusions was slow to heal. But that old life had given up the ghost, and a new one had taken root . . . slowly at first, sending up tentative shoots from deep within.

Only to have them unfurl into breathtakingly beautiful blossoms, all the more exquisite for the unexpected ranges of hues and textures. Family, friends . . .

*And Wrexford.*

Shading her eyes from the sunlight, Charlotte stopped to stare out at the sloping fields leading down to the lake and, behind it, the leafy stand of trees, the breeze-rippled colors ranging from soft shades of newborn green to flutters of dark sage and smoky emerald.

The earl was colored in the same complexities. Some shades were easy to discern, while others dipped and darted, defying the eye. There were moments when she thought she could clearly see the hues of his heart. And there were moments when dark-on-dark shadows seemed to swirl up and block the view.

"Then again, I'm sure that I, too, appear to be a maddening collage of conflicting shades."

Charlotte felt a wry grimace pull at her lips. *Ye gods.* For two people who claimed to have a modicum of intelligence, they seemed to be making a hash of things. . . .

Feeling a little lost, she wandered out of the gardens and turned down the footpath leading to the stables. Hoots of laughter floated over the high boxwood hedge. The children were already up—the earl had given them permission to play with a litter of puppies—and as she slipped through the opening in the greenery, she saw they had all been let loose to play in one of the empty paddocks. Amid all the hilarity and the squish of mud, her approach went unnoticed.

After moving quietly to a spot half-hidden by a stack of

newly cut hay, Charlotte leaned up against the fence to watch. She found herself smiling. . . .

And then, to her utter surprise, she felt the salty prickle of tears.

She forced herself to breathe in and out. Her emotions were clearly in a humble-jumble tangle—

"You're up early."

The soft earth had muffled Wrexford's steps. He looked like he had just come from riding. The wind had snarled his hair and whipped a flush of red across his cheekbones. Mud spattered his doeskin breeches and well-worn boots, giving him a slightly raffish air. . . .

Charlotte quickly looked away, hoping to hide the confusion tugging at her thoughts. "As are you."

He settled himself next to her, shoulder brushing shoulder, and peeled off his gloves.

They watched in silence for several long moments before he shifted slightly. "By the by, you're crying."

"A-am I?" She looked down at the ground, not wishing to dampen the mood of exuberant good cheer. "A bit of straw must have blown into my eye."

Wrexford reached out and took hold of her chin. "Here, let me help," he murmured, tilting her head up to face him. "Blink a few times and then look up."

His finger brushed lightly at the corner of each eye. "Better?"

"Much," answered Charlotte, quickly turning back to the children cavorting with the puppies.

She felt his gaze remain on her face.

*Shouts. Barks. Laughter.* Pure and joyous as the dancing sunlight.

"I'm sorry." She hitched in a breath, and suddenly emotions refused to stay pent up any longer. "It's just that I'm thinking of . . . of a great many things."

"Such as?"

How like Wrexford to cut to the heart of a problem. Somehow, the simple question gave her the courage to confess her fears.

"Such as . . . how carefree our urchins look, and . . . and how in a few days they will go back to stews, where . . ."

To her consternation, her voice broke.

The wind ruffled through Wrexford's hair. "Good Lord, you don't think I intend to send them back, do you?" He allowed a small smile. "Cook is in need of a kitchen helper, and Alice would be a good match. Skinny likes horses and will fit in with the stable boys, while Pudge and One-Eye Harry can learn gardening. They will all, of course, attend school and have a choice about their future . . ."

He stopped abruptly. "You're still crying."

"I . . ." *How to explain?*

"The future," Charlotte stammered. "The other night, I watched for the second time as you came within a hairsbreadth of death. Once again, we were extraordinarily lucky. But Luck is fickle!" She blinked, feeling pearls of salt fall from her lashes. "What about the next time?"

"The future holds infinite uncertainties." His mouth curled up at the corners. "That is why one of the best-known Latin aphorisms is *Carpe diem.*"

*Seize the day.*

"Do you think I'm not terrified for you, and how often your courage and compassion lead you into awful dangers?" continued Wrexford. "You're a beacon—that bright glimmer in the night which helps me find my way when I'm feeling lost." He drew in a measured breath. "I'm not sure how I would bear the darkness without your light."

Their eyes met.

"A weakness, no doubt. However, as you well know, my weaknesses far outweigh my strengths," he added.

"As do mine," she said softly. "But perhaps we've come to

know each other well enough not to be fearful of showing our vulnerabilities to each other. Flaws are what makes us human."

Charlotte hesitated, trying to find just the right words to express the feeling bubbling up inside her.

*Oh, be damned with finding just the right words.*

*Carpe diem.*

*Seize the day.*

Throwing caution to the wind, she flung her arms around him and pulled him close. "You are . . . you are . . . impossibly perfect just the way you are. I can't imagine my life without you in it."

"You can't?" Wrexford shifted, his boots kicking up a tiny clot of mud. "Then perhaps . . ." He hesitated, his green eyes rippling for just a moment with a look of naked vulnerability, which made her heart give a fluttery lurch.

"Then perhaps you'll consider marrying me."

Was the breeze playing tricks with his words?

"Y-you are p-proposing to me in the middle of a dung-filled barnyard, with a bunch of little savages running amok all around us?" stammered Charlotte.

"It appears I am." Wrexford gave a crooked smile. "Are you offended?"

"On the contrary . . ." Charlotte touched her fingertips to his cheek, feeling the warmth of his sun-bronzed skin pulse through her skin. "It's so outrageously wonderful that I might consider saying yes."

"You might?"

The enormity of what he had just suggested hit her like a stallion's kick. She felt a little light headed. "Yes, but . . ."

"But what?" Wrexford pulled her closer. "You have to admit, we fit together," he whispered. "In every way that matters."

She held him close, savoring the steady beat of his heart, echoing in harmony with hers.

"I do apologize for the barnyard proposal," he said after several moments. "I imagine it's not nearly as romantic as your first one."

"Oh, fie, Wrexford." Charlotte made a wry face. "Anthony didn't propose. It was *I* who suggested we elope." A sigh. "He would never have dreamed of being so . . . devil-be-damned bold."

"You deserve to be swept off your feet." And with that, he suddenly seized her in his arms and threw her over his shoulders, much to the glee of the children.

"Wrexford! Put me down!" Her cry was muffled by a mouthful of wool and the exciting barking of a half-dozen hairy little hounds.

"Come, we've dithered long enough over this." He set her on her feet, but his nonchalant laugh held a note of uncertainty—and perhaps a note of longing. "It's a simple answer— yes or no."

And yet saying a single syllable would change everything. "Is it *really* that simple?"

Charlotte watched Wrexford's face pinch in thought. She loved the look of fierce concentration that took hold of him when he pondered an intellectual challenge.

Sunlight flickered through a scudding cloud. A barn swallow swooped low, chasing the fat black flies buzzing around the paddock. And then a smile slowly softened the chiseled angles of his features.

"Perhaps that's the crux of the whole conundrum. The most profoundly complicated questions in Life can have the simplest of answers," said Wrexford. "Love is one of the inexplicable little beauties of the universe. A fundamental truth that makes absolutely no sense."

He looked at her through the fringe of his dark lashes. "Unless you listen to it with both your heart and your head, and make those two opposing organs sing in harmony."

"Yes," mused Charlotte.

"Yes?" A tiny tic pulled at the corner of his mouth. "Is that a yes?"

And in that instant, all her doubts flitted away.

"Yes."

He drew her close. "Go away, Weasels," he called to the pile of hay. "I wish to celebrate our betrothal by kissing Lady Charlotte without two chortling little beasts making a mockery of it."

Doubled over in laughter, Raven and Hawk dug themselves out of their hiding place and scampered back to their friends.

And then his lips touched hers.

*A kiss.* Or perhaps it was a revelation, reflected Charlotte, once her thoughts fluttered back to coherence. She hadn't imagined one could feel such a profound connection of body and spirit.

Wrexford's breath feathered against her cheek. "Shall we go back to the house and tell our friends the news?"

"Yes," answered Charlotte. "I think that a splendid idea." She watched a leaf swirl up in a gust of air and slowly float back to earth. "And then I suppose we shall have to start thinking about . . . about what comes next." Her gaze lingered for an instant on the faraway flickers of sunlight dancing on the horizon. "A great many things will change."

"They will," agreed Wrexford, twining his hand with hers. "But why don't we just take the future one step at a time."

# AUTHOR'S NOTE

Those of you familiar with my Wrexford & Sloane series know that I like to weave in an important development in Regency science/technology as a main element in the mystery. And for me, one of the most fascinating concepts of the era was that of the "Computing Engine." For this story, I've used the real-life Charles Babbage and his Analytical Engine as inspiration.

The new ideas and new technology of the Industrial Revolution were turning the early nineteenth century world upside down. It was an exciting time for someone with imagination, and Babbage—a brilliant mathematician and engineering genius, was one of the new breed of scientific thinkers leading the charge. His mind was constantly spinning with ideas on how to improve the ways things were done, and he used his practical skills to achieve many great accomplishments, from pioneering technical advances for lighthouse signaling to fine-tuning track designs for the first railroads. But it was while working on a way to create accurate mathematical tables that his genius really kicked into high gear.

Babbage was frustrated that many of the tables, which were calculated and typeset by hand, had so many mistakes. So in 1821, he decided to design one. You can read more about Charles Babbage and his Engines—and why mathematical tables were so important—on my website (andreapenrose.com) under the Diversions tab.

My fictional Professor Sudler is based on Babbage, and while my story is set a number of years earlier than the actual building of Babbage's prototype, geniuses are often ahead of their time!

As a side note, Lady Cordelia's mathematic skill and creative genius for programming the fictional Computing Engine is an homage to Ada Lovelace, another fascinating real-life luminary of the Regency era. The daughter of bad-boy Romantic poet Lord Byron, Lovelace was a math prodigy, and after meeting Babbage through a mutual friend, she worked with him for a number of years, helping him develop his Differential Engine, as well as his more advanced Analytical Engine. She is credited with realizing that the punch cards which had been created to control the intricate weaving patterns of the new steam-powered Jacquard looms could be used to program a Computing Engine, and she also wrote a math sequence that is considered the first computer program.

One last charater note—William Hedley and his "Puffing Billy" are also both real, and the prototype locomotive was first used by Wylam Colliery, where its success helped spur the development of the railroad. (So Sheffield did indeed make a very savvy investment!)

As for the financial machinations by the villains, those too have some basis in fact. Their arbitrage scheme (arbitrage being, as noted, the simultaneous purchase and sale of an asset to profit from differences in price in different locales) is loosely modeled on a remarkably well-developed smuggling and arbitrage market for silver and gold which developed in Spain, reaching its height early in the eighteenth century.

Spain, through its New World colonies, led the world in silver and gold production from 1493 to roughly 1820. Spain also, like most countries then, subscribed to "bullionism": the economic theory (now abandoned) that a nation's wealth is defined by the amount of precious metals it owns. This led Spanish policymakers, first, to mandate price ceilings for gold and silver (allowing purchase by the Crown at an artificially low cost) and, second, to prohibit the export of the metals once they were received from the colonies.

A remarkably sophisticated network of merchant banking houses developed, however, to illegally buy metals at low prices in Spain to be smuggled to higher-priced markets in Northern Europe. As in this story, bills of exchange were used to move money and profits around European financial centers separately from the physical goods. High-tech for the day, double-entry accounting practices distributed the gains among those participating in this illegal commerce.

Superb research has been done by economic historians uncovering the detailed recordkeeping this scheme required (records were kept even of the exact pricing in these illegal markets!), analyzing the economics involved and tracing the genealogical ties purposefully developed by the participating merchant banks. As I have noted before, fact can at times be as strange as fiction. The story of this Spanish market makes for riveting reading, especially for those interested in a dollop of economics.

Both the opium smuggling from India into China, and the Chinese Emperor's iron-fisted control of the tea trade—including the stricture that all tea had to be paid for with silver—described in the plot are based on historical fact, as is the description of how foreign merchants did their transactions. As for the East India Company, it was once the most powerful and feared economic institution in the world, but during the Regency era, the British government passed a number of laws regulating its practices, which forced it to adjust its old ways of doing business. As my characters point out in the story, a world experiencing momentous changes in so many aspects of life offered exciting opportunities—both for doing good and doing evil.

—*Andrea Penrose*

Read on for a special preview of the next Wrexford & Sloane mystery...

# MURDER AT THE ROYAL BOTANIC GARDENS

*The upcoming marriage of the Earl of Wrexford and Lady Charlotte Sloane promises to be a highlight of the season, if they can first untangle—and survive—a web of intrigue and murder involving the most brilliant scientific minds in Regency London . . .*

One advantage of being caught up in a whirl of dress fittings and decisions about flower arrangements and breakfast menus is that Charlotte Sloane has little time for any pre-wedding qualms. Her love for Wrexford isn't in question. But will being a wife—and a countess—make it difficult for her to maintain her independence, not to mention, her secret identity as famed satirical artist A.J. Quill?

Despite those concerns, there are soon even more urgent matters to attend to during Charlotte and Wrexford's first public outing as an engaged couple. At a symposium at the Royal Botanic Gardens, a visiting botanist suffers a fatal collapse. The traces of white powder near his mouth reveal the dark truth— he was murdered. Drawn into the investigation, Charlotte and the Earl learn of the victim's involvement in a momentous medical discovery. With fame and immense fortune at stake, there's no shortage of suspects, including some whose ruthlessness is already known. But neither Charlotte nor her husband-to-be can realize how close the danger is about to get—or to what lengths this villain is prepared to go . . .

*Coming in October 2021 from Kensington Publishing Corp.*

# PROLOGUE

The floral fragrances—a symphony of subtle sweetness—swirled with the earthier scents of mist-damp leaves and the nutrient-rich soil. The gentleman closed his eyes for a moment and drew in a deep breath.

*The essence of Life.* There was nothing more beautiful, mused Josiah Becton as he stood very still in the shadows and let the warm air caress his cheeks.

Moonlight flickered through the soaring glass-paned walls of the magnificent conservatory, its silvery softness twining with the gold-hued glow of the lanterns hung among the exotic greenery. The faint sounds of a string quartet—was it Mozart or Haydn?—floated out from the assembly room attached to the rambling structure, the lilting notes punctuated by discreet laughter and the crystalline click of champagne glasses.

It was all so . . . elegantly civilized, this international symposium of botany scholars and wealthy patrons of science, gathered at London's legendary Royal Botanic Gardens in order to share their knowledge for the good of mankind.

Becton slowly released a sigh. "But I am far more at home in the wilds of the world, where the flora and fauna have not yet been disturbed by the footsteps of men. Exploring . . . searching . . . learning . . ." His words trailed off as he meandered down the brick pathway, delving deeper into the vast assortment of specimens gathered from around the globe.

The music gave way to the whisper of the leaves and the drip of water feeding a section of succulents from the West Indies. His steps brought him to a smaller room that housed the treasures brought back from the islands of the South Pacific by Sir Joseph Banks, the noted scholar and adventurer whose tireless efforts over the years had established the Gardens as the leading repository of botanical specimens in the world.

"Ah, the South Pacific," murmured Becton, bending low to examine the lush colors of a tropical flower. "Perhaps the Antipodes should be my next destination. Granted, it is so very far away . . ." A twinge of regret pinched at his chest.

*So little time, so much to know.*

"I see you are admiring the efforts of Sir Joseph." Fronds rustled as a gentleman slipped past a cluster of leafy brake ferns.

"He is an inspiration to all of us who believe the natural world holds unlimited potential for improving the lives of all people."

"Ah, but you, too, are an inspiration, Mr. Becton."

"That's very kind of you to say. But such praise is undeserved. I'm merely a curious traveler who is happiest in the solitude of the jungles or mountains." He quirked a wry grimace. "I've always been far more comfortable with the company of plants than people."

His companion chuckled. "I fear that a passion for science makes all of us odd fish."

Becton smiled.

"Your work has always been quite special—ye heavens, your solitary journeys have taken you where few others have managed to go! Everyone here is eagerly awaiting the lecture on your explorations through the northern reaches of Spanish empire in South America, and all your fascinating experiences. The sense of wonder . . ." His companion allowed a pensive pause. "And discovery."

"Yes," agreed Becton. "As a fellow man of science, I know you understand that such opportunities can simply take your breath away."

"Indeed, indeed." A muted rustle of well-tailored wool. "Come, I took the liberty of bringing along some champagne. Let us raise a toast." His companion offered him a glass. "To Discovery!"

"Thank you, sir, but no." Becton waved away the wine. "The marvelous botanical specimens here are intoxicating enough."

"Nonsense, my good fellow. You have crossed the ocean from America to be here for this grand occasion. Surely that calls for celebration—and the effervescence of champagne!"

"Alas, the years of traveling under constant adversities like heat, cold and pestilence have taken their toll on my constitution. My physician forbids the use of strong spirits."

"Sparkling wine is hardly strong spirits," protested his companion. "A few sips to acknowledge the spirit of collegial friendships that have brought us here from near and far surely can do no harm."

The lantern's glow danced over the cut crystal coupe. Becton watched the tiny bubbles beckoning like a myriad of diamond-bright points of fire.

"Quite right," he agreed, taking the proffered glass. "With so many dark forces at play in the world—war, disease, hunger— we must celebrate the light of knowledge and the hope it brings for the future."

"To scientific triumphs that will change the world," said his companion with a beatific smile.

Glass kissed against glass, setting off a sonorous ring.

"A lovely vintage, don't you think, Mr. Becton?"

"Yes, I—" A sudden strangled cough cut off his words.

"F-forgive me, I seem to be . . ." He reached out a hand to steady himself on one of the display pedestals, only to feel his knees begin to buckle.

" . . . Feeling unwell," he gasped as he slumped forward, spilling the rest of his wine. A fierce pain spiraled through his gut, drawing a guttural moan. Everything was turning black as Hades. His head was spinning . . .

His companion pulled the glass from his spasming fingers. "It's all right," soothed the man's voice. It sounded very far away. "All your mortal aches and pains will soon be over."

Another drunken lurch, as Becton felt himself sinking, sinking into the darkness . . .

A thud echoed in the muffled crack of terracotta pots as his thrashing arm knocked several specimen plants to the stone floor.

"Rest in peace," murmured his companion, crouching down beside the American explorer's still-twitching body. "Your discovery will live on—I promise you that." His voice was solemn, but betrayed not a ripple of remorse. "Though it won't be you who reaps the rewards that will come with its fame."

The gentleman waited for the final death throes to cease before shifting the crystal stems of the two glasses to one hand and beginning a methodical search of Becton's waistcoat pockets.

"*Eureka.*" He smiled as he extracted a small brass key. "Thank you for making this easy."

The display room was once against quiet as a crypt, the moist air undulating through the fanciful silhouettes of the plants as they settled back into a peaceful slumber. Rising, the gentleman smoothed the wrinkles from his trousers and disappeared into the gloom.

A bevy of footmen, resplendent in their royal livery, circulated through the crowd, discreetly ringing hand bells to signal that the gathering in the conservatory's reception room was coming to an end and the guests were to exit and make their way along the graveled walkway to the nearby Kew Palace, where a gala supper was soon to be served.

"The bells are quite unnecessary," said one of the governors of the Royal Society, the illustrious scientific organization that had created the symposium. "Once the pop of champagne corks ceases, everyone will quickly understand that it's time to move on." He waggled his brows. "I understand that a very fine claret and German hock are to be served at the banquet. After all, man cannot live on the fruits of knowledge alone."

The quip drew a round of chuckles from the small circle of scholars standing with him.

The governor gave a courtly wave toward the brass-framed glass double doors. "Shall we proceed, gentlemen?"

Other groups were also beginning to drift toward the exit, still engaged in lively scientific discussions with frequent terms in Latin echoing amid English, French and German.

"Has anyone seen Mr. Becton?" asked the leader of the American delegation, after sweeping the room with a searching look.

"I believe I saw him wander off into main conservatory, Dr. Hosack." A vague wave accompanied the answer. "It looked like he might have been heading for the section that houses the South Seas specimens collected by Sir Joseph Banks."

Hosack smiled. "Becton tends to lose all track of time when distracted by plant life. I had better go fetch him. He's absent-minded enough to forget all about supper."

"We'll come with you," offered a pair of Royal Society members. "It's easy to lose your way if you're unfamiliar with the twists and turns of the walkways."

The three of them set off, but no sooner had they passed through the first display when a shout of alarm shattered the stillness.

"A physician!" came the panicked cry. The thud of boots

echoed like gunfire against the night-dark glass panes. "Help, help! A physician is needed!"

"Ye gods." Hosack started to run, only to skid to a stop as he rounded a turn and came to a fork in the walkway.

"This way!" One of the Royal Society members grabbed his sleeve and pulled him to the left. The lamplight tuned jumpy as they raced down the narrow slate-flagged path, setting off a dance of jagged shadows.

"Help, help!" A gardener burst free of the gloom, his face tight with fear. "A gentleman has collapsed near the South Seas specimens and I . . . I think he ain't breathing—"

Hosack gave the fellow a hard shake. "Take me there— quickly, man, quickly."

Drawing a steadying breath, the gardener nodded and turned.

Palm fronds slapped at their coats as they shouldered through a cluster of tropical trees. And then the lush vegetation gave way to a display alcove filled with tiny treasures—

A body lay sprawled on the paving stones, half shadowed by the marble pedestals.

Dropping to his knees, Hosack touched a finger to his friend's throat, but one look had already told him that he wouldn't find a pulse.

"Damnation, he's gone," he muttered, feeling a sharp stab of both anger and regret at the unholy bad luck of the Grim Reaper's choosing Becton at this of all moments. "Why now?" he added in a whisper just loud enough for his own ears.

A brusque cough. "My condolences, sir," said one of the Royal Society's members. "I heard mention that your friend had a bad heart."

"He did suffer some troubles while in the wilds," acknowledged Hosack. "Though of late, after proper medical care, he was much improved."

"I'll go alert the head watchman and arrange for the body to be moved to a more . . . appropriate place until a mortuary wagon can be summoned," came the reply.

"I'll stay with you, sir—" began the other Royal Society member.

"That's not necessary. I'm no stranger to death." Hosack sat back on his haunches. "I'd rather you go along with your colleague to inform the rest of the American delegation of the unfortunate incident—discreetly of course, as I've no desire to ruin the evening for the other guests—and help them organize their carriage for the trip back to Town. I don't imagine Mr. Becton's friends will be in any mood to make merry tonight."

"Very good, sir," they responded, and quietly withdrew, taking the spooked gardener with them.

"Damn, damn, damn." Smacking a fist to his palm, Hosack added a more colorful oath. Becton had hinted that his presentation at the symposium would reveal a momentous discovery—one that that might indeed be called a miracle, for all the lives it would save.

*And now?*

Hosack sighed and shifted his gaze . . .

A puddle of liquid gleamed in the flickering light of the lantern hung on a nearby stanchion. Strangely enough, the surrounding flagstones were dry as dust. He stared for a moment longer before inching forward and leaning down for a closer look.

The whiff of grape-scented alcohol ticked at his nostrils. Wetting a finger in the spreading rivulet, he touched it to the tip of his tongue.

*Champagne.*

Frowning, Hosack looked around for broken bits of glass. *But where was the crystal coupe?*

A conundrum—and one that seemed to defy logic. As a rational man of science, that bothered him. Ignoring the chill seeping through his trousers, he remained on his knees, crawling around to search beneath the display cases.

Perhaps the gardener had picked up the coupe—though it was highly unlikely that the delicate glass could have survived the fall. Or perhaps . . .

His thoughts were interrupted as a harsh burning sensation suddenly had his mouth on fire.

Stirring a wash of saliva, he puckered and spit. *Holy hell— what the devil was going on?*

Hearing the sound of approaching footsteps, he quickly blotted up the rest of the wine with his handkerchief and stuffed it in his pocket before crawling back to his friend's corpse and studying the half-open lips, now frozen in death.

*A bad heart be damned.*

Unless he was much mistaken, the tiny telltale flecks of white powder indicated it wasn't the Grim Reaper's blade that had cut his friend's life short.

The mortal blow had come from some earthly hand.